Boycotts & Barflies

a novel by

Victoria Michaels

OMNIFIC PUBLISHING
DALLAS

Omnific Publishing
P.O. Box 793871, Dallas, TX 75379
www.omnificpublishing.com

First Omnific eBook edition, February 2010
First Omnific trade paperback edition, February 2010

Library of Congress Cataloguing-in-Publication Data

Michaels, Victoria.
    Boycotts and Barflies / Victoria Michaels – 2nd ed.
    ISBN 978-1-936305-00-1
    1. Young Women—Fiction. 2. Bet—Fiction. 3. Bar—Fiction.
    4. Portland—Fiction. I. Title

10 9 8 7 6 5 4 3 2 1

Book Design and Cover by Barbara Hallworth

Printed in the United States of America

"Love isn't something you find. Love is something that finds you."
— Loretta Young

To my husband who inspires me and makes me laugh,
to my kids who love me, and to my family and dear friends
who encourage me to try new things.
I have been truly blessed to have all of you in my life.
Also, to everyone who knows what vjgm means … thank you.

Chapter 1

Grace Park found herself on yet another bad date… the story of her life, or so it seemed. The Italian restaurant was dimly lit, with the smells of garlic and tomatoes filling the air around her. The clanking of dishes rang in her ears as she intently studied the red and white checkered tablecloth underneath her fingertips. She pushed the crumbs that fell from her breadstick into a small pile, all the while wondering just how much longer she would have to endure this torture. The long black waves of her hair hung around her face, providing a veil of privacy as she escaped into her own little world, trying to pass the time. She glanced up when she heard her name called and saw her date, Tony, looking at her with an irritated expression on his face.

"Sorry, I zoned. You were saying… something about that new computer program at work? I'm listening, I swear."

Tony worked for an insurance company—not the most exciting of careers to discuss over dinner. He had been driveling on endlessly about accident rates in the Pacific Northwest since they had arrived at the restaurant. There was nothing particularly attractive about the man; his brown hair was cut very short to his scalp to hide just how much it was starting to thin at the crown, even at his young age. His brown eyes were hidden behind thin, wire-framed glasses that looked a bit too small for his face, and his skin was so pale that with his narrow build, one might wonder about his health. Work consumed his every waking hour, and to him, it was utterly fascinating. To the rest of the world, however, Grace included, it was boring as hell.

Grace casually glanced at her watch and realized she had only been there for thirty minutes. It only felt like an eternity. She silently cursed herself for not having the nerve to make up another excuse when she ran into him outside the elevator of their apartment building. Unfailingly persistent, Tony had asked her out for the fifth time in a month, and even though it shouldn't have, the question caught her completely off guard. It had been a really long day and she hadn't seen him coming quickly enough to be able to prepare a believable lie. Before she knew what happened, the word "sure" had slipped out of her mouth, and now, as a result, she was enduring the longest and most boring night of her life.

She shifted uncomfortably in her seat and again glanced at her watch, wondering how long it would be until she would get her reprieve. *It shouldn't be much longer*, she told herself. Like an answer to her unspoken prayer, Grace's cell phone rang in her pocket. She peeked down at the small, silver object and noticed the caller ID.

Thank God! I'm almost free…

"I'm so sorry; I need to get this. I told Meg not to bother me unless it was an absolute emergency."

Yes, Grace was using one of the oldest tricks in the book: having her girlfriend call midway through the date with an "emergency" so she could bail if it was a disaster or the guy was creepy. This date qualified on both counts. Unfortunately for Grace, these bail outs seemed to be happening a lot on her dates lately; so much so, in fact, that she made sure she went to church regularly so God wouldn't be tempted to actually give her mom a real illness as a punishment for all of the lying that she had been doing about her mother's health.

"Meg, I told you not to call unless it's an emergency. I'm on a date with *Tony*." Grace gave an apologetic smile and mouthed the word "sorry" to him for extra effect.

He shrugged like it was no big deal and took a sip of his wine, watching the waitress in a low cut sweater bend over and pour wine at the table next to them.

"So, does he suck as badly as I said he would?" Meg giggled into the phone. Grace heard Bianca scream in the background, "I warned you!"

"I had no idea," Grace answered vaguely, trying not to burst into laughter and tip off Tony that the call was anything but a serious emergency.

"Oh, come on! He practically has 'dull' tattooed across his forehead, and he's the worst dresser. So, you need a rescue, right? What story are you going to use today? Mom's in the hospital, Mom took a nasty fall, or Mom got hit by a bus? You know those would require extra prayers this week," Meg teased.

"That's terrible," Grace quipped back, biting her cheek to keep from laughing. A giant smile would not sell an emergency to Tony, and right now she was desperate to get out of this dinner. She sucked it up and prepared for an Oscar-worthy performance.

Tony looked confused as he watched her, trying to decipher her end of the conversation and get some idea of what the call was all about.

Grace sighed into the phone and pressed the receiver more tightly to her ear to hide Meg's cheery voice as much as possible.

"OK, it's that bad, huh? Going for maximum impact, ready to bolt immediately? Well, I don't know what you were thinking in accepting the date; he isn't even cute, Grace. Just because he lives in the building doesn't mean you have to go on a date with him. You should have just said no or told him we were lesbians... or something. God, we seriously need to discuss raising your standards when it comes to men when you get home. Put him out of his misery. Go with the naked mom story. The movie starts in fifteen." With that parting bit of advice, Meg hung up on her. Fortunately for Grace, Meg talked incredibly fast, so it only took her seconds to relay the entire message.

At the end of Meg's tirade, Grace dropped her head into her hands and prepared to sell her sad story to Tony.

"Of course I understand... No, thank you so much for letting me know, Meg. I'll meet you there," Grace said into the silent phone. Then she snapped it shut and tossed her napkin onto the table.

"Tony, I have to go." She proceeded to replay her favorite sob story of her schizophrenic mom who had forgotten to take her meds and was found naked in a phone booth downtown. Grace turned on the waterworks, a gift she had that came in quite handy at times like these. A few apologies and a doggie bag later—no point in wasting perfectly good food when there were starving people in the world, not to mention the fact that leftovers were Meg's required payment for saving her—and Grace ran out of the restaurant into the chilly Portland air. *Free at last, free at last,* she thought with a smile on her face as she happily jumped into her car and cranked the radio. With new-found excitement, she made her way home to join her two best friends and get as far away from Tony as possible.

Grace smelled the popcorn as soon as she stepped off of the elevator.

Meg and Bianca must be close to starting the movie, she thought as she rushed down the hall, not wanting to be late.

"Hi, honeys! I'm home." Grace came through the door and gently tossed her keys into the wicker basket on the counter.

Meg and Bianca were perched on the couch, remote control and popcorn in hand. "Grace," they squealed in delight, "you escaped!"

Bianca, Meg, and Grace had been best friends for nearly four years. They met during their sophomore year of college, and after a horrible time living with insane roommates in the dorms, they decided to get an apartment together their junior year and had been living together ever since.

Bianca and Meg graduated with undergraduate degrees in interior design and currently worked at Baker Design House in downtown Portland. They had been there for the last year and a half, and even though they were only twenty-four years old, they had started to make quite a name for themselves. They were becoming two of the most highly sought after young designers in town.

Grace was the same age as her friends, but she was still in school and would be graduating in June with her Master's in Literature. In the meantime, she was teaching English Lit classes at the local community college. The classes she taught didn't make her a ton of money to live on, but her parents were very supportive of her education and were helping her financially until she finished her degree and could get a full-time job at the university.

Even with successful jobs and graduate level educations, the girls still found themselves failing with men. These days, they were in the midst of a "dating drought" as they liked to call it. It seemed none of them could find a decent guy for any sort of long term relationship. They had been going on a series of random dates that ranged from bad to disgusting on the date scale. Lately, their Friday nights involved one or two of them ending a bad date early, a big bowl of popcorn, and a "chick flick" to take their minds off of their misery.

Grace glanced over at the couch and saw the leggy redhead stretched out there, flipping through a magazine. "Bianca, what are you doing home already? You had a date, too. How'd you get home before me?" Bianca had left for her date at the same time as Grace, but she had already been home and screaming in the background when Meg called Grace at the restaurant.

Bianca blushed furiously at the question. She had very high standards when it came to guys. To Bianca, chemistry with a guy was everything, and if she didn't feel it immediately, she wasn't going to wait around for it to blossom. That was Bianca. She was a strong, beautiful woman, and she needed a man that was her equal; that was just how she was wired. If it was a blind date, she always had the guy wear a red rose on his lapel so she could check him out before she actually went so far as to introduce herself to him, giving her the option to walk away if she wasn't attracted to him. Of course, even the good looks and chemistry would only get a guy so far. He'd better have a brain and a personality to back it up, or she would leave him the first chance she got.

Meg wasn't nearly as bad as Bianca, but she was a hopeless romantic, looking for her one true love, convinced she would know him on sight. Her personality was quirky and wonderful. She too went on many first dates, but very few second dates for just that reason. Sometimes Grace envied Meg's faith in true love and happy endings more than she cared to admit.

Bianca laughed darkly, and then launched into the story of her disastrous date as the previews played on the TV. "You know I hate blind dates. I did it as a favor to this girl at work, and after seeing this guy, I'm not sure I'm going to ever speak to Cindy again! He was this scrawny blond guy with a cheesy mustache! I mean really, when have I ever liked a guy with facial hair? Ugh! I gave the hostess twenty dollars to tell him I threw up in the parking lot," she said, completely unashamed of her actions.

Bianca was not one to waste her time with being nice; she always cut to the chase. Grace was glad Bianca liked her, because she wouldn't want to be on her bad side.

The girls joined Grace in the kitchen and plopped down onto the bar stools across the counter. Grace smiled as she looked at them, so opposite in looks but similarly dazzling.

Bianca's long, red hair hung down past the middle of her back, thick and straight. Her blue eyes were mesmerizing and framed with thick, lush eyelashes. Blessed with a wonderful metabolism, she had a curvy, womanly body to die for without ever going to the gym. Women were jealous of her; men were enamored instantly. Throw in a pair of killer legs that went on for miles, she was gorgeous.

Meg was average in height, but next to Bianca's long legs, everyone looked tiny. Her small frame and currently chocolate brown hair made her a much more exotic beauty. Always a work in progress, she changed her hair color as often as some women changed their nail color. Last month it had been platinum blond with pink highlights. No matter what, her deep blue eyes shone under the veil of her thick hair, twinkling with life, just like Meg herself. While average in stature, Meg had one of the biggest personalities you would ever come across. Everyone she ever met remembered her. Her smile lit up a room, and people just naturally gravitated to her warmth and happiness.

Grace placed the foil swan with her leftovers in front of Meg. "Thank you for saving me from Tony the Dull," she said with a bow as she stood across the counter.

"No problem, but next time, please listen to us when we tell you someone isn't right for you. We're designers, for goodness sake; we can tell when things go together and when they don't. It's what we do." Meg rolled her eyes and dramatically snapped the neck of the swan, digging into the leftovers. It was her silliness that Grace loved most about her.

"So I guess we're the big losers this weekend, Bianca. At least I got a decent appetizer out of it and Meg got a foil swan of lasagna." Grace laughed, trying her best to be a "glass half full" girl.

Bianca shrugged her shoulders. "True, but that's also an hour of your life you'll never get back, an hour wasted—on a dork. I, however, spent my hour productively shopping! Look at these fabulous shoes I found." She squealed as she threw her foot into the air revealing a sleek black stiletto.

After an extensive discussion about the versatility of black patent leather heels in one's fall wardrobe, Grace let out a loud sigh. "Girls, what are we going to do about all these losers we've been going on dates with? Where are all the good guys hiding?"

Meg laughed. "If we just keep going, eventually we will have dated every loser in the greater Portland area, and then, by process of elimination, we'll finally come across the nice guys."

"Yes, but we might be eighty years old by then, in a nursing home, eating pudding, and making Popsicle stick sculptures," Grace teased.

"Oh, can we be roomies in the nursing home?" Meg asked excitedly. "Then we can wear our Juicy sweat suits and make all the other old people jealous of our fabulous style."

"Enough about getting old and wrinkly, please. Let's focus on the here and now, where we're twenty-four and looking fit and fantastic. I'm with Grace; I'm tired of kissing frogs. I really want to make out with a handsome prince,"

Bianca whined. "Is that really so much to ask? One sexy, gorgeous, mentally stable, gainfully employed guy with an amazing personality, that doesn't smell like mothballs or live with his mother?" Her eyes glazed over as she began to daydream about her perfect man.

Grace glanced over at Meg and found her deep in her own fantasy as she gracefully swayed with an invisible dance partner, probably named Mr. Right. Struck with an idea, Grace went to the refrigerator, took out three beers, and opened them, placing one in front of each of the girls. "I propose we go on a boy-boycott until the new year," Grace said as she happily waved her beer in the air. "Who's with me?"

Both of her friends considered the idea for a few seconds before smiles crept onto their faces. Meg, of course, had questions. "What are the rules of a boy-boycott? No dates, I assume, but what else? Can we kiss random boys? What if they kiss us? It doesn't happen to me much, but Bianca gets that a lot, so I figured I'd ask..."

"Hold on a minute, Meg. Let's make a list!" Grace dug in the drawer for a pen.

Bianca snatched a notebook off the nearby desk as Grace tossed her the pen she found. "OK, Boy-Boycott Official Rules," she wrote across the top of the page.

Rule number one: No dates.

Rule number two: No tongue kissing with boys. Closed lip kissing is fine. If a guy crams his tongue down your throat unexpectedly, it doesn't count, unless you kiss him back. (AKA Bianca's rule)

Rule number three: No sex... of any kind. If you wouldn't want to see your parents do it, that counts as sex and it's off limits.

Rule number four: Each of us puts $200 into the pot. If you break the rules of the boycott, you lose the money. The last person(s) standing gets the money to spend on a hot new pair of shoes to be worn on her first date of the new year and gets eternal bragging rights about her superior will power.

Bianca flipped the paper around so Meg and Grace could read it and check to see if they agreed with all of the rules. They quickly scanned the list; Grace was the first to sign the paper, followed by Meg, and finally Bianca. Grace ran into her room, her wavy black hair flowing behind her as she grabbed her wad of emergency cash. She slammed $200 onto the counter. Meg and Bianca disappeared for a few minutes, and then did the same. They hid the winnings in the cookie jar and tucked it into the back corner of the counter.

"To the boycott!" Grace cheered as she raised her beer high into the air.

"To the boycott!" Bianca and Meg toasted in unison.

❧

The smoke in the club was starting to burn Michael's eyes. He glanced to his left and found Jack and Ryan sitting on the nearby bench with a bleached blonde draped over each of their laps. Candy and Sandy were a set of twins from California with incredible bodies but about as much personality as a toilet seat.

"Mikey…," a voice whined in Michael's ear.

He turned to his right to see Donna, brainless friend of the twins and his date for the evening, pouting, inches away from his face.

"Mikey, why aren't you paying attention to me?" she asked as she snaked her way into his lap.

Because you're dull, dim, disgusting, drab, desolate, demonic… he thought to himself. *Nice use of the letter D, Michael.*

Michael flashed a dashing smile that he knew, from years of experience, would allow him to get away with anything and said, "Donna, my name is Michael, not Mikey. Please try and remember that; I'm tired of reminding you." Michael looked out the corner of his eye and saw Jack start laughing as Candy—or was it Sandy?—played with his hair.

"Come on, Michael, let's dance," Donna squealed as she jumped to her feet. "I love this song," she shouted over the music, pulling on Michael's arm.

"I don't dance, sorry."

Ryan raised his eyebrow suspiciously. He knew Michael was lying, and that he actually loved to dance, but obviously Michael didn't believe Donna was even worth the walk across the dance floor.

Michael looked at both Jack and Ryan and pressed two fingers to his temple which was their universal sign for "bail."

They both laughed and stood up somewhat abruptly, knocking Candy and Sandy off their laps. "Sorry, ladies, Michael has a migraine. We need to be going. Thanks for a pleasant evening. We'll…see you around," Ryan said as he gallantly kissed Candy's hand—or was it Sandy's?

They went through the motions of exchanging phone numbers, although the one Michael gave to Donna was to a local pizza joint, not his apartment. That was his signature way to end a bad date and he felt absolutely no guilt about doing it. He figured at least she'd end up with a great place to order pizza from.

A few kisses on the cheek later and they were in Jack's truck, flying down the highway.

❧

"What the hell were we thinking, guys? If I had to listen to one more story about their ridiculous sorority, I was going to stab myself." Michael shuddered at the memory. The evening had been filled with countless tales about rushing and pledging, things he loathed beyond words.

"Hey, man, it was twins! I had to go for it. You never know, sometimes twins can be a lot of fun. Of course this time, not so much… God were they stupid or what? You know Candy actually asked me if she was the first girl I'd ever picked up at work. Can you imagine?" Jack laughed. "So I said, 'Of course, sweetie, only you,' and she totally bought it."

Ryan, Jack, and Michael had known each other for years. They met their senior year of college as they all finished their degrees in business management. About eighteen months ago, they'd started tending bar at a local nightclub to allow them to research a business venture they were interested in pursuing together. The Vault was a great place to work. They made easy money as bartenders, and working with their buddies was a major bonus.

On more than one occasion, the guys had taken out girls they met at work. They lovingly referred to them as the "barflies." Some of their co-workers probably considered them major players for their free-wheeling ways, but they were twenty-six years old and good-looking, so they used what they had to their advantage. The funny thing was, even though they took out a lot of girls, very few of the dates turned into relationships. More often than not, the girls ended up being bubble heads, and the guys left them sitting in some nightclub, never to see them again. Tonight had been no different.

Since it was common knowledge that Michael always kept his refrigerator stocked, Jack and Ryan parked the car and followed him up to his apartment for a late night snack before heading back to their place. Jack and Ryan lived in your classic bachelor pad, with a pool table instead of a dining room table and more beer in the refrigerator than food. Michael, however, liked his privacy and had always lived alone. He loved Ryan and Jack; he just couldn't live with them.

Three beers and a package of mini corn dogs later, they were sitting around Michael's kitchen table, questioning if there were any decent girls in the Greater Portland area.

"Look at us. Just how lame are we? It's not even midnight on a Friday night, and here we are, huddled around the table, eating junk food and drinking beer—alone," Michael complained. Of course, hanging out together was a far better option than being out on a disastrous date with another brainless bimbo. Deep down, Michael knew he needed something…something more in his life, someone special.

"We do look like losers, I'll give you that. I mean, we're good-looking guys! What's wrong with us?" Jack asked with irritation as he ran his fingers through his dark spiked hair. Of the three of them, Jack had the most outgoing personality. He could probably talk a plant into coming back to his apartment if he put his mind to it; he was that charismatic. Girls loved his large frame and well-defined muscles, and Jack loved flexing them for anyone who was interested. He was the playful, big brother type, and everyone who met him wanted to be his friend.

Michael glanced over at Ryan, who was flipping through the Arts section of the newspaper, and smiled. In contrast to Jack, Ryan was more the strong, silent type—a real gentleman and a self proclaimed romantic. When he dated a girl, he often put her up on a pedestal, treating her like a queen, probably a result of being raised by his strong, southern mother. The girls swooned over his long blond hair with its natural highlights and his ice blue eyes. Where Jack was big and broad shouldered, Ryan was the tallest of the three men, and while muscular, his height made him appear exceptionally lean.

Michael had always been described by people as the boy next door that every mom wanted her daughter to go out with in high school. He was very smart, did well in school, and was voted most popular guy in his senior class. In college, he always had girls throwing themselves at him, but of the three, Michael was the most picky when it came to dating. He was not about to waste his time with someone he didn't feel a connection with no matter how beautiful she was, so he developed his routine of only giving his phone number to the girls that he felt something for, ones that intrigued him. The rest got the number to the pizza joint. His blue eyes made the girls melt, and they loved to run their fingers through his dark brown hair, which he always kept on the long side and purposely messy.

Ryan looked at Michael over the top of the newspaper and shrugged in response to the question, but Jack was right. They *were* good-looking, and tons of girls hit on them every night at work. Unfortunately, they weren't girls a guy could have a conversation with that lasted more than three minutes. Their skills were more in the physical realm, rather than the intellectual. Definitely not the kind of women they'd ever dare take home to meet their mothers, that's for sure.

Ryan thought about it for a second as he chewed on his last corn dog. "You know, I don't think there's anything wrong with us. What's that one song? 'Looking for Love in all the Wrong Places.' I think that's our problem. I mean, my mom keeps bugging me that I'm never going to meet a nice girl at the bar. According to her, nice girls wouldn't be caught dead picking up a guy in a bar because they're off at the museum or the library. Maybe she's right."

Jack's mouth fell open in shock. "You're not seriously suggesting we go trolling the library for chicks? Or a museum … Wait. Like an art museum, or are we talking a history museum? I could tolerate the dinosaur bones and war relics, but modern art will just give me a headache. A red dot on a white canvas isn't 'a representation of a woman's struggle in a male dominated society;' it's a red freakin' circle!" Michael and Ryan nodded their heads in agreement with Jack's artistic tirade.

Michael considered Mama Bartlett's point for a minute. Most nice girls didn't hit on bartenders at the bar; it seemed like a reasonable assumption. It only followed suit that libraries and museums wouldn't be filled with bimbos and brainless twits. Sure, one or two would probably sneak in from time to time, but you had to actually know what a book was to be at the library, and you had to be able to appreciate art to be at a museum.

Slamming his hand on the table, Michael said, "I think we should give it a try. What the hell do we have to lose? Let's go look for the nice girls in town. No more barflies. If we meet them at the bar, they're off limits." He glanced back and forth between Jack and Ryan, trying to gauge their reactions to his unorthodox suggestion.

Jack was more interested in chugging his beer than answering the question. Ryan, however, looked deep in thought.

"I'm with Michael, no more barflies. Bring on the smart girls," he said with great enthusiasm. "Jack?"

Both Michael and Ryan knew it was an all-or-none proposition. The only way it would work was if Jack agreed and they were all in this together.

A grin came across Jack's face. "Care to make it a little more interesting … say, with a small wager?" His eyebrows arched up playfully, daring the guys to accept the challenge.

As childish as it sounded, the guys loved making bets. They'd bet on the weather, how much snow they'd get over the winter, if Jack would go home with a blonde or a brunette. If there was something to bet on, they definitely found it.

"What's the bet, Jack?" Michael asked, his interest now piqued by the possibility of a little friendly competition.

"Well, don't they say sex ruins a relationship? And we are looking for quality girlfriends, right? So, we each put a couple of nights' worth of tips in a pot, and the last guy to have sex wins the money. That helps make sure none of us cheat or go have some meaningless quickie with a barfly. Sound reasonable?" Jack offered.

"Sure, let's do it," Ryan and Michael agreed. They both knew that this probably wouldn't be easy, and that they were all going to have to be out of their element by looking for nice, intelligent girls, but they were all ready to give it their very best effort.

Michael, for one, loved a good challenge, and this was sure to be just that. Smart girls were … well, smart. He just hoped they weren't smarter than he was. Besides, who knew what they may find if they actually looked for love in all the *right* places.

Chapter 2

It was still early when Grace woke up to the strange sensation of her bed vibrating underneath her as the sun streamed brightly through the window. "Are we having an earthquake?" she mumbled into her pillow, refusing to open her eyes.

"Nooo," a giddy voice sang from the edge of the bed.

"Well, then, unless you're Brad Pitt and you're trying to wake me up to make sweet love to me, go away!" Grace threw the covers tightly over her head, and with her arms, she braced for the wrestling match that was certain to ensue.

Meg, however, was never one to play fair. Instead of fighting to free Grace's head to get her out of bed, she pulled up the bottom part of the comforter and attacked Grace's ticklish feet.

"Wake up! Come on, Grace, get up! We have things to do today."

Grace groaned and sat up in bed. "What do we have to do today? It's Saturday. Saturdays were made for sleeping in. Why am I up at…" she glanced at her clock, "oh my God, eight-thirty in the morning? Are you insane?"

Before she could throw the blanket back over her head, Meg scooped it up and ran into the family room. Grace streaked after her in a T-shirt and underwear and tackled Meg somewhere near the coffee table.

"Ha! I win. Give it back, Meg. I'll see you in a few hours," Grace teased as she triumphantly dragged the blanket back into her room and locked the door.

"Drop the blanket," a menacing voice said in Grace's ear.

"Argh!" she screamed as she jumped into the air, flapping her arms to fend off the possible attacker.

Laughter filled the room as she opened her eyes to see Bianca flop across the bed in hysterics. Her bright red hair was splayed across the sheets. "Grace…that was priceless…your face…" she said in between gasps for air.

"My loving roommates, ladies and gentlemen. One tries to freeze me to death by stealing my blanket, and the other tries to give me a heart attack, all before nine a.m.!" Grace sat down on her bed with an angry huff.

Meg tapped on the door. "Can I come in now please, Grace? It's not fair. Bianca is in there." She whined like child, hoping to wear her friend down.

Grace rolled her eyes at Bianca then strolled over to the door, propping it open a crack. "What's the plan for today, before I allow you to enter?"

"Just a little shopping, silly, now move." Meg shoved open the door with her shoulder and leaped inside to join Bianca on the bed.

☙

Shopping with Bianca and Meg was an experience not to be taken lightly. If they hadn't majored in Interior Design, their second choice for an occupation would have been fashion. They were up on all the latest trends and looks coming off of the runways. They gave the phrase "fashion forward" a whole new meaning. However, Grace preferred to dress for comfort, a concept that was completely lost on those two. If she was being totally honest with herself, she dressed for invisibility. Attention was the one thing Grace could do without. Bianca and Meg, on the other hand, dressed to be noticed the second they entered a room.

Their clothing choices illustrated the differences between the three women perfectly. Bianca and Meg were self-confident and self-assured women who turned heads in a crowd. They wore whatever they wanted and got away with it. Bianca, with her curvy shape, long legs, ice blue eyes, and long mane of red hair that men longed to run their fingers through, commanded every room she entered. She made sure her clothing highlighted her assets as much as possible, and every outfit was topped off with a gorgeous pair of stilettos that made her even taller.

Meg was average height, but with blue eyes and dark hair, her classic beauty allowed her to pull off clothes like no one else. She was artsy and creative not only with her clothes but also with accessories, each an expression of her mood of the day. You never exactly knew what to expect with her. She could go into her room to get ready for a date and come out wearing a blue wig just because she felt like it. Once you met Meg, you never forgot her exuberance and energy. Her clothes reflected her playful side, her sense of whimsy, and her flair for the romantic.

Compared to Bianca and Meg, Grace felt absolutely average. Her long black hair had a few dull red highlights, but other than that it looked like everyone else's she passed on the street. There was a hint of a wave to it, making it messy and utterly untamable in her mind. She wasn't rail thin, either; she had hips and breasts, both of which she felt were too big, so she tried to hide them as whenever possible. Grace believed that guys would never look at her the same way they looked at Meg and Bianca. She lacked the grace, the confidence, and the daring. The men that Meg and Bianca attracted were the good-looking model types. Grace believed her "type" was more along the lines of the accountants and computer geeks of the world. Her clothes sealed the deal—they were always conservative and modest, making her look as average as she felt.

"Fine, I'll go shopping, but I get two vetoes this time instead of the usual one, got it?" Grace insisted, her conditions set in stone.

Her friends grudgingly agreed to her terms. They knew Grace could be extremely stubborn. If they went too overboard with their clothing suggestions for her, Grace could call into effect her veto and replace one item of their liking with one item of her own. If they played their cards right, they could usually get Grace into a more flattering outfit. Pushing her too far, though, usually resulted in her getting something dreary she could hide her cute shape under.

"Go shower and we'll head out." Meg ran out of the room to prepare for their day of shopping.

"What in the world do you have against fabrics with Lycra in them, Grace?" Meg shouted in the middle of the store as she waved a stretchy blue shirt in her friend's face. They had been at the mall for hours, trying on too many outfits to count. There were so many, in fact, that Grace's head started to spin.

"That shirt clings to me, and I prefer things that flow." Grace had already used both her vetoes of the day, so thankfully she wasn't the proud owner of leather pants or a red sequined tube top. Now, she was on her own, and without a veto, and it was up to her to persuade Meg to choose another shirt. Unfortunately, Meg and Bianca weren't easily swayed, especially when it came to clothes.

"You wear everything a size too big so you can hide your body. This looks amazing on you. It shows that you actually have some sexy curves there, honey," Bianca said as she looked Grace up and down, smirking.

"You're getting this and these jeans to go with it, no arguments. All your vetoes have been used." Meg victoriously danced over to the cashier and handed the girl her credit card. "This outfit is on me. I guarantee that when you wear it, it'll be a night to remember!"

With the final item jammed into the bag and paid for, they headed to lunch. The server brought over their drinks, and Grace had sucked down her whole glass of iced tea before she even had time to realize how thirsty she was.

"So, Grace, Meg and I have something we'd like to talk to you about," Bianca said with a bit of hesitation in her voice.

Grace looked suspiciously at both of her friends, waiting for one of them to begin.

"OK, here's the thing. Since we have a few weeks left in our boycott until we're allowed to date, we thought it might be a good time for you to…um…broaden your horizons when it comes to guys. We think you should use these weeks to, let's say, loosen up a bit?" Bianca chose her words carefully, waiting to see if Grace was going to haul off and hit her.

Instead, Grace gave her a rather confused look. "Huh?"

"Dear, sweet Grace," Meg began, "men are like a buffet. There all sorts of different 'flavors,' if you will, for you to sample. Exotic, spicy, foreign, hearty, sweet. However, you tend to keep going to the comfort food section of the buffet. How many times can you eat fried chicken before it makes you sick? Haven't you ever just wanted to walk over and grab a handful of something different?" Meg asked excitedly as she leaned across the table. Her hair framed her face as her blue eyes sparkled.

Grace took a deep breath then answered. "So, let me see if I understand you. Over the next few weeks, you want me to 'grab' a handful of some foreign guy? Wouldn't that be against one of our rules or something?" she challenged as she sucked the last sip of tea from her glass, unable to look Meg or Bianca in the face.

"Come on, Grace, we're serious. You keep choosing these dorky, boring guys. Cadavers have more personality than most of the men you go out with.

You could do so much better!" Bianca spoke with such sincerity, Grace almost believed her.

But then, she looked at Meg's beautiful face, her winning smile, and Grace crashed back to reality. "Thanks, girls, I know you mean well, but you two can eat from any part of the 'buffet' and no one would question you being there. I'm just not in your league, never have been, never will be. Can we drop the topic please?" Grace tried to hold in the tears that she felt creeping into the corners of her eyes.

"How can you say that? You are a great catch—funny and beautiful, smarter than both of us combined, loving and kind … Any guy would be lucky to have you. All we're suggesting is that you raise your standards a little. Try flirting with a few guys you might not normally flirt with. What's the big deal? You can't go on a date with them anyway, and if you get rejected, who cares? You know you're going to go home with Bianca and me no matter what, so no harm done. Come on, Grace, we'll help you. Right, Bianca?" Meg glanced over to the vibrant redhead for support.

Bianca nodded her head vigorously in agreement, her blue eyes wide with hope.

"Please, Grace, for me, will you just try?" Meg unleashed the full power of her pouty lip on Grace and, of course, she caved.

"Fine, I'll try. My face may be permanently red after this little lesson, however, and I make no guarantees that I will be able to pull it off. Of course, if I'm going to go outside my comfort zone for the next few weeks, you two will be joining me. When I think of a little 'character expanding activity' for each of you, you have to go with the flow, no complaints. Deal?" Grace raised an eyebrow, daring them to disagree.

"This boycott could be quite interesting for all of us," Bianca whispered with a playful smile.

☙

The next few weeks of the boycott were actually quite fun. Without having to worry about getting dates for the weekend or dreading blind dates, the girls' stress level went down considerably. Their weekends turned into one big "Girl's Night Out," and they would literally open the phone book, close their eyes, and point to pick a new club to try.

Bianca and Meg were teaching Grace the finer points of flirting. Playful banter, hair flips, and the casual touch on the arm were fast becoming a part of Grace's social repertoire. So far, she had flirted with a body builder who could lift four hundred pounds, who even Bianca had admitted later was intimidating. There was the professional soccer player from Brazil—from the "international section" of the man buffet no doubt—and the guitar player with hair as long as Grace's. Needless to say, they'd had pleasant conversations, but none of them were exactly her cup of tea. Her friends, however, were proud of her willingness to try and talk to these guys, and they gave her a standing ovation when the soccer player gave her his phone number before heading back to Brazil.

On Wednesday, when Grace got home from class, she found Bianca on the couch with her nose pressed into the latest issue of *Cosmo*.

"Guess what? I thought of something new I want you to experience during our boycott. Are you up for it?" Grace asked, a huge grin plastered across her face.

Bianca lowered the magazine and looked suspiciously over the top of the pages. "What is it?" Her eyes narrowed as her brows pulled tightly together.

"Football!" Grace beamed happily. "I got three tickets to a Seahawks game this weekend. Feel like a road trip?" Grace pleaded as she bounced excitedly on to the couch. Sports were not Bianca's thing by any stretch of the imagination, but Grace loved football, mainly because her dad was a huge fan, and his love of the game had rubbed off on her.

"Oh come on. Just think about it—big, muscular guys in tight pants. I know you can appreciate that. I'll even bring binoculars for you, and there's shopping there too." She didn't mention every item for sale had a Seahawk on it—Bianca didn't need that much information.

"Fine, I'll go. But if some stupid football fan spills beer or nachos on me, I'm so gonna smack the hell out of them."

Grace threw her arms around Bianca and shouted toward Meg's room. "Meg, she said yes! It looks like we're going on a road trip this weekend!"

Another night at work, and yet another barfly was trying to hit on Michael as he stood behind the bar.

"Are you sure I can't make you change your mind? We could have a lot of fun together," she whispered as she reached out and touched his bangs, slowly brushing them off his face. Her long blond hair cascaded over her freckled shoulders as she leaned across the bar.

"Sorry, but I have a girlfriend, and she's a real bitch. Oh look, here she comes. Hi, honey." Michael waved over at Vicki, one of the servers at the bar.

Vicki was a nice girl, but her twelve facial piercings and purple hair often terrified people at first glance. She gave Michael a slightly confused wave back until he casually nodded his head at the blond and she took the hint. Her eyes lit up with understanding, she blew Michael a kiss and then glared at the barfly beside him.

"*That's* your girlfriend?" the barfly asked, completely stunned.

"Yep. I told you she's a bitch. Last time someone hit on me, she broke the girl's nose," Michael muttered under his breath dramatically.

"Oh, look at the time! Hey, I gotta run. My friends are waiting for me … Um, see ya," she said with one more quick glance in Vicki's direction before she sprinted out the door.

"Shoo, barfly, shoo." Michael heard Jack laugh as he mockingly waved the woman away with his hand.

Ryan just shook his head. "I thought you might cave there for a second, Michael. She was really cute."

"I'm not losing two hundred bucks that quickly! Give me some credit please." He laughed as he wiped down the top of the bar. The lights had just come up; last call was over. Finally, it was time to start closing down shop. Jack began washing glasses while Ryan took inventory.

Vicki came over and smacked Michael in the back of the head. "What the hell was that about? Can't you just tell your admirers to go away all on your own? I'm gonna to start charging every time you make me blow you a kiss, Michael. It's so lame. Now if you want, I'd be happy to punch them or perhaps even spit on them. That's more my style." Vicki laughed as she cracked her knuckles to prove her point. She had the toughest exterior, but underneath it all, she was a really loyal friend, which is the main reason why she and the guys got along so well.

Michael gave her a big hug. "Thank you for saving me. You know you love being my pretend girlfriend. Steve even gave us his blessing." Steve was her very large boyfriend. He was a six-foot-five biker covered in tattoos, and he looked like he could eat Michael for breakfast. One night when he was at the bar, the guys had told him of their bet. Steve had laughed for a few minutes, convinced they'd all fail miserably, and then offered Vicki's services as their "personal fly swatter."

Vicki poked Michael in the shoulder. "So, have you guys found what you are looking for yet? How much longer do I have to do this? Last night I had to save those two, tonight it was you, Romeo. You guys better spend the next few days hunting for some nice girls. Don't you have this weekend off? " she asked, faking irritation.

"Yeah, we finally have a free weekend. If we're lucky, we'll have found some nice girls before Monday, and your fly swatting days will be over," Michael said to her with a wink.

"Yeah, good luck with that, boys," she said with a wave as she ran over to Steve who was standing in the doorway grinning at her.

"Bye, Vicki! Bye, Steve!" Jack yelled as he watched them clasp their hands together and walk out of the bar.

It was close to three in the morning when Ryan and Jack finally dropped Michael off at home. He placed his keys on the counter and immediately crawled into bed, pulling the covers tightly over his head, sleep being the only thing on his mind. As usual, he flipped on the radio and drifted off to sleep.

Michael was still in a deep sleep, having the most wonderful dream, when the phone started ringing.

"Damn it!" His eye peeked out from under his blanket, temporarily blinding him with the bright morning sun. He glanced at the clock as he started swatting his hand toward the sound of the phone. Eventually, Michael knocked the receiver off the cradle and heard it crash to the floor.

"Crap!" he shouted. "I'm coming, just a minute … stupid phone," he mumbled as he grabbed the receiver and rolled back onto the bed. "It isn't even noon yet. This better be important," Michael growled into the phone.

"How much beauty rest do you need, pretty boy?" Jack quipped, his booming voice wide awake and chipper.

"It's not beauty rest I need, Jack. What I need is time away from the sound of your voice!" Michael yelled into the phone.

"Dude, I have delicate ears, you know. Hey, Ryan, you talk to the crab."

The phone hit something hard before Ryan's groggy voice mumbled, "Michael?"

"Did he just wake you up too?" Michael asked, now somewhat amused.

"Yes, do you want me to wait until you get here so we can kill him together, or should I finish him off myself?" Ryan asked with a laugh.

"No, wait for me. I want to see him suffer. So what the hell is the reason for the early wake-up call?" Michael sat up in bed and tried to stretch out his still weary muscles.

"All I know is, he ran into the room and jumped on my bed, blabbering something about going hunting today."

"Hunting? Like with guns? Don't you usually have to get up well before noon to do that? And I think we need a license or something." Michael was completely confused now. They had never gone hunting before. Hell, they hadn't even so much as gone fishing.

The extension picked up on Ryan's end, and he heard Jack's voice. "We're going hunting for girls, you idiots! Get yourselves clean and smelling good; don't embarrass me. Today we're going to begin our intensive search. Get a move on. You have an hour!" Then he hung up his extension.

"OK, Ryan, I better go make myself 'smell good' for some mystery nice girls that we probably won't even meet today. See you soon." Michael laughed as he hung up the phone. Jack could really get into things sometimes, so Michael couldn't help but wonder where they would be hunting on today's little adventure.

Michael pulled up in front of Jack and Ryan's apartment a half hour later only to find them waiting outside on the sidewalk, pacing. Jack hopped up front while Ryan slid into the backseat. "Hey, Mike, ready for some fun?" Jack asked as he rubbed his hands together in anticipation.

"Where are these nice girl hunting grounds you spoke of earlier?" Michael asked, playing along with the hunting theme.

He took in a dramatic breath before saying, "To the library, my friend!"

After driving in circles for nearly twenty minutes, they found a branch of the Portland Metropolitan Library not far from their apartment. The guys climbed out of the car, ran their fingers through their hair, and went inside. It was relatively empty as they walked through the lobby. A number of senior citizens were gathered in some chairs off to the side for some type of workshop.

Michael elbowed Ryan and pointed. "Look, all the nice girls have gray hair. Who knew?" Ryan let out a laugh while Jack rolled his eyes in irritation.

"Guys, come on, it's like a nightclub. You have to work the room, see who's here, and mingle. You know what I mean?" Jack signaled like a stewardess showing where the emergency exits were on a plane. "Let's check the place out and find the action."

Michael and Ryan just shook their heads. "Lead the way, Jack. This is your show," Michael said as he held out his arm.

After a minute of looking around at the signs, Jack decided to head off to the fiction section. Having no real game plan, they wandered aimlessly up and down the aisles, occasionally glancing at the thousands of books they passed. The only people they crossed paths with were a man in his late forties flipping through a book on kitchen remodeling, an elderly woman who was looking for the restroom, and a three-year-old boy who had escaped from the children's section of the library and was hiding on a shelf from his now-panicked mother who was screaming his name.

"Great hunting grounds, Jack. Ryan, you better call your mom this afternoon and let her know the nice girls are most definitely *not* at the library." Jack and Michael snickered, imagining the possible conversation between Ryan and Mama Bartlett.

"This place is so boring!" Jack whined. "I mean, who needs all these books? Do they have magazines here too?" he asked hopefully, looking to Michael for the answer.

"Yes, Jack, they have magazines at the library too. A number of different ones, for your information," Michael said still laughing.

Jack's face lit up with a wicked smile. "Do you think they have *Playboys* here?"

Ryan rolled his eyes. "Jack, I highly doubt the public library stocks back issues of pornographic magazines." Jack laughed and slapped Ryan on the back.

Michael reached up and grabbed a book off the shelf and briefly flipped the pages before returning it to its original location. "Why don't you ask someone about the *Playboys*, Jack, if you're that curious?" he teased, never thinking Jack would actually do it. Before Michael could stop him, Jack darted out of the aisle and rounded the corner.

"If he finds porn in this library, I swear, I'll buy the first round of beers tonight," Ryan said laughing.

❧

After successfully getting the girls to agree to go to the Seahawks game, Grace threw on one of her cozy cardigan sweaters and headed out to pick up the tickets from her friend, Amanda. She had completed her Master's degree at the university with Grace and had been in most of her classes. Amanda was working this afternoon, so Grace headed over to meet her. Sure enough, Amanda was sorting through the books in the return bin, making nice, neat piles from the terrible mess at her feet.

"Grace! How are you today?" She gave a weary wave from behind the huge stacks of books in front of her.

"Hey, Amanda! Wow, looks like the book return threw up over here. What's up?" Grace started gathering books into her arms and placed them up on the counter, trying not to mess up the piles that Amanda had already organized.

"It's that time of the year when we send out our missing book notices. I guess a lot of people did some searching and found books under their beds this week." She chuckled as she blew a stray piece of hair from her face and continued sorting.

"How's the PhD coming?"

A half-hearted smile crossed her friend's face. "It's sucking the life out of me, but it'll be worth it, right?"

Grace laughed, once again happy with her decision to take a year off and teach before diving into her PhD as well. "Yeah, it'll be a piece of cake. So, I came to grab those tickets from you, if that's still OK?" Grace asked eagerly, leaning against the counter.

"You actually talked Bianca into going, huh? It was the hot guys in tight pants speech that sealed the deal, wasn't it?" Amanda asked with a big smile as she tamed her brown curls back into a ponytail.

"Yes, that and the promise of shopping. I just hope she likes Seahawks green!" Both of them laughed as they imagined Bianca dressed from head to toe in Seahawks gear. Of course, if anyone could wear it and make it look hot, it would be Bianca.

Amanda reached for her purse and dug around until she found the tickets. "Have a great time. I was hoping to be further along on my dissertation by now, but with things being so busy here, I've gotten behind. I'm just glad you'll be able to use them," Amanda said with a smile. She glanced around at all the books and sighed. "Well, I guess I better get back to sorting."

"You know what? I have some time before I'm meeting Meg. How about I help you get some of these back on the shelves before I leave?"

"You're a lifesaver! I have a date with John tonight, and I don't want to be stuck here too late." She pushed the two biggest piles in Grace's direction. Lucky for Amanda, Grace had spent so much time at this library, she was an honorary employee. She knew the Dewey decimal system as well as any librarian in town.

Grace walked behind the desk, dragged a book cart over, and after checking each book back in with the bar code scanner, she began loading the cart. Reaching into her purse, Grace searched for her glasses and a rubber band. She threw her hair up into a tight bun, hoping to keep it out of her face as she sorted the massive pile. When her cart was full, Grace headed off to the book stacks.

The cart was finally starting to look about halfway empty when Grace flopped into a nearby reading chair to take a short break. She tucked a piece of hair that had fallen out of her bun behind her ear.

I must look lovely, Grace thought to herself as she stood up and stretched. She had started to head down the next aisle when she saw three heads bobbing behind the other side of the bookcase. Grace could tell by the deep voices that it was a few guys, and they were snickering for some reason.

Idiots, she thought as she climbed up onto the stool and got back to work. The thick book about Sherman's March to the Sea fell off the cart with a loud thud.

"Crap," Grace mumbled as she climbed down to pick it up. But before she could bend over and get to the book, a large, masculine hand reached down and picked up the book for her.

"I think you dropped this," a deep voice said in Grace's ear.

Startled, she spun around to see the massive man standing inches from her face. He was as tall, dark, and handsome as they came, with dark spiked hair and light stubble covering his chin and cheeks. His body was covered with muscles that showed through his tight fitting T-shirt. She took a step back, suddenly feeling intimidated, and removed the book from his hand.

"Um, thank you very much. Glad it didn't land on your foot." Grace laughed as she nervously gnawed on her bottom lip.

"No problem," the big guy said as he stood there and continued staring at her.

"Can I help you with something?" Grace asked, trying to sound casual.

"Where do you keep the old issues of *Playboy*?" he managed to ask with a straight face. Someone coughed loudly from behind the stack.

Grace bit her cheek to keep herself from bursting into laughter. "Sorry, champ, no *Playboys* here. I do have some medical books over in the reference section you could probably see some boobs in, but they'll probably be pretty old and saggy. Sorry. Do you know where the reference section is?" She pointed over his head, doing her best to look serious as she took another book off the cart and climbed back up the stool. While Grace turned her back to hide her smile, she heard a low, sexy voice begin teasing the big guy.

"There you are! We thought you got lost, this being your first time in a library and all."

Grace spun around to see a striking guy with dark brown hair and piercing blue eyes joke and slap the big guy on the back, then casually lean against the book stack. Grace couldn't pull her eyes away from him; he was absolutely gorgeous. His brown hair was longer, with a hint of wave to it, and hung slightly into his eyes, his smile was breathtaking, and his eyes were deep and mysterious. After a few seconds, she realized she had been holding her breath and gasped for air. As she did, the third member of their party, a tall, slender blond guy joined them, suddenly making things feel very crowded in the narrow aisle. Grace took a step higher up on her stool as she tried her best to regain her composure.

"Shut up!" the big guy hissed to his friends as Grace grabbed another book and put it onto the shelf. He cleared his throat. "Um, thanks, but I think I'll pass on the saggy, medical boob books. So, what's your name?" he asked in husky voice that Grace assumed he intended to sound sexy, though it didn't really work for her. He was way too forward for her liking.

Grace glanced over at his friends and realized the guy with the blue eyes was smiling at her. Unexpectedly, she felt her heart start racing in her chest. "My name?" Grace was so flustered she couldn't think straight. "Wait a minute…" Suddenly, something struck her as odd about this whole situation.

What were three exceptionally good-looking guys doing wandering around in the library in the middle of the day, which one of them had all but admitted he had never set foot in before today, unless…

"Did you guys hear somewhere that libraries are good places to try and pick up girls? Was it on the news again? Just so I know… are you actually hitting on me in the middle of the library?" Grace asked incredulously, now grinning as the men shifted uncomfortably in their spots.

The look on the big guy's face was priceless. His mouth hung open while his friends doubled over in silent laughter, politely remembering they were still in a library. Somehow, Grace kept herself from laughing. She glanced back at her cart and realized there were still a ton of books to get through, so sadly, she decided it was probably time to wrap up this little chat.

"Listen, you seem like a nice enough guy, so I have a suggestion for you. Why don't you try to find a nice strip club, and then you can get girls and boobs all at the same time. Not many women here at the library are going to flash you their boobs, sorry. We library girls like to leave a little something to the imagination." Without waiting for his response, Grace took the cart and quickly pushed it past them, leaving the big guy speechless and his friends still shaking with laughter. The guy with the blue eyes stopped his laughing as she passed by and gave her a sexy smirk, tipping his head to her.

Well done, Grace, she thought to herself. *Bianca will love this story.*

With her heart still pounding in her chest, and unable to believe she had been so bold with three complete strangers, Grace hurried off a few aisles away to catch her breath. Out of the corner of her eye, she saw a very large figure storm down the main walkway toward the door. She watched a second longer and then saw a beautiful pair of blue eyes looking down the aisle at her, obviously still amused.

Grace didn't know what possessed her to do it, but before she could stop herself, she winked at him, her mouth turning up into the biggest grin. He returned her smile, waved, then dashed off after his friends. Adrenaline coursed through her veins in reaction to his smile, her whole body awakened. Grace had to stop herself from running to the end of the aisle just so she could watch him walk away. She took a few deep breaths to clear her head and told herself to stop swooning over the complete stranger, but when she finally got her wits about her, she dove back into the books, still unable to wipe the grin off her face.

Michael put the keys into the ignition and exploded with laughter.

"That went … well," Ryan managed to get out between breaths.

"Your face, Jack …" was all Michael could sputter.

Jack cursed. "Your mom's idea sucked, Ryan! That girl wasn't very nice," Jack mumbled as he changed the radio station.

Michael's thoughts drifted back to the beautiful woman who had taken on Jack and left him speechless in the aisle. No one ever stood up to Jack. His size alone was intimidating, and yet this girl, with her dark brown eyes, not only stood up to him, but she did it without blinking. And from the way the corners of her beautiful mouth twitched, she seemed to find the whole exchange just as hilarious as Michael had.

She was intriguing, she was beautiful, and from what Michael could tell, she had a sense of humor. *Maybe there are nice girls at the library*, he thought to himself as he started the car and drove Jack and Ryan back to their apartment.

Chapter 3

The drive to Seattle was a riot. Once the girls climbed in the car, they never stopped laughing. Grace loaded their favorite songs on her iPod, and they spent the two and a half hour drive singing along, doing elaborate hand motions to go along with the beat. Driving down the highway, they would get the funniest looks from the other cars they passed, but they hardly noticed because they were simply having a blast.

Grace held the tickets in her hand as they skipped toward the entrance gate. The guy scanning the tickets looked at them and smiled. "Wow, these are great seats, ladies. Follow the signs for Club Level to the elevator. Enjoy the game." He motioned them through the turnstile and they headed left, following the bright blue signs overhead.

An older gentleman in a blue-green sports coat stood in front of a set of elevators marked 'Club Level Seating.' The girls smiled and proudly showed him their tickets. With a nod of his head, he held open the doors to the elevator and wished them 'good day' as they began to close.

When the elevator doors opened again, the women were overwhelmed by the delicious smells of the mouthwatering food that they found arranged on a huge table to the right. The buffet was surrounded by smaller tables, each covered in long, white tablecloths. The usher who greeted them as they exited the elevator explained that the buffet was complimentary to all Club Level Seating guests and told them to help themselves to whatever they wanted.

"These are amazing tickets Amanda gave us," Grace mumbled as she looked over at her friends in awe.

Bianca and Meg nodded their heads in agreement as they headed over to make themselves a plate of food and order a drink from the bar. They settled at a table which overlooked the stadium. On their plates, they had piled everything from chicken wings and mini quiches to pasta, Caesar salad, and roast beef sandwiches. Even with all that food, there were still things on the buffet they hadn't even looked at yet. The food was delicious and tasted like it had been prepared at some swanky restaurant rather than at a football stadium.

Meg ate her fill then happily sat back in her chair, looking around at all the excited fans as they milled past on the way to their seats. "Oh look! I want one of those foam fingers, Grace. Where do we get those?" Meg asked with a huge smile, her childlike wonder getting the best of her.

"I bet there's a souvenir stand somewhere on this level that carries them. Why don't you go wander around and we'll wait here for you?" Grace grinned as Bianca just looked up in horror at the thought of Meg wielding the foam monstrosity.

Meg squealed, grabbed her purse, and ran over to a gentleman who was proudly waving his foam fingers over his head. After a quick conversation, he smiled and pointed Meg in the direction of the stand where he'd purchased it. She waved then took off like a shot into the crowd.

Grace and Bianca were just about to go search for their missing friend, when suddenly a flash of blue approaching the table caught their attention. Out of the corner of their eyes, they saw a girl wearing a Seahawks hat, jersey, scarf, and, of course, foam finger, waving frantically in their direction.

"Meg?" Bianca gasped in shock as she lifted the bill of the cap to get a good look at the girl's face underneath. "What the hell happened to you? Did you stumble into the locker room and get turned into the honorary team mascot?" she asked in revulsion.

"No, Miss Party Pooper. I'm just trying to show some team spirit. Look, I got you hats, too!" In Meg's hand were two baseball caps, identical to the one she was wearing.

Bianca looked disgusted, certainly imagining what the hat would do to her beautiful hair, which she'd spent a ridiculous amount of time styling this morning. She held the hat between two fingers and examined it like she was checking it for lice.

Grace, on the other hand, shrugged and whipped her hair into a quick pony tail, pulled it through the back of the hat, and put it proudly on her head. "Go Seahawks!" she yelled, pumping her fist into the air, which delighted Meg.

Bianca rolled her eyes and grudgingly put hers on backwards, growling, "Yeah, go birds…"

They quickly finished eating, threw away their trash, and started off to find their seats, which to their utter surprise, were in the front row. They were on the Seahawks' side of the field—the fifty yard line was directly in front of them, giving the girls the best seats in the house. As the Seahawks players warmed up, the girls couldn't help but scope out the fine physical specimens running around on the field before them.

Bianca had the binoculars pinned to her face most of the first half, rating the behinds of all the Seahawks players. Having chosen her favorite player by his splendidly muscular butt, she decided mid-way through the second half that she wanted to buy his jersey from one of the shops in the stadium.

Grace promptly handed Bianca a ticket stub so she could get back up to the club level and find their seats after her little outing. Not in the mood to shop, Grace and Meg stayed put, enjoying the rest of the extremely close game.

Nearly a half hour had passed when Bianca finally came back, wearing her new hat, the number eighty-eight jersey, and a totally pissed-off look on her face.

"What the hell happened to you?" Meg asked cautiously.

Other than her furious face, Bianca looked absolutely fabulous in the jersey. Somehow, she had managed to alter the shirt by cutting it so it was more like a half-shirt rather than a bulky football jersey. In her hand, she clutched a small bag of popcorn as she flopped down into the seat next to Grace.

"Ugh. Guys at football games are such pigs! You're not going to believe what happened to me." There was nothing but venom in her voice as she spoke. "So, I leave the club level in search of my jersey, which I find, no problem. After a little trip to the bathroom and a few minor alterations, it was finally wearable. I changed and started heading back this way when I decided to stop at a concession stand before I came back because the popcorn smelled so good. While I'm standing in line waiting, out of the blue, the guy next to me leans over … and grabs my ass!"

Meg and Grace burst out laughing because they both knew exactly what Bianca did when guys touched her without permission: she decked them.

Not missing a beat, Bianca continued with her story. "I turned around and said 'What the hell do you think you're doing?' and he gave some lame excuse about not trying to grab my ass, he was trying to grab *his wiener*. Can you believe it? What a freak show this place is!" She was so furious, she was almost shouting, and by now, her story had got the attention of a few of the people sitting nearby. Many of them were now chuckling and had turned toward Bianca to listen to the rest of the story.

"He actually…he said he was trying…to…grab his wiener?" Grace gasped while trying not to hyperventilate, she was laughing so hard.

"What did you do?" Meg squeaked out between laughs. Even though she already knew the answer, she wanted to hear Bianca say it.

"I decked him, of course. He was pretty big too, but he should have a nice black eye by morning! You know he had the nerve to try and follow me up here? Luckily, Mitch, that sweet guy in the green coat, stopped his regular-admission-ass at the elevator," she said with a humph.

"Sorry you were molested at the football game, Bianca. I really thought it'd be fun," Grace said trying to keep a straight face by biting her lip until it almost bled.

"Don't worry. I'm having fun, perverts and all. And actually, he was kind of cute, for a perv…" Bianca gave Grace a big hug so she knew she wasn't really mad. "Really, how can I be in a bad mood when I'm surrounded by so many muscular guys in tight pants?"

They spent the last few minutes of the game laughing about Wiener Guy, as they had lovingly named him. With their hats, popcorn, jerseys, and foam fingers in hand, the girls filed out of the stadium after an exciting day at the game and began the long trip back to Portland, laughing about the adventure they had managed to have on their trip to Seattle.

So, the quest to find a nice girl over the last week hadn't been going very well for the guys. After the fiasco at the library, Jack refused to even so much as touch a book; most certainly he was still reeling from the beating his ego took at the hands of the 'naughty librarian,' as they referred to her. Michael often found himself thinking about the woman in the library, wondering if he might be able to casually bump into her if he went back for a visit. The guys spent their weekend off getting some much needed rest and relaxation, but when Monday night rolled around, it was time to get back to the bar.

Michael was the first one to arrive at work. Ryan and Jack came flying in fifteen minutes late, full of apologies. "Sorry, dude, it's not my fault. Jack took a little longer than normal to get ready this evening," Ryan whispered, tilting his head subtly in Jack's direction, a small grin on his face.

Michael was about to ask what made Jack take so long when Vicki came screeching over to the bar. "Oh my God, Jack! What happened to you? Did you get into a fight?" She had grabbed his face and pulled it closer so she could inspect him.

Jack's face turned red at all the attention Vicki was paying to his little injury, one Michael and Ryan both knew Jack desperately wished he could make disappear.

"Really, it's no big deal. I just…um…ran into something. It was an accident, a misunderstanding." He was being evasive, which made Vicki even more suspicious as she pulled the dark sunglasses off his face.

She wheeled around and faced Ryan. "Did you do this to him? Did you guys get into a fight this weekend?"

His lips tightly pursed to hide the smile that was trying to escape, Ryan silently shook his head no. Michael could see his friend was using all his concentration to keep a straight face. Jack watched from behind Vicki, waiting to see if they'd both keep their mouths shut.

With Ryan's denial, she turned her anger toward Michael. "How could you?"

"Stop yelling at us, Vic, we didn't do anything. Stupid over there picked a fight with *someone* at the football game yesterday, that's all. And for the record, it was all his fault." Michael looked at Jack who mouthed a silent 'thank you' from behind her back.

"Well, you look like hell, Jack, and that makeup you tried to plaster on it isn't covering anything!" She stormed off in a huff and went to help the other servers set up their stations.

Without a word to Jack, who was putting back on his sunglasses, Michael picked up his clipboard and started going through the evening's checklist. Ryan walked in the back, still snickering, while Jack got started on changing the kegs.

If Vicki only knew the real story behind Jack's eye, she'd be laughing her ass off, Michael thought as he finished getting things ready to open the bar.

The Vault was packed that night. There were three parties going on, plus it seemed like half of Portland decided to come there, for some unknown reason. Michael had felt a migraine coming on all night, but he tried to shrug it off. Knowing how busy they were, he didn't want to leave Ryan and Jack one man short. He was desperately trying to hang on, but when he broke out in a cold sweat and threw up in the trashcan, Michael knew it was time to go home.

❧

The next morning, with his migraine a distant memory, Michael felt much better and decided to give the guys a call to apologize for leaving them short-handed last night.

A very groggy Jack answered on the third ring. "What?"

"Hey, Jack, it's me."

"Oh, man, how you feeling? Did your head finally explode?"

"Thanks for the concern, Jack. Sorry to disappoint you, but I'm fine. I was going to apologize for having to leave last night, but now I don't feel so bad," Michael snarled, but his anger had no effect on Jack, except to make him boom with laughter.

"So how was it last night? Did I miss anything good?" he asked when Jack's laughter had died down a bit.

"Oh, you missed it. Ryan almost lost his money last night!" Jack's voice became much more animated and Michael could hear him moving around in bed.

"What happened? And with whom?" Michael sat up, his interest now piqued. Ryan was very selective when it came to women so he knew this had to be good. Before he could ask another question, Michael heard Ryan pick up another line at their place.

"For the last time, Jack, I did not almost lose my money. Nothing happened, so shut up about it. You two gossip like a couple of old ladies," Ryan snapped.

"This is a private conversation, Mr. Nosy. Did Michael call you? No, he called me, so get off the phone!" Jack yelled.

"Will one of you just tell me what happened?" Michael interrupted.

Jack decided to start the story. "So, I was minding my own business—"

Ryan interrupted. "He was flirting with a bachelorette and her friends at the bar, letting them touch his muscles. Shamelessly trying to earn some extra tips is probably more accurate. Minding his business, my ass!"

Jack loudly cleared his throat. "Anyway, where was I? Oh yeah, I look over at Ryan and he's all frozen like a deer in headlights, looking across the bar at this chick. She was cute, too; super blond hair, nice little body." Ryan cursed at Jack under his breath. "He was so preoccupied with her, a customer threw a maraschino cherry at his head to get his attention."

Michael couldn't help but laugh at that mental image.

"Wait, it gets better. The girl must have seen him looking at her like some sort of freaky stalker, but still saunters over and orders a drink from him. He's so distracted by her that instead of putting the soda for her rum and Coke in the glass, he pours it all over his shoe and damn near flooded the bar."

"The nozzle malfunctioned, you moron. I hit the fill button and the stream of Coke came out, and then it wouldn't stop. It had nothing to do with being distracted." His voice got all sappy at the end.

"Mike, I swear, he actually had drool coming down the side of his mouth! Aarrrgghh! Stop it, Ryan … Get away. I'm telling the truth, I saw you drool … Damn it, put down the fucking pillow."

Michael heard the phone drop to the floor then slide across the hardwood while the two of them apparently wrestled in the background. A long string of profanities later, there was the sound of a slamming door and the click of a lock.

Jack returned to the phone victorious. "I'm back. Dude, I'm telling you, he was so hot for this girl. She was cute—a real artsy type. I don't think he even said a single word to her. Then, when I jokingly called her a barfly, he put me in a headlock. We may need to hold an intervention for him or something."

"Well, I sure am sorry I missed all the fun. You know what I think Ryan needs? I think he needs a quick trip to the gym to work out all his aggressions … or his pent up *energy*. You in? I'll pick you guys up in twenty minutes."

When Michael pulled up to their apartment, Ryan climbed in the backseat and Jack jumped up front. Michael couldn't resist the urge to tease Ryan a little more. "So, Ryan, seriously, you're falling for a barfly?" Michael felt a sharp smack the back of his head and a lot of cursing from the back seat. Jack's deep laughter filled the car as they headed off to the gym.

Chapter 4

*G*race adjusted her headphones, making sure they were securely on her ears before she walked out of the locker room. With her iPod, towel, and water bottle in hand, she headed over and claimed one of the open treadmills. After setting the resistance level, she draped her towel over the bar and started jogging at her usual brisk pace.

The treadmill faced a mirrored wall, so as she ran, Grace could watch the people moving through the gym behind her. Her eyes stopped on one of the television monitors where a local sports program was running highlights from that weekend's Seahawks game. Thoughts of Wiener Guy and the black eye he had to be sporting popped into Grace's head, making her chuckle as she continued on her run.

Michael, Jack, and Ryan had been working out for about a half hour when Michael decided it was time to try and get some more information out of Ryan about the mystery girl he had met at the club the night before.

"So, Ryan, are you going tell me anything about the girl?" Michael sat down and took a break on the weight bench.

"Can't … talk … lifting … heavy things," Ryan gasped as he thrust the dumbbells over his head, completing seven more reps before he stopped. As Michael sat and waited for him to finish, he couldn't help but notice a beautiful blond with huge, cosmetically enhanced breasts wandering around the free weights.

She was trying to be subtle in her tight white T-shirt, but every few seconds, she'd glance over in Michael's direction and smile.

She circled a few more minutes and then made her way over. "Excuse me; you look like a big strong guy. Can you show me how to lift these weights properly? I wouldn't want to hurt myself," she giggled, lamely twirling a piece of her hair.

He noticed Jack across the room preening in a mirror. "See that guy, the one fixing his hair? Ask him. He's really good with the weights; he can teach you all kinds of things." Her eyes grew wide with excitement and she chased off after Jack, like a dog in desperate need of a bone.

Ryan started laughing. "Not nice to sick her on poor unsuspecting Jack. Not nice at all."

"Give me a break. He loves this kind of thing—just look at him." Michael pointed over at Jack, who was already standing behind the girl, helping her lift the feather-light weights over her head, while she blatantly flirted with him.

Ryan put his weights down and sat next to Michael on the bench, prying open his bottle of water.

"So, I'm waiting," Michael prodded again.

"There's nothing to tell, Mike. I saw this girl at the bar. She was absolutely gorgeous, and for some reason, I just panicked and couldn't produce a coherent thought, much less speak. My emotions got the better of me. I also may have been distracted and spilled some Coke on my foot," he admitted with a sheepish grin.

"Did you get her name, a number, anything?" It was rare for Ryan to be rendered speechless by a woman. He was always so cool and collected. For him to be flustered was a very big deal.

"No, not that it would have mattered anyway. We do have a little wager about no barflies, and since I met her at the bar, she's off limits, remember?" Michael could tell Ryan was disappointed, but he didn't know her at all. She could have a pea-brain like the rest of the bar girls for all he knew.

"Don't worry, man. If it's meant to be, then you two will meet again." Michael grimly chuckled as he slapped Ryan on the back. Then he looked down at his empty water bottle. "I'll be right back. I need a drink." As he left the bench, he was still laughing about Ryan's predicament.

☙

Thirty minutes and a bottle of water later, Grace was finally done with her run and happily stopped the treadmill so she could catch her breath. Beads of sweat had started dripping down her forehead so she gave her face a quick wipe with her towel. Knowing she still wanted to do a few more machines before she left, Grace found her empty water bottle and headed over to the water fountain to refill it. While she was walking, her favorite song started playing on the iPod. She cranked the volume as she approached the water fountain, enjoying the tune.

Singing to herself as she held the water bottle in the continuous stream of cold water, Grace waited until it was filled all the way to the top before screwing the lid on tightly. She bent over the fountain and took a quick sip for herself, then quickly turned to head back over to the machines when she crashed into something hard, or rather some*one* hard.

Two strong arms reached out and caught Grace as she found herself in the embarrassing position of having her sweaty face and body clamped against some strange man's chest. "Oh! So sorry!" she said without even looking up, feeling her cheeks flame with embarrassment. Grace took a deep breath and nervously glanced up to see what unfortunate soul she had just thrown her not-so-fresh self at. To her complete surprise, she was met by a smiling face with a familiar pair of sparkling blue eyes looking down at her.

In what looked like slow motion, the man opened his mouth and she watched his lips move but Grace couldn't hear a single word. "Huh?" she said, and for some reason that amused him because he started to laugh. Grace realized that she was still pressed up against his chest and started to back away when his hand shot out and brushed against her cheek. Her heart started beating wildly in her chest at the contact. She felt like she had just run the fifty yard dash, simply from his light touch across her skin.

His fingers looped around her head phones as he gave them a gentle tug, freeing the buds from her ears and sending loud music spilling into the air around them. He leaned into her. "Can you hear me now?"

Grace gasped when she finally heard his deep, smooth-as-silk voice in her ear. *The music!* Grace scolded herself. She was mortified when she realized that it had been up so loud she couldn't hear a word that he had said and that she had probably screamed her apology at the top of her lungs.

"Yeah, I can hear you. Sorry about that before," she mumbled as she forced herself to step away from his hard and deliciously masculine body. She stared at him, completely drawn in by his hypnotic blue eyes. They were so perfect, and so familiar for some reason. As her heart continued to flutter in her chest, Grace realized who he was and why he looked so familiar. He was one of the guys from the library. He looked different in less clothing … much better, in her opinion.

He seemed amused as she stood in front of him, temporarily rendered mute by his presence. "Yeah, I know. You already said that. Actually, you more or less yelled it at me, but I still got the message. No harm. Apology accepted." Two people came up and stood behind him. Grace immediately recognized them as his friends from the library, but the big guy with the black hair now sported a nasty black eye. The one with the long blond hair leaned against the wall and watched.

"Hey, Playboy, long time no see." Grace laughed as the big guy came and stood next to her. Playboy was the nickname that Meg and Bianca had given him after she told them the story of his ridiculous quest to find porn at the public library.

The look of confusion on his face was priceless, and it quickly changed into one of panicked concentration. Grace could tell he was racking his brain trying to place where he knew her from … a one night stand, school, the supermarket, his apartment building … She could see him ticking off the possibilities in his head at a rapid rate with no success.

In his defense, the last time he'd seen her, Grace's hair had been up in a tight bun, she'd had her glasses on, and she'd been standing on a stool in baggy everyday clothes. Her loose ponytail and the much tighter gym clothes she was currently wearing were likely throwing him off. Needing help, he looked over at his friend with the baby blue eyes. But his friend was too busy looking curiously at Grace as if he too was trying to figure out who she was. Grace blushed under the intense scrutiny.

Needing a distraction, Grace glanced up at the tall blond who suddenly started smiling widely. Apparently, he remembered her and was happy to sit back and watch this little scene play out for his own amusement.

"Do I … did we … have we met before?" The big guy stammered after a few hand gestures back and forth between himself and Grace.

"Yep," she said smugly, nodding her head and dragging out his torture a bit longer by not offering any additional information.

"Where did we meet?" he asked, completely puzzled.

"Well, you said it was your first time—" Grace started, stopping abruptly, trying not to give too much away and also trying not to break out into a fit of laughter when she realized the double meaning in her reply. She meant his first time at the library, but then she stopped, making their acquaintance sound rather… intimate.

The tall blond was leaning against the wall, openly laughing now. Grace saw his friend with sexy blue eyes glance over at him and then glance back at her, still trying desperately to put the pieces together and figure out the joke he was missing out on before Playboy caught on.

Grace gave him a quick wink and a smile and that's when it all clicked.

Recognition washed over Blue Eyes' face as he made small 'o' with his lips and ran his fingers through his thick, brown hair. Rather than help Playboy out, he decided to join in on the fun and egg her on a little more. "Come on, Jack, don't tell me you can't remember your first time?"

"Suzy Linert from West High?" he asked, his brows furrowed together as he looked at Grace. "I thought you were taller."

"Nope, sorry. I'm not Suzy." Grace let out a fake, frustrated sigh. "You're such a playboy. I guess I didn't make that much of an impression on you. Oh, well. Congrats to whoever gave you that black eye. Enjoy your workout, guys." And with that, she headed off to the upper body machines to end her workout. She didn't dare turn around to see Playboy's face or his friends', but Grace smiled when she heard the deep laughter coming from behind her, knowing they had finally decided to let him in on the joke.

"What the hell just happened? Did I sleep with her or something and I can't remember it? She's pretty hot. I doubt I'd forget that…" Jack said, scratching his head in confusion.

Ryan was the first to find his voice. Michael was distracted by the mystery woman as she walked away. Her long, glossy black hair bounced behind her while her curvy hips swayed gently from side to side, mesmerizing him.

"She's the girl from the library, you idiot! The one you asked for the Playboys," Ryan managed to croak out.

"Damn, she's much hotter without the glasses," Jack said absently as he looked over his shoulder at her retreating form. "Think I have any chance with her?" Michael and Ryan shook their heads no.

When Michael finally caught his breath and was able to pull himself together, he filled up his water bottle and headed back over to the weights.

Through the rest of their workout, Michael found himself completely distracted by the woman from the library. He was pleasantly surprised when he caught her looking over his way on more than one occasion. For some reason, when their eyes met, he couldn't look away—especially when her cheeks flushed with embarrassment. Intrigued, he wanted to know more about her, at the very least get her name and number before she disappeared again.

Staring at the woman instead of spotting Jack as he bench pressed some ridiculous weight, Michael nearly killed him. He was so distracted by her that he didn't notice Jack's face turning purple until he felt a quick kick in the shin.

"Damn it, Michael, I could have died here, and all because you have the hots for the 'naughty librarian,'" Jack teased as he followed Michael's gaze and found her bent over a machine doing arm curls. "Check out the rack on her."

Michael punched Jack in the arm. "Quit staring." They watched her hop off the machine then head toward the women's locker room.

Jack smiled. "Yeah, you don't have a thing for her at all, do you?" He teased Michael and then yelled, "See you around, Suzy!" Jack waved his hand in the air when she turned around to see who could possibly be shouting.

She just smiled wide, showing off her dimples, and waved as she walked around the corner, disappearing into the locker room.

"Come on, Mike, you should ask her out. She's not a barfly." He turned to their friend for backup. "Ryan, come talk some sense into him; he listens to you." Jack waved Ryan over into their little conversation.

"Michael, go for it. She seems smart and funny and she doesn't take crap from any of us which, I have to say, is rather refreshing. Just think how much fun it would be to watch her confuse Jack again." Ryan couldn't resist getting one parting jab in at his friend who was fixing his hair—again—in the mirror.

"Well, I hate to break up the 'slam on Jack' fest that's going on, but I'm hitting the showers. Let's be ready to leave in fifteen, 'kay?" Jack grabbed his towel and started walking away. "Oh, and Michael, you better ask her out. If you don't, I will." He gave Michael a sinister grin and headed to the locker room.

"She thinks you're a pervert! She'd never go out with you," Michael yelled, causing a few people to stop their workouts and stare at Jack as he walked away laughing.

Ryan put a comforting hand on Michael's shoulder. "Jack's right, you should ask her out. She seems like a normal human being. It might be a really nice change of pace for you. And, if you or Jack don't ask her out, I just might," he finished with a smile. "I'm done. My suggestion is to hang by the women's locker room and see if you can catch her on her way out."

"Thanks." Michael nervously walked in the direction of the locker room and sat down against the wall. He nervously ran his hand through his hair and waited. *I look like some kind of stalker lurking outside the women's locker room,* he thought to himself with a laugh. *What is wrong with me?* He was rarely put in the position of pursuer, but something told him that this time would be different. It was his turn to do the chasing, and this woman was the one he wanted to catch.

When Grace sat down on the bench in the cramped locker room, she had the biggest grin on her face. The last twenty minutes of her workout she had spent shamelessly checking out the guys from the library. Whenever she found herself peeking over at them, the one with the gorgeous blue eyes would catch her staring and flash her a smirk. Every time he smiled at her, Grace's stomach filled with a thousand butterflies. She blushed as she remembered how delicious he looked in his tank top and those gym shorts that left little to the imagination.

Remember the boycott, Grace, remember the boycott, she would repeat to herself as she worked the machines. But for some reason, she couldn't stop herself from glancing over, just to see the sweat glisten off his shoulders as he thrust the weights into the air or the delicious sliver of his abs that his raised shirt exposed.

She skipped to the showers and quickly jumped in, letting the hot water run down her back, soothing her stressed muscles. Grace scrubbed the sweat from her body and her hair as the scent of coconut filled the shower. Under the water, she found herself smiling whenever she thought about him ... his eyes, his muscles, his hair falling into his eyes, the sweat. She couldn't help but remember how good it felt to be pressed up against his body, the feel of those strong arms of his as they held her tight against his chest.

The boycott, Grace, a great pair of shoes and eternal bragging rights ... plus he's way out of your league, she told herself, snapping herself sharply back to reality as she climbed out of the shower.

She threw on a tight black T-shirt and some jeans. As she dried her hair, she couldn't help but wonder what it would be like to kiss those full lips of his. *I can fantasize, can't I? No rules about that in this damn boycott.* She finished dressing and then put all her toiletries and sweaty clothes into her backpack. With a sweatshirt around her waist, she took one last glance at herself in the mirror and headed out of the locker room.

I wonder if they're still here. Grace thought to herself. *Bad Grace! Bad Grace!* Her breath caught in her lungs when she turned the corner and looked up to find a gorgeous man leaning against the wall outside the women's locker room, waiting for her.

"Hey," he said pushing himself off from the wall, moving toward her.

"Hi," Grace said shyly, praying that she wouldn't blush too badly as she talked to him.

He was perfection. Bianca and Meg's league of perfection. Even now, covered in sweat, he was beyond handsome. His hair had that intentionally messy but still perfect look to it. His body was toned and fit, and Grace knew that because she remembered exactly how it felt when she was pressed against it earlier. As a matter of fact, she couldn't stop thinking about the way his arms felt wrapped around her or the heat that radiated off his chest. The butterflies returned full force and her face turned red.

"Sorry about Jack. He can be an ass sometimes. Well, most of the time, actually. I just hope he didn't offend you the other day at the library," he said with an apologetic smile on his face.

"No, he was fairly harmless. But thanks," Grace said as she flung her backpack over her shoulder.

Her light-hearted answer made his smile grow wider. "So, if you want to wait a few minutes, we can go grab a coffee."

She was too stunned to speak. Her entire body screamed yes, but as she opened her mouth to speak, Grace's brain quickly silenced the chorus. "Sorry, I can't. I'm boycotting men until the new year." Grace smiled playfully as she forced herself to walk away from him, even though all she wanted to do was stay there and get lost in his eyes a little longer. She only got a foot or two away when she felt his strong hand touch her shoulder.

"Wait, can I at least get your name?" he asked, sounding hopeful.

"Call me Suzy," she laughed. And with that, Grace headed out the doors of the gym and hurried off to her car.

Michael stood there, too stunned to move. *Well, that went well,* he thought as he slumped back and banged his head against the wall.

"Ha ha, looks like Mikey's sleeping alone tonight. She's immune to your charms, isn't she?" Jack boomed from behind him. "I like her even more now."

"Shut up, Jack. I was sleeping alone anyway thanks to our little bet. And, I may have been shot down by 'Suzy,' but at least I didn't let a girl give me a black eye!" Michael shot back.

"How many times do I have to tell you the whole thing was an accident?" Jack fumed as he stormed toward the exit.

"Sure, Jack, because that kind of thing happens all the time," Michael scoffed as he grabbed his bag and followed him to the car.

Chapter 5

"Oh, Susan, she just walked in the door. Hang on; I'll get her for you." Meg sighed in relief as Grace opened the door of their apartment. As always, she tossed her keys into the basket on the counter and grabbed the phone from Meg's extended hand.

Meg simply shook her head and laughed, mouthing the words 'good luck' to Grace.

"Hi, mom. How are you?" Grace asked tentatively. Her mother typically called every day, most of the time to share some random gossip from back home about people Grace vaguely remembered or ones she hadn't seen since high school. As much as Grace hated to admit it, sometimes she would just let the machine pick up in order to be spared the pain of chatting with her mother.

"I'm fine. Were you teaching?" Susan asked quickly. The other annoying thing about talking to her mom was that she turned into a fast talker whenever she called. Susan could talk at the speed of light just to get the conversation over as quickly as possible, all in the hopes of saving fifty-seven cents on her phone bill.

"Yes, I just got home. So, what's up?" Grace waited for her to get to the point of the day's call. Perhaps her old art teacher from high school had died and she was going to read the obituary, or even better, it could be a wedding announcement for someone she'd hated in high school, and probably someone who Grace knew for a fact had slept with half of the football team.

"You'll never guess what happened. One of my old friends that I haven't seen in forever called. She's moving to Spokane. Isn't that great?"

Flipping through her mail, Grace could hear the excitement in her mother's voice. "Wow, Mom, that's great," she mumbled as she glanced down at her Visa bill. *Damn, all that shopping with Meg,* Grace thought.

Susan started her speed-talking again, but Grace missed the first part of her wild rambling because she was busy waving the bill at Meg, pointing at the total. Grace started paying attention again when she caught the words, "My friend's son … Portland … date."

"Whoa, Mom. Stop right there. Listen, there's something you should know. I'm boycotting boys for a while." There was silence on the line, then hysteria.

"Mom, why are you crying?"

"So who is it? Is it Meg or Bianca?" the woman asked between sobs.

"Meg or Bianca what, Mom?" Grace was confused by Susan's over the top reaction. *Damn, I really should pay attention when she fast talks.*

"Which one of them turned you into a lesbian?" she sobbed into the phone.

Grace burst into laughter. "Mom, Meg, Bianca, and I are not lesbians, I swear. We've just been dating too many losers, so we're taking a little break from dating men for a few weeks, but not forever, OK?" Bianca laughed as she walked in on the middle of Grace's bizarre conversation with her mother.

"Well, when this silly boycott is over, I'm going to give you his number. I gotta go to yoga class. I love you!" Before Grace could say good-bye, the line went dead.

Meg giggled. "So, now she thinks we're lesbians?"

"Apparently. Maybe I should have let her keep thinking that. At least she wouldn't give my number out to any guys for a while." Grace sat down on one of the kitchen bar stools and expectantly looked at her friends. "So, what's on the agenda for this evening, ladies? I don't have a class to teach until late tomorrow. Do you want to go out?"

Meg jumped to her feet, clapping. "I know the perfect place! We can get a bite to eat and dance and—"

Bianca interrupted with a smirk on her face. "And see the guy you haven't stopped talking about since you met him last night? Is *that* where you want to go?" she asked suspiciously.

With a shameless smile on her face, Meg started jumping up and down whining. "Please, please, please, please …"

"See, this is what happens when you go out to a bar with one of your clients instead of us—you fall in love," Bianca said sarcastically as she batted her eyelashes and put her hand over her heart.

"Come on, Bianca, let's go check out Mr. Wonderful, a man she can't date for another three and a half weeks," Grace teased while Meg continued pleading.

"Fine," Bianca said grudgingly. "But there better be some other cute guys there for me to look at, because if I have to watch you make goo-goo eyes all night, I may throw up!" Meg picked up a pillow from the couch to launch at Bianca, but the redhead took off for her room before it even left her friend's hand.

After an hour filled with showers and general beautification, they were ready to hit the town. Bianca was in a short red dress that showed off her incredible legs. The dress accentuated her hair which she kept long and poker straight. Meg wore a long sweater with a pair of leggings, and a few new magenta streaks in her black hair when she emerged from the bathroom. Grace had been physically forced into a black patterned miniskirt, with a black, off the shoulder top and a pair of knee high black boots. They had put hot rollers in her hair to accentuate the curls, so her long ebony locks had some extra spring in them as they headed out the door.

When the girls entered The Vault, Grace noticed that it looked like any other bar they had been to over the course of their boycott. The dance floor was on the lower level, with the tables wrapping around on the second floor in a 'U' shape. The long bar was against the far back wall with a two-story blue lit wall behind it. The place had a very cool vibe once you were inside. Meg led the way upstairs to a table where they could sit but still see both the bar and the dance floor. Grace watched as Meg leaned over the rail and peered toward the bar.

Bianca caught the puzzled expression on Grace's face and laughed. "She's looking for Mr. Wonderful. Apparently, he's one of the bartenders."

Grace chuckled when Meg flopped down into the chair beside her. She could tell by Meg's expression that he wasn't there. "Well this sucks! No eye candy for me to look at while I eat," Meg pouted.

Trying to sound encouraging, Grace said, "It is still kind of early, Meg. Maybe he'll be here later." That seemed to do the trick because a smile returned to her face when Grace tugged on one of the magenta streaks in her hair. "Love the color."

The menu they found on the table had an extensive selection of mixed drinks. Grace was still scanning it when their server came over to the table. "Hi, I'm Vicki and I'll be your server. How are you ladies doing tonight?" she asked.

Grace looked up and saw a beautiful woman standing confidently next to their table, slipping coasters onto it. The first thing that anyone who looked at her would notice was the mane of purple hair she wore with pride. After the hair, it was impossible to ignore the numerous facial piercings that adorned her skin. Even with all the hardware decorating her face, she was still gorgeous, and her smile miraculously made her seem less intimidating.

All of a sudden, Meg blurted out, "Cool piercings. How many do you have?"

"Eighteen, but you can only see twelve of them," Vicki said with a wink.

Meg's eyes got wide. "Cool," she said again in awe. "Did they hurt? Because I cried my eyes out when I was a kid and got my ears pierced. I can't imagine how much it hurts to get your eyebrow pierced."

"That wasn't the most painful one I have…" She grinned as she watched Meg's eyes get big with understanding. "So, can I get you ladies something from the bar?"

Meg almost popped out of her seat. "Oh, can you get me that tall, blond, gorgeous guy that was working last night? The one with the ponytail? I'll take him with a few maraschino cherries on the side."

Grace smacked her hand to her forehead in embarrassment while Bianca growled, "Meg, please."

Fortunately, Vicki was very laid back and appreciated Meg's exuberance. "Oh, Ry. Yeah, he's a cutie. He'll be here in about a half hour. That's the early shift." Vicki patted Meg's shoulder, "Don't worry, honey, I'll let you know when he gets here." Meg started grinning from ear to ear and wriggling in her seat.

When she saw Meg's enthusiasm, Vicki felt like she should let the girl know what she was up against. "Of course, I should tell you, that he and his buddies—the other two bartenders—they've sworn off dating girls from the bar. Normally, I wouldn't share that bit of info and I'd let you make a fool out of yourself, but for some reason, I kinda like you…"

"…Meg," she answered, offering Vicki her hand.

"Yeah, I like you, Meg."

"Well, I like you too, Vicki, and you know what's ironic? The girls and I are in the middle of a boy boycott until the new year, so we can't date them either! It's perfect!" Meg beamed in satisfaction.

Vicki just laughed. "Yeah, it *is* perfect. I can't wait to see this one play out. OK, let me get you some drinks and I'll be back to take your order." Vicki wrote down what they wanted, and then headed down to the bar.

When their server was out of earshot, Bianca ripped into Meg. "What the hell was that? 'Bring me the guy from the bar'? Have you lost your mind?"

"Oh, come on, Bianca. I know I can't date him so calm down. There's no harm in just window shopping. It's like visiting the puppies at the pet store. You go and look at them, and they're so cute, they make you smile. They get all excited to see you and they lick your hands and face, then you go home without one. I just wanted to look at the puppy. Is that so wrong?" she asked with her best pouty face.

"Yes, Meg, that's wrong on too many levels to explain right now," Bianca laughed. Grace just nodded her head in agreement.

Vicki returned with three drinks, all fruity and colorful, just how the girls liked them. Before she left, she took their food order and put a red reserved plaque on the table.

"What's that for?" Grace asked, having never seen one before.

"Oh, that's so you ladies can go down and dance while you wait for your food, or … mosey down to the bar later … if you wanted to for some reason, and that way no one will take your table," Vicki said with a warm smile.

"Wow, thanks." Grace was touched by the gesture.

"I like you ladies. You seem … nice." She smiled at her own private joke then headed off to her other tables.

"Well, you heard the lady. Let's go dance, girls!" Bianca exclaimed as one of her favorite songs started pulsing through the club.

The girls ran down the stairs and joined in the crowd that had gathered on the dance floor. Bianca and Meg had been teaching Grace new dance moves as part of her 'raising your standards' education. She was getting to be a pretty good little dancer if she did say so herself. Grace's erotic gyrations and hip shaking looked almost as attention grabbing as Meg's.

The trio spent the next twenty minutes dancing under the flashing lights of the club. Men weaved in and out around them, occasionally joining them for a dance, then moving on. Bianca even accepted a phone number from one of the guys they met on the dance floor.

As they sat down back at their table, Grace sucked down her Cosmo. She was so hot from dancing, she wished she had a glass of ice water, but another Cosmo would probably quench her thirst as well. Bianca and Meg finished off their drinks too, and when Vicki arrived with their food, the girls quickly ordered another round of drinks.

Grace didn't realize how hungry they all were until she looked up saw both Bianca and Meg were already done with their food. The only things that remained on the table were a few stray bread sticks in a basket. Like an answered prayer, Vicki appeared again, grinning from ear to ear, with a fresh tray of drinks.

"Here you go, ladies. Meg, yours was made special by your favorite bartender." Vicki gave her a wink as she placed the glass in front of her and walked away. Meg jumped out of her seat and flew to the rail, her eyes scouring the bar.

Grace knew from her high pitched squeal the moment Meg found him. Curious to see what all the hype was about, Bianca and Grace ran over to take a peek. From a distance, with his long blond hair and thin build, he looked strangely familiar to Grace. Before she could figure it out, Bianca started screaming, "It's him. Oh my God, it's Wiener Guy!" She waved her finger wildly down toward the bar.

"Where? Are you sure it's him?" Grace asked, trying to follow her bouncing finger.

She leaned over Grace's shoulder and pointed to the second guy behind the bar. With his dark, spiked hair and light scruff across his chin, Grace's eyebrows shot up in recognition. "See, he has a black eye!" Bianca whispered excitedly.

As Bianca and Meg started rambling, Grace stood frozen in place. She wasn't listening to a word they said. Her eyes were fixed on the third person behind the bar: the perfect male specimen with the baby blue eyes from the gym.

Completely shocked, Grace stumbled back into her chair and grabbed her Cosmo, downing it in one gulp. Bianca and Meg watched with confused expressions on their faces.

"What the hell is going on with you?" Bianca asked.

"Those guys…I kind of know them. Bianca, Wiener Guy is the guy that asked for Playboys at the library. And Meg, your lover boy, Ryan, is one of his friends, and the third guy down there…he's the guy from the gym *and* the library…the one with the sexy eyes that makes my skin tingle whenever I think about him." Her head started to spin and her heart started racing. Grace didn't know if it was from the shock of seeing them or the two Cosmos she had chugged in the last twenty minutes.

Eager to catch a glimpse of the guy that had Grace all flustered, Bianca sprung to the rail and checked out the guy from the gym. "Grace, he's hot! Why didn't you go have coffee with him?"

"Because we have a stupid boycott in effect, Bianca! That, and I figured he was way out of my league," she said sadly, glancing down at the bar in time to see his gorgeous white smile as he talked to his friends.

"Oh, stop it, Grace, he's definitely in your league! He's just the kind of guy you should be going after, if we weren't boycotting guys right now, that is," she said as she returned to her seat.

"Funny thing is, I told you that I thought you'd like the Playboy before we even knew he was Wiener Guy. His name is actually Jack, and he is most definitely your type, minus the ass grabbing and the facial hair. He's got an incredible body and seems really laid back," Grace said, looking at Bianca with a smile. Then she turned to Meg and gave her a little more information. "And Ryan is really cute and nice, too, Meg. He was the first one to recognize me from the library," Grace laughed encouragingly.

Peeking over the rail, they spied on the guys as they began their shift. Grace watched Bianca evaluating Jack. The smirk on her face told Grace that he had caught her eye, but the ass grab incident would be hard for Bianca to put aside unless the guy did some major damage control.

"I think I have a newfound appreciation for facial hair," Bianca sighed as she watched Jack twirl a bottle of vodka in his hand.

"Like what you see, ladies?" Vicki laughed when she found the three of them hanging over the rail, gawking at the guys.

"You're just the lady we needed to talk to. Do you have a minute to sit with us?" Meg begged, patting the seat beside her.

Vicki shrugged her shoulders, sat down, and started chomping on a bread stick. "What do you need?"

"For starters, how well do you know them?" Meg asked as she leaned in, like Vicki was about to share her deepest secrets.

"Well, I've known them for a year, I guess. They're nice guys—smart, employed, and all with college degrees. They've dated girls they meet at the bar, but it rarely goes anywhere. Michael's big trick is he gives a 'dud' the number to a pizza joint instead of his real phone number when she asks for it. Then a few weeks ago, for some odd reason, they swore off barflies—that's what they call girls they meet in the bar—and are now on a 'quest' to meet nice girls."

Grace started laughing. "I guess that explains why they were trolling for girls in the library when I met them."

Vicki's jaw hung open. "They went to the library?"

"Oh, you haven't heard the half of it," Bianca chimed in with a laugh.

They spent the next ten minutes telling Vicki all the different run-ins they'd had with the guys over the last week. She almost lost it when she heard that Bianca was the one who gave Jack the back eye.

"He told me he got into a fight with some drunk guy at the football game. What a liar!" Vicki roared with laughter. "Oh, and by the way, Grace," she pointed at the bar and grinned, "the guy from the gym? His name is Michael."

Michael… that's a sexy name. She glanced down at the bar for a little peek. Michael was bent over, wiping his hands on a towel under the bar. The muscles of his back were rolling under the tight black shirt he was wearing, making Grace's heart kick into high gear.

"So Vicki, would you like to help us have a little fun with the boys?" Meg's eyes twinkled as she rubbed her hands together like a villain in a movie.

"Oh, I would love to get them. Ever since this crazy bet went into effect, I've had to be 'pretend girlfriend' and fight off all the barflies throwing themselves at them while they're at work. You know how many kisses I've had to blow at their sorry asses? How can I help?"

They all put their heads together and decided that they would put their plan into action tomorrow night. Vicki confirmed that the boys would all be working then and she would be there to help out too if the girls needed her. There was one last thing Grace needed to do before they left for the evening.

"Vicki, can you go down there and tell Michael that a friend of Suzy's wants his number? Just make sure that Jack and Ryan are distracted when you do it, OK?"

"You know he's going to give you the number to that pizza place, right?" Vicki asked, unsure what exactly Grace was up to.

"Yeah, I know. I just want to see where he likes to get his pizza from." Grace's face gave away a hint that she might have ulterior motives in asking for the number.

Vicki picked up on it and grinned. "I knew I liked you girls for a reason. They aren't going to know what hit them."

The three women watched breathlessly through the railing as Vicki sauntered down to the bar on her mission. "Michael," Vicki said as she scooted down to his end of the bar. Jack and Ryan were under the bar checking the connections to the kegs.

"What's up?" Michael asked while he was digging a couple of beers out of the ice chest to fill an order.

"I have a customer requesting your phone number, big guy," she punched his arm playfully.

Michael's eyes rolled wondering who was hitting on him now. "I have to say, that's very unlike you, Vic. Aren't you supposed to be discouraging girls from asking for my number right now, oh great fly swatter?" he asked suspiciously.

"Hey, she offered me twenty bucks. Even I have a price!" she said with a laugh.

Michael grabbed a napkin off the bar and started to scribble down the number for Mama Rosa's when she added, "Oh yeah, I was supposed to tell you she's a friend of Suzy's? I don't know what the hell that means, but just passing along the info I was paid to share."

His hand stopped moving on the napkin. "Where's this girl sitting?" Vicki motioned upstairs and to the left. Michael spun around and started searching along the rail to see if it could be her, the woman from the library and the gym, the one he hadn't stopped thinking about for days. As he searched, a small girl with black hair caught his eye as she waved furiously at him, but she was alone.

Probably a different Suzy, Michael thought to himself. He finished writing the number then tossed it at Vicki.

"Next time, I want a cut of the money," he snarled.

"Thanks, grumpy. You're just too cute for your own good," she said as she tucked the napkin into her pocket and headed to the kitchen to pick up an order.

"Meg, get down!" Grace growled through her teeth as Meg gracefully dangled herself over the rail and continued waving like she was on a parade float. "OK, enough. You're laying it on a bit thick, don't you think?" Grace tugged on the back of Meg's sweater sending her toppling to the ground.

She laughed and came back to sit at the table. "He is really cute, Grace. I would totally approve if we weren't boycotting boys right now," she said with a giggle.

Vicki came back up a few minutes later, laughing as she sat down. She slid a white napkin from the bar across the table to Grace. A phone number was scrawled on it with the letter 'M' above it.

"Here you go. I thought his neck was going to snap when he spun around to look for 'Suzy's friend.' His first question was if Suzy was with her. Good call having Meg wave. That threw him off. Then he just looked pissed and scribbled the number."

Grace grabbed her phone and dialed the number written down on the napkin. The voice on the line said, "Mama Rosa's Pizza. Is this for pickup or delivery?"

She snapped her phone shut and looked at her fellow conspirators.

"Perfect…"

Chapter 6

race, will you please stop being so damn stubborn and come out?" Meg rammed her shoulder into the bathroom door as Grace continued to hold it shut.

"No, I'm *not* wearing those pants you have in your hand. They hardly cover my ass, so if I bend at all—"

"If you bend, some hot guy will get to peek at your cute little butt. Would that be the worst thing ever? I bought an adorable thong you can wear under the jeans," Meg slid the lacy scrap of fabric under the bathroom door.

"I'm not wearing that either," Grace yelled into the door.

"Fine, then go commando for all I care, but you will wear these jeans and this blue shirt. If not, I'm going straight to the bar and giving *Michael* your phone number and telling him that you want to have his babies!"

The door opened a crack. "You wouldn't dare."

"Try me, Grace, just try me," Meg growled, her eyes narrowed to slits, emphasizing just how serious she was.

Grace flung open the bathroom door, ready to have a face-off with her roommate, but then changed her mind. Their whole experiment was about taking chances and she intended to throw caution to the wind for once and be daring like her friends. "Give me the damn clothes." She held out her hand in defeat. Meg jumped up and down with joy, piling the clothes into Grace's arms.

"You won't regret this Grace, I swear!" she said as she clapped her hands together happily.

"I already do, Meg, believe me." Grace gathered the offensive clothes and stormed off to change.

☙

A half hour later, the women gathered in the family room, all dolled up and ready for a night on the town. Grace was wearing the low rise skinny jeans and blue shirt that Meg had bought for her at the mall, minus the thong of course, which Grace had lovingly flung back at her like a rubber band. Commando was far better than floss for her rear.

"Not wearing the thong? How risqué of you, Gracie," Meg giggled.

Meg was dressed in a short white baby doll dress with silver accents along the braided straps and bodice. Her outfit was completed by a pair of strappy silver heels. The flow of the dress made her appear even more graceful when she moved. The pale shade of the dress accentuated Meg's skin, making it look absolutely radiant.

Grace looked over at Bianca, who had just entered the room, and did a double take. "Honestly, you are the only person I know who could wear that outfit and make it look so damn hot! He's going to die when he sees you," she laughed.

"That's the plan," Bianca said as she winked and proceeded to check her red mane one last time in the mirror.

Bianca elected to wear her Seahawks half shirt/jersey from the football game. This time, however, she wore nothing under it, exposing the tanned skin of her flat, bare stomach. She went with a jean miniskirt that made her already perfect legs look five feet longer. She finished the whole ensemble off with the black patent leather heels she'd bought when she skipped out on her date weeks ago.

"Let's go have some fun," Meg said excitedly as they grabbed their purses and headed downstairs to the parking lot. With the music cranked up all the way, Meg pulled into traffic and they sped downtown to The Vault. Vicki told them that the guys were working the later shift again, but Grace wanted to get there a little bit before Michael arrived so they had time to safely get out of sight and set the plan in motion.

When they walked into the bar, Bianca immediately became the center of attention. Cheers of "Go Seahawks!" followed her through the club. Anyone else would have been embarrassed at all the attention. But for Bianca, it was like air. She took it all in and it made her happier, more confident. Halfway to the bar, Vicki spotted them. "Ladies, how nice to see you again. I have a table ready for you. Come on, let's get you three upstairs and let the games begin!"

She led Grace and her friends to the same spot they'd had the night before. The little red reserved sign was already on the table when they arrived. The girls ordered drinks and an appetizer to tide them over until the boys showed up for work. Grace's stomach was doing flips, but she couldn't tell if it was from nerves or the fact that her pants were so tight, the blood wasn't properly flowing to the lower half of her body.

Tired of checking her watch, Meg wanted to go downstairs and dance for a few songs to kill some time until the boys arrived. Grace and Bianca followed her lead and they stayed on the dance floor until Vicki texted Grace.

They're here!

The three women slid through the huge crowd and made their way back to the table. Grace sat down and dialed the phone number that Michael had given the night before.

"Mama Rosa's Pizza. Will this be for pickup or delivery?" a voice asked. Grace had to plug her ear so she could hear over the loud music of the club.

"Delivery, please."

"Address?"

"Do you know a place called The Vault?"

"Sure do."

"Well, I work there and we are having a party for the staff. I need ten large pizzas with everything but anchovies on them. You can drop them off at the bar. Ask for Michael, and have the delivery guy tell him Suzy called the order in for him."

While she was placing the order, Grace couldn't help but look down at the bar where Michael was working feverishly to serve drinks. He looked incredible in a tight black T-shirt with The Vault logo across the chest and a pair of snug fitting jeans. His hair kept falling into his eyes as he bent down so his hand was constantly raking it back off of his face. Even when he was busy, he managed to have the most perfect smile on his face. Grace was watching him take a drink of water from a glass behind the bar when she was abruptly snapped back into reality.

"Hello? Miss? Are you there? It will be there in twenty-five minutes, and I asked if you wanted your total." The person on the phone was clearly irritated.

"Not really, Michael can worry about that, thanks!" Grace quickly clicked the phone shut and smirked at Bianca and Meg. "Now, let's see if he has a sense of humor."

All of the dancing earlier had made the girls hungry and thirsty, so they easily finished off the appetizers and drinks they had ordered. Vicki came over a short while later and joined them. "I'm on break, so I thought I'd hang out up here with my girls and get a better view of things down below. Can I just tell you that I've been looking forward to this all day? My boyfriend thinks your plan is genius."

The next ten minutes were spent listening to Vicki's stories from working at the bar over the past year. Some of them were so funny she had them howling at the ridiculous things that happened at The Vault.

"How much longer until the pizza gets here, Grace?" Bianca asked, glancing down at the front door, sipping on her second margarita of the evening.

Grace quickly checked her watch. "About five minutes, if they're running on time."

Meg went to the rail to watch Ryan again. She had been sneaking peeks at him since he walked in the door. Abruptly, she turned around, her mouth open in visible horror. "That bimbo is hitting on Ryan!" Her hands were firmly planted on her hips as jealousy washed over her face.

Vicki stood on her chair and looked for herself. "Don't you worry; they don't call me the fly swatter for nothing," she laughed and gave Meg an encouraging nod before heading back down the stairs. Grace and Bianca joined Meg at the rail to watch Vicki in action.

She stormed over to where Ryan was talking to the bimbo, slammed her notebook onto the bar, and started waving her arms wildly. Grace couldn't hear any of the conversation over the loud music, but by the look on the girl's face—and Ryan's for that matter—Vicki was playing the part of bitchy girlfriend perfectly. Meg started laughing when the girl tried to leave so fast that she stumbled over her own feet, falling and spilling a drink on her shirt. The last thing they saw was her scurrying to the restroom, glaring back over her shoulder at Vicki.

Michael and Jack were both doubled over in laughter while Ryan just stood there, still a bit shocked. He threw his hands into the air at Vicki, wondering what the hell that was all about, when Grace's attention was pulled away by a guy in a bright purple jacket carrying a tall stack of boxes. As he moved through the club, he would occasionally disappear into the crowd, but the pile of pizzas stayed ever visible. He moved closer to the bar and Grace held her breath, waiting for their reaction.

Ryan and Vicki were still in the middle of a heated conversation when the delivery guy set the pizzas on the bar and pulled out a long strip of paper, no doubt with Michael's name on it, and the total for the order. Jack walked up and asked the guy something, then pointed to Michael who was busy pouring a drink. Jack must have called Michael's name because his head snapped up and his eyes got big when he saw the huge pile of pizzas sitting on the bar. Slowly, he walked over and started talking to the delivery guy.

Vicki saw the pizzas and looked up in the girl's direction and laughed, but then quickly covered her mouth with her hand so no one noticed. Grace looked back at Michael who was now shaking his head no over and over again. The delivery guy leaned over and showed Michael the piece of paper and whatever he said made Jack and Ryan explode into laughter. Vicki ran her fingers through her hair and when her hand was hidden beside her head, she flashed the girls a big thumbs-up.

Mission accomplished.

Meg, Bianca, and Grace started laughing as Michael threw up his hands in frustration and pulled out his wallet, tossing the guy a wad of cash. The delivery guy looked like he was apologizing, but Michael had already walked over to the pizzas and shook his head, probably wondering what the heck to do with them.

Ryan and Jack seemed thrilled by the whole situation. They threw open a box and began happily eating. Michael stood there, rubbing the back of his neck over and over again in obvious anger.

"He's so cute when he's frustrated," Bianca whispered to Grace.

"Yeah, he is cute, isn't he?" Grace's eyes were following Michael as he started moving the boxes of pizza off the bar top one by one and onto a nearby table. He looked inside the first one then made a face. He moved on to the second and made another face. After looking in the third box and rolling his eyes, he sulked away, apparently not a fan of pizza with 'the works.'

❧

Onions. Why did it have to have onions? Michael asked himself as he shook his head in disgust. He looked over at Jack and Ryan who were thoroughly enjoying the little gift from the elusive Suzy.

Does this mean she likes me or hates me? Michael asked himself. *I gave the stupid number last night to Vicki … She was the one who asked for it and mentioned Suzy.*

Michael saw Vicki looking up to her area of tables upstairs and she was … laughing? "Vic!" he called sharply. She turned to face him and immediately wiped the smile off her face, trying to play dumb.

"That was really nice of you to get pizza for everyone." The twinkle in her eyes gave her away.

"Anything you want to tell me? I know you're up to your eyeballs in this. Trying to teach me a lesson or something?" Michael pointed a thumb at the pizzas. "Did I do something to piss you off?"

"Me? No. I swear. I didn't make the call."

"But you know who did …"

She shifted her feet as Michael watched her intently, picking up on the tension in her body language and the guilty look on her face.

"Maybe I have an idea," she mumbled, then nervously glanced up to her serving area with a smirk on her face.

That's when it hit Michael. "She's here, isn't she!"

It all made sense. She'd been here yesterday—Suzy. She'd sent Vicki for the number and she decided to teach him a lesson about giving out a fake phone number to girls. When Michael turned back to Vicki, she had taken off like a bat out of hell up the stairs to her tables.

"Jack, Ryan, I need to take a quick break!" Michael shouted down the bar to his friends, as they continued stuffing their faces with pizza.

"Wait, where are you going, Michael?" Jack asked.

Michael wanted to chase after Vicki and find Suzy, but first he needed to explain to his friends why he was ditching them behind the bar. "Suzy's here. I think Vicki has made a new friend. I need to run upstairs and see for myself if it's her. I'll be right back."

❧

The women had watched helplessly from above as Michael went over to Vicki and started waving his hands furiously at the pizza. "Uh-oh. This can't be good," Meg said as she tapped her fingernails on the handrail.

The girls exchanged anxious glances and quickly sat down. They tried to peer through the bars of the rail to get an idea of what was going on, but when they looked back at the bar, Vicki was gone.

"Where did she go?" Bianca asked, trying to get a better look down at the floor level. All of a sudden, Vicki ran over to the table.

"Our cover's blown! He saw me laughing and looking up here; he knows something's up. He's coming up to my section of tables to look for 'Suzy.' Run, ladies, run!"

Faster than Grace ever thought possible in three inch heels, they leapt out of their chairs and hurried down the set of stairs that were farthest away from the bar but led down to the dance floor. There were tons of people packing the floor so they assumed they'd be safe and almost impossible to find.

By the time Michael made it upstairs, Vicki was calmly helping a table in the corner, but he could feel her watching his every move. He scanned the room: two old guys, some older women, and a bachelorette party. Those were her only tables, and no Suzy in sight. As Michael was about to go back downstairs, he noticed one empty table with a reserved sign on it. They hardly ever used those; only for special occasions. Vicki saw Michael walking toward that table and ran over to intercept him.

"Michael, don't spoil their fun. You'll see her when she wants you to. And trust me—she wants you to see her. Go back to work." She gave him a playful shove, and then walked away.

He went to the rail near the reserved table and looked down at the bar. Jack and Ryan looked up trying to get an indication if he'd found her, but Michael just shrugged and threw up his empty hands.

While the girls were dancing, they each took a post to watch. Meg kept an eye on the bar, so she could tell when Michael went back to work…and keep an eye on Ryan at the same time. Bianca watched the staircase in case he decided to search the dance floor, and Grace kept her eyes fixed on the railing near where they had been sitting, the scene of the crime.

After their narrow escape from Michael, Grace saw him lean over the rail very close to where their table was located and begin looking down at the dance floor. Thankfully, they were across the room where the lighting wasn't the greatest so he wouldn't be able to see them. Still, Grace ducked her head down, letting the long waves of her hair fall over her face to hide, just in case. He didn't look nearly as mad as Grace had thought he might after her little prank.

There was only that brief glimpse; then Grace didn't see him again. Bianca was certain that he hadn't come down the stairs, but Meg couldn't see him at the bar yet, either. They were playing really good music at the club so they were perfectly content to stay in the cover of the dance floor a while longer until things cooled down. Bianca and Meg took the opportunity to teach Grace a few new moves. More specifically, Bianca insisted that Grace practice her booty drop, because, as she so lovingly told her, "Grace, you look like my grandma tying her shoe, not like a woman doing a sexy dance move."

Meg leaned over and shouted, "I can't stand it anymore. I need to know if he remembers me. I'm going to march over there and order a drink from Ryan. Oh, there's Michael. He's back at the bar! I'll go spy on him and see if I can hear what he's saying about the pizzas. You guys stay over here and I'll be right back." She skipped away from her friends with a huge grin on her face, her white dress flowing behind her.

Grace turned around and nearly shouted to Bianca over the loud music. "She's not winning our bet. Those shoes are as good as mine!"

Bianca raised her eyebrows high in the air, taken aback by her friend's comment. "And what about me? Am I chopped liver or something?"

"I hate to break it to you, but you never stood a chance in this one, Bianca. You like boys way too much," Grace teased, until she felt Bianca give her rear a hard whack and she let out a yelp.

"Just for that insult, this whole next song, you have to practice your grinding moves on me! Show me what you got, girl."

"Cyclone" by T-Pain came on and everyone on the dance floor started moving and gyrating together. Grace insisted Bianca stand behind her while she danced, especially in the low cut jeans she was wearing. One wrong bend and Grace was certain a cheek might just fly out. The last thing that she wanted was some random guy looking at her butt.

Grace and Bianca were having a great time; the beat was slow and sexy, making it an easy song to move to. Bianca danced right behind Grace and helped her hips find the right beat when she occasionally got off track. While she danced, Grace had a view of a small section of the bar and could see Michael every so often when he walked past. Whenever she saw him, Grace would become distracted and stop dancing, ending up off beat, which would annoy Bianca to no end. When she tried to do a booty drop toward the end of the song, Bianca growled.

"Come on, Grace, you can do better than that," she scolded in her ear. "Now here's the perfect song for you." The DJ put on "Hot in Herre" by Nelly, one of Bianca's favorites. "OK, listen to the music and just think of some really hot guy, and pretend that you're dancing for him. Impress me, and I won't bother you again for the rest of the night. I swear!" She held up her hand like a good little girl scout and crossed her heart.

Grace rolled her eyes. "Fine, I'll unleash the full potential of my dance moves on you, but if I start to look like I'm having a seizure or something, please stop me. And whatever you do, stay behind me. These pants leave little to the imagination and I'm self-conscious enough as it is." Grace felt Bianca snuggle up right behind her, which made her relax more.

Trying to get in the right frame of mind to dance, like Bianca recommended, Grace closed her eyes. She thought back to the gym, when she was pressed up against Michael's chest, remembering just how good that felt. The memory of the hard planes of his body, the heat that was coming off his skin … it was just the inspiration Grace needed. She started dancing, imagining Michael watching her as she started slowly moving her hips with Bianca's.

"That's it, Grace. Keep it up, girl!" Bianca said encouragingly in her ear. "Now drop it, and remember—arch your back on the way back up."

The first one was a disaster and Bianca started laughing. "Do you have a back condition or something? What the heck was that? Try another one."

Glancing over at the vast blue wall, Grace and Bianca saw a small flash of white that appeared to be sitting on top of the bar. *What the hell is Meg doing up there?* Grace's view was temporarily blocked by the people dancing around her. She got up on her tip toes to see if it was in fact Meg up there. When she'd stopped moving, though, she felt Bianca's hands firmly grab on to her hips, moving her body in rhythm again.

"Sorry, Bianca, I thought I saw Meg. I'm dancing, I'm dancing," Grace mumbled. *I better give her what she wants or I'll be doing this all night.*

Never taking her eyes off the bar, she once again found her thoughts drifting to Michael, letting the beat of the music lead her body. She threw her hands over her head and did the best few minutes of grinding of the night. Bianca let out an approving whistle behind her, letting Grace know that she managed to impress her.

Grace was still scouring the bar for Meg when she felt Bianca brush the hair over her shoulder and lean in to say something in her ear.

Instead of hearing Bianca, though, Grace heard a deep, husky voice say, "Thanks for the pizza, Suzy." His hot breath tickled her neck while his fingers held her in place as he rocked her hips tightly against his.

Immediately Grace's heart thundered in her chest and her body broke out in goose bumps as his hands moved slowly up and down her sides. She was totally mortified when she realized who she had been grinding her ass against for the last few minutes.

Grace spun around to see Michael, a sexy smirk on his face, standing so close there was barely an inch between them. With her face feeling like it was on fire, she breathlessly whispered, "Michael." His eyes were the color of the sky on a clear summer day and even more intense than she remembered.

He didn't say a word but continued moving his body with hers, beat for beat, not allowing Grace's embarrassment to end the erotic dance they found themselves enjoying. His hands returned to her hips and his eyes wandered over her body as if examining every curve and swell of her feminine figure.

On the verge of losing control, Grace glanced over his shoulder and found Bianca standing a few feet away, laughing her ass off. She mouthed "You're dead" to her friend, then looked back up at Michael's perfect features, hoping he didn't notice just how badly she was trembling from his touch.

Big mistake.

"Aren't you supposed to be working?" she blurted out, flustered not only by his proximity but the intensity of his gaze. She took a step away from him, trying desperately to separate her body from his and clear her head. But when she backed up, Michael simply took one step closer, closing the small distance that Grace had created.

With a masculine confidence that set her body on fire, Michael stood there, gazing at her. "I *am* working. I better go back or Jack will have my head. But you know where I'll be if you want to talk or anything." His darkened eyes once again swept down her body, then returned to her face as a sly grin crossed his lips. "Oh, and thanks for the dance. It was really…hot." He reached down and took Grace's quivering hand, kissing the top of it before winking at her and heading back to the bar.

She couldn't move, couldn't breathe, couldn't think. She just stood there, her knuckles tingling from where his lips had made contact with her skin, her legs—jelly. Bianca came running over laughing. "Sorry, Grace, but I have to do whatever I can to win those shoes, and I think that just increased my chances of winning big time. You guys looked so hot together on the dance floor!"

Still unable to form any intelligible speech, Grace took off up the stairs, back to the table where she snatched up both her own Cosmo and Meg's, downing both of them in huge gulps. When her breathing and pulse returned to the normal range, Grace glared savagely at her so-called friend. "That was evil, Bianca! How long was he behind me? Do I even want to know?"

Shaking her head no, Bianca bit her lip to hide her grin but answered anyway. "We switched when you stopped dancing. I thought for sure you'd notice, but you were distracted by something at the bar. The man jumped right in and put his hands on your hips and got you dancing again. That was the hottest thing I've ever seen. You really must have been *feeling* it." She cracked herself up while Grace found herself blushing, again.

The pieces all began to fall into place in her head. It had been Michael that whistled at her when she was dancing, and those were *his* commanding hands on her hips. *Shoot me now. Just kill me,* Grace thought as she flung her face down into her hands. *On the plus side, he did say the dance was hot.*

When she regained her composure, she looked at Bianca and said, "That was evil and I *will* get you back somehow."

"I told you, I'm just trying to increase my chances of winning the shoes. There's nothing wrong with that." As Grace came down from her adrenaline rush, she and Bianca burst into laughter. They settled down, and then Grace remembered what had distracted her earlier. She jumped up from her chair and looked over the rail to the bar where she found Meg, sitting on the corner of the bar, with a notebook in her hand taking drink orders from customers and barking them out to Ryan, who happily ran around filling them.

Grace looked over her shoulder. "Bianca, come check this out!"

"That little shit! What's gotten into her?" Bianca peered down at Meg from the railing, watching her not only flirt with Ryan, but Jack as well.

"I have no idea, but I guess he remembered her. Come on, let's go make Jack's day! Your turn to have some fun."

Bianca whipped a mirror out of her purse and quickly fixed her hair and put on a fresh coat of lipstick. "Let's do this," she said with a wink and an excited gleam in her eye.

Grace had to muster all of her courage to walk down to the bar and talk to Michael after what had just happened out on the dance floor. Every time her mind wandered back to it, she felt the blood rush to her cheeks and she began fanning herself from the intense heat radiating off her skin. If it was possible to die from embarrassment, Grace was sure she'd be in the ICU.

Somehow, she managed to force one foot in front of the other and strolled up behind Michael, who was leaning with his back to the bar, talking to Jack. "Michael!" she shouted right behind him. His hands flew up into the air as he spun, nearly spilling the drink in his hand. At first, his face was annoyed, until he saw it was Grace. Then his expression changed to a sexy smirk.

"Trying to kill me this evening? First the dance, and now you're screaming at me? You know there's only so much excitement my poor heart can take." He dramatically put his hand over his heart. "So what brings you here? Did you miss me?" he asked as he leaned over the bar, his eyes twinkling.

The deep tenor of his voice made Grace's knees weak, and she couldn't stop looking at the sexy curve of his red lips. "No, I came to apologize for, you know … rubbing myself all over you before. If it makes you feel any better, that was the most embarrassing moment of my entire life, and you were able to witness it." Grace grinned uncomfortably, hoping the floor would open up and swallow her whole. "Sorry that you had to endure that."

"Endure? Actually, I rather enjoyed myself." *God, why does he have to be so gorgeous?*

"Yo, Suzy!" she heard Jack boom from the other end of the bar. "Thanks for the pizza!" In all of her mortification over the impromptu dirty dancing incident, Grace had completely forgotten about the pizzas, but that discussion would have to wait for a few minutes.

Out of the corner of her eye, she saw Bianca heading toward them. Without thinking, Grace grabbed Michael's hand on the bar and pulled him closer. "Trust me; you're going to love this. See the girl over my shoulder that looks like a Seahawks cheerleader?"

Michael leaned to the left so he could get a peek at Bianca. His face looked slightly frightened as he nodded his head yes.

"Just watch a master at work," Grace whispered and let go of his hand, instantly missing the contact. She shyly folded her hands on the bar and waited as Bianca approached.

Jack had his head ducked under the bar and was rummaging through a large box when Bianca slapped both hands on the bar top and leaned over to get his attention. "Excuse me. Can I get a drink, please?" she purred, her long red hair dangling seductively over one shoulder.

Without even looking up, Jack held up one finger which frustrated the hell out of Bianca. She was using her best stuff here, the things that made every man stop in his tracks and take notice, yet Jack wasn't even paying attention.

"Does he know her?" Michael whispered, leaning his head closer to Grace. His warm breath blew across her ear.

Any time he moved near Grace, her heart thundered in her chest. "Kind of…"

At that moment, Jack finally looked up from the box and saw Bianca, looking every bit the Seahawks pin-up girl, draped over the bar on front of him. His eyes went from her face, to her cleavage, and back to her face in the span of one second.

Then he froze and his eyes grew wide. The box he took out from under the bar crashed to the floor sending about a thousand straws to scatter at his feet. Grace heard Ryan cursing down at the other end.

"Oh my God! It's you…" Jack mumbled.

"How's the eye?" she asked pointing a beautifully manicured finger at his face.

Michael turned to Grace. "*She's* the one who gave him the black eye?" He was unable to hide the joy and amazement in his eyes at this discovery.

"Yep, she did. She's got a wicked right hook." Grace watched Jack start stammering as he tried to apologize to Bianca. She stood, tall and statuesque, with her hands firmly planted on her hips, but one corner of her mouth turned up slightly.

"No, wait, I really am sorry. I would never grab…I mean, OK, I guess I probably would have grabbed *you*. I mean, look at you…wow…but not in the line at the football game…and I probably would have waited until I at least knew your name. Hi…nice shirt. Go Seahawks?" he sputtered random words out of his mouth, trying to gauge how much trouble he was in with the fiery redhead in front of him. He nervously began raking his hand over his beard, trying to get a read on her.

Michael and Ryan watched their friend flounder awhile longer; then they had to come over and rub it in. "Jack!" Michael strolled over and patted him on the back. "Introduce us to your friend. She seems to be quite the football fan. Did Jack tell you we were at the game this weekend?"

Ryan finally caught his breath and added, "Were you by any chance at the game too?"

Jack started furiously wiping down the bar, trying to not pay attention to the conversation that he knew was going to live in infamy, but Bianca wasn't letting him off that easily. "Why, as a matter of fact, we *were* at the game this weekend, weren't we girls?" she looked over at Grace and Meg, who nodded in agreement. "That's where I met your friend here."

As Jack continued wiping off the bar, Bianca grabbed his arm. "Would you like to tell them the story of how we met, or should I?"

His face went white, his dark brown eyes pleading with her to not tell them anything, but Bianca was having fun watching him come unhinged. She took a deep breath and started the story. "Well, I had just gone and bought my jersey and was on my way back up to the club level when I decided to stop at the concession stand and get some popcorn. So I'm standing in line, minding my own business, and as the guy hands me my popcorn, I feel someone reach over and grab my ass." She glared in Jack's direction as he opened his mouth to protest, and silenced him with her hand over his mouth before a sound escaped.

"I turned to him and said, 'What the hell to you think you're doing?' and he turns to me and says, 'I wasn't trying to grab you; I was trying to grab my wiener.'" Bianca couldn't go on with the story because Michael and Ryan collapsed onto the bar in hysterics.

"Tell me you didn't say that," Ryan begged, wiping the tears from his eyes.

Jack pried Bianca's hand off his mouth and held it in his. "Wait, that's not exactly how it happened. Can I please tell my side of it?" Grace and Meg were on the edge of their seats while Michael and Ryan gasped for breath.

"Go ahead, Jack, I'm sure your explanation will make it all better," Michael laughed.

"OK, so you guys know that after the long drive, I was starving. So I went down to the concession stand, too, and I must have been next to her in line, but I didn't notice her." Bianca let out an angry huff at the thought of any man not noticing her.

Jack picked up on her irritation and smiled. "I was watching the television so I wouldn't miss the game. You were on the other side of me. Otherwise I definitely would have been checking you out, trust me." He gave Bianca a confident wink that finally made her smile.

"So anyway, when I got to the window, I ordered a large hot dog—you know, the third-of-a-pound ones—because I was hungry and had been thinking about this hot dog all game. The guy tells me I was pretty lucky because I got the last one. When he handed me the hot dog, I also went to pick up the hot pretzel I had to get for someone," he glared at Ryan who saluted him with his middle finger, "and when I turned, the hot dog slipped out of my hand and I went to catch it, but I missed and I guess that's when my hand accidentally grabbed your ass." He looked at Bianca apologetically.

"So your lame excuse about grabbing your wiener was true?" Now Bianca was in hysterics.

"Yes, and that's what I tried to explain to you before you decided to deck me," Jack said, pointing back up at his bruised eye. "Then, when I tried to follow you to explain, you sicked the elevator boy on me, and I was stuck looking like some perverted ass-grabber with a black eye."

Grace's cheeks burned from laughing. At some point during her hysteria, she must have taken a hold of Michael's hand because she became very aware of the fact that they were touching and just how good it felt when he gave her hand a squeeze. She nervously slid her hand away from his and looked up to find him watching her.

"So how much of Jack's story did you know?" Grace joked, trying to take his focus off of her.

"He told us he accidentally grabbed some girl's ass, but he left out the part about his wiener. That sounds so bad. No wonder she decked you, Jack," Michael said as he looked down the bar. "In his defense, he did whine the rest of the game about not getting to eat his hot dog."

"Shut up, Mike. Why don't you and your girl *Suzy* there go enjoy some pizza?" Jack snarled as he turned his attention back to Bianca who wanted to get a closer look at her handiwork. Jack happily leaned closer and allowed her to run her fingers gingerly over the bruise under his eye, basking in her tender attention.

Jack's comment snapped Grace out of her Michael-induced haze. "Oh gosh, here." She pulled money out of her pocket and held it out to Michael, who stood there looking puzzled.

"What's that for? My pain and suffering because of the dance?" he teased.

"Very funny. No, it's for the pizzas." Grace dropped the money onto the bar, but he pushed it back to her.

"I'm not taking your money."

"Take the money. The look on your face was worth every penny. And from what I could tell, you don't seem to like pizza with the works very much." She pointed her thumb in the direction of the pile of pizzas that some of the other employees were now helping themselves to.

"Not a big fan of onions, sorry," Michael said while quickly getting a few beers for one of the servers.

"Yeah, it would probably make it difficult to make out with all your barfly groupies if you have onion breath." Grace bit her lip to keep from laughing at the shocked expression on his face.

"How did you know about barflies? Never mind—Vicki. I need to have a little chat with my friend later," he said, looking up at her section of tables. He smiled and turned his attention back to Grace with a wicked grin.

"And for your information, there's only been one girl I've met in the last few weeks that I wanted to kiss. However, the first time we met, it wasn't here at the bar, so she isn't really a barfly, even though she seems to be becoming a regular here." He playfully raised an eyebrow as he continued unleashing the full power of his charms on her. He moved closer, and with a sexy male arrogance, waited for her reaction to what he said.

Grace felt her face getting hot, in part from embarrassment, but also from the thought of what it would be like to kiss Michael, wondering how his lips would feel against hers, how they would taste. Flustered, she nervously played with a strand of her hair and tried to hide her face to keep him from seeing how his words had affected her.

Desperate to change the subject, she tried to deflect his attention. "So, I want to know how many times you've had pissed-off girls send you pizzas from this place." She glanced over at the stack of Mama Rosa's boxes.

He laughed. "Never."

"No one ever called an order in for you before when you gave them the bogus number? Why not?" Grace asked in amazement.

"Probably because they weren't nearly as clever as you," he half whispered. Michael glanced down at the money which was still sitting in front of him. "Please take this back. I don't want it. I gave out the number; I should be a man and face the consequences."

"But I feel bad. I stuck you with a bunch of pizzas you won't even eat. The least I could do is pay for them."

"You know what you can give me instead of money?" His eyes had that naughty twinkle in them again. Grace's heart fluttered when he began slowly running his thumb over her wrist.

"I'm not kissing you."

"Who said anything about a kiss?" he asked innocently.

"I'm not giving you my phone number. I don't know you that well. You could be a stalker or something."

"I don't want your phone number either. Well, I do, but that's not what I want right now."

Completely confused as to where he was going with this, she narrowed her eyes suspiciously. "What do you want then?"

"Your real name, please. I've seen pictures of the girl Suzy that Jack was with, and let's just say he wasn't very 'selective' for his first time, if you know what I mean. Every time I call you Suzy, I see her face, and it's starting to make me ill. Besides, you seem to already know my name, so I think it's only fair that I know yours." He stood, confidently waiting for her answer.

Grace sat on the stool quietly and continued to twirl a piece of her hair around her finger, making him wait. He looked nervous, like she might actually turn him down, so she decided to put him out of his misery. "I don't know if I want to tell you that yet. I kinda like you calling me Suzy."

"Hey, Michael! Hey, Grace!" a voice came from over her shoulder.

Meg.

Grace rolled her eyes in disgust. "Thanks, Meg!"

Michael laughed out loud and clapped his hands together. "Grace, Grace, Grace. Now that fits you much better," he said as he tucked a stray piece of hair back behind her ear, his fingers brushing lightly against her cheek, sending a wonderful chill down her spine.

"Grace, we need to get going. Come on, Bianca, the boys have work to do, and it's getting late." Meg handed Grace her coat, which she threw haphazardly over her shoulders, not wanting to leave. She continued looking at Michael, memorizing every detail of his face. She knew she would be seeing him in her dreams tonight, those icy blue eyes, the strong line of his jaw, her fingers threaded into his long hair.

Michael's smile faded into a frown, not even trying to hide his disappointment at Meg's words. "Do you really have to go? Can't you just stay until we close? We could go get something to eat."

Jack walked over and echoed Michael's request.

"Sorry, boys, but we have to go. We need our beauty sleep. Ladies, shall we?" Meg pointed toward the door. Grace saw her wink at Ryan as she strolled away from the bar. Bianca blew Jack a kiss, and Michael quietly said, "Bye, Grace."

"Bye, Michael. I'll see you soon." She squeezed his hand and gave him a warm smile. Her words somehow seemed to make him happier.

"Promise?" He smirked.

"Yeah, I promise." She gave him a small wave, and yet again, she had to force her feet to walk away from him, because for some reason, she was inexplicably drawn to him. Her body knew what it wanted, but her head kept getting in the way.

What she really wanted to do was sit at the bar all night long and watch him as he worked, watch the way he smiled when he looked at her, or the way his muscles flexed when he carried a new tray of glasses out to the bar. She just wanted to be near him, for as long as possible, but unfortunately her time for tonight was up.

"See you soon," she whispered as she took one quick look over her shoulder and saw Michael leaning against the bar, watching her walk away.

Chapter 7

When the cold evening air hit their faces, the girls were snapped out of their silence. Grace unlocked the car and they all quickly climbed in and cranked the heat. Before she pulled out of the parking lot, she had to ask the question that had been bugging her since she forced herself to walk away from Michael.

"Remind me again why we just turned down an offer to grab food with three drop dead gorgeous men? And I know … the boycott. But it wouldn't have broken any of the rules."

Bianca nodded her head in agreement and patiently waited for Meg's answer to the burning question of the moment.

"Ladies, think about it. We're playing hard to get. Hard to get is far more attractive to men than clingy and desperate, wouldn't you agree?"

Grace thought about it and offered a quick, "Sure, but—"

Bianca threw her hands up in the air. "Fine, we're playing hard to get. I understand that part. But eventually we *are* going to let them catch us, right?"

They spent the rest of the drive home in a comfortable silence, each of them deep in their own thoughts about what had happened at The Vault. Grace unlocked the door to the apartment, tossed her keys into the basket, then told the girls, "Get your PJs and pillows and meet me on the couch in ten minutes." They both smiled and hurried to their rooms to change.

Grace opened her bedroom door and threw herself down onto the bed. She couldn't help but smile as she thought back over the night's events: Michael's face when the pizza arrived, the way he whispered in her ear on the dance floor, the feel of his strong hands on her hips, the hilarity of Bianca and Jack retelling the wiener story while Meg sat on the bar helping Ryan serve drinks. But nothing made her smile more than the memory of how it felt to be in Michael's arms. That was something she was certain she'd never forget.

Grace grabbed her pajama bottoms and a T-shirt and quickly changed. With a pillow under her arm, she headed out to the couch, where Meg was sitting, bouncing with excitement. Bianca disappeared into the kitchen to make some popcorn, and then came out and joined them.

Unable to remain silent another second, Meg finally burst. "Oh my gosh, that was so much fun, and they're just great." She started clapping her hands together. "Bianca, you and Jack are so cute together and Grace…wow. Talk about chemistry!"

Bianca rolled her eyes at Meg's comment. Grace, however, turned a bright shade of red.

"Get a grip, Meg, he's still the Wiener Guy, you know. One conversation doesn't make a love connection, and he's got facial hair," Bianca tried to blow it off, but Grace could see she was trying way too hard to sound uninterested.

"Nice try, Bianca, but we both saw it, and I for one distinctly heard you use your 'sexy' voice. You only use that if you're interested in someone." Grace looked at her suspiciously, and the uninterested façade was replaced with a huge smile that spread across her face.

"God, he's so cute…and dense…but I can work with that. I think I might need an intervention because, God help me, I think his scruffy beard is sexy. And Grace, you saw him exercising! I may need to go to the gym with you." Bianca began fanning herself at the thought of seeing Jack, sweaty and working out.

Grace turned her attention to Meg who was throwing popcorn into the air and trying to catch it in her mouth. "So, I take it Ryan remembered you?" A piece of popcorn hit her in the nose and toppled onto the floor.

"I'll say he remembered me. He was getting drinks for someone else, so I just hopped up onto the bar and waited for him to notice me." Meg giggled with excitement.

"How very subtle of you," Bianca teased.

Meg just tossed a piece of popcorn at her which Bianca easily swatted to the ground. "You know I don't do subtle very well, Bianca."

Bianca laughed. "Really? I hadn't noticed."

Meg ignored Bianca and continued with her story. "Anyway, when he finally came over, all he said was, 'I was wondering when I'd see you again,' and I said, 'The sooner the better.' Then I introduced myself as Meg Tomlin, the girl of his dreams."

Grace's mouth dropped open in shock. "I swear I'd kill to have your self-confidence for a day. Wow," she commented, shaking her head from side to side.

"Oh please, Grace, I saw your little 'bump and grind' routine with Michael. You didn't look insecure at all when you were rubbing yourself all over him. I could feel the heat all the way over at the bar." Meg giggled as Grace lunged for her.

With a pillow in her hand, Grace playfully whacked Meg over the head as things snowballed into an enormous pillow fight. She was standing over Meg with two pillows in her hand, when a thought suddenly jumped into her head.

"Meg, you were over at the bar. Why in the world was Michael even on the dance floor to begin with?" Meg sat there, looking extremely guilty as Grace waited for her answer.

"Meg, spill!"

"Well, when I was sitting on the bar with Ryan, Michael *may* have recognized me from last night when we asked for his phone number, and he *may* have asked if I was a friend of Suzy's…" She looked to Bianca for help, but Bianca was too engrossed in the story herself to run any interference.

"And?" Grace pressed on, holding the pillow up a little higher as a threat.

"And I may have said yes, I knew you. Then, Gracie, he got all cute and excited and he wanted to know if you were at the bar tonight. So I might have mentioned you were in the far side of the dance floor, wearing a blue sweater, tight jeans, and no underwear. Oh yeah, and I mentioned that you were dancing with a Seahawks fan." Meg threw her hands defensively over her face as the pillow left Grace's hand on a path to her head.

"Are you insane? You told him I wasn't wearing underwear?" Grace wasn't sure Meg could even hear her over Bianca's hysterical laughter.

"Oh, stop it, Grace! You loved every minute of it—ouch! I was just helping. You should be thanking me—ouch! He just about jumped over the bar to go find you—stop hitting me!" Meg begged as Grace pummeled her with pillows.

Then Grace turned her attention to Bianca. "And did *you* say anything I need to know about?" she asked with raised eyebrows as she took a few steps closer to Bianca. Bianca's eyes were cautiously fixed on the pillow in Grace's hand.

"He asked if he could cut in and—ouch! I didn't even tell you yet! I might have said something along the lines of 'Go get her, tiger; she's been wanting to grind on you all night. Better bring your A game.' Stop it, Grace! I can't breathe," Bianca squawked from underneath a pillow.

"Just when I thought I couldn't be more embarrassed, you two just prove me wrong. This is so much worse than I thought it was two hours ago. I need a new alias," Grace rambled out loud to herself.

The trio spent the next two hours talking and laughing about everything that had happened over the last few weeks. From establishing the boycott, to the boys, and now to counting down the days until the stupid game was over so they could go on a date with these fabulous guys. No one was willing to concede the battle; someone would be crowned the winner.

All three of them were too stubborn to just cancel the wager, so as Grace climbed into bed for the evening, she devised her master plan. She decided her best chance for success was to push Meg and Ryan or Jack and Bianca together as quickly as possible. The sooner they disqualified themselves, the sooner Grace could find out if Michael was really interested in her, or if it was simply the thrill of the chase.

Over the next two days, Bianca and Meg were swamped with work. The holidays were always a busy time of year for them. For grace it was the opposite; the university was on break so she had nothing but time. As a result, she spent most of the day alone. She even tried to kill some time and sneak to the gym to see if she could 'accidentally' run into Michael, with no luck. Thursday night, Meg flopped onto the couch after yet another long day of work and wanted to plan some fun for their weekend.

"What are we doing tomorrow night?" Meg asked.

Bianca came and joined them on the couch, eating a bowl of cereal. "Would it be too desperate to go to The Vault?" Bianca asked hopefully, but when Meg rolled her eyes, she knew the answer.

"Yes, Bianca, if we went there we could just paint desperate across our heads." Meg sighed. "Wait, I have a great idea! Let's go see a movie and then we'll do dinner after that. What comes out tomorrow?" She grabbed the newspaper and started planning the rest of their weekend.

❧

"Meg, we're going to a dark, sticky movie theater. There's no reason for all this primping, unless you've changed your mind and decided we can go to The Vault tonight. In which case, Bianca and I are going to kill you because we are completely underdressed!" Grace bellowed at the closed bedroom door.

She looked helplessly at Bianca, who decided to try banging on the door while screaming to see if that would light a fire under Meg's ass. "We need to leave in exactly five minutes or we won't have time to get popcorn. And you know I can't sit through a movie without popcorn and candy, so get a move on."

Meg chose that moment to throw open her door. "Stop the screeching girls; I'm ready." Meg strolled out of her room and showed off her long, mahogany wig of the evening. "Perfection takes time, ladies," she said with a curtsy.

Grace drove like a madwoman to make it to the theater in time. She knew if they missed the previews, Meg would whine for an hour, and if Bianca didn't have time to get her popcorn and candy, there'd be hell to pay. She'd bought the tickets online and was able to quickly print them out at the kiosk, leaving them with five minutes to spare before the previews were scheduled to start.

A large refillable tub of popcorn, three large sodas, one bag of licorice, a box of chocolate, and an order of nachos later, the girls dashed into the theater just as the lights were dimming for the previews. Meg slipped into the third row and sat down near the center. "Do you think we have enough food?" she whispered as the first preview started.

"We have enough food to feed a family of six for a week, Meg." Their giggles were immediately shushed by a woman a few seats down.

Bianca glared at the woman and shushed her right back.

"How scary is this movie supposed to be?" Grace asked when the creepy music started with the opening credits.

"It's a horror movie, Grace. You're guaranteed to have nightmares for a week," Bianca whispered in her ear. Grace began nervously munching on her tray of nachos as mysterious shadows crept across the screen. To her right, Meg was shaking her candy around in the box, and on her left, Bianca was balancing a huge bucket of popcorn on her lap while clutching a package of licorice in one hand and reaching for her soda with the other.

A few minutes into the movie, the eerie music returned and Grace started to tense up, knowing something scary was about to happen. She was completely engrossed in the movie when a couple of hard candies whizzed over her shoulder and bounced off the seat back in front of her, landing in her nacho cheese.

"What the hell was that?" she hissed to Bianca. "Damn kids," Grace mumbled as she turned around in her seat to find the little culprits. There was no one directly behind them, but three rows back a young couple was laughing. Grace gave them a dirty look, and then turned back to the movie.

"This movie is kinda intense, don't you think?" Meg whispered in her ear as yet another person disappeared into the mist. With her hands pressed tightly against her eyes, Grace nodded her head while peering at the screen through a small gap in her fingers.

"Why the hell do these stupid people always go off alone when people are disappearing?" Bianca mumbled, gnawing on her long licorice rope. As Grace reached over to grab one from her bag, a handful of popcorn sailed over their heads and scattered into their laps.

"What the hell?" Bianca's loud exclamation caused the woman down the aisle to start shushing them again. "Hey, someone's throwing popcorn at us, lady. So mind your own business," she snapped at the woman.

Grace spun around in her seat to search for the culprits and again, the only people laughing were the young couple three rows up. She flipped them off, which for some reason made them laugh harder, and then she turned back around in her seat.

"Who's throwing stuff at us?" Bianca growled. Meg was giggling in her seat as her friends fumed. Apparently, she was safely out of range of the popcorn-throwing lunatics behind them and found the whole thing rather amusing.

"There's a couple, three rows up, who keep laughing. They're the only ones around," Grace whispered, getting even more irritated.

The girls turned their attention back to the screen, hoping the shenanigans would stop. In the movie, the white clouds of mist were still rolling in. More people disappeared as they were climbing through a pitch black building, trying to elude the mist. Terrified, Grace was clutching her tray of nachos with both hands, holding her breath. The mist came closer and closer, and then, all of a sudden, she felt something warm blowing on the back of her neck and broke out in goose bumps.

It's your imagination, Grace, chill out! It's a movie. No deranged killers are in the theater, her brain tried to tell her body, but her frantically beating heart refused to listen. Her hands were trembling and she was about to turn around when a deep voice said in her ear, "Who goes to a movie and orders nachos?"

That was all the scare her heart could handle, and Grace screamed. Not just any scream, but a bloodcurdling 'someone's killing me' scream as she tossed her nachos up into the air. Her outburst startled Bianca so badly that she knocked the popcorn off her lap and onto Grace. Meg, on the other hand, was laughing so hard, she dropped her box of candy, sending chocolates cascading all over the floor.

Grace spun around in her seat to find Michael, Ryan, and Jack howling in the row directly behind them. *Where the hell did they come from?* Then she realized most of the people in the theater had erupted into hysterical laughter, including the couple she had flicked off just minutes ago.

"What the hell do you think you're doing? Were you trying to give me a heart attack?" Grace snarled as she threw two huge handfuls of popcorn at them.

"I didn't know you were that scared…oh my God…the nachos…they went everywhere…" Michael laughed the words between gasps.

"You suck! And you owe me some new nachos—and refill the popcorn, jackass." She threw the now empty large popcorn bucket back at him. Michael was still laughing as Grace watched him stumble out of the theater.

Jack leaned over to Bianca. "Are you scared? If you want, I could come sit next to you, and help you feel safe…" His voice trailed off, hoping she would take the bait.

"I can promise you, Jack, that I wouldn't feel the least bit safe sitting next to *you* in the dark. I've seen the crap you're capable of in broad daylight, let alone a dark movie theater. Stay back there. *That* will make me feel safe," Bianca quipped without even turning her head to look in his direction. The girls heard him huff and crash back into his seat. Grace glanced over at her friend, and Bianca gave her a quick wink.

On the other side of Grace, Meg and Ryan continued whispering back and forth with their heads tucked together. Every so often, Meg would let out a loud giggle, causing the shushing to begin all over again.

Michael returned a few minutes later with the new bucket of popcorn and some nachos. "Here you go, Grace, one tray of nachos, the strangest movie food ever sold. Did you know that you've been the only person all day to order nachos? I asked the girl. She said it typically takes them three weeks to go through a whole vat of liquid cheese." He kept rambling on about how gross the nachos were, so Grace did the only thing she could. She dipped one of the corn chips into the bright orange cheese and crammed it into his beautiful, open mouth.

"Taste the deliciousness that is liquid cheese, Michael." Grace laughed, as she turned back to face the screen. She could hear him still mumbling behind her.

"Disgusting…"

Bianca swatted Jack's big hand away as he reached over her shoulder trying to sneak some popcorn from the freshly filled bucket.

"Ouch," Jack whined, but Bianca just glared. "Hey, I'm hungry."

"Maybe you shouldn't have thrown all your popcorn at people."

Wisely, Jack changed his approach. "May I please have some popcorn, Bianca?" His good manners won her over, and she reluctantly held the bucket up so he could reach the buttery kernels. "Thank you, B."

Grace felt a gentle tap on her shoulder. When she turned around, Michael's face was right there, his lips curled into a sexy smirk. The light from the screen accentuated the two dimples that framed his smile. She was caught off guard by how close he was and just how delicious he smelled.

His breathtaking smile broke her out of her trance, and she stammered, "Wh- What?"

"I still have the horrible taste of molten cheese in my mouth. May I please have a sip of your drink?" he pleaded with not only his voice, but with a pout of his full, bottom lip that Grace suddenly wanted to take a bite out of.

Grace couldn't help teasing him a little bit. "You don't have any communicable diseases do you? When was the last time you sucked face with some skanky barfly?"

He rolled his eyes. "My lips are clean, I swear. Would you like to check for yourself?" he asked wickedly as he puckered up.

"Ew. No thanks. Here you go." Grace handed him the soda. "Now if you don't mind, I would like to see the end of this movie."

Grace settled into her seat and looked up at the giant screen, trying to focus on the end of the movie, but her mind was only interested in one thing: Michael. Just knowing he was sitting directly behind her, whispering to Jack, was driving her crazy. She strained her ears to try and hear what they were talking about, but with no luck.

Then he started tapping his foot into the back of her chair. When he realized she was annoyed by it, he leaned up again and whispered "Sorry" into her ear. Feeling his warm breath on her neck made Grace shiver. She began imagining him sitting next to her and burying her face into his chest during the scary parts of the movie. He would put his arm around her protectively and it would be … perfect.

Boycott, money, shoes, boycott, money, shoes. Grace repeated her new mantra in her head.

She heard Bianca let out a frustrated sigh beside her. Neither of them was the least bit interested in the movie now. They had something far more interesting sitting behind them, capturing their complete attention. Having no idea what was going on in the movie any more, Grace leaned over to Meg who still had Ryan whispering in her ear.

"I'm going to go pee. I have no idea what the hell's going on in the movie anyway."

Meg snickered. "Paying attention to something other than the movie, are you?" she teased.

"Go back to whispering with Ryan. By the way, you know you want to kiss him; too bad you can't," Grace snarled before she stood up. Meg stuck out her tongue as Grace stormed away.

She ran to the bathroom and glanced in the mirror as she washed her hands and sighed. *Had I known we would be seeing Michael, I definitely would have worn something different.* Unfortunately, as Grace looked at her reflection, she was just in an old pair of jeans and a T-shirt, nothing spectacular. She ran her fingers through her hair quickly to try and make minimal improvements to it. As she applied a fresh coat of lip gloss, Bianca stormed into the bathroom.

She paused when she saw Grace's primping and smiled. "Prettying ourselves up, are we?" She placed her purse on the counter.

"What are you doing in here, Bianca?" Grace asked, trying to change the subject.

"Same thing as you—hiding and beautifying." She leaned back against the sink and sighed.

Grace put an understanding hand on her shoulder and mumbled, "I know. Trust me, Bianca, I know. A little scary, isn't it?"

"He's just so damn irresistible." Bianca swept the tube of lipstick across her lips and then tossed it back into her purse. The pair put the finishing touches on their faces and headed back to the movie.

When they opened the doors to theater twelve, they stopped dead in their tracks. Michael and Jack were leaning up against the back wall in the dimly lit hallway, smiling.

Grace took a deep breath to try and keep from blushing but failed terribly. Michael chuckled and waved them over to where they were standing.

"Hey," she said casually as she dug the toe of her shoe into the carpet.

"Hey. So, I take it you are not enjoying the movie. Is it too scary for you?" A teasing grin spread across his face.

Grace glanced over at Bianca and laughed. "Something like that, yeah."

"So, what are you ladies doing after the movie?" Jack asked, trying to sound casual. Grace laughed, Michael just rolled his eyes.

"We're going to go get something to eat," Bianca answered quickly. "What about you?"

A huge grin broke out on Jack's face. "What a coincidence. We're going to get something to eat, too. Would you ladies like to join us?"

Grace guessed they could have said they were getting pedicures and Jack would have insisted that was what they were going to do too. She could see in his face just how much he wanted to spend time with Bianca.

"That would be fine with me, but Bianca, we'd better check with Meg and see," Grace said hesitantly.

Just as she said that, the movie ended and a mob of people started crowding the hallway they were currently standing in, trying to get to the exit. Grace felt Michael grab her hand and pull her close to keep track of her in the crowd. She felt his hard body press against hers as they navigated through the narrow space.

Breathe, Grace, breathe, she said in her head.

They lost Bianca and Jack in the crowd, but Michael found them standing over in a corner and waved his hand up in the air. Grace looked back over her shoulder, trying to find Meg and Ryan, who should have been exiting the theater any minute, but there was no sign of them. Michael continued leading her over to Bianca and Jack, her hand tightly clutched in his.

"Did you two see Meg yet?" Grace asked.

Instead of answering, Bianca looked down at Grace's hand which was still entwined with Michael's and smiled. Suddenly self conscious, Grace slid her hand out of Michael's grasp and glared back at her friend.

"Don't look for them anytime soon. Ryan has this thing for staying until the very last credit rolls, something about acknowledging the hard work of everyone involved in the filmmaking process. I don't get it. All I know is he's the last guy out every time." Jack laughed.

While the four of them stood there waiting, Jack nonchalantly slipped his arm around Bianca's shoulders. A small grin crossed her face as she snuggled up against his chest. When she saw Grace looking at her cozied up to Jack, she scowled and shrugged off his arm.

The door to the theater swung open one final time, and out came Ryan with a very chipper Meg perched on his back getting a piggyback ride. Grace looked at Bianca, who returned her stunned expression; then they burst out laughing. "Is that against any of the rules?" Grace asked between laughs.

"Unfortunately, I don't think so," Bianca chuckled.

"Damn. Thought we had her for a second."

"What are you two talking about?" Michael asked as he and Jack exchanged a confused look.

Grace skirted the subject. "We'll tell you about it at dinner, right, Bianca?" Bianca nodded her head in agreement.

"You don't want to check with Meg anymore?" Michael asked, pointing over in her direction.

"No, she doesn't get to decide this one." She grabbed Michael's hand this time and led him over to Meg and Ryan, who were laughing at a poster of a coming attraction.

"Hey there, love birds, are you guys ready to go?" Grace asked, giving Meg a big smirk. She immediately hopped off Ryan's back and put her hands on her hips.

"Where are we going?" she asked with a suspicious tone to her voice.

"We're going to get some food and, guess what, so are the guys! What a coincidence," Grace said with over-exaggerated surprise.

Meg shook her head side to side. "I know you two *desperately* want to go get food."

"There's nothing 'desperate' about the need for sustenance. Why don't you just *cling* back onto Ryan and we'll head to the car. I think a good table for six people is *hard to get*," Bianca sneered. She raised her eyebrow daring Meg to say no to her request, but even Meg knew to back off when Bianca was this adamant about something.

"Fine. Where are we meeting?" Meg asked. Grace looked at Bianca in confusion. They hadn't gotten that far in the planning yet.

The first restaurant that Grace could think of popped out of her mouth. "Mi Casa."

Meg looked confused. "We're going back to our house? Are you cooking?"

Grace shook her head slowly. "No, Meg, that Mexican place on third, with the 'Margaritas by the Yard,' remember?" Of course she probably couldn't remember—she'd gotten pretty drunk last time they went. So had Bianca…all part of Grace's plan.

"Oh, I love that place. Yeah, let's go there!" She held out her arms to Ryan who slung her over his back and headed for the doors.

Grace felt Michael lean over her shoulder. "Want me to carry you to the car, too?"

She bent her finger for him to come a little closer. "If you're lucky, I'll let you carry me somewhere one day…but first you have to catch me!" she teased as she let go of his hand and ran for the door.

Chapter 8

"Can we get a pitcher of margaritas on the rocks, four salted glasses, and two 'yards of margaritas' for my friends, please?" Grace ordered the drinks for the group and something more special for Meg and Bianca.

"Wait!" Meg chirped. "I am not having one of those yard thingies. I remember what happened last time, Grace. Nice try. Bianca, you don't want one either." She looked up at the waitress and waved her hand. "Just bring six glasses, please."

Darn you, Meg! So what if last time you drank a yard of margaritas you made out with the waiter? And who could forget the way Bianca shoved her tongue down the throat of the guy at the next table?

Michael was sitting to the left of Grace at the huge circular table, scouring the menu. Before the server walked away, he quickly ordered an appetizer for the group. "Can we get an order of chicken nachos too, please?" The waitress nodded her head as she jotted it in her notebook. He leaned over to Grace, and smiled. "I thought you should try some *real* nachos for a change, minus the molten cheese from a can."

Grace opened her mouth to make a smartass comment, but was interrupted.

"Before I put this all in the computer, how are we splitting the check?" the waitress asked as she looked around the table.

"One check, and I'll take it," Michael answered. Of course, everyone had something to say about that.

"No, no, no. We need to split it, just take the whole thing, and at the end, split it in half," Bianca insisted.

The waitress nodded and walked away while the group continued to argue.

"Just let us pick up the check. After all, we're crashing your dinner. It's the least we can do." Jack tried to argue, but Bianca shook her head no.

"Thanks for the offer, but if you pay then this could be considered a 'date' and we can't have that, now can we, ladies?" Meg said as she glared across the table at Grace and Bianca.

Michael mulled the comment over in his head then turned to Grace. "So at the gym, when you said you weren't dating until the new year, you were serious?" he asked in amazement. Grace looked at him and blushed as she nodded her head yes. "Did all three of you agree to that?" he asked incredulously.

Jack quickly looked at Bianca, who was nodding her head along with Meg.

"Care to share the details?" Ryan asked Meg.

"Well, we had been going on dates with total losers, especially Grace, but that's a completely different story. Anyway, we decided no dates until January, made a few ground rules, and put some money on it." Meg shrugged and munched on some chips and salsa.

"So what are these *rules*," Jack asked Bianca suspiciously. Grace could tell he wasn't excited at the prospect of rules cramping his style.

"Well, no dating obviously, no tongue kissing…" Jack smacked his hand down on the table and gave Michael a 'you've got to be kidding me' look. Bianca giggled and continued. "No sex of any kind—if you wouldn't want to see your parents do it, it counts as sex. Then we each pitched two hundred dollars into the pot for the winner to spend on a gorgeous pair of shoes."

Shoes or sex, shoes or sex… which do I value more? Grace pondered the question in her head. *Maybe I need to be more specific. Shoes or sex with Michael, shoes or sex with Michael. Of course that's assuming that Michael actually wants to have sex with me.* The argument raged in her head. She made the mistake of glancing over at Michael, who still had her fixed in his smoldering gaze, making her heart flutter out of control.

"Six hundred dollars for a pair of shoes? Are you serious?" Jack boomed. "That's crazy."

"No, it's not. That's a fabulous pair of shoes to be worn on her first date of the new year," Bianca said with deep desire lacing her voice. "I'd do just about anything for a great pair of shoes," she mumbled as she put her margarita glass to her lips.

Grace let out a big laugh when she noticed Jack's mouth was hanging open as he watched Bianca's tongue drag along the edge of her glass, sensually licking the salt off the rim. "She's totally serious, too, you know," Grace whispered as she leaned over to Michael. The brilliant blue of his eyes at times was too much for her heart. The way he looked at her was wicked and sinful and she loved it. She nervously grabbed the margarita that the waitress had poured, and took a big sip to distract herself.

She felt Michael's arm snake around her back and finally come to rest on her chair. He leaned in close and put his lips up to her ear, barely grazing her earlobe. "And what would *you* do, Grace, for a great pair of shoes?"

I think my heart may have actually just stopped. Grace froze, her entire body in knots as she reminded herself to breathe.

She was seconds away from losing all control and saying 'screw the shoes,' but instead, Grace used some common sense and chose sarcasm to hide her true feelings. "Wouldn't you like to know?" she whispered back at him as she looked up through her long eyelashes. Another one of those slow, sexy smiles that Grace couldn't resist came across his face, and she found herself smiling right back at him.

Through the rest of dinner, Michael would 'accidentally' brush his hand against her arm or back or leg as he adjusted his chair. Each time he touched her, no matter how innocent the contact, Grace's heart would pound and her skin would tingle. At one point, she had to excuse herself to the restroom to catch her breath. Being that close to him was driving her crazy and sending her libido into overdrive.

Everyone had a fantastic time at dinner. Jack was hilarious, and Ryan and Michael were armed with a never-ending supply of funny stories about him. Meg and Bianca continued to suck down the margaritas, and then with some prompting from Michael, thought it would be funny to share a few embarrassing tales about Grace.

"So, Meg, tell me about some of the losers Grace has dated in the past that led to the boycott," Michael asked a very tipsy Meg.

"Meg." Grace gave her a warning look, which she must have missed while she was tonguing the rim of her margarita glass. Ryan's wide eyes were glued to Meg's tongue as it leisurely trailed along the edge of her rotating glass.

"Michael, you have no idea the magnitude of losers she has dated. Bianca, help me, there are so many to choose from. Top five had to be…Oh, I know! Remember that guy who was the greeter at Wal-Mart?"

"Wait a minute. That one doesn't count. I had no idea that's what he did for a living until after our date. The next day I went to Wal-Mart and he was the one who handed me my cart. I changed my phone number that afternoon," Grace admitted sheepishly. The boisterous laughter of the guys turned a few heads from the surrounding tables.

"Don't forget the slew of insurance salesmen and the accountants. Dull, dull, dull—especially the one accountant that made you split the bill for the entire date with him down to the penny, including sales tax and gas money." Bianca howled, wiping her eyes with her napkin.

"I almost forgot about the mortician. Grace, do you remember that one? After dinner he took her back to his place and it was a funeral home. Grace had nightmares for a month about that guy."

Of course Meg would mention Dead Fred.

Jack actually left the table, he was laughing so hard, while Michael leaned back in his chair, with tears streaming down his face. Ryan's whole body, shaking with laughter, was draped across the table.

"My personal favorite was that poet guy, remember him? The earthy one who was so 'natural' he wouldn't wear deodorant, eat meat, or bathe every day, all in an effort to supposedly save the environment. He gave us a lecture one time about how we should all be concerned with the ozone layer and our part in depleting it. Tell Michael what kind of car Stinky Pete picked you up in for your date." Bianca sat back in her chair and waited for Grace to finish the story

"A big ass Hummer," Grace giggled quietly. "And for the record, his poetry sucked. Most of it was about a stupid goldfish."

As Meg opened her mouth to start into another story about her friend's pitiful dating experiences, Grace decided to change the topic to one that was guaranteed to shut Meg up. "Do you want me to ask if Hector is working tonight?"

Meg spit her margarita out of her mouth at just the mention of his name. Bianca's eyes bugged out of her head and immediately took the hint that Grace was done being the butt of the jokes, quickly changing the subject. Meg, however, nervously scanned the restaurant for any sign of Hector.

They hardly even paused to touch their food, which wasn't surprising considering how much they were laughing and all the junk food they had eaten at the movies. The server brought over a bunch of boxes and the leftovers were saved, giving everyone lunch for the following day. It was getting late; the restaurant was nearly empty by the time they decided to call it an evening.

"We should get a move on, ladies," Grace said quietly as she paid the girls' half of the bill even with the boys' vigorous protests.

"Wait," she heard Michael say as he rummaged in his pocket for something. He pulled out his cell phone and placed it in her hand. "Can I get your phone number?"

Grace grabbed his cell phone and tossed him hers in return. She quickly programmed her home and cell numbers and then, while Michael was arguing with Meg about how it wasn't against the rules at all to exchange phone numbers with a 'friend' in case of emergencies or a flat tire, Grace quickly programmed the perfect ringtone to go with her number, one she hoped would make him laugh when he heard it.

She snapped the phone shut and handed it back. "Here you go." As Michael dropped her phone back into her purse, Grace eyed him suspiciously. "No pizza places, right?"

"Depends if I'm interested in you or not. I only give my *real* number to women I'm interested in. I guess you'll just have to wait and see." He smirked and wrapped his arm around her shoulders.

Grace looked across the table and saw Jack fixing his hair and slipping on his shades for a picture with Bianca on her phone, no doubt to go with his phone number. Meg and Ryan had their heads huddled together again, whispering. She couldn't help but notice what a perfect couple they made. He was more on the quiet and reserved side and she was as flamboyant and artsy as they come. Opposites who were definitely attracted to one another.

"Ladies, we are out of here!" Grace stood up and went to grab all the leftovers, but Michael beat her to it, insisting he carry them to the car for her. He politely held open the door to the restaurant as they stepped out into the crisp evening air which made Grace shiver.

They piled the leftovers in the trunk before Grace made her way to the driver's side door. "Thanks for tagging along on our dinner. It was a lot of fun." There was no way to stop her growing smile as Michael slowly slipped his arms around her waist, pulling her closer to him. Grace's stomach filled with butterflies like she was a teenager again.

"I had fun, too. Will you do me a favor and call me when you get home so I know you made it in safely?"

When she opened her mouth to protest, he placed a finger over her lips and whispered, "Please?"

All rational thought went out the window and Grace was left staring at him all glassy eyed. Like an idiot, all she could do was look up at him through her thick lashes and nod her head yes. She didn't even notice that Meg and Bianca were at the car until she heard "Let's roll, Grace!" from Meg as she slammed the back door of the car.

"Bye," she mumbled to Michael as she left the warmth of his arms and climbed into the driver's seat. Before Grace closed the door, he stuck his head in. "Drive safely please." With a wink he shut the door and headed to where he had parked his car.

Her face still flushed from being in Michael's arms, Grace peeked over at Bianca before she put the key into the ignition. "Oh. My. God!"

Bianca clapped her hands together. "See, Grace, isn't it fun to hang out with a guy that isn't as dull as dishwater?"

Drive safely please. The words echoed through Michael's head as he replayed the last thirty seconds in his mind, again. Grace's face had been inches away from his and it took all his strength not to kiss her right then and there. He knew she had her ridiculous boycott rules, not to mention two hundred dollars on the line. As Michael walked over to the car where Jack and Ryan were waiting, he decided he was going to have to find a way to get around some of those silly rules.

"Dude, we're freezing! Are you done cozying up to Grace?" Jack growled as Michael unlocked the doors.

"You're just mad because you found out tonight that you can't impress Bianca with your legendary kissing skills like you were planning on doing. Guess you're going to have to get her attention the old fashioned way: earn it."

Ryan patted Jack on the back. "Just be yourself. Wait, let me rephrase that, be on your best behavior until you can kiss her."

"I can be just as charming as you, Ryan, so shut it! You and Meg looked pretty cozy over at your end of the table. One more margarita and she probably would have crawled into your lap man! Ouch!"

"Watch it," Ryan growled after smacking the back of Jack's head.

Michael glanced over at Jack and the two exchanged a surprised look over Ryan's overreaction to a simple joke, which of course made Jack annoy him even more.

"Ryan loves Meg, Ryan loves Meg…" he chanted. This time, Ryan reached forward and messed up Jack's beloved hair.

"There's an easy way to see how much you like her, Ryan. Out of curiosity, what did you set as your ringtone on Meg's phone?" Michael asked, glancing back at him in the rear view mirror. Ryan looked very embarrassed and refused to speak. They all knew his soft spot for music would give them a hint of how deeply he felt about this woman he just met.

Jack picked up on it and whipped around in his seat. "Yeah, what's the song, man?" he demanded, but still Ryan kept his mouth shut, unwilling to share.

"You know we'll find out," Michael laughed, "and then it will be ten times worse."

"Fine, I'll wait then. Consider it my stay of execution!" Ryan joked.

It must be good for him to be so stubborn and not give it up, Michael thought. Jack was thinking the same thing, judging by the raised eyebrow being cast in his direction.

Michael pulled in front of their apartment. "Last chance to confess, Ryan."

"None of your business, Mike." He slammed the door behind him without a goodbye.

Jack ducked his head in the window. "If you find out from Grace, you *have* to tell me, and if I find out, I'll give you a call. What do you think it could be?"

"I'm a little afraid to guess. You know him, probably something sappy. See you tomorrow!"

Jack gave the roof of the car a tap as Michael drove back to his apartment. On the trip home, he glanced at the cell phone on the seat beside him at least five times to make sure he hadn't missed Grace's call.

❧

The girls made it home in record time. Before the door was even all the way open, Meg barked, "Couch—ten minutes!" and then took off in a mad dash for her room.

Grace happily slipped out of her extra tight jeans, then washed her face and changed into pajamas. She managed to be the first one to reach the couch. As she waited for the girls, she remembered that she had promised to call Michael when she got home.

She ran over to the counter where she had left her cell phone. Scrolling through the contacts, she found the entry for 'Michael Andris.' He listed his cell phone, home phone, work phone, and somehow threw in the number for Mama Rosa's under 'other' which made Grace laugh out loud.

Not knowing if he was home yet, she decided it would probably be safest to call his cell phone first. It rang three times, and then she heard Michael laughing. "Hello? Nice ringtone by the way."

"Do you like it?" Grace asked, assuming that was the source of his laughter.

He chuckled. "Yeah, it's perfect, thanks! I'm a big Pink fan you know."

"I thought it was appropriate with your bet and all," she teased. Meg had walked into the family room now and was staring at the blushing Grace on the phone, grinning from ear to ear.

"I take it you made it home in one piece?"

"Yes, we did."

"Good. So what are you doing right now?"

"Meg has called a meeting on the couch, so I assume we'll be gossiping about these three hotties we had dinner with tonight."

Meg yelled from her corner of the couch, "Hi, Michael!"

"Tell Meg hello. You girls have fun; gossip away."

"OK, thanks. Sweet dreams."

"I'm sure they will be tonight. Good night, Grace. I'll talk to you soon."

Pulling her long black hair into a ponytail, she didn't want to look up at either of her friends who were both staring at her, anxiously awaiting the juicy details. The grin on her face gave away who Grace had been talking to. With bright red cheeks, she mumbled, "Michael said hi, Meg."

"And?" Bianca waited for the play-by-play of their brief phone conversation.

"And, nothing. He asked me to call him so he knew we made it home in one piece. That's it." Grace answered the question quickly as she set her phone back on the counter, hoping they'd drop the subject.

"So, what did you make your ringtone on his phone?" Meg asked with a sly smile.

"'U + UR hand' by Pink." The room filled with giggles. Grace turned to Bianca who had been messing extensively with Jack's phone. "What did you make yours on Jack's phone? I saw you smiling."

"'I Touch Myself' by the Divinyls." She grinned wickedly.

Grace almost fell off the couch laughing and wished she could be there to see Jack have a heart attack when she eventually called.

"Did you tell him?" Grace gasped out between laughs.

"Nope. Meg, did you put one in Ryan's?"

"'You Drive me Crazy' by Britney Spears," Meg said, still giggling. "I can't wait to see what they put in our phones. Promise me that no one will peek. Let's wait until they call, deal?"

Grace and Bianca nodded their heads in agreement in between fits of laughter.

"OK, girls, we need to have a conference. I want to take a scientific poll. Cover your eyes, please." Meg waved her hand at both of them when neither complied with her request. "Just trust me."

Grace and Bianca were confused, but covered their eyes nonetheless. Meg, they both assumed, covered her eyes as well.

"Who's considering bailing out of the bet right now? Raise your hand and keep it up until I say drop it."

Grace went back to her debate from earlier—shoes or dating Michael, shoes or kissing Michael, and then finally, shoes or the remotest chance of sex with Michael. There really wasn't any question; her hand went up immediately. She actually was planning on telling them she was forfeiting the bet tonight.

Curious to see what the others were thinking, Grace peeked between her fingers only to find Meg and Bianca both with their hands high in the air. They too were peeking to see the results of the poll.

Grace dropped her hand. "Well, now what do we do?" It would be hard to declare a winner if everyone quit the game.

Meg got a devilish smile across her face. "I was afraid of this. That means there's only one thing to do. We up the ante, ladies!"

"What?" Bianca shrieked. Grace could tell she was counting on this whole bet going away by tomorrow or at least having the option to bail.

"Define 'up the ante,' Meg."

Experience had taught them that Meg's mind worked in strange and sinister ways.

"To make sure we stick to our bet, we need to put in more money, double the bet."

"Another two hundred dollars? Are you serious?" Grace asked in amazement.

"Totally serious. Look, these guys are great, and don't get me wrong, I like Ryan a lot. A lot more than I want to admit even, but I think we should all take it slow to make sure. Upping the bet will do that."

"If you make us up the ante, I want something in return," Bianca spoke up. "A renegotiation of one of the rules, if you will."

"You can't have sex, Bianca," Meg said bluntly.

"I know that, idiot, but if I'm putting four hundred dollars on the line, I want to make sure he's worth it. I want one kiss. A real kiss, with tongue and all. I'm not losing all my money for some guy who kisses like a wet fish. And a few pecks on the lips within the current rules won't tell me squat!"

The best part of her argument was that she was totally serious. If Jack couldn't curl her toes with a kiss, he was out. He needed to have the power to turn her legs to jelly and make her swoon or she wouldn't waste her time and would happily focus on the shoes.

Meg pondered the proposal for a long time, and then a wicked grin came over her face. "Fine, Bianca, I accept your renegotiation. My counter offer is a 'kiss and tell' clause. After each of us gets our kiss, we have to share all the delicious or gory details. Do we have a deal?"

Meg was the first to put her hand out, followed by Bianca and finally Grace.

"I'm glad we got that settled, ladies. I'm going online to look for a fabulous dress to go with the shoes because I'm *so* going to win this," Meg said with confidence.

Right as she turned for the computer, her cell phone started ringing on the table. When she heard the song that came on as the ringtone, her face turned bright red and she flew over to answer it.

"Hello?" she said quietly, and then Grace heard her sigh "Hi, Ry," as she closed her bedroom door.

Grace and Bianca broke into hysterics. "Did you hear what he made his ringtone? Was that what I think it was?" Bianca asked in between laughs.

"Boyz II Men? I swear, I thought she was going to die on the spot. I bet she's kicking herself for upping the bet now," Grace barely squeaked out before she shoved a pillow over her face to hide her hysterical laughter.

❧

Her peaceful night's sleep was disturbed, as usual, by Meg's shrieking. "Grace!" she screamed as she flung herself onto the bed, clutching Grace's cell phone which was playing 'Hot in Herre' by Nelly.

"Thanks, Meg. Is that to remind me that I made an ass of myself the other night with Michael?" Grace yawned as she stretched.

"No, you idiot! It's Michael on the phone—that's his ringtone." She chucked the phone at Grace, nearly hitting her in the face. "Well, answer it!" She was bouncing up and down on the bed with excitement.

Grace took the phone and checked the caller ID, seeing Michael Andris in big bold letters. *I'm not dreaming.*

"Hello?" Her voice was tentative, her heart pounding in her chest. *What a way to start the morning!*

"Good Morning, Grace. Did I wake you up?" his husky voice asked, sounding very much like he had just woken up himself.

"No, technically Meg woke me up with her screaming. Nice ringtone, by the way."

"It just *recently* became a favorite song of mine."

His shameless flirting caught Grace off guard and she couldn't help but giggle. "Recently, huh?"

Meg, noticing her friend's embarrassment, threw herself at Grace, trying to get close enough to hear what Michael was saying to put such a smile on her face.

"Hang on a second. I need to take care of Meg." Grace put the phone down on the bed and screamed. "Meg Tomlin, did I bother you last night when *Ry* called? No! Leave, or I'm going on eBay to find an old Boyz II Men shirt, and I'll wear it every time you're anywhere near him. Get out!"

Annoyed that her fun was ruined by her stubborn friend, Meg stomped out of the room, but not before shouting, "Bye, Michael. Watch out, Grace is *not* a morning person!"

She took a deep breath and picked the phone back up. "Sorry about that, and for the record, I *am* a morning person—when I'm woken up the right way, that is." All she heard was his deep laughter on the other end of the phone. "Glad I could amuse you this morning."

"I'm sorry, Grace, but that argument with Meg was too funny." He pulled himself together. "So, why exactly are you going to buy used clothes on eBay?" he asked with great curiosity.

"Oh, nothing. Ryan called last night, and when Meg heard the ringtone he used, she almost burst into flames on the spot."

"What was it? Jack and I asked him last night, and he refused to tell us. Hold on. Let me get Jack in on this. Give me a second to set up the three-way call, OK?" Grace heard him click over and when he came back, she heard the phone ringing at Jack's apartment.

"God damn it, Michael. Do you know what time it is and, more importantly, do you have any idea what Bianca and I were just doing in my dream?" Jack groaned into the phone.

"Good morning, Jack," Grace said sweetly into the phone.

"Who is this, and why are you calling from Michael's phone?"

"It's Grace, you idiot! And I'm so telling Bianca you're having naughty dreams about her."

"Shit. Hi, Grace, you gave me a heart attack. Wait, where's Michael? In the shower?" he asked suspiciously.

"Right here, dumbass. It's a three-way call. Grace has some info you might like to hear, about a certain someone's ringtone."

"Awesome! Did Ryan call Meg? What's the song? We gotta know so we can give him shit for it. It's sappy, isn't it? I bet it's sappy."

Grace wasn't sure where Meg was, so she whispered, just to be safe. "Well, he called last night, and his ring tone was 'I'll Make Love to You' by Boyz II Men." She had to move the phone far away from her ear because of the volume at which they were laughing.

"He did not," she heard Michael wail.

"He is such a sap," Jack boomed.

Bianca stuck her head in Grace's room just then, to find out why Meg was in the family room stomping around and swearing. Grace motioned for her to be quiet and then put the boys on speaker phone, quickly whispering in Bianca's ear who she was on the phone with as well as passing on the nugget about Jack's dream. When the guys finally stopped howling, Bianca pulled out her cell phone and dialed Jack's cell.

"So, Jack, have you talked to Bianca yet?" Grace asked. Suddenly, music started playing in the background—the ringtone that Bianca had programmed into Jack's phone.

"Jack, do you need a moment alone?" Michael asked, laughing again.

"No way." The girls heard Jack chuckle. "Damn she is one hot—Hello?"

Behind her, Grace could hear Bianca wishing Jack a good morning.

"Who is he talking to?" Michael asked.

"Bianca. That was her ringtone you just heard."

Jack finally came back to the phone. "Um, guys, hey, I gotta go. I got a call on my cell I need to take. I'll catch you later!" Immediately, Jack hung up.

"Can you tell her to call him about every hour? That should send him right over the edge. It might just help you win those shoes."

Grace was distracted from her conversation with Michael when she caught part of the conversation between Bianca and Jack. "Gross, Bianca! Get out of here if you're going to do that! And at this hour of the morning? Jeez!"

"What's wrong?" Michael asked with great interest.

"I think she took Jack's ringtone too seriously last night," Grace laughed. "I don't need to listen to those two have phone sex this early in the morning."

"He called her last night?"

"Yep. Right after Ryan called Meg."

"And what is his ringtone? Is it as bad as Ryan's?" he asked cautiously.

"'Talk Dirty to Me' by Poison."

They laughed for a few minutes before Michael calmed himself and could speak clearly. "Thank you, Grace."

"For what?"

"For making me laugh my ass off before ten in the morning. I don't think that's ever happened before. So what are your plans for today?"

"Not much. Meg will probably drag us to the mall and then tonight we're having a movie night. We'll watch a bunch of girl movies and eat ice cream. A real female bonding day. How about you, do you guys have to work?"

"Yes, unfortunately." He sounded genuinely disappointed.

"Well, just make sure you stay close to Vicki and let her swat the hell out of the barflies tonight, OK?" Grace teased.

"Don't worry; I'll keep her by my side all night," he chuckled.

"Good."

"I should probably get going."

She could hear him climbing out of bed, and her mind went right in the gutter. *I wonder what he's wearing.* Grace gave herself a mental slap and snapped her to her senses.

"Will you do me a favor?" Grace asked shyly.

"Anything for you." His voice was low and sexy. Grace could practically see the smirk on his face.

"Keep your phone on you tonight, just in case, you know, I want to say hi. OK?" she almost whispered.

"I promise. And Grace?"

"Yes?"

"I'll miss you too."

Grace hung up the phone and picked up her pillow. Pressing her face tightly to it, she screamed.

I am so going to lose this bet!

Chapter 9

Their afternoon trip to the mall was an adventure, to say the least. Meg led them through store after store in search of the 'perfect outfit' for the next time they saw the guys. The girls stood in countless dressing rooms, trying on more outfits than Grace cared to remember in their never ending quest for glamour excellence.

The stress of finding clothes was often relieved by fits of laughter caused by a ringing cell phone. Furious giggles broke out across the ladies dressing room at Nordstrom's when their ridiculous ringtones reverberated through the small space. 'I'll Make Love to You' started playing for all to hear until Meg could rummage through her purse to find her phone. Of course, that was nothing compared to the whistles that they heard when 'Talk Dirty to Me' blared out of Bianca's dressing room unexpectedly.

Grace managed to find quite a few things she liked even with all the distractions, and she was pleasantly surprised that she didn't have to argue with Meg nearly as much as she normally would have. They came home with an armful of packages, ready for their movie night to begin. Grace went to her room, put away all her purchases, and changed into the perfect fashion choice for the evening's fun: sweatpants and a black cami.

With Bianca's help, Grace managed to make spaghetti, salad, and garlic bread for dinner, while Meg ran out to rent the movies. She was busy draining the pasta when she heard the door slam and found Meg was grinning from ear to ear, clutching a movie box in her hand.

"What did you get there, smiley?" Bianca teased.

Meg ran into the kitchen and thrust the box at their faces. When Grace read the title, she burst out laughing.

"'On the Rocks'? You got 'On the Rocks'? The bartender movie? I wonder what or *who* could have inspired that choice?" Grace laughed.

Meg just smirked and skipped off to set the table.

Over dinner and a nice bottle of wine, they spent the hour discussing their new favorite subject—the guys—and their dream shoes if they each were to win the bet. Meg and Bianca seemed much more confident than Grace that they would be the last woman standing. Grace tried her best to fake confidence, but she knew in her heart that she was taking it day by day, trying to focus on the prize, which she often had to remind herself were the shoes, not Michael. In her opinion, he was still way out of her league.

When the last dish was put into the dishwasher and the final sip of wine from dinner had been drunk, Meg squealed and ran over to set up the movie. Bianca opened a new bottle of wine and poured each of them a healthy glass before they plopped themselves onto the couch for the evening's festivities.

The movie began and the girls found themselves giggling a lot, thanks to the wine, as they enjoyed the somewhat bizarre plot. Bianca and Meg began giving their harsh critique of the actors.

"My yummy bartender Jack is much hotter than that guy," Bianca gloated. "I mean come on, he's skin and bones. Does he even have any muscles at all on that body? Now Jack can really fill out that T-shirt they wear. And when he pops on his sunglasses…" Bianca dramatically fell back onto the couch and sighed.

"And who's that old guy? Does anyone think he's sexy?" Meg scoffed at the poor actor having to play the role of the lead actor's sidekick. Even Grace had to admit, he did leave a bit to be desired.

While the plot was, at best, lame, when the bar scenes came on they all squealed like teenagers, then got very quiet, each of them lost in their own personal fantasies about the guys dancing around behind the bar at The Vault, looking unbelievably hot, while the girls shamelessly ogled them. They had cracked open their third bottle of wine as the next bar scene came on, bottles and glasses flying through the air.

Meg started laughing. "I wonder if the boys can do that."

Without even thinking and spurred on by the wine, Grace reached into her pocket and yanked out a cell phone, giggling. "Let's find out." She quickly dialed Michael, knowing that he had promised to keep his phone with him at work. Meg and Bianca paused the movie and waited to see what exactly Grace had up her sleeve.

"Hello?"

"Hi, Michael."

"Hi, beautiful."

"Are you talking to me, or some girl at the bar?" A tipsy Grace giggled in the phone.

"Of course I'm talking to you. Don't be silly. Hang on a minute; I can't hear anything. This new DJ likes to play his music at a deafening level." Grace heard him put the phone down and yell something to Jack. He mumbled something that Grace couldn't quite make out. Then everything became very quiet and she heard a door close.

"OK, I'm back. So, do you miss me already?" he teased in a sultry voice.

Grace blushed while Meg and Bianca started laughing, breaking her out of her little trance.

"Yes, I do but that's not why I called. So listen, the girls and I were watching this movie. You may have heard of it ... 'On the Rocks?'"

He started howling with laughter. "Yes, unfortunately, after being a bartender for quite some time now, I'm quite familiar with that box office bust. So what do you want to know? I think I can guess, but I want you hear you say it."

"We want to know if you guys can do those cool tricks they did in that one scene in the movie?"

"Yes."

"You can? Holy crap!" Grace was sure he could hear the awe in her voice, but she didn't care. Her mind was running wild with visions of Michael dancing around behind the bar. Meg and Bianca vibrated on the couch beside her, nearly bursting with excitement.

His low chuckle made her heart race. "Would you like us to show you?"

"Girls, Michael said they can do it, and he wants to know if we would like them to show us." Grace held the phone out so Michael could get the full effect as they let out their girlie screams.

"Does that answer your question?" she laughed.

"OK, but you should know we don't perform for free. It'll cost you," he said mysteriously.

"Wait. Let me put you on speaker for this." Grace clicked the button on the phone and immediately Meg and Bianca started saying hello to Michael and laughing hysterically.

"Ladies, are you drunk by any chance?" Michael asked, suddenly suspicious of all the insane laughter.

"Yes, no … well, probably," Grace stammered. He said something under his breath that she swore sounded like *perfect* but she couldn't be sure.

"OK, so listen. Jack, Ryan, and I are quite talented at bar tricks, and we would be willing to do a little performance for you, but I mentioned to Grace that we don't work for free, so it will cost you. I have to talk to them, and then I'll get back to you with our price."

"Fair enough," Meg giggled as she tried to juggle some plastic cups like in the movie. "We'd pay big money to see that, trust me."

"I'm counting on that."

Grace laughed and took Michael off speaker. "Hello again," she sighed into the phone.

"Hello. Are you having fun with your friends?"

"Yes, we are. So has Vicki been busy this evening in her swatting duties?"

"I have no idea. I decided to just ignore them all, but I think she did go after a girl who was leering at Jack a bit too much for her liking."

"Good, Bianca will be happy. Sorry we kept you on the phone so long; I know you're busy. I better let you go," Grace said sadly, even though she really wanted to talk to him for another hour, or ten.

"Yeah, I'd better get back to work. Jack is already going to give me hell because I had my phone on me in case you called." His deep laughter sounded rough and sexy. Actually, every sound from his mouth seemed to be sexy to her these days.

"Will you call me when you get home?"

"Grace, it'll be really late. I have to close tonight, and you'll be sound asleep."

"Please, I don't care. I just want … to know you made it home in one piece." She cleverly used his own words from the other night back on him, which made Michael laugh.

"Fair enough. I'll give you a call to say good night, how's that?"

The sweetness of his words made her head spin. "Perfect. Bye, Michael."

"Bye, beautiful."

Grace hung up the phone and found Bianca and Meg smiling at her.

"What?"

"You do know that whenever you're talking to him, you get this big smile on your face, right?" Meg teased. Grace felt her cheeks go red as her friend leaned over and gave her a big hug. "I'm happy for you."

"Thanks."

After a few more hours of painting nails and watching movies, it was time for bed.

A combination of too much wine and the late hour made it impossible for Grace to keep her eyes open any longer, even though she desperately wanted to wait up for Michael's call. Both Meg and Bianca had received calls already, so they were on cloud nine by the time they went to bed.

Grace gave them a hug and then, quite literally, stumbled into her bedroom. Already dressed for bed, she grabbed her cell phone and crawled under the thick covers. From the kitchen, she could hear the clanks of wine bottles being thrown in the trashcan and then Meg's and Bianca's bedroom doors closing as they retired for the night. Smiling, she drifted off to sleep, waiting for Michael to visit her in her dreams.

Soon enough, she was enjoying the sweetest dream; Michael was driving her to his apartment and they were laughing and holding hands. He smiled and turned some soft music on the radio when all of a sudden it changed and words from "Hot in Herre" blared from the dashboard. Immediately, she woke herself up and began searching for the phone.

"Michael?" she whispered in her raspy voice, glancing at the clock with one squinty eye and saw it was four a.m.

"I told you that you'd be asleep," he chuckled.

"I don't care. I just wanted to hear your sexy voice. So shoot me," Grace sighed. *Did I just say that out loud? Great...* She heard springs squeak on the other end of the phone as he crawled into his bed, snickering.

"Go to sleep, Grace, I'll see you sooner than you think," he whispered into the phone.

"OK," she yawned. "Good night, Michael."

"Good night, Grace."

❧

The next morning she wandered out of bed sometime around noon. Her head was pounding, and she had absolutely no desire to eat a thing. All the wine from the night before left her with the hangover of the century. Meg and Bianca must have recently woken up as well, because they were both still bleary eyed, savoring cups of coffee.

"Good morning, ladies, do we all feel like shit this morning?" she asked as she joined them at the table, snagging a piece of toast from Meg's plate.

"Total and complete shit," Bianca mumbled, pushing her bowl of cereal away. "By the way, you were sleep talking again, well, more like sleep yelling this time."

"Sorry, what was it? My shopping list, reciting the Declaration of Independence, or another conversation with my mom?" Grace bit into the piece of jelly-covered toast, hoping it would settle her stomach.

"Um, no. It was mostly…" Meg shot Bianca a smirk across the table.

"Mostly what?" Grace was confused. Usually her nighttime ramblings made no sense.

"Michael's name." They both burst into laughter.

Her face turned bright red. "What exactly did I say?" In a panic, she racked her brain trying to remember her graphic dream from last night.

"His name. A lot. And loudly. If I didn't know any better, I might have assumed that he was maybe, um, in there with you," Bianca squeaked out.

"I'm going to my room to die now. I'll be drowning myself in the shower, washing the layers of embarrassment and humiliation away. It might take a few days. I'll see you then." Grace got up from the table, leaving them to their boisterous laughter, and slammed the door to her bedroom. In the bathroom, she started the shower, turning the water up as hot as she could get it. While she waited for the temperature to get warm enough for her to climb in, she grabbed the new bottle of conditioner that was sitting out on the dresser and heard her cell phone beep.

She dove onto the bed and dug around for the phone, but it was all twisted up in the sheets from last night. When she managed to get it free, there was a new text message:

Exercise is a great way to get over a hangover. – M

Grace quickly replied:

I'll have to try that, thanks. – G

Suddenly, instead of being nauseous, her stomach was filled with an excited swarm of butterflies. Her heart pounded, knowing that she was going to be able to see Michael today. It seemed like a lot longer than one day since they had been together, but Grace missed him more than she could have believed possible in such a short time.

With newfound purpose, she grabbed the conditioner, jumped in the shower and quickly scrubbed her hair and body into a good lather. She didn't know exactly when he was going to the gym, but she figured it had to be soon, so she hurried and got dressed in the cutest workout clothes she owned.

When she in walked out of her bedroom, she found a nervous looking Bianca sitting on the couch, also dressed for the gym. Grace raised an eyebrow at her suspiciously, knowing that Bianca hardly ever went there. She has been blessed with amazing genetics and everyone absolutely hated her for it. Her pleading look told Grace to just go with whatever she said and not draw attention to her sudden interest in physical fitness.

"You two going to the gym?" Meg casually asked when she came out of her room a minute later, a sleek black wig on her head.

"Yeah, there's a new kick boxing class I told Bianca about and she wants to go check it out. Besides, I looked online and working out is supposed to be a great way to work the toxins out of the system. Do you want to come with us, Meg?" Grace asked casually as she snatched an apple out of the basket on the counter and took a bite. Bianca sent her a panicked look, but Grace knew they had about as much chance of Meg coming with them as they had of winning the lottery, twice. Especially since she had just painted her nails and done her hair.

"No thanks. You two go sweat away your hangovers. I'm going to shop my toxins away. It's almost Christmas and I have a ton left to buy." Meg was flipping through the colorful ads in the newspaper, looking for gift ideas.

Relieved to have dodged the bullet, Bianca looked at Grace and winked.

"OK, then we'll see you later, Meg." Grace tossed her cell phone in her gym bag, grabbed her keys, and the two of them headed out the door.

Grace glanced at Bianca as she drove, noting the big smile on her face. "So, I take it you got a text message too?"

She nodded her head. "When I was in the shower. I was sitting on the couch trying to figure out how the hell I was going to convince Meg that I wanted to go to the gym out of the blue when you came out and I knew I was saved."

"So we aren't breaking any rules here, are we?" Grace asked hesitantly.

"No! We are going to the gym to workout. That's definitely not a date. And we'll tell Meg we saw them there, no lies."

Grace thought about it and had to agree that they were in no real violation of any rule she could think of, so when they came home, Meg couldn't complain.

The girls parked the car and went straight to the locker room, trying to be casual as they anxiously scanned the gym looking for Michael and Jack.

"Damn, they aren't here yet. Now I have to actually work out! I'm going to do that step aerobics class that just started. What about you?" Bianca asked as she grabbed her towel and water bottle.

"I'll go run a few miles on the treadmill. I have a lot of, uh, pent up energy to get out of my system," Grace mumbled. Bianca laughed and said she'd see her in thirty minutes when her class was over.

Grace grabbed her stuff and went back toward the treadmills she'd used earlier in the week. She popped in a pair of ear buds, cranked the music, and started running.

About ten minutes into the run, she could hear Jack's booming laughter fill the gym and her already-pounding heart started flying even faster in her chest. *Don't look, Grace, don't look, play it cool,* she tried to tell herself, but then she made the mistake of taking a sip of water and glanced in the mirror to find Michael watching her from across the gym.

His smile grew bigger when she gave him a little wave as she continued running. He held up one finger to signal he'd be right back and then disappeared into the locker room.

Grace quickly checked herself out in the mirror. Her cheeks were a little pink from running and thankfully she wasn't completely covered in sweat. She turned the speed of the treadmill down a notch to make it easier to catch her breath. If he happened to come over, she didn't want to be panting like a dog. Full of nervous energy, she snatched the water bottle out of its holder and took another sip, trying to calm herself before Michael reappeared. She had almost accomplished her task, when a booming voice came from the right. "Grace, fancy meeting you here!"

"Hi, Jack. Yes, what a total coincidence," she said in mock surprise. Jack stood between her treadmill and the vacant one to the right. Michael hopped up on the empty one and stood there silently smirking while watching Grace jogged beside him. Her arms broke out in goose bumps under his intense gaze. Her face immediately got hot and she needed to distract herself.

Jack looked around the gym. "So did you, um, come here alone?" he asked, trying to sound casual.

"Why, no, I didn't, Jack. It just so happens that Bianca joined me today. I have to say I was quite shocked, since she despises getting sweaty. Well, through exercise, that is," she teased.

Jack took a second to process what Grace said, then smiled wickedly. "Well, where is your sweaty friend? I'd like to say hello."

"She's over in the classroom. There was some strip aerobics class she was dying to take." The words had barely finished crossing her lips when Jack spun around and sprinted over to the large window.

"There's no strip aerobics class here." Michael laughed glancing over at the large glass window.

"I know that, and you know that, but Jack sure didn't." Grace watched Jack press his forehead against the glass and then look over at them with a confused look on his face before shrugging and continuing to watch with a big smirk, clearly enjoying the view.

"So, are you going to stand there and stare at me all day or are you going to run?" she asked Michael, praying he'd choose to run because his staring was starting to drive her crazy.

"Actually, I like watching you, but if you insist, I suppose I could run today." He looked clueless as he stared at the buttons on the treadmill, making it obvious to Grace he had never operated one before.

"Push the green one to start it. Right there, yeah. And then run." She pointed to the top of the console and encouraged him to press the button. The machine hummed and Michael stumbled; then he started jogging, much slower that she was going, but at least he was moving.

"So, do you like to run?" he asked, trying to make small talk even though it was extremely difficult while running on the treadmill for the first time in months.

"Yes, I like to work on my endurance and stamina. It comes in very handy you know." She gave him a flirty wink.

Shame on you, Grace! Remember the boycott—and the shoes, Grace, the shoes.

"I can definitely see where your *stamina* training could come in handy." The seductive tone of his voice made her stomach do a flip. "However, weight training can also come in handy for when your task requires more power."

I am not having this conversation. Not with this guy, in this gym. And oh, wow, now he's getting sweaty. Shoes, money, bragging rights, shoes, money, bragging rights, she reminded herself.

There wasn't much she could say to that without embarrassing herself even more, so she decided against a snappy comeback and continued running, stealing a quick glance at Michael now and then when he wasn't paying attention. Grace looked briefly toward the weights and noticed Jack with two enormous dumbbells raised over his head. Bianca's class was due to finish up any minute and while Michael seemed to be holding his own on the treadmill, she could hear him starting to huff and puff.

She flipped off her machine and took a long drink of water before she climbed down. As soon as her treadmill stopped, Michael shut his off too. He doubled over, with his hands pressed onto his knees, trying desperately to catch his breath.

"How was your run?" Grace smiled and patted him on the back, encouraging him to stand up to help him breathe.

"Fantastic, great, never better. And yours?" he asked as he continued to gasp for air, his hands locked behind his head while he paced back and forth.

"Not bad. I stopped a little early because I didn't want that vein on the side of your head to explode. Looks like you need to work on your stamina if you hope to keep up with me." She grabbed her water bottle and wrapped her lips around the opening as Michael looked on, mesmerized.

Bianca emerged from her class, and Grace watched her shamelessly make a bee-line for Jack. Bianca was fluffing her hair, licking her lips, and sticking her chest out a little more than usual as she approached.

Look out! She's a woman with a mission. Grace was laughing to herself when she felt two arms wrap around her waist.

She spun around to find Michael's perfect smile looking down at her.

"Now I've got you. Let's see if your stamina is enough to beat my brute strength." He locked his wrists behind her back and pulled her close, a cocky smile on his face.

"You're assuming that I want to leave," Grace said softly as she pressed her body tighter against his. Michael's eyes lit up with excitement as she gave him a coy smile. She felt his body relax as his hands moved to her hips, his eyes fixed on her pouty lips.

That's when she pushed him away.

"Nice 'brute strength' you've got there, Michael." She smirked. Michael gave her a playful smile and started walking straight at her. Grace took a few steps back and found herself pinned to the wall. She held her breath as he leaned in close enough for her to feel his hot breath on her neck.

"Cheater."

"A girl's gotta do what a girl's gotta do. It was either that or knee you in the groin and scratch your eyes out like I learned in self-defense class. I decided to take it easy on you this time." She laughed, ducking under his arm to make a hasty escape. "Come on, I need to see if Bianca is behaving herself. If not, my odds of winning the bet go up exponentially," she said happily. Michael laughed and followed her over to the bench where Bianca sat admiring a very sweaty Jack from a safe distance across the room.

"Hey, Jack." Grace gave a wave in his direction as she sat down next to Bianca. Michael went over and joined his friend while the two women sat, taking in the magnificent view before them. "Hi, B," Grace mumbled.

"Hey."

"How long do you think we can just sit here and blatantly stare at them before they realize we're ogling them?" Grace asked, somewhat distracted by Michael's twisting torso.

"Not sure, but I do know that if Jack starts doing those squat things again, I'll need to leave the room." She fanned herself for dramatic effect as she winked at Jack. Grace could only nod her head in agreement. When the guys started doing pull ups, the women had reached their limits of self control.

Bianca reached over and grabbed Grace's hand in a panic as Jack bent over to select a heavier weight, his shorts becoming snug in all the right places. "Grace."

She laughed. "I'm right here with you, Bianca. Just think Manolo Blahnik, Jimmy Choo … We can do this."

The pair stood up and tried to casually wave goodbye to make a fast exit, but as soon as Jack saw them get up, he waved them over.

"Hey, guys, we're going to call it a day and hit the showers," Grace said eyeing the locker room door.

Jack smiled and took a step toward Bianca, whispering something in her ear that made her blush three shades of red. She bit her lip and slowly shook her head no.

Grace glanced at Michael who shrugged his shoulders, looking just as confused as she was. "Thanks for suggesting the gym. I feel much better. I think I ran all the toxins out of my system."

Michael wiped his face with his towel and laughed. "Good. I'm glad you feel better, Grace. And see? We both accomplished something: you increased your stamina, and I worked on my strength."

Her eyes wandered over his arms and chest, taking in the thick, glistening muscles exposed by his form-fitting tank top. His body was definitely built for both strength and sin.

"I … uh … see them," Grace muttered somewhat incoherently.

Michael reached for her hand. "You can't tell anything about muscles by looking at them, Grace. You really have to *feel* them to appreciate them." Before she knew what was happening, he took her hands and ran them across his rock hard abs. "What do you think?" he asked innocently even though his actions were anything but.

"Wow." Grace exhaled loudly as her fingers danced over his sculpted body.

The flustered look on her face must have been the reaction he was hoping for, because the biggest grin came over his face. As Grace looked down, her hands were clinging to the sides of his tank top for dear life. She gasped in embarrassment and released his shirt. "We need to go, Bianca. Now." Grabbing her friend's arm, she whipped her around, heading for the locker rooms as quickly as possible.

Once inside, Grace sat down on the bench, her heart racing, and stifled the urge to squeal like a schoolgirl. Instead, she opted for the very mature, "Oh. My. God!"

Bianca kept chanting "Manolo, Manolo, Manolo, Manolo" as she rocked back and forth, gripping the seat of the bench with white knuckles.

"Do I even want to know what Jack whispered in your ear? You actually blushed, do you know that? I don't think I've ever seen you blush before, Bianca."

"When you said we were hitting the showers, he … he asked me if I needed any help," she said breathlessly. Grace couldn't help but laugh, knowing it took every ounce of Bianca's self control not to throw herself at Jack right there in the middle of the gym. If it wasn't for the bet, security would have been called to the women's locker room by now for sure.

Grace heard her friend start to mumble as she grabbed her toiletries and stormed off to the showers. "Stupid boycott. What the hell was I thinking?"

The time under the hot stream of water allowed Grace to clear her head and focus on the task at hand: winning the bet. She just had to make it three more weeks. Twenty-one simple days. She could do this. While she was conditioning her hair, she decided that if she just kept at least a foot between herself and Michael at all times, that would help tremendously. Her head would remain clearer if she wasn't inches from his face, and his lips—especially his lips.

Bianca looked refreshed as she exited the shower, towel wrapped tightly around her head, hiding her long red locks. They chatted about who they still needed to shop for Christmas gifts for in their families, and decided to try and squeeze in a quick trip to the mall sometime this week to finish up. Meg would be thrilled.

Their hair dried and bodies moisturized, they went back to the lockers to put on clean clothes. A familiar song that now made her heart race started playing as Grace threw on her jeans. Bianca's eyes were huge as she waited for Grace to answer it.

"Michael?"

"Where are you?"

"In the locker room. Why?"

"Oh, good. I thought I'd missed you. I'll see you in a minute."

"What was that about?" Bianca asked suspiciously as Grace slipped the phone into her bag, smiling.

"I have no idea. I think they thought we'd left already. He said he'd see me in a minute." Grace shrugged and finished dressing. With their bags packed, the girls headed out of the locker room to find Michael and Jack waiting for them.

Both men had showered and dressed too, their hair still damp on their heads. They were leaning against the wall, their gym bags in a pile on the floor. Big smiles welcomed the girls as they approached.

"You two are the slowest humans on Earth!" Jack laughed.

"Looking this good takes time, Jack. Are you complaining?" Bianca sauntered over and leaned against the wall next to him.

"Nope. No complaints here. Come on, let's walk." He took Bianca by the hand and led her toward the front door.

Michael gave a small nod to his friend and then turned his attention back to Grace.

"I'll meet you at the car," Bianca called over her shoulder with a wave.

"So," Grace nervously looked at the ground. "What's up?"

"Nothing. I just wanted to see you before you left." He reached out and gently took her hand in his and pulled her a little closer. They were barely Grace's recommended twelve inches apart, and her head was already starting to swoon at the clean, spicy smell of his soap.

"Oh," she mumbled. For some reason, when his fingers laced through Grace's, she instinctively tightened her grip on his warm hand. The smile on his face grew bigger.

"Did you know that Meg gave Ryan a printed copy of the rules for your boycott?"

Grace laughed and shook her head. "It doesn't surprise me, though. She taped a copy to my mirror this morning."

"Well, she did, and I've been studying them and have found a few loopholes." There was a playful twinkle in his eye, like a child who was about to go do something mischievous.

"Loopholes?" Grace probably sounded more excited than she should have, but if he found loopholes, then there was a chance they might be able to spend some more time together without losing the bet. Even more importantly, it meant that Michael was looking for ways to spend time with *her*. Just knowing that made her knees weak.

"Yes. For example, you can't go on a date with me, but there's nothing in the rules that says I can't just show up every single place you go and join you. Like today, this was totally legal. I didn't invite you here; I merely suggested a remedy to your ailment, and our paths crossed."

"Amazing how that keeps happening. So basically you're going to become my stalker?"

That made him laugh. "Yes, your own personal stalker. I've also made a few other discoveries about the rules, but I'll tell you about those later," he teased.

"Well, I've also been thinking about the boycott, and I have a few ideas myself. Care to hear them?"

"Absolutely."

"I know we still technically have three weeks until New Year's Eve, but that's only if no one wins before that. If I could, you know, knock out my competition, then it wouldn't be that long until I could go on a real date with *whoever* may want to ask me."

"I like how you think. Maybe we could combine our efforts and see who we should try to crack first."

"Sounds like a plan. Who's your weakest link?" She asked the question, but there was really no need to; she already knew the answer.

"Jack, of course. Yours is Bianca, I assume?" He laughed.

Grace nodded to confirm his guess. "She is, but she's also the most devious, so no one can know our little arrangement or God knows what they'll do to me in retaliation." Her eyes grew wide with fear, remembering back to this morning and her sleep talking. If they shared information like that with Michael, Grace would die. "Actually, all I think we need to do is have them spend more time together and they'll naturally cave on their own."

"Are we a team?" Michael leaned closer, breaking through her self-imposed safety zone.

"Definitely," she said quietly as she gave his hand a reassuring squeeze to confirm their pact.

"Let's go check on the two of them. With any luck they're making out in the parking lot already." Michael laughed as he picked up Grace's gym bag as well as his own and carried them outside, never letting go of her hand.

Bianca and Jack were snuggled together next to her car. When Jack saw Michael, he jumped back and rubbed his hand against his beard. Bianca pointed at the trunk. "It's open," she said brusquely to Michael so he could put Grace's bag in it.

"We'd better get home before Meg sends the troops out looking for us." Grace leaned back against Bianca's trunk and smiled.

"I'll call you later, if that's all right?" Michael asked.

"Absolutely," she murmured, dazed by his sexy smile and the fact that he kept moving closer to her.

He put his mouth to her ear and whispered, "Bye, Grace." As he moved away, his lips grazed her cheek, making her shiver.

If she hadn't been leaning all of her weight on the car, she probably would have fallen over, her body turning to jelly. Grace closed her eyes for a minute to get herself under control when she heard Michael chuckling.

"What's so funny?"

"As much as I hate to say it, I need my hand back, Grace."

She looked down and saw that she was still clinging to his hand, their fingers entwined. Immediately, she released her grip on him and turned bright red. "Sorry!"

He raised his newly freed hand, brushing it against her face. "Don't be. I'll talk to you later."

"Bye," she said numbly as she held onto the car, watching them walk to the truck and climb in, laughing about something Jack said.

"Grace, come on, we need to get home," Bianca said sharply, breaking her out of her trance.

When they were in the car, Grace dug her nails into the dashboard as Bianca peeled out of the parking lot. "What's the hurry?"

"I need to get home. I have something to *tell* you," Bianca said cryptically as she stopped at a red light, clutching the steering wheel.

"Oh my God! Tell me you kissed Jack!"

She looked at Grace and nodded her head slowly, her eyes dancing with joy.

"Meg is going to flip out."

Chapter 10

She *so* wants you." Jack laughed as they climbed into the truck. Michael turned and finally got a good look at his friend, surprised by what he saw. "I wouldn't talk, man, if I were you. Pink's a stunning color on you." Michael didn't even try to hide his laughter at his friend's sparkling lips. Jack grabbed the mirror and examined his face, wiping the gloss away with his sleeve. Michael's head turned when he saw Bianca's car fly out of the parking lot like a bat out of hell.

"Follow them." He motioned to Jack as he pulled out of the parking space. "Care to explain your glossy lips?"

"I don't know what to tell you. One minute I was talking, and then next she had me pressed against the other car. She said something about how she renegotiated the rules and had one real kiss to last her until New Year's that was totally legal and that I shouldn't make her regret using it. And then she was all over me, but in a really good way, you know what I mean? It was one hot kiss."

"So, Bianca got Meg to change the rules. Interesting." Michael couldn't help but smile when he realized this meant that he too had one kiss with Grace, one kiss with those pouty lips to last until New Year's Eve.

"So, why am I following them exactly?" Jack asked as he cut across traffic and made a sharp left.

"I don't know. I just wanted to know where they live, and I'm thinking about doing something nice for Grace."

"Aw, you're falling for her. That girl has you wrapped around her little finger. You know, Bianca told me she loves flowers. Let's find out where she lives and you can send her some. Women love romantic gestures like that."

As much as Michael hated to admit it, Jack was right. Grace would like the flowers, and then she'd call to say thank you and he could ask her about this change in the rules—and the possibility of a kiss. A wicked smile crossed his lips as he urged Jack to drive faster.

They followed behind the women at a distance until they pulled over in front of a brick apartment building. Jack wrote down the address, and the men headed to the nearest florist. A sweet older woman was behind the counter when they walked in. She heard the door chime and looked up from her magazine.

"Hello, boys, I'm Mary. May help you?"

"My friend here is trying to impress a young lady he wants to date. Can you help him pick out a special bouquet of flowers that might help him get the girl?" Jack asked in his most charming voice. The woman glowed with excitement and eagerly took Michael's hand.

"For a young lady. Oh, I see… Can you tell me something about her? That will help me pick the perfect arrangement." She smiled as she took her thick framed glasses off her face.

"Well, she's beautiful, and smart. Witty and charming and clever. Very clever. She makes me laugh whenever I'm around her and she constantly keeps me on my toes. And when I have her in my arms, I never want to let her go." Michael stopped for a minute, totally stunned by his own admission. Jack was smiling next to him, nodding his head as Michael rattled off random things about Grace.

"He usually isn't so sappy," Jack joked to snap Michael out of his stupor.

"She sounds like a very special young lady. I know just what to make for her." She led them over to a table where she had a picture of a spectacular arrangement full of rich, colorful roses. She smiled as Michael nodded his head in agreement.

"That's perfect," Michael muttered.

"Do you want to take it yourself or have us deliver it?" Mary walked behind the table to start on the arrangement right away.

"If I had you deliver the flowers, when would she get them?" he asked, hardly hiding his urgency. He really wanted Grace to get them as soon as possible, to let her know he was thinking of her because he didn't know when he would get to see her again otherwise.

"Marty!" she yelled toward the back room. An older gentleman walked out, smiling, a sandwich in his hand.

"Yes, Mary, my dear?"

"This young man is getting a beautiful flower arrangement for his young lady. I think he would like her to get it right away. How soon can you deliver it?" she asked sweetly, smiling at him and casting Michael a quick wink.

"As soon as I finish the delicious dinner you made me, dear." He waved his sandwich at them with a twinkle in his eye before returning to the back of the store.

"Thank you very much. She's very special to me," Michael said as Mary finished up the arrangement.

"I can tell dear, I can tell," she said as she patted his hand.

Mary finished the most spectacular bouquet in record time, and Marty was already waiting for the address before she handed it to him. Jack went over and gave him all the information while Michael tried to fill out the small card that would accompany the flowers. He sat there for a long time, struggling with what to write. He didn't even know how to put his feelings for her into words; they were so new to him.

"It gets easier when you finally admit it to yourself," Mary said quietly as she put the finishing touches on the flowers with a knowing smile. "Until then, why don't you just let her know you're thinking about her? She would really like to know that."

Michael filled out the little card and handed it to a smiling Mary. She tucked it safely into the arrangement, closed the clear paper around the flowers to protect them, and handed the bundle to Marty who happily headed out the door.

"Thank you so much for everything." Michael reached down and lifted her hand to his lips giving it a small kiss.

She grinned brightly. "You're quite the charmer, aren't you? That young lady doesn't stand a chance." She shook her head while Michael smirked guiltily.

"I hope not." He reached into his wallet and paid for the flowers, adding a hefty tip for Marty for the quick delivery. Mary started shaking her head to refuse.

"Have him take you out to dinner on me, for all your help. Please," Michael insisted.

"Thank you, dear. Good luck with your endeavor."

Jack started walking to the door after thanking Mary once more. As Michael was about to follow after him, Mary stopped him and took his arm, whispering, "There is nothing more wonderful than falling in love." She gave his arm a pat then sent him on his way, smiling.

"Meg! Meg! Meg!" Grace and Bianca screamed as they threw open the door to the apartment and tore inside. Their roommate had been sitting peacefully on the couch, going through her purchases, but their screams scared her so badly, she fell onto the floor.

"What the hell are you shouting about?" she spat at them as she climbed back to her feet. Her friends simply clapped and squealed like lunatics.

"Bianca kissed Jack. She has to kiss and tell! Come on! Hurry up and move that stuff off the couch," Grace said, waving her hands over the seat. "Sit, sit, sit." Grace commanded Bianca to the couch. Meg instantly flung her shopping bags across the room and was now bouncing in anticipation. They sat on the floor like two school children, waiting to hear a story from their teacher.

"How was it?" Meg begged, unable to stand it another second. Bianca took a deep breath as a dreamy smile danced across her face.

"Amazing..." She sighed and blushed.

"Bianca Quinn, are you blushing?" Meg gasped. Grace laughed in the background of course, having already seen her blush earlier at the gym, but Meg was floored.

"Oh stop it, Meg! It's an involuntary reaction. I have no control over it."

"Details, Bianca, we need details!" Grace pleaded.

She quickly explained how she and Grace had run into Jack and Michael at the gym and the highlights of their workout. Then she got to the good part.

"After we left Grace, we walked out of the gym and found his car so he could put his bag inside. Did you know he has one of those big ass trucks?" A mischievous grin spread across her face as she paused in her story, remembering the amusing details. "And did I mention it was the most spectacular shade of blue?"

Meg and Grace exchanged knowing smirks. Bianca had countless tricks up her sleeve when it came to men, but her most potent and unexpected was her ability to sexualize the most mundane things—especially colors.

"What did you do?" Meg shook her head in disbelief, knowing that smile on Bianca's face was nothing but trouble.

Unashamed, Bianca shrugged. "I told him how much I liked the color of his car." Lost in the memory, her eyes glazed over as she began telling them about her brief, romantic encounter with Jack ....

"Let me throw my stuff in the car," Jack said as he led her over to his truck. Bianca stopped in her tracks when she saw the sun gleam off of the perfectly waxed blue paint job. Not a fingerprint or speck of dirt could be found on the thing; it was impeccable. She ran her hand over one of the oversized wheels as he opened the door.

"This is yours?" she asked in amazement.

"Yep." He chuckled when he saw her dazed expression. "Do you like it?"

"Yeah. It's gorgeous. The color constantly changes in the sunlight. What shade is it exactly?" she asked, bending down to examine the flecks of green that faintly mixed with the vibrant blue.

"Blue?" Jack said more as a question that a statement of fact.

Bianca's lips curved up into a sinful smile. Shaking her head in disagreement, she lightly caressed her fingertips over the side of the truck. "I work with colors all day; it's what I do. A shade this spectacular wouldn't be called something as boring as *blue*." With a little extra sway in her hips, she walked around the truck and bent over to take a closer look—and give Jack a better view of her body. "A color like this is more ... sensual," she whispered as Jack stood gaping in front of her.

A long moment passed while his eyes hungrily raked over Bianca's body, taking in every exquisite curve she was proudly showing off. Finally collecting himself, Jack snapped out of his trance. "Well, since you're the expert," he said as he made his way up beside her, his body purposely brushing against hers, "what would you name this color?"

Bianca paused, ran her tongue over her bottom lip, and then smirked when she noticed he was holding his breath, waiting. "This color is exotic, like a cross between a sensual sapphire," she stepped closer to him, allowing her chest to nearly touch his, "and an emerald erotica." Her smile widened as Jack's lips parted and his hands fisted at his sides.

As she stared at his full lips, all Bianca could think about was her one free kiss.

God, he's sexy. Do it already! her body screamed. *Stop with the naughty fantasies, girl. Think about the shoes,* her head screamed right back.

Somehow sensing her inner struggle, Jack wrapped his arms around her, pressing his body to her until there was no space between them. Bianca could feel every rope of muscle in his chest and began wondering how decadent his skin would taste.

"Well," Jack lowered his head and whispered in her ear, "what would you call the color of my truck, then?"

She heard the husky tone of his voice, but Bianca's mind was a million miles away. *I get one kiss. That's totally within the rules. Why not now? His hair is wet and he smells so good. Plus, I know his body is cut from marble perfection.*

"P-peacock lust." The words fell from her lips in a rush, and he grinned wickedly as his hands began to slide down lower on her back, settling firmly on her hips.

As if propelled by an unknown force, she allowed her body to melt into his, her legs nearly going limp from the feel of his strong arms wrapped around her waist. Jack took a step backwards, pinning himself against the car behind him. She gently pressed her body against his, fisting a handful of his sweatshirt in each hand.

"So listen, I did some renegotiating of the rules and basically I get one real kiss, with no boundaries, between now and New Year's when this ridiculous bet ends. Don't make me regret using it. Understand?" She grinned seductively as she inched closer and closer to his lips.

To show he understood every word she said, he took charge, possessively pulling her even closer. He held her in his arms so tightly, she couldn't move an inch. His lips turned up into a sexy grin and before she could stop herself, Bianca kissed him. Her arms went around his neck, holding on for dear life. Their mouths moved together in perfect harmony, instantly taking her breath away. His lips were so warm and gentle even though the kiss had more passion in it than she had ever imagined possible in a single kiss. The gentle scratch of his beard against her cheek set her body on fire.

Jack seemed surprised by the jolt that went through him as he kissed her. There wasn't time for slow and gentle; this kiss was about fire and possession. His tongue swept past her lips and took command of her mouth, pouring everything he had into those few short moments they had together.

Bianca felt her knees give a little and her head spun when she reluctantly pulled back, ending their all too brief kiss.

"Wow…" she muttered.

"Wow doesn't even come close," Jack said, as stunned as she was by what just happened between them. He slowly ran his thumb across her now swollen bottom lip and chuckled.…

Bianca touched her lip as Jack had, still lost in the beautiful memory, while Grace and Meg sat silently on the floor at her feet. She closed her eyes and, with a smile on her lips, replayed the kiss one more time in her head.

"And did his oral skills meet your incredibly high standards?" Grace asked, even though the way Bianca was beaming gave it away.

"Absolutely. I mean the things he did with his mouth. If I made a list of the ten best kisses of my life to date, he completely blew them out of the water. I was tingling by the time we came up for air. I can't even explain. It was…it was…" Bianca trailed off trying to find the words. Meg had become very quiet next to Grace, but then finally spoke.

"It was…the kiss of a lifetime," Meg mused as she absently brushed her fingers across her own lips. Grace and Bianca exchanged a shocked look.

"Meg Tomlin! Did you kiss Ryan?" Grace shrieked. Meg glanced around uncomfortably and eventually nodded her head up and down very slowly.

"Where did you see him?" Bianca grilled her friend, wanting every single detail of the encounter.

"I bumped into him at the mall. I was in a store and saw him waving at me through the window. We spent the next hour shopping, and he insisted on following me home to help carry all the packages I bought." She waved her hand at the colorful parcels that were scattered on the floor.

"When he brought up the last bag, I was walking him to the door, and I don't know what came over me. He had just been so wonderful and I just felt so happy. I curled my finger at him and he bent down to see what I wanted. When his face got close enough, I grabbed his face and kissed him. He slipped his arms around my waist, picked me up off the floor, and gently held me in his arms as he kissed me back. It was incredible."

Grace's mouth was actually hanging open by the time Meg finished. She was so happy for both of her friends, happy they had found someone special and taken advantage of their one kiss. She noticed they were both staring at her expectantly, waiting for her to make a confession of her own.

"Sorry to disappoint you, girls, but I didn't use my free kiss yet." Grace tried to play it off as no big deal, but on the inside, she was holding back a flood of tears that threatened to ruin their happy moment.

"Well, that's OK, Grace. It's no big deal. You're probably smarter to wait." Bianca put a loving hand on Grace's shoulder to reassure her.

"Yeah, it's smarter," she muttered as she headed for her bedroom. "I'm going to go lay down. My head is bothering me again."

As soon as Grace reached the safety of her room, the tears fell uncontrollably. She slid to the floor and let her insecurities consume her.

Smarter to wait. Yeah, that way I don't make an ass out of myself. Why in the world would someone like Michael ever want to be with me? He's perfect and could have any girl he wants. There's nothing special about me. It's all a game to him; the chase is fun for men. But when he catches me, he'll be disappointed, I know it. Grace continued to beat herself up until she heard a small tap on the door.

"Honey, are you OK?" Meg gently pushed open the door and found her friend in a heap at her feet. Grace felt Bianca's arms wrap around and hug her tightly into her arms.

"Grace, it's all right. Why are you so upset? Did we do something or say something?" she asked, searching for a reason for the tears.

"I'm just being stupid. It's nothing," she managed to get out between sobs. "I really am happy for both of you." Grace smiled, but her eyes still showed her pain.

"Please talk to us," Meg pleaded. She took Grace's face in her hands and started wiping away her tears.

"I'm just so … I don't know. I really like Michael. So much so, that quite frankly it scares me sometimes. I can't explain it. But in the back of my mind, I keep telling myself he's so out of my league. Let's be honest. There's very little about me he could possibly find attractive other than the fact he can't have me right now. I think what he really likes is pursuing me, and I'm afraid that if I kiss him, things will change. Maybe he'll come to his senses and it will be over, and it all will have been a dream." Tears once again were streaking down her face, but now there was a chain reaction effect, and Bianca and Meg started crying too.

"Grace, please listen to me. He likes you. He is chasing you, but I have a feeling when he catches you, he's never going to let you go. Ryan even said he's never seen him act this way before. Never! Bianca, help me here."

"She's right, Grace. I wish you could see how you two are together—it's unreal. There's this electricity that charges the air around you. You are two parts of a whole, in many ways completing each other. He watches you all the time—he never takes his eyes off of you. And he's always touching you, or holding your hand. He feels it too, Grace." Bianca's voice was gentle as she tried to explain the things she saw happening between them.

"I know you're scared; you've been burned before. I think we're all terrified to some extent. But Grace, if you want to find love, you have to be willing to put your heart out there—and trust Michael to take care of you. Your face just lights up when you're around him." Grace thought back to Michael today at the gym and smiled. "Or if you're thinking about him," Meg teased.

Grace wiped the tears off her cheeks as she calmed herself down. "Thank you both. I know I sound like a lunatic. I've only known him a few days, but I can't explain it. I'm terrified that something will happen and I won't ever see him again and I don't know what I would do if that ever—"

"Hush, Grace, it's fine. It will be all right. If it's meant to be, it will all work out. Just have some faith," Bianca whispered as she lovingly stroked Grace's hair. The doorbell rang and Meg hopped up to see who it was.

"Thanks, Bianca. I don't know what I'd do without you two." Grace sighed as she pulled her face way from Bianca's tear-soaked shirt.

"Grace, come here please," Meg sang from the kitchen. Bianca held out her hand to help Grace off the floor. "Come on. Let's go see what the little nut wants now. I have to change my shirt anyway."

They laughed and made their way out of the bedroom. Both women stopped in their tracks when they reached the kitchen. On the table was the biggest bouquet of flowers Grace had ever seen, and next to it was Meg, bouncing up and down like she had springs on her feet.

"That must have been one hell of a kiss there, Meg. What did Ryan do?" Grace asked in awe of the massive arrangement in front of her. Bianca leaned across the table and pressed her nose into the petals.

"They aren't for me, Grace. They're for *you*!"

> *Always...*
> *thinking of you.*
> *M*

Grace held the card in her trembling hand and read it over and over again until the meaning behind the words actually sank in. Michael was thinking about her. Was it possible he was thinking about her as much as she was thinking about him? Grace felt her face start to smile as she allowed herself to finally believe his words. Meg and Bianca sat patiently until she looked up from the card and back to their awaiting faces.

"Let me see it!" Meg whipped the card out of Grace's hand and held it out so she and Bianca could read it together.

"We told you, Grace, he's crazy about you too! And look at these flowers, they're spectacular. Does this make you feel a little bit better?" Grace slowly nodded her head up and down and threw her arms around Meg's neck. Grace laughed when she heard Bianca start grumbling.

"Figures. I give Jack one hell of a kiss and I get nothing. Come on, he had to drive Michael to the florist for God's sake! Would it have killed him to throw a rose or something my way?" She shook her head in mock anger as Meg laughed. "You better go call lover boy and thank him. He's probably camped out by his phone, waiting to hear from you."

Grace kissed both of them on the cheek, scooped up her enormous flower arrangement and headed for her room. With the door closed, the aroma of roses slowly filled her bedroom. She lay down on her bed to call Michael, still grinning. The phone only rang once and he answered.

"Grace?"

"Hi. I got your flowers. Thank you, they're so beautiful."

"Not as beautiful as you, but they'll do. You're very welcome by the way." His silky voice gave her chills.

"So what made you buy me flowers?"

"I wanted to do something nice for you, and it's a loophole I found."

"What's the loophole?"

"Well, there's nothing in your rules that prevents me from buying you gifts. If I do, the customary thing is for the recipient to call the person who sent that gift and thank them. So I get to talk to you more without raising any suspicion. I'll bet Meg was even the one who told you to call me, right?"

"I knew there was a reason I liked you, Michael Andris."

"You like me?" he asked enthusiastically, like he had no idea.

"Yes, Michael, I like you." *You have no idea…*

"How much?" he teased.

"What are we—twelve? I like you a lot. Isn't that good enough?"

"Yes, actually it is. Just for the record, I like you too, but way more than a lot!" Again, Grace found herself blushing.

"Hey, give Jack a bit of advice. For future reference, if he's standing next to you at the florist shop, and you're getting me flowers, he should throw a fern or something Bianca's way to keep himself out of trouble." She heard Michael chuckling over the phone.

"I'll try and remind him of that next time."

"They really are gorgeous."

"Just like you."

Grace spent the next hour on the phone with Michael, talking about anything and everything. She found out that he, Jack, and Ryan wanted to open a bar. It sounded like they had a bunch of really great ideas and had been taking this last year to learn all the ins and outs of running a bar at The Vault. He also apologized because he was going to be really busy over the next few days trying to talk to different investors.

Their conversation then turned to Christmas and their family traditions. Both of them were only children and were used to being dragged to different relatives' homes to celebrate with the whole family. Grace heard about his twin cousins setting the Christmas tree on fire one year with a can of hairspray and a lighter. Her family wasn't nearly as exciting. Her mother liked to invite friends and neighbors over as her way of filling the house with the Christmas spirit. She told him how Susan had an unhealthy obsession with mistletoe during Grace's teen years which led to some very awkward kisses with neighborhood boys.

As the hour drew to a close, Meg stuck her head in to ask Grace a question and shrieked. "You're still on the phone with him, Grace? How long have you been talking to him?" She stood in the doorway, her foot tapping furiously.

"I gotta go. *Mom* says I've been on the phone too long and I have homework to do. I don't want to get grounded." Grace stuck her tongue out at Meg, who in turn gave a small humph and slammed the door as she left.

"Sorry I got you in trouble, Grace." His laughter made her stomach do a happy flip.

"I'll live. I guess I'll talk to you tomorrow." She was a sad at the thought of not talking to him any longer, which Michael picked up on immediately.

"How about if I wake you up in the morning? What time would you like your wake-up call?" he asked cheerfully.

"I have to run errands all day, so how about nine-thirty, if that's not too early for you."

"That will be fine. I'll talk to you in the morning, Grace."

"Bye, Michael. Thanks again for the flowers."

"Just look at them and think of me. Goodbye."

Chapter 11

Somewhere around two in the morning, it hit. The vomiting and fever caused Grace's body to shake violently for the next few hours. She was crawling back into bed for the fifth time after dashing to the bathroom that morning, when her phone rang. It was Michael.

He was very sweet and concerned when she told him she was sick. He even wanted to come over and take care of her, but considering she actually looked worse than she felt, Grace decided against it. Instead, she told him to call later for an update. Meg and Bianca came in and checked on her before they left for work and took the stack of papers from Grace's dresser that they were going to drop off at the university for her.

Armed with a box of tissues, a glass of Sprite, and some toast on her night-stand, Grace spent the day sprawled out on her bed, praying for her illness to pass quickly and thanking God that for once she was punctual and had graded her students' finals the previous week. She could think of nothing worse than grading papers while she was sick.

Grace spent the next two days in bed, sick as a dog. At one point she thought she might not recover and was convinced that she had contracted Ebola or some other rare and horrible virus intent on her destruction. Every day at lunchtime, Michael called the deli down the street and had them deliver two different kinds of soup to her apartment. He also called three times a day just to check on her even though she still refused to allow him to come visit. If she was asleep, Meg would give him the update then wake her up so she could say a quick hello. Hearing his voice always made Grace smile so Meg wasn't about to argue.

When the sun rose Wednesday morning, Grace woke up feeling better than she had in days. She managed to sleep through the night without incident and even felt hungry when she finally climbed out of bed. She shuffled into the kitchen where she was met by the smiling faces of Bianca and Meg.

"She lives!" Meg squealed.

"How do you feel today?" Bianca asked, smiling as Grace reached for the box of cereal on the table. "You actually look human."

"I'm starving. I feel like I haven't eaten in days. So what have I missed while I was incapacitated? I don't suppose either of you has lost our little bet yet?" Grace asked, hoping both would confess and she could call Michael. Now that she wasn't throwing up, she missed him terribly. But when they both grinned and shook their heads no, she mumbled her frustrations with a mouth full of cereal.

"Sorry to disappoint you. The bet is still on, and those shoes are calling my name." Meg twirled her spoon around her coffee mug.

"What day is it anyway?" Grace had lost all sense of time.

"Wednesday. Two weeks and five days until New Year's ... but who's counting?" Bianca sighed and glanced over at the calendar. She was beginning to crack; Grace could see it on her face.

"We have to go to Seattle today for that hotel remodel and actually have to spend the night, possibly two. We have to finalize the interior finishes with the client and approve some of the paint samples so they can get started this weekend," Meg said sadly. "Sorry we're bailing on you, but I'm glad you're at least feeling better."

"That's fine, I'll just hang out around here today and maybe go shopping tomorrow for your Christmas presents, that way you *might* be surprised this year." Meg was so nosey, it was impossible to keep anything from her.

They gathered their suitcases by the door as Grace finished her breakfast. She was rinsing out her bowl and putting it in the dishwasher when Meg sat down on one of the stools at the counter and sighed.

"I really don't want to go on this trip right now."

"Ryan withdrawal?" Grace teased. Meg smirked and nodded her head.

"It's already been two days since I've seen him and now two more. This sucks." She pouted, putting her head down on the counter top.

Grace stroked her silky, golden hair. "Maybe we'll just bump into them when you get back. When are they planning on doing their little performance for us anyway?" She had been so sick that most of her conversations with Michael had involved her grunting and answering questions about what she had managed to eat that day. She hadn't even thought to ask.

"Apparently they wanted some time to 'practice' before impressing us with their skills. They also wanted to do it on a weeknight when the bar wouldn't be too crowded, so Ryan said sometime early next week."

Grace laughed, still not believing they had talked the guys into doing it.

"Cool. When you two get back, we'll have to go shopping for something to wear."

Meg's head flew up off the counter and she slammed the palm of her hand to Grace's forehead, a look of panic on her face.

"What are you doing?" Grace asked.

"I was just checking to see if you were delirious! You, Grace Park, actually *want* to go shopping for an outfit? Since when do you care about what you wear?" she asked, raising an accusing eyebrow.

Grace blushed. "Since Michael came along. Happy?" She covered her face, embarrassed that she was tuning into such a girl.

"Tremendously. Bianca, guess who wants to go shopping for a new outfit when we get back?"

Bianca had just walked into the room with her jacket on. "Is she delirious?" she asked, looking at Grace with concern. "Maybe we should stay."

"No, I think she's in love," Meg sang. Grace grabbed a piece of toast from the counter and flung it at her head.

"I hate you both." Grace sneered and then hugged her friends before they walked out the door.

"We love you, too. Behave while we're gone," they said with a wave, closing the door.

Grace sat down on the couch and turned on the TV, but there was nothing that held her attention. Bored, she walked back into her room to find a book when a small silver object on the nightstand caught her eye—her cell phone. She glanced at the clock; it was 9:15. Michael had been calling her every morning at 9:30 so she decided to take a chance and call him first this morning.

"Grace? Are you all right?" Michael said anxiously when he answered.

"Never better. How are you today?" A smile crossed her lips at his concern. "Much better now. You really had me worried, you know."

Grace heard a small beep through the phone. "Hang on, I have another call. It's Meg." She clicked over to the other line. "What do you need?" she asked quickly.

"Hello to you too, Grace," Meg said in a hurt voice. "Where's the fire?"

"Sorry, I'm on the other line with Michael." *Crap, here it comes.*

Laughter filled Grace's left ear. "Bianca, you owe me five dollars! I told you she was going to call him as soon as we left. Behave, young lady. Reread those rules if necessary. I wouldn't want you to lose."

Grace didn't even listen to the rest of her harassment before she clicked back over to Michael, mumbling "Bitch" under her breath.

"Who's a bitch? Me?" Michael asked somewhat taken aback.

"Not you. It's Meg."

"Why is she a bitch? Aren't she and Bianca on a business trip?"

"They just left, but they made a small wager and Meg won. That's what the call was for."

"What did they bet on?"

"They bet on me … if I would call you as soon as they walked out the door. Meg won because I did." Grace rolled her eyes and banged her fist against her head, wondering why she had admitted that to him, but she figured Ryan probably would have told him later.

"Well, I'm glad you called, too. Did I tell you I've missed you?"

Who sounds this sexy at 9:20 in the morning?

"No, or you might have, but I was too busy burning up with fever to remember. I miss you too," Grace said shyly. It still surprised her how connected she could feel to someone she'd only known for a short time.

"So what are your plans for the day?"

"Actually, I was going to hang out here for one more day, stay in my pajamas and read a book."

"You know what would go great with a book? Some hot chocolate. There's this coffee shop down on Henderson, right by your place, that has the best hot chocolate. It's Jack's favorite. It might be a good way to start your day."

"I'm still in my pajamas, Michael, and I really need a shower," she said sadly. There was no way she could run out looking like death for an 'accidental' meeting with him.

"Not a problem. I happen to know that Jack won't be able to find his keys for at least…fifteen or twenty minutes. He keeps losing them you know," he joked as she heard keys jingle in the background.

"Well, then, that does sound like a great way to start my day. I have to hang up now. That hot chocolate is calling my name." Before she even hung up, Grace was on her feet and rummaging through her dresser looking for something to wear.

"Bye, Grace."

"Bye, Michael."

She threw the phone onto her bed and giggled with excitement. *What the hell is wrong with me?* Grace turned on the shower and stripped out of her clothes, jumping in before the water had heated up all the way. As the cool stream turned hot on her skin, Meg's words kept ringing in her ears: "I think she's in love." The more she thought about it, the more her heart pounded. Was she falling in love with Michael? Was that even possible? The answers were yes and yes, but there was no way she was going to admit that to herself right now.

Of course the nagging voice in the back of her head had a question of its own. *But was falling for Michael really a good idea?*

Refusing to allow her inner demons to ruin her day, she buried the voice deep in her head and smiled, thinking about seeing Michael again, feeling his arms around her…

Shoes, boycott, bragging rights!

Adequately flustered, Grace went back to the job at hand. She scrubbed the shampoo into her hair and rinsed it out as quickly as she could. With a towel tightly wrapped around her head, she flew into her room and grabbed some underwear, jeans, a bra, and a long sleeved T-shirt. When she was dressed, Grace glanced over at the clock. She still had five more minutes before she needed to walk out the door.

At the speed of light, she dried her hair and tried to quickly put on some makeup so she didn't look deathly pale. Her hair wasn't cooperating so she threw it up in a ponytail and grabbed the Seahawks hat Meg had bought her at the football game, tucking it on top of her head. *I think I read somewhere guys think girls in hats are sexy.*

She scooped up her keys, jumped into the car, and made it to the coffee shop in record time. When she arrived, Grace went directly to the line, not daring to scan the room for Michael. She ordered a large hot chocolate and made her way over to a couch nearby. There was a newspaper on the coffee table in front of her, so she started flipping through it, checking the holiday ads for gift ideas, when she felt the couch shift beside her.

"Hello, sicko! Nice hat," Jack's voice boomed from her left. Instinctively, she turned to the right and was rewarded with the smile that she had been craving for the last two days.

"Hello, beautiful," Michael said as he sat down, his body so close, their thighs brushed against one another's. Grace felt her cheeks turn pink when she couldn't stop the goofy grin that appeared on her face.

"Hi," she said breathlessly. *God, have I missed him.*

"Hi, Jack. I wore the hat just for you," Grace teased. She felt Michael's arm wrap around her shoulders and pull her closer to him. Her heart began to race out of control.

"Funny running into you here," Jack said, glancing over at Michael who just rolled his eyes.

"I was in the mood for some hot chocolate and heard this place had the best." Grace batted her long eyelashes innocently. Michael gave her shoulder a little squeeze which made her body melt into him even more.

"Yeah, sure." Jack shook his head and tucked his sunglasses into his coat pocket. "Crap, I forgot my phone in the car. I'm going to go grab it; I'll be right back. Don't eat my muffin." Jack pointed a finger at Michael in warning.

"What's wrong with him?" Grace asked as she watched Jack scamper out the door.

"I have no idea. I honestly wasn't paying any attention to a word he said. For some reason I was … distracted." The silky tone of his voice was hard enough to resist, but then, he started stroking the back of her neck, which sent her head spinning.

"Michael," Grace whispered as she closed her eyes, enjoying the feeling of his fingers running down her neck and along her shoulders ever so slowly.

"Sorry. I'll behave. I just missed you, that's all," he chuckled quietly.

"I really missed you too. But if you keep doing *that* …" Grace didn't dare finish the sentence. Instead, she rested her head on his shoulder and breathed deeply, perfectly content for the first time in days.

☙

Outside, Jack stood in front of the coffee shop and pulled his phone from his pocket, quickly dialing.

"Hello?" he heard her sexy voice say.

"Hey, babe. It's me."

"Do you miss me already?" she purred into the phone. *God, this girl drives me crazy. She'd totally be worth losing $200 over, but she really wants those damn shoes. Focus, man.*

"No, I mean yes, I miss you, but that's not why I'm calling. Michael and I went to grab some coffee before our meeting and guess who we ran into? Your girl, Grace."

Bianca squealed into the phone. "Did she kiss him yet?" she asked eagerly.

"No, I don't think so."

"Well, if she didn't lose the bet or use her free kiss, why are you calling me?" she asked somewhat annoyed.

"Because you should see the two of them, he can't stop touching her. Like now, he's got his arm around her on the couch and he's running his fingers down the back of her neck. She is totally staring at him, too!" Jack peered into the window of the shop, praying Michael wouldn't catch him spying.

"Jack says Michael and Grace are having trouble keeping their hands to themselves," Jack heard Bianca explaining to Meg. "We might be able to give them a little push and get them out of the contest! Then it'd be just you and me, girl!" Jack could hear what sounded like a high-five slap over the phone. "I'm back. Listen, Meg and I are going to work on this. We have an idea. You just keep an eye on the love birds, and if they violate any of the rules, you call us, OK?" Jack could hear the excitement in Bianca's voice.

"Will do. So, what are you wearing?" he asked playfully, trying to catch her off guard.

Apparently, it worked.

"I'm in the car with Meg," she hissed into the phone.

"So what?"

"I'm wearing a shirt and pants, you idiot," she barely whispered.

"I mean under your clothes. What are you wearing?" Jack heard her gasp at the question and started laughing.

"Damn it, Jack. I need to go. Shut up, Meg, I am *not* blushing. I'll call you later, Jack."

"Bye, babe." He hid the phone in his pocket, and with a big grin on his face, walked back into the coffee shop to check on the love birds. *The sooner we get them to lose, the sooner I get to see Bianca in that red number she was talking about,* he thought as he opened the door.

Ten minutes later, Grace was still curled up comfortably next to Michael and wished she could stay with him all day, but she knew he and Jack had a meeting about some properties for their bar. Michael glanced at his watch and then towards the door.

"Where the hell is Jack?"

She sat up and looked out the window behind them to see Jack closing his cell phone. "It looks like he made a call. Here he comes." She pointed toward the door and in walked Jack, grinning like the cat that swallowed the canary.

"If you two are done hanging all over each other, we need to get going, Mike." Jack smirked, drawing a glare from his friend.

Michael leaned closer and said, "I'll call you later," and then kissed Grace's cheek. It was a small and innocent kiss, but it made every cell in her body crave more. Her mind was lost in a delicious daydream as she mumbled something incoherently that sounded like "uh-hum." Michael chuckled with masculine satisfaction at the effect he had on her.

She watched them leave the coffee shop, but it wasn't until they drove away that she felt the cramp in her hand from where she had been clutching the leather cushion of the couch since Michael's lips had touched her cheek. Grace took a deep breath to clear her head, and walked out to her car unable to think of anything but Michael.

The rest of her afternoon was spent at home, doing one of her least favorite but most needed chores: cleaning the apartment. She put on her best bumming-around-the-house pajamas and dug into the mountains of laundry and stacks of dishes that had piled up while she was sick. Meg and Bianca definitely weren't known for their housekeeping skills.

The girls had called in the afternoon to let Grace know they arrived safely in Seattle and gave her the name and number of the hotel where they were staying, in case of an emergency. After she talked to them, Susan called to talk her ear off for the next hour that, as usual, felt like ten. She did her usual fast talking, which made it so difficult to fold and sort laundry while on the phone because Grace actually had to pay attention to what her mother was saying. She let Susan know she would be coming up the Saturday before Christmas and that Bianca was coming with her. Meg planned to fly home and visit her parents back East, but Bianca's family would be on a cruise to the Caribbean, which she decided to pass on this year. Susan blabbered about getting the guest room ready for her.

Of course, Susan had to ask about the boycott and see if they had finished their "pretend lesbian phase." Grace told her no, they were still experimenting and through some cosmic stroke of luck, Susan actually believed her. She was so gullible sometimes. To wrap up the call, Grace had to endure the list of all the guests who would be parading through their home over the holidays. Most of the names she didn't recognize, so she simply grunted in agreement when actually, she was searching for the mate to the sock in her hand as she finished folding her laundry.

At five o'clock, she laid down on the couch to watch some mindless television and relax as her busy day finally caught up with her. She had just settled into a show on the deadliest snakes of Australia, when she was startled by a knock on the door. She sprang up from her seat and hurried over to answer it.

"Who is it?" Grace asked when she didn't recognize the guy on the other side.

"Pizza!" he called out.

"I didn't order any pizza," she said as she peeked out from behind the door to find a delivery guy from Mama Rosa's staring her in the face.

"Whoever called told me to tell you it was paid for, so take it." He thrust the box at her before she could protest then waved his hands as she searched the pocket of her pajamas for a tip. "That's been taken care of too. Enjoy your pizza, miss."

Still confused, Grace took the box into the kitchen and set it on the counter. She peeked inside to see what kind it was and started laughing. Inside was an extra-large pepperoni and sausage pizza, which she absolutely hated, but the pepperonis were arranged into a big "M" shape. She was still laughing when she picked up the phone.

"Hello, beautiful." Even though it was how he always answered the phone when she called, her heart would still flutter at the sound of his voice.

"Why do I have an extra large pizza with a big pepperoni 'M' on it?" Grace asked accusingly.

"I have no idea. Why do I have a pizza with 'the works' in my hand from Mama Rosa's when we both know I hate pizzas with everything?" he laughed.

"Meg," Grace hissed into the phone.

"What? Why do you think she did this?"

"Oh, I don't know for a fact that she did, but think about it. You get my favorite pizza, and I assume this is your favorite pizza, and of course the big 'M' makes me call you and—" Suddenly everything started making sense in Grace's mind. "Sh-she's trying to knock *us* out of the bet. That little sneak! I bet Bianca's in on this one, too."

Michael laughed. "OK, fine. She's trying to be sneaky. What am I going to do with this pizza in the meantime?"

"Bring you, the pizza, Ryan, and Jack over, and we'll have a little party, on Meg and Bianca."

"I'll call the guys and we'll be there in ten minutes."

"See you then." Grace hung up and then quickly dialed Meg's cell, which went straight to voice mail.

"You little rat. You and Bianca are both dead for this pizza stunt. Just so you know, I invited Michael, Jack, and Ryan over to eat so there will be no date or romance. Ha! And while they're here, I'm going to let the boys snoop through your bedrooms, so hopefully you've hidden any juicy items safely away. Tell Bianca that I know she was in on this too and I *will* get my revenge." Grace snapped the phone shut and laughed, imagining their faces when they listened to her message.

Grace's excitement changed to panic when she caught her reflection in her flannel pants and T-shirt. Under normal circumstances, she wouldn't be welcoming guests in her current state of dress, but she was still recovering from being sick and wasn't getting dolled up in four minutes flat for anybody. She did run to the bathroom to do what she could—put on more deodorant, brushed her teeth, and combed her hair out of courtesy to her guests—but that was her limit.

Trying to calm her nerves, Grace decided to do the one thing that was always able to distract her: she sat down and played a video game. Bianca was actually the secret fanatic and the one who turned her on to the brainless addiction, but Grace was a fast study and was soon able to keep up with her. As she was about to finish the sewer-zombie level, she heard a ruckus at the door.

"Come in!" she yelled from the family room. Grace glanced over to see Michael carrying a pizza box and Jack with a bunch of beer. "Hi, guys, just give me a second. I must kill…this last zombie…" she said as she focused on the screen intently. "God, I love this laser," she mumbled to herself.

Jack came running over to the television. "No way! You play? Ryan, check this out!" Jack threw himself to the floor next to her and started coaching her through the level.

"Finish for me." Grace flipped the controller to him and headed over to find Michael who was putting the beer in the refrigerator.

"Whoa, Grace, you're playing at a legendary skill level? Holy shit!" Jack yelled from the other room.

"If it's too hard, you can stop and change it back to easy." The temptation to give Jack just a little grief was too much for Grace to resist.

"He takes his status as a gamer very seriously. You may have just started a war." Michael offered the warning, not having any idea how capable she was of defending herself. She gave him a wink and a hug.

"What was that for?" he asked laughing.

"No reason," she answered with a smile. "Come on, you guys. Let's eat this pizza."

Grace put out some plates for them, and they made themselves at home. Ryan and Jack grabbed a few pieces and ran back to the couch to play video games while she and Michael chose to sit at the counter.

"How many controllers do you have?" Ryan called.

"Four, and yes, I will play head-to-head if you want, but I warn you, I'm really good. Or we can do teams," Grace said, winking at Michael.

"OK, teams. But you get Michael. He sucks." Ryan laughed.

Twenty minutes later, Grace had single-handedly beaten both Ryan and Jack into oblivion.

"Who taught you to play like that?" Jack asked when it was all over, totally stunned.

She shrugged her shoulders. "Bianca." A number of different emotions danced across Jack's face: wonder, shock, amazement, and, finally, lust. *Apparently another reason for him to want her.*

Grace patted Jack on the head as she stood up and laughed. "I'm going to warm up some soup." She headed into the kitchen, taking the leftover chicken noodle soup out of the refrigerator and bent down to find a pot to warm it up in. When she stood back up, Michael was in the kitchen, leaning against the counter, watching her.

"Yes?" she asked as she dumped the soup into the pot.

"Nothing. Just watching. Is that OK?" He pushed himself off the counter and inched his way closer.

"Um, sure, watch away." Grace grabbed the wooden spoon and started nervously stirring. She could feel him creeping closer and closer, until she felt his body make contact with her back. He leaned his head to the left and gently pressed his lips to her neck.

"What are you doing?" she sputtered, trying to control her ragged breathing.

"I'm not violating any rules by doing this, don't worry. It's another loophole."

Thank God for loopholes, Grace thought, her hands starting to shake as she stirred.

"Here, let me help you with that." He took his right hand and reached around Grace's body, putting his hand on hers, helping her stir the soup on the stove. His left arm snaked around her waist.

"Michael…" she quietly moaned.

"Yes?"

But before she could answer, he started kissing her shoulder and across the back of her neck to the other shoulder. "That is so…not…fair…" Grace gasped as she leaned her body back into his, her knees going weak when she felt his muscular arms wrapped around her.

His mouth moved up to her ear and she could hear his breathing picked up as he whispered, "Did I tell you how sexy you look in your pajamas? You know what would make it even sexier? If you were wearing something of mine." He gave a little tug on the side of her shirt, and Grace couldn't take it anymore. Even though she was blushing from all the attention and loving every minute of it, her body was screaming for things she couldn't have. Trying to regain control of her raging hormones, she spun around to find the biggest grin on his face.

"*You* need to take three steps back, mister," she said, poking him in the chest. He held his hands up in surrender and took three of the smallest steps possible away from her. "That kind of thing isn't going to help us win the bet. As a matter of fact, that kind of thing will make me lose it, right here and now, on the kitchen counter, while Jack and Ryan watch," Grace hissed, which only made his smile grow.

"Really?" His eyes twinkled with excitement.

"Yeah, really. Now, come on, haven't you noticed? Jack's on the phone giving someone, I'll guess Bianca, the play-by-play. I feel like I'm in some horrible porno." Grace turned and glared at Jack, who tried to hide the phone under his leg. "If you want to watch something, Jack, go to channel eight hundred twenty-three. The code to unlock the porn is *Bianca*!" she yelled.

"Gotta go!" he said quietly and clicked the phone shut.

Grace took the soup and carefully poured it into a bowl. "You, stay here." She pointed at one side of the counter in the kitchen. Michael obediently stood in that spot and watched her take the soup and walk around to the stools to the other side of the counter and sit down. Grace hoped that the wide piece of granite between them would be enough distance to allow her to maintain a coherent thought around him. When Michael leaned his chest across the counter, baby blues blazing, she knew she was in trouble.

I am so screwed.

"OK, we need a plan, Michael. They're obviously all conspiring against us. Here's my suggestion. Do you guys work on Saturday?" He shook his head no as his lustful eyes burned into her. "So, when Bianca and Meg get back, we need to get them all together somehow." Grace tapped her spoon on the counter as she plotted. Out of the blue, she came up with a great idea. "Jack needs to offer to go to the Home and Garden Expo with Bianca. Just tell him that nothing gets her worked up like new paint colors and interior finishes; he should be all over it. She already gave him a little taste of her 'creativity' the other day when they kissed. I'll go so it won't be a date, and I can do a little spying. If he plays his cards right, she should be putty in his hands. Then you need to get Ryan to let Meg drag him around the mall, and you can go with them. Holiday sales should push her to the edge."

Michael's forehead crinkled in concern. "When do I get to see you?"

"You don't, but I'll have my phone, so call me. Focus on the end result: the sooner we get them out of the bet, the sooner we win."

He took the spoon out of her bowl and took a sip of soup. Then he slowly licked his lips to get the last drop off the side of his mouth.

"Yeah, we really need to hurry up and win this bet," Grace groaned as she turned on her heel and went back over to the couch.

Jack and Ryan had figured out that Grace had been kidding about the porn channel and had gone back to playing games. She sat safely on one end of the couch and pointed at the opposite end when Michael came over to sit. He rolled his eyes and sighed, but sat on his corner, twirling a piece of hair on top of his head as he stared at Grace with a flirtatious expression on his face.

Even with all the yelling Jack and Ryan were doing, Grace found herself getting really sleepy. When she could barely keep her eyes open, she crawled across the couch and laid her head in Michael's lap. He gently stroked her hair and arm as she laid there with him, relaxing her completely. In a matter of minutes, Grace was sound asleep.

She heard quiet voices and felt herself jerk awake. "What's going on?" Disoriented, Grace rubbed her eyes, trying to get them to function. Michael's arms were around her, as she felt him lift her off the couch.

"We're going home, sleepy head. You need your rest," he said sweetly, as Grace nuzzled her head to his chest.

"Jack, Ryan, wait. Before you leave, go snoop around in the girls' rooms; you never know what you might find. Jack, top drawer; Ryan, top shelf in the closet, blue box," she managed to get out before Michael had her inside her bedroom, laying her down in bed.

Grace shimmied under the blankets and settled her head down on the pillow so she could see Michael's face. He perched himself on the edge of her bed, looking at the flowers he had sent, which were sitting on the dresser.

"Good thing you were already in your pajamas or I would have had to change you," he teased.

Grace swatted him weakly with a pillow. "You wish."

"Yes, I most certainly do!" he laughed, making the bed shake gently.

"I wish you could stay. I don't like it when you leave," Grace whispered.

"I don't like leaving you either. It gets harder every time." The sincerity of his admission made Grace smile.

"Thanks for coming over tonight and keeping me company." Exhaustion began to take over as she stifled a yawn. He brushed the hair off of her face and kissed her cheek.

"You really are the most beautiful creature I've ever seen, Grace. Sleep well." She closed her eyes and heard the squeak of the bed springs as he stood up to leave.

"Good night, Michael," she whispered.

"Good night, Grace," he said as he shut the door.

Chapter 12

This blows! – G

Trust me, this blows more. – M

Just call me already. My fingers hurt. – G

"What were we thinking?" Grace asked, as the phone finally rang in her hand.

"This was your plan, there, chief, not mine. As I recall, I protested because I wouldn't get to see you at all today," Michael grumbled.

"Where are you now?" she asked as she climbed on an ergonomically designed stainless steel barstool.

"I am lying on a bench outside some underwear store," Michael sighed.

"They're in there alone? Are you nuts? Meg could be doing some sexy fashion show for him or dragging him into the dressing room. Get in there and keep an eye on them!" Grace nearly shouted at him.

"Please don't make me go in there. A single guy should not enter that place alone. The sales girls are downright scary. Now, if *you* were with me that would be totally different."

"Well, I'm not. Get your butt in there. The whole reason I'm here and you're there is to get them to break; so go make a few suggestive remarks to fire up Ryan. Someone has to cave." *And I'll be damned if it's me,* Grace thought to herself.

She heard a groan as Michael stood up from his bench. "Fine. I'll go in, but you're staying on the phone with me. Going in … Oh lord, here comes the sales girl to help me." Grace could hear the little tramp's flirty voice on the other end of the phone.

"Can I help you, sir?"

"Um, no. I'm just looking for my friends. There they are! Thank you."

"If you need anything, my name is Jenny. I'd be happy to help you." The woman stressed the "anything" a bit more than Grace would have liked.

"Michael," she shouted into the phone, "go find Meg and stop flirting."

"I wasn't the one flirting and unbuttoning my blouse at a customer," he replied.

"She did what?"

"That's what you get for sending me into this store alone. OK, I see them. Meg's shopping for, um, things..." His voice trailed off.

"That's really specific. What things? And where's Ryan?"

"Ryan has a pile of lace panties in his hand right now and looks like he wants to die. I think Meg is looking at... What *are* those? Head bands? Oh, nope, thongs. Now she's moving over to the really tiny pajama section. Uh-oh, here comes that barracuda again."

"Sir, have you found anything you like? I'd be happy to try on that garter belt for you so you can see what it looks like on." Grace heard the evil little voice purr in the background.

"Michael, why do you have a garter belt in your hand?" Grace teased.

"What? No, I don't. Sorry, miss, I don't need any help, but thanks," Michael sputtered.

"My name's Jenny. What's yours?"

Grace fumed as she heard the woman giggling. "Get out of there. You're obviously too cute for your own good. If that girl follows you, let me know, and I'll call in Meg for backup." Grace laughed when she heard him sigh in relief.

"Freedom!" He sighed heavily as she heard the bags he was carrying crunching over the phone. "I'm now back safely on my bench, but that salesgirl is staring out the window at me. I think she just blew me a kiss. So how's the design expo?"

"Hell on Earth. How many shades of brown does one person need to see? Bianca's made us walk at least ten miles, and of course she has to stop at every single booth and ask questions, making it take twice as long. Who cares about a shower door that squeegees itself?" Grace grumbled as she watched people stroll past.

"How are Jack and Bianca? Anything happening there?"

"Oh, they've been whispering back and forth the entire time. Jack gets a big grin on his face every time she starts moaning over a new fabric or something."

"So what are you doing?" Michael asked, worried about Grace's sanity.

"I'm sitting out on some barstool that's supposed to be the perfect design for the human body, but it's sure making my ass hurt. Holy crap, the thing costs two thousand dollars! Are they serious? But I swear if one more guy here tells me he 'has something he wants to show me' or calls me 'Little Lady,' I might punch someone."

"At least you aren't carrying around five shopping bags."

"At least you don't smell like a new carpet. I'm getting dizzy from the fumes."

"Wait, Meg has made her purchases, and Ryan has a goofy grin on his face. That's good, right? Ugh, Pottery Barn. I don't need to go in there, do I? I see a bench near a television. I'm going to sit over there. There's nothing sexual about Pottery Barn, right?"

"There is to Meg. All those coordinated items can whip her into a frenzy. She's an interior designer, for God's sake. Oh man, Bianca just found this gorgeous copper soaking tub that's big enough for two and she's climbed in. She's writhing around in it with her head thrown back, and Jack's clutching his chest! Gotta go!"

"Bye, Grace."

"Bye, Michael."

Back at her apartment, Grace flopped down onto the couch after spending the entire day wandering the design expo with Bianca and Jack. She had blabbered on and on about the different models of everything from toilets to light fixtures, and Jack hung on Bianca's every word while Grace stomped around behind them like an angry child at the grocery store. By the end, she realized her plan to catch them in a compromising position behind one of the booths had failed miserably.

Jack and Bianca were locked in an epic video game battle when the apartment door flew open. Michael stood in the doorway, glowing, like a man returning home victorious from battle, his arms draped with an obscene number of shopping bags.

"Michael!" Grace smiled as she launched herself onto his arms. He dropped the bags to the ground and wrapped his arms tightly around her waist, lifting her up onto her toes. She gave him a big kiss on the cheek as she squeezed his neck with all her might. "You survived!"

"I'll go shopping with Meg more often if that's the welcome home I get." Michael laughed as he kissed the top of Grace's head and put her feet back firmly on the ground. "You do smell like new carpet."

"If you two are done, some of us would actually like to get through the door now," Ryan teased as he came into the apartment with yet another armful of bags.

"Grace, wait until you see what I got you," Meg sang as she came through the doorway.

"It better not be that pile of panties Ryan had in his hand earlier," Grace said, carefully watching her reaction. She turned and raised an accusing eyebrow.

"Spying on us, were you?" she said as she walked closer to her friend, waving her index finger in Grace's face. "Shame on you." Then she turned on Michael. "And you, her accomplice. Sorry to disappoint, but I was a perfect little angel, wasn't I?" Meg said smugly. Ryan nodded his head in agreement as he continued delivering the bags into her room.

"Better luck next time," Grace mumbled to Michael as he motioned her over to the recliner with him. He sat down and held out his arms for her to join him.

"Another loophole," he beamed. Grace happily crawled into his lap and snuggled her head against his chest, playing with the buttons on his shirt. Meg came out of her room, opened her mouth to protest, and then scowled at Michael before stomping off to her room.

"I told you so." Michael laughed triumphantly.

Grace closed her eyes and enjoyed being so close to him, feeling his breath on her forehead and listening to his gentle heart beat as they relaxed together. She wasn't sure how long they sat there before she heard him sigh.

"You have to go, don't you." Grace pouted.

"Unfortunately, we do. How will the drunks get fed otherwise?" he asked sarcastically.

"Can you stay five more minutes? Please?" she asked, unleashing her pleading eyes on him. He glanced at his watch and caved.

"Fine, we can stay … ten minutes. Then I'll have to drive, oh, sixty miles an hour to get us to work on time. That should be fine. Ten minutes. Got it guys?" Jack gave him the thumbs-up from his spot on the couch with Bianca. Ryan yelled "Works for me!" from Meg's room where they were apparently unloading Meg's purchases and putting them away. Michael winked and twirled a piece of Grace's hair around his finger. "Happy?"

"Yes, very." Grace placed her head back onto his chest and relaxed for the last few minutes they had together before the guys had to go to work. She felt his warm hand caressing the length of her back as she relaxed further into his body.

The ten minutes passed, and again, Grace felt him glance at his watch. Jack didn't move from Bianca's side when Michael cleared his throat, and Grace gripped his shirt even tighter to try and hold him in place.

"Fine, five more minutes, but now I have to drive eighty miles an hour and we'll still be five minutes late. Hopefully, no one will notice," he mumbled as his fingers laced with Grace's. He pulled her hand to his mouth and began kissing a trail from her wrist, up to her shoulder.

"Gotta love the loopholes," Grace said softly.

"Is that legal?" Jack asked from the couch.

"Yes, you idiot. So why don't you take a page from Michael's book and figure out a few ways around these stupid rules?" Bianca snarled.

All too soon, the five minutes were over. "Come on, guys. Ryan, we need to roll," Michael yelled.

Ryan came out of Meg's room, holding a wide array of hanger shapes and styles across his arms, looking like a six-foot-three coat rack. Meg quickly snatched them off his arms and gave him a peck on the cheek before he put his jacket on.

"Have fun at work," Grace said as Michael searched his pocket for his keys.

"Unless you're there with me, there's nothing fun about work." He quickly brushed his lips over hers. Grace stood there, stunned because he had never kissed her on the lips before. His mouth had felt soft and gentle as it moved against hers, and she realized she wanted him to do it again. Her face must have shown her shock because he smiled. "That's allowed, Grace, remember? I'll call you later."

"Bye."

"Bye, beautiful."

&c;

"Bianca, where the hell is she?" Grace asked as she hopped through her bedroom, trying to cram herself into the new pair of black skinny jeans.

It had been the longest four days of their lives, waiting for the night of the big bar show. Michael said Wednesdays were typically less crowded at The Vault, so they would be able to do the show without throwing the whole club into chaos. Bianca was in Grace's room, clamping yet another bangle bracelet around her wrist and cursing Meg for running late as well.

"She had a meeting about the courthouse lobby remodel, but she knows they're coming to pick us up soon. If she's not ready, then we'll have to drive ourselves," Bianca said, pouting. Grace could tell she really wanted to ride with the guys so she could cuddle up with Jack in the car. As Bianca opened her cell phone to call Meg again, they heard the door fly open and the rapid clicking of Meg's heels across the hardwood floor as she made a beeline for her room.

"I know! I'm late. I'm going to jump in the shower. I will be ready, though! Warm up the blow dryer!" she screamed. "Stupid, blabbering bureaucrats!"

In an amazing show of speed and skill, Meg was ready to go in eighteen minutes flat. It was her personal world record. She beamed proudly as she sprayed the last puff of perfume onto her neck and took another second to fluff her hair one last time. "And with three minutes to spare," she bragged proudly, glancing at the clock as she put on a fresh coat of bright red lipstick.

"OK, ladies, are we prepared for this? I have a feeling they've got quite the production planned from what Ryan said." Meg grinned. "Tonight could be the night someone falls by the wayside."

"Not gonna be me," Grace said emphatically.

"Me neither," Bianca added with conviction.

"I'm just saying… They're pretty irresistible under regular circumstances. But throw in some music, lights, alcohol, and them shaking their asses, it might just be too much to bear." Meg winked at Grace when the two of them caught Bianca looking deep in her own personal daydream.

"Do we know what their demands are for this little performance?" Bianca asked when she came to her senses.

"No. Apparently Michael will tell us when they pick us up. If we agree, then there's a show. If not, no bar tricks."

Meg's brows furrowed suspiciously. "Has he said anything to you, Grace, about what they expect as payment?"

"I never even asked," Grace laughed.

"He's a tricky one, that Michael. I don't trust him. I think that's why he's waiting until the last minute to tell us. He's got something up his sleeve." Meg tucked her cell phone into her purse and snapped it shut.

"Actually, I think he's trying to make sure *you* go along with it, Meg. I doubt Grace and I will put up much of a fight no matter what they ask for," Bianca said with a smirk in Grace's direction. Grace had to laugh because it was true. Meg was the consummate rule keeper while she and Bianca were constantly looking for ways to bend the rules to their advantage.

Before the discussion could go any farther, there was a loud knock on the door. The girls gave a silent scream as they squeezed hands. Grace put her hands to her cheeks and felt the warmth of the blush rushing to her face. *Please, God, let me make it through tonight,* she silently prayed as she took a deep calming breath. Meg danced over to the door to reveal the guys, all looking incredibly sexy in their black leather jackets and jeans, with grins plastered on their faces.

Jack let out a low whistle as he entered the apartment. "Ladies, you look incredibly hot this evening." His eyes spent extra time looking Bianca up and down.

"Thanks, Jack. See, there are these cute bartenders at the club, and we're kinda trying to get their attention," Grace said, laughing as Michael came over and wrapped his arms around her. She could smell the leather from his jacket as he pulled her closer.

"You look stunning," his husky voice whispered in her ear, "and you have my undivided attention."

"I know. That's what's driving me so crazy right now," she whispered into his coat, not expecting him to hear. When Grace felt his fingers lift her chin up and she looked into his darkened eyes, she knew by the devilish smile on his face that he'd heard every word.

"Michael, we need to talk business," Meg barked, tapping her purple nails on the kitchen counter. Michael's hand slipped into Grace's as they walked over to the kitchen and joined their friends.

"OK, Meg, here are our demands for the show to happen." Michael looked at his partners in crime, who were both nodding their heads in support. "Breakfast, tomorrow."

"Breakfast? You want us to make you breakfast tomorrow?" Meg asked incredulously. "That's it?" Grace saw relief wash over her. In Meg's opinion, they were getting off easy. She'd assumed Michael would demand something much worse.

Grace peered back at Michael and could tell by his eyes that it wasn't as benign a demand as Meg thought.

"No, we want to be able to feed each of *you* breakfast, tomorrow. Alone." Grace felt him give her hand a small squeeze.

There is no way she's going to go for this. Great. No show. Grace felt her stomach drop.

"Alone constitutes a date, Michael. No can do."

"How is eating breakfast a date? No one goes on breakfast dates. Dates are afternoon or evening activities; this is a breakfast meeting. Just a meeting. We have some things to discuss with you ladies, privately."

He should really go into sales because I am totally buying his line of bullshit. Grace looked over at Bianca who was biting her lip, staring at Jack and anxiously awaiting Meg's decision. Meg, however, was locked in an intense stare down with Michael, who just smiled sweetly at her like a choir boy, the picture of innocence. Ryan kissed the top of her head, and Grace saw Meg's resolve fade a bit.

"And what do we have to discuss at this meeting?" She sneered. Ryan bent over and whispered a quick explanation which seemed to appease her, but she wasn't completely convinced.

"A breakfast meeting you say? Breakfast traditionally ends at 10:30 a.m. so we need to be home by then. Got it? All other rules are to be enforced. If we're even one minute late, we're out of the bet. Ladies, do you agree to these terms?" Before she even finished her sentence, Bianca and Grace were nodding their heads in agreement.

"Excellent," Michael said as he extended his hand to Meg to make the arrangement binding with a handshake. Jack and Ryan looked impressed with Michael's negotiating skills. When Michael turned back to face Grace, he looked absolutely thrilled.

"Then let's go, ladies. We have a show to perform. We'll go warm up the cars. Meet us downstairs," Ryan said as he jingled the keys in his hand and nodded to the door. Michael and Jack followed close behind.

When the guys were out the door, Grace turned to Meg. "Well, you were very accommodating. I have to say that I'm shocked you agreed to the whole thing."

"Come on, Grace, I thought Michael would've come up with a better plan than that. He didn't think that through very well. They're working tonight, not until close, but well past midnight, so they're going to be exhausted and probably sleep in late. With our ten-thirty curfew, they'll only have time to feed us and then have to bring us home. The score for today is Meg: one, Michael: zero," Meg said proudly. Bianca looked at Grace with an annoyed look on her face, like it was her fault Michael's plan sucked.

What was he thinking? Meg's right; they'll be exhausted after work. I finally get to be alone with Michael, and he's going to be a zombie. Great! Still, Grace couldn't shake the feeling that she was missing something. Michael was smarter than that. She'd just have to be patient and wait.

When they got to the club, the guys brought them through the employee entrance around the back of the building. As soon as they walked in the door, Vicki came rushing their way.

"Chicas, long time no see! How are you? Are these boneheads behaving themselves?" she asked, eying Jack in particular.

"Hi, Vicki. We've missed you too. You'll be happy to know they actually are behaving," Meg said with a wink. "We brought you something." She pulled a large gift from behind her back and held it out to a very surprised Vicki.

"Merry Christmas from Grace, Bianca, and, of course, me," Meg said, pointing at herself and smiling. Vicki's eyes grew huge as she looked at the package. She popped off the bow first and stuck it in the middle of Ryan's chest. Like a little kid, she quickly ripped off the shiny red paper, tossing it carelessly to the ground.

"Oh my God! These are the most bad-ass boots I've ever seen in my life! Steve is going to shit himself." She threw the box down and held the boots in her hands, admiring them. Michael nodded his head in agreement.

The girls had searched the greater Portland area for the coolest pair of motorcycle boots they could find that just "screamed" Vicki. These were black leather, and around the ankle were a studded harness and a shiny number seven buckle. Everyone laughed as Vicki kicked off the boots she'd been wearing, tossed them into the trashcan, and jumped into her new ones.

"How'd we do on the size?" Grace asked.

"They fit like a glove," Vicki purred. She kept looking down at her feet and smiling. "You ladies are unbelievable." She then turned to the boys and in a very motherly voice said, "If you bozos blow it with them, I'll personally hunt you down and kick you square in the balls—with these fabulous boots." All three of the guys rolled their eyes at her, but when she took a step toward them, they threw up their hands in surrender.

"We're glad you like them, Vicki. You're the world's greatest fly swatter, you know. Thanks for everything," Bianca said as she looked lovingly over at Jack. The girls exchanged hugs with her as the guys ran off to change for work.

"Come on, I have your table waiting for you." Vicki led them upstairs to the table they'd sat at on their first night at The Vault. The little red reserved sign sat on the table where their view of the bar would be the best in the house. Vicki sat down in one of the chairs and propped her foot on the table so she could admire the boots—again. She started rolling her pant legs up asking, "So, have they told you anything about what they planned?"

"No. What have you seen?" Meg asked clapping her hands together in excitement. "Have they been practicing? Are they any good? Has anyone gotten hurt from the flying bottles?"

"Yeah, we've had quite a few things broken and glasses have been flying around here lately as they worked out the kinks. I think they really want to impress you." She laughed. "Of course, I get the feeling they could spin in a little circle and say *ta-da* and you'd be happy."

"They're a pretty impressive trio." Grace laughed with Vicki as they watched Meg and Bianca wave to Jack and Ryan from the upper rail.

"I gotta go work, I guess. I'll bring you some food. Go down there and dance for a while until it's time for the show." Vicki headed downstairs with a new strut in her step thanks to her boots. Grace saw her stop and show them to one of the other servers before disappearing through the kitchen door.

"Grace? Grace Park?" she heard a male voice say from the next table. Grace turned to see a big, red-haired guy who looked vaguely familiar. He was sitting with another guy who she knew she'd never seen before. The redhead stood up and came over to their table.

"Grace. Do you remember me? Liam, Liam Sullivan. We met at your mom's house over the summer." He held out his hand as Grace racked her brain, trying to remember him. Then it dawned on her—her mother's annual pool party, which had also become her annual "find Grace a boyfriend" party. She was notorious for inviting only her friends with sons Grace's age, hoping to play matchmaker.

"Hi, Liam. I remember you now. The pool party, right?" She smiled and he nodded his head, staring at her chest. "What are you doing in Portland?" She couldn't remember a thing about him other than his spindly legs and that he was extremely boring. *Looks like nothing's changed*, Grace thought as he sat down in the open chair and waved his friend over to the table as well.

"Grace this is Rick. Rick, this is Grace Park. Our moms are good friends."

"Nice to meet you. These are my friends Bianca and Meg."

Ugh, Sullivan had been one of the names Mom had rambled on about the other day on the phone. I think they're coming to the house while I'm home for Christmas. Great…

"Actually, I just got a job down here working for Newman Insurance. I work as an actuary." He continued rambling and pointing at Rick, but Grace wasn't listening. *Oh God, flashbacks to dates with boring guys. Why is he still talking? How much cologne does one man need to wear on his body? And that Rick guy is creepy, looks almost weasel-like.* Her head was starting to throb when she finally saw Bianca looking like she was going to deck Liam if he didn't shut up.

Meg threw back her chair and squealed. "I love this song. Sorry, guys, we're gonna go dance for a while. Nice meeting you!" And with that, she and Bianca darted away, leaving Grace with the two bookends. Rick's eyes followed Meg as she made her way onto the dance floor. Liam, of course, was still talking.

"Your mom was supposed to give you my number so we could meet up sometime." He leaned closer, and Grace saw him reaching for his cell phone. "Can I get your number?" he asked, holding up his phone. Without thinking, she took it from his hand and entered the only number she could—Mama Rosa's.

Hey, he's new in town, at least he gets the number for the best pizza joint in Portland out of this, she told herself as she quickly gave it back to him. *I have to make a break for it.*

"Here you go. Sorry, but I really need to get down there to my friends. It- it's Meg's birthday. I'll see you around." Happy her lie had worked, she gave him a pat on the hand and smiled at Rick. "Nice to meet you! Take care." And with that, Grace ran for her life all the way to the dance floor where she found Meg and Bianca happily dancing.

"Thanks for leaving me back there. Nice friends you two are," she fumed as she joined them, "abandoning me in my hour of need."

"Oh come on, Grace, before Michael, you would have found him perfectly acceptable dating material," Meg teased, throwing her head back and laughing.

That was before Michael. Grace's eyes scanned the bar, searching for his perfect face. When she found him, he was talking to Ryan and laughing about something. His hand was on Ryan's shoulder and he was smacking his other hand on the bar. His smile was absolutely contagious. *How did I ever get so lucky?* Grace asked herself now, smiling. He was all she wanted, all she needed.

"Come on. Let's dance over there where the view is better." Bianca grinned as they wiggled their way closer to the bar. Grace was in the middle of learning a new dance move from Meg when she felt someone lurking behind her. She immediately glanced at the bar and saw Michael hard at work. *It's not him. Who the hell?* Around her shoulder came Liam, while Rick was creeping up behind Meg, watching her move to the music.

"Can we join you, ladies?" Liam asked in a smooth voice.

Bianca, apparently in need of some entertainment, said with a flirty laugh, "Sure, guys, join us!" Meg and Grace both glared at her, but Bianca shrugged and kept dancing a safe distance from the two intruders.

Liam started dancing right in front of Grace, blocking her view of not only the bar, but of Meg and Bianca as well. His body thrashed around and amazingly he managed to accomplish the incredibly difficult feat of dancing completely off beat. Mortified to be dancing anywhere near him, and even more embarrassed for him, Grace tried to move away, but he only followed her. She realized it was probably good that she couldn't see Bianca or Meg because she might have burst out laughing at the absurdity of it all. She tried to look at the floor, allowing her long hair to fall over her face as a protective cocoon from his offensive dancing, but Grace could still see his shoes, flailing around in front of her. She tried casually scanning the room, looking at the person next to her, the ceiling, over his shoulder—anywhere other than directly at his face. He, on the other hand, stared mostly at Grace's breasts, which only strengthened his status as a major creeper in her book.

Grace did some evasive ducking move and managed to move in front of Liam with her back to him. *He's probably staring at my ass now, but at least I can't see him doing it,* Grace thought as she danced. Meg was on her right and Bianca was on her left, waving her arm wildly to get Jack's attention. Once Jack saw their predicament, he gave Michael's shoulder a shove and pointed to the girls. Together, they doubled over in laughter at the sight on the dance floor.

There was an odd shaking sensation that she knew could only be Liam vibrating around behind her, but Grace couldn't bring herself to look at what the hell he was doing back there. Annoyed by all the laughter, she flipped the guys the bird, which only made them laugh harder.

Liam "accidentally" bumped into her and grabbed her waist. "Sorry," he mumbled in her ear. She could smell the nachos he had eaten on his breath.

Shuddering in disgust, Grace turned to Meg and found her shooting Rick dirty looks to try and repel him, but he seemed to somehow find it a turn-on and moved closer to her, doing some horrible popping moves he must have seen originally in a music video. Out of nowhere, Ryan appeared like a knight in shining armor and scooped Meg up in his arms, taking her over to the safety of the bar. Grace, on the other hand, remained with Mister Touchy who continued grinding his body against hers. When she felt his hand graze her rear, she snapped. Digging into her pocket, Grace pulled out her cell phone and dialed.

She couldn't make out the exact words through all the laughter when Michael picked up. She was standing twenty feet away, glaring at him while Liam stroked her hair.

"Is he … is he … petting you now?" Michael gasped.

"Yes, and he was petting my ass a minute ago. I'm glad he's moved farther north!" Grace growled, watching Michael wipe the tears out of his eyes. "I'm glad this is so amusing to you."

"Does he suffer from a neurological disorder that causes him to have erratic muscle spasms? And how does he manage to dance completely off the beat like that?" Even Grace had to laugh at that one. Liam's dancing skills were impressively pathetic.

"Can you please come save me? Please?" She was in the middle of her plea when she saw Michael's mouth hanging open as he looked over her shoulder at Liam. "What is he doing?" she asked, suddenly paralyzed with fear.

"He's pretending to smack your ass! Don't turn around, whatever you do."

"Michael Andris, you better get *your* ass out here and save me!" Grace hissed into the phone.

"Come on, honey, he looks like he's really enjoying himself. Look out—he's preparing a spin move!" As Michael said the words, Liam's body flew in front of hers, a huge grin on his face. He turned around so Grace was facing his back. He probably intended the move to impress her, however when he did his version of a booty drop, he looked like he was crapping in the woods rather than doing a seductive dance move. She looked over at Michael and Jack, who were both hysterical now. Bianca had abandoned her long ago and was now standing at the bar with them.

Grace found herself alone, dancing with a moron.

Liam finished dumping his load on the dance floor and turned back to face Grace. She still had the phone pressed to her ear, waiting for the laughter to stop. Somehow encouraged by the look of horror on her face, Liam came right up along side of her and started rubbing himself on her hip.

That was it.

"Michael. Michael, can you hear me?" She saw him look up and nod his head as he laughed. "He just rubbed his *junk* on my leg. What do you think about that?" The smile immediately left his face. Grace breathed a sigh of relief when Michael slammed the phone onto the bar top and catapulted himself over the top of it. She folded her phone shut and counted the seconds until her rescue. Liam, completely oblivious, continued gyrating against her hip.

Michael stalked over to where they were dancing while Grace glared at him. "It's all fun and games until some creeper rubs his penis on my leg, huh, Michael?" He didn't say a word. He simply bent over, wrapped his arms around Grace's knees and hoisted her over his shoulder. She could feel the blood rushing to her head as she dangled mid air, screaming in surprise as her hair fell into her face.

Even upside down, Grace had no problem hearing Michael's parting words to Liam. "Stay away from her. Don't look at her; don't even think about her. If she appears to you in your dreams, wake up and punch yourself in the face for me. Come near her again, and I'll cut your nuts off and put them in a jar on my mantle. Do we understand each other?" Liam, too stunned by the threat to say anything, simply stood there looking dumb.

Grace looked up as Michael turned and gave Liam a lame parting wave as they disappeared into the crowd.

A man on a mission, Michael walked past the bar and continued down the hallway until they came to a door. "Where are you taking me? Put me down!" Grace demanded as she kicked her legs wildly. All he did was laugh and tighten his grip. When they were in a small room with a couch, a television, and a coffee machine, her feet finally hit the ground.

"Thank you for the caveman style rescue," Grace started to sneer, but then she realized how incredibly close Michael was standing to her.

"Are you going to say anything like 'Sorry I left you out there with a creepy guy, Grace' or 'I'm an idiot, Grace, please forgive me'? How about 'Grace, are you all right?' Any of those would be a great place to start." The more enraged she got, the wider he smiled.

Finally, he moved toward her and put his hands on either side of her face. "Grace, are you all right?" His voice was deep and husky, and the seductive tone of it set her body on fire. She tried to stay mad at him, but the longer he looked at her with those piercing, sexy eyes, the harder it was. With him so close and smelling so good, it was damn near impossible.

"Yes, I'm fine. Just completely grossed out, that's all," she said with a smile. "Do you have any hand sanitizer handy?"

"What am I going to do with you? Every time you try to dance, you have a run in with an uninvited man." He smiled and brushed the hair out of her face.

"Well, it's only happened twice. Once it was horrifying, but the other time it was…pretty great." Grace sighed as his thumbs gently caressed her cheeks. She took a moment to enjoy the sensation of his hands on her face.

"Do me a favor. Don't move," he whispered as he looked down at her.

Grace's entire body froze. Unable to even breathe, all she could do was stare into his mesmerizing eyes and wait. He crept closer and when he was an inch from her face, she closed her eyes. As she did, Grace felt the explosive warmth of his lips on hers. Every part of her body was tingling as the adrenaline raced through her bloodstream. He held her lips tightly against his for a second, and then as quickly as the innocent kiss began, it ended.

"Impressive," Grace murmured, her eyes still closed, their foreheads touching.

"Thank you," Michael laughed. "Are you still mad?"

"If I said yes, would you kiss me again?" she asked coyly.

"I can kiss you like this whenever I want, Grace. It's allowed."

"Then kiss me again, please." And before she even had time to finish the sentence, his lips were on hers again, her head swimming. "I could get used to this," she mumbled against his lips.

"Me too."

"Hey, guys what are you do—" Jack stopped in his tracks then turned on his heel and headed for the door. "Never mind. As you were. Bianca!" They heard him yell as he ran down the hall.

Grace took Michael by the hand. "Come on, before Jack tells her we were rolling around naked back here." Before they walked out the door, she took a second to wipe the hint of lipstick off of his lips with her thumb.

Back at the bar, Michael pointed to an empty stool. "Sit here, so I can keep an eye on you." He winked then kissed her cheek and slipped back behind the long, polished bar. Grace sat quietly, watching him make drink after drink. He slid a Cosmo with extra cherries over to her when he had a free minute to keep her entertained.

Meg and Bianca flew to her side. "So did you do it? Do you have anything to confess?" Their eyes were wide with excitement. Grace shook her head no and kept her attention on Michael who was lifting a heavy tray of clean glasses from the back. The muscles of his arms tensed and flexed as Grace smirked and plucked a cherry from its stem with her teeth.

"Wait a minute, Jack said you kissed Michael. He saw you." Bianca stood poised with her hands on her hips.

"I did kiss him, but just on the lips. I kept my tongue to myself, and that's within the rules." Grace smiled, remembering how wonderful it felt to have his sinfully delicious lips on hers. Meg and Bianca just continued to look at her with puzzled expressions.

"Why are you still waiting to use your kiss?" Meg asked.

"The back room of the club is not the way I imagined our first real kiss. I'm saving it." Grace shrugged, unable to explain it any better than that. Of course, the underlying reason was a bit more complicated than that. She just hoped her answer was enough to appease them for now.

"You're stronger than I gave you credit for, Grace. You may just win this thing," Bianca complimented her. "Do you want to dance?" she suggested, giving her arm a small tug.

"You two go; I'm done dancing for now. You never know who may still be lurking on that dance floor." Grace laughed, remembering the spastic dancing of one Liam Sullivan. Unafraid of the hazards of the dance floor, Meg and Bianca smiled and headed off into the crowd. As they disappeared, a new group of girls claimed the seats beside Grace at the bar. *Total barflies,* Grace thought to herself then began eavesdropping on their conversation.

They cackled on about how cute the bartenders were, each picking their favorite. Grace was glad Bianca was safely off dancing when the one girl started mentioning all the things she wanted to do to Jack. Bianca would have most certainly ripped her limb from limb had she heard any of it. Grace watched as they tried to flirt with him, but the most Jack would do was politely smile, and then he moved to the other end of the bar. Ryan wasn't paying them any attention either; he was off to the side and had a glass in his hand that he kept twirling, probably practicing for later.

Michael, however, kept looking down at Grace and smiling like she was the only person in the entire bar. Every time their eyes met, her cheeks turned red, but she couldn't look away. He started walking over in her direction and the girls next to Grace thought they'd finally gotten his attention. But when he continued past them, without a word, and stopped in front of Grace, their smiles disappeared.

"Hello, beautiful," he said with a smile on his lips as he kissed the top of Grace's hand. She heard the girls next to her mumble, "Bitch."

"How's your evening going?" she asked, watching the barflies become angrier by the second.

"Not too bad. There's this gorgeous woman at the bar who keeps checking me out. It's a little distracting at times, but I have to say I kinda like it."

"I hear you kissed her tonight," Grace said, playing along. "How was it?"

"I believe she said it was impressive, but I thought it was more along the lines of... exquisite."

It was pretty darn exquisite, Grace thought, her pulse racing at the memory. Before she could catch her now ragged breath to say anything, Ryan came over and interrupted them.

"Twenty minutes until show time. Grace, you may want to go hunt down your girls." He looked down at their still interlocked hands, smiled, and then patted Michael on the back. "Or maybe not just yet."

"I better go get them," Grace agreed, not wanting to let him go.

"I hope you like the show," he said with a sexy smirk on his face. He leaned over the bar and whispered in a seductive voice, "We have something very special planned for you ladies afterwards as well."

Shoes, money, eternal bragging rights, shoes, money, eternal bragging rights...

Chapter 13

The music stopped, except for a low beat playing as the DJ started to speak to the crowd. "Hey, guys, this is your DJ, Maxwell, and I wanted to welcome you all to The Vault!" The crowd cheered wildly with excitement as the spotlight illuminated the man behind the elaborate control board. "We have a special treat for you. Our bartenders here at The Vault have decided to impress us with just a few of their bar tricks tonight. I've been watching them practice, and I can assure you this is going to be one hot show!" Again, the crowd started screaming and people began pushing toward the bar to get a better view.

The girls were safely up at their table with the best seats in the house for the show. The guys weren't behind the bar yet. They had disappeared into the back to change. Grace was so excited, she could only imagine what was going to happen next. When she looked over at Bianca and Meg, they too were nervously smiling in anticipation, their eyes scanning the room for a glimpse of Jack or Ryan.

The crowd continued to mill around quietly until the spotlight shone on the end of the bar where Michael, Jack, and Ryan now stood, looking absolutely edible. Meg screamed, while Bianca threw her fingers in her mouth and let out a shrill whistle that immediately caught the guys' attention and earned them an enthusiastic wave.

Jack was standing there in a skin tight, black tank top that showed off his muscles perfectly for Bianca to enjoy. His arms were folded, making his chest and biceps look even more striking, if that was possible. A huge smile was on his face as he waited for the show to begin. Bianca stood at the rail, licking her lips at the sight of him.

Ryan was also dressed in a black designer T-shirt that showed off the definition in his chest, but his was more modest, leaving a bit of mystery underneath. He was casually flipping a silver drink shaker in his hand with smooth and confident movements, like he did it all the time. There wasn't the slightest sign of nerves in him. Meg was clapping, stopping only to blow Ryan a kiss from time to time.

Then there was Michael. He was standing off to the side, alone. He had changed into a form fitting black long sleeve button down shirt that fit him like a glove. It was untucked at the bottom and he was rolling up the sleeves as Maxwell addressed the crowd. The top three buttons were left open, exposing part of his chiseled chest. He pushed the sleeves up over his elbows and ran his hand through his hair. He looked up to the girls' seats and gave Grace a wink and a nod that made her heart flutter wildly.

Shoes, money, eternal bragging rights, she reminded herself, yet again.

"Thank God we're all the way up here," Grace said to Bianca who was standing next to her, tapping her nails frantically on the rail. All of her pent-up energy was about to burst from her body.

"Grace, do you see them? I can hardly breathe," Bianca gasped as though she were about to hyperventilate.

"Take a deep breath and relax." Grace put her arm around Bianca and patted her shoulder in support. Meg smiled knowingly from her spot on the rail and pointed down to the bar. "You don't understand, Grace. I ... I think I'm in love with him." Bianca said the words so quietly Grace couldn't be sure she heard her right over all the screaming, but the pink in her cheeks told her she had. Before she could respond to Bianca's confession, the show started.

"Ladies and gentlemen, it is my honor to give you our bartenders: Michael, Jack, and Ryan! They wanted me to tell you that this performance—and song— goes out to Suzy and her friends." A few girls in the crowd, probably named Suzy, started screaming, thinking the show was for them, but Grace and the girls knew the truth. The guys walked behind the bar and took their places. Jack was on the far left, Michael in the middle, and Ryan was on the right side of the bar, closest to the girls.

A few whistles and cat calls later, Maxwell cranked the music and Kid Rock's "So Hott!" blasted through the club.

As the music started, the guys began clapping their hands over their heads in beat with the drums of the intro, trying to get the crowd into it. The spotlights flashed in perfect rhythm. Soon, people were following right along, clapping their hands. Tons of girls started screaming as Jack jumped onto the bar top and pumped his fist to the beat, like the lead singer at a rock concert. The electric guitars kicked in, causing the boys to start dancing.

Grace had assumed they were good dancers, considering they worked in a bar surrounded by music all the time, but to see them moving together was a completely different thing. Their hips slowly rocked from side to side and hit every beat in the song. It made her memory of dancing with Michael all the more exciting. Their shoulders swayed and they smiled back and forth to one another, clearly enjoying themselves. Seeing them so at ease in front of that many people was an unbelievable turn-on.

Jack jumped off the bar top and each of them grabbed a liquor bottle from behind the bar and, in unison, they started flipping them around in their hands at amazing speeds. Grace watched Michael as he would throw a bottle behind his lower back with the flick of his wrist and it would fly up over his shoulder. Somehow he would catch it in front of himself every time, grinning from ear to ear. He could also flip it high over his shoulder and catch it blindly behind his back at a breakneck pace.

Ryan was flipping two bottles around like a master juggler, one in each hand. Things were flying back and forth, arcing from side to side. Jack's tricks were unbelievable as well. He would flip a bottle into the air and catch it by balancing it on the back of his hand, which he held out flat in front of himself. He would give his wrist little flick, and it would fly in the air and again land perfectly balanced on his hand. One time, he even managed to balance it upside down by the narrow bottle top, rather than the wider base, and the crowd went wild.

The song and the lights pulsed on, only adding to the heat of the performance. When Grace heard the provocative opening line of the song, she smiled and blushed profusely, knowing the guys meant it to be a message especially for them. She squeezed Bianca's hand as they watched in utter and complete awe. Meg was jumping along with the beat, never taking her eyes off of Ryan.

As they performed their tricks, they were in constant, graceful motion. Gliding and shaking, each movement complimented the music, while the tricks they were performing took not just their hands and arms, but their entire bodies. Their legs, hips, and thighs moved just as much as their upper bodies, much to the girls' personal enjoyment. Grace was stunned by the speeds at which their hands were able to move as the bottles swirled between their fingers and rotated through the air and how effortless they made it all look. Michael continued bouncing a bottle off his bicep and catching it in his hand before launching it back into the air. The concentration on his face had Grace biting her lip.

Ryan put down his liquor bottles and grabbed four of the silver mixing cups he'd been working with all night. He began juggling them high into the air, never dropping a single one. Jack and Michael stood next to him and the two did some tandem moves flipping the bottles back and forth to one another, over their shoulders and under their legs. When Ryan caught all four cups he had been juggling in a tall stack, the place went crazy again. He moved over by Michael and Jack who were lining up three glasses on the bar top.

A bottle flew from Ryan's hand, over Michael's head, and Jack caught it upside down by the neck and poured a long, sexy shot into a silver mixer cup. He flung the bottle back to Michael who did the same into his shaker before placing the bottle back under the bar. The exchange of flying ingredients back and forth between the three of them continued until each had a shaker full of liquid. Climbing up onto the bar top, they slowly shook the drinks up, singing and dancing along with the song.

It was impossible to hear the music and watch the show and not dance along with them. As the guys stood on the bar top, singing, they each stared up at the girls and gave them seductive smirks that drove all three of them crazy. Grace simply could not take her eyes off Michael—he was breathtaking. There were girls screaming at his feet, and yet she didn't think he even glanced at them once. His eyes were fixed on Grace's exclusively.

As the song started to wind down, they reached below and grabbed a glass off of a tray that Vicki was holding high into the air for them. They each filled a glass with the liquid from their shakers, look a small sip, and returned them safely onto Vicki's tray for delivery. When Michael's smiling face paused and looked back up at Grace, giving a little nod of his head, she knew the drinks were for them, special delivery.

Be strong, Grace, it's almost over. Hang in there!

The guys stood on the bar top as the song ended and took their bows from the screaming crowd. Bianca whistled again, louder than anyone in the club, while Meg and Grace clapped wildly and waved their arms over the rail. Vicki appeared behind them and handed each of them their drinks. "A little present from the boys. They said if you liked the show, drink them fast and come meet them down at the bar."

Grace looked at Bianca and Meg, who were just as flushed as she was after that amazingly sexy show. They raised their glasses in unison to the guys and quickly downed them in one gulp. The boys applauded from below and waved for them to hurry up.

The trio sprinted down the stairs as fast as they could. It took them a few seconds to mill their way through the crowd that was still gathered around the bar, but when Grace finally saw Michael, she ran and threw herself into his awaiting arms.

"Hello there, beautiful," he laughed in her ear. "Did you like the show?"

"It was impressive," she said again as she nuzzled her cheek against his neck.

He threw back his head and laughed. "You say that a lot."

"That's because a lot of things about you are very, very, impressive. Sexy, too, but I'll tell you about that stuff in … just over twelve days." Grace laughed as his lips met hers. Before she knew what she was doing, her fingers gripped the back of his head and pressed him closer to her. When her lips started to part, she released him and jumped away. "Sorry about that!" she said sheepishly.

Michael had a proud smile on his face. "I must have done a good job to get that kind of reaction out of you."

"Yeah, you did really well," she said shyly as he held her hand tightly. The six of them were gathered together off to the side of the bar, talking about the show and reliving the highlights. Grace noticed three of the other bartenders who normally worked the early shift were back tending bar.

Confused, she turned to Michael. "What are they doing here? It's not that busy tonight. Why would they need six of you?"

"They're here to take over for us. We called in a favor." The look of surprise on Grace's face made Michael smirk. "Did I forget to mention that?"

"So you guys have the rest of the night to hang out?" she said excitedly, now bouncing like Meg.

"Yep, there's just one more thing we need to do first. I need a little help. Are you game?" Grace was so enthralled by him, she couldn't say no. Even though the mischievous grin on his face should have set off her warning flags, she agreed. His face lit up with excitement as he quietly responded, "Excellent!"

What did I just get myself into?

Grace heard Maxwell clearing his throat on the microphone. "Did you guys enjoy the show?" he asked the crowd, who responded with thunderous applause and whistles. "Awesome job, gentlemen!" The boys took another bow for the applauding patrons and gave everyone a wave. "To thank you for a job well done, we wanted to give you a little gift. Did you find some volunteers?" Maxwell asked and Grace felt her hand being hoisted into the air by an ecstatic Michael. She glanced over at Bianca and Meg who were in the same position with their hands high in the air, looking equally confused.

"OK, then, ladies, could you please head over to the bar? Make some room for them people." The crowd slowly parted as people cleared a path to the front of the bar for them.

Grace leaned over to Meg and Bianca. "What the hell is going on? Did they say anything to either of you?" They both shook their heads no and the closer they got to the bar, the more anxious the three of them looked. Behind the bar, the guys stood, absolutely beaming. Jack was pulling out a bottle of tequila and arranging shot glasses on the bar while Ryan gathered up a handful of lime wedges and a shaker of salt. Michael smiled as he wiped down the top of the bar, mouthing the word "loophole" to Grace. Her body immediately exploded with a mix of fear and excitement.

"Who's up first?" Maxwell asked. Ryan pointed at Meg and gently tapped the top of the bar, coaxing Meg up with his finger. She stood there paralyzed for a second until Bianca elbowed her in the side.

"Time to start the body shots!" Maxwell cranked the music and the crowd went crazy. Def Leppard's "Pour Some Sugar on Me" thundered through the club as Meg slowly climbed onto the bar top and hesitantly laid down.

Her face turned five shades of red as she lay there. Ryan leaned down and brushed her hair out of her face then whispered something in her ear. She shyly hiked up the bottom of her shirt and laid her trembling palms down flat on the bar. Part of Grace was laughing at the sight of her friend waiting to have Ryan do a body shot off of her, the other part of her was absolutely terrified, knowing her turn was coming up. She glanced over at Michael who was watching her reaction anxiously. When Grace smiled and playfully shook her head from side to side, he gave her a wink which started that wonderful tingly feeling running through every inch of her body.

Jack handed Ryan the salt and he slowly licked a small section of Meg's stomach, which quivered when his tongue made contact with her skin. She let out a small squeal that Grace could hear over all the screams of the surrounding crowd who had all crammed closer, wanting a good view of what was going on. Ryan continued pouring a small pile of salt onto the damp spot on her stomach.

"Ready?" Ryan asked before he put the lime wedge into her mouth.

All she managed was a warning, "Ryan…" and then she was holding the lime between her teeth, waiting for him to do his worst.

Michael handed him a shot of tequila which Ryan held carefully in his hand. He smiled down at Meg and leaned back over her stomach. Grace could see him licking Meg's skin gently where the pile of salt was positioned. When he got every last grain of salt into his mouth, he threw back the shot and moved up to her mouth. Meg's eyes were huge as he came closer and Grace noticed her hands were clenched into tiny fists as she did her best to stay in control under these extreme circumstances. Grace's heart was racing just watching it. She couldn't even imagine what it was going to feel like when Michael did that to her.

Ryan's lips met Meg's as he bit into the lime and lingered. Meg's hands flew up to his head and she twirled his hair in her fingers for a minute before he pulled away from her, grinning triumphantly. Once again, the crowd screamed at the completion of the first body shot.

Ever the gentleman, Ryan put one arm under her knees and the other around her waist and lifted her off the bar top, setting her down safely behind the bar with him. Her blond hair was scattered in every direction and as she smoothed it down, Jack looked at Bianca with a seductive grin and patted the top of the bar. Bianca shocked everyone when she shook her head no and pointed at him while patting the bar top. Grace didn't think it was possible for Jack's grin to get any bigger, but it did. Ever the showman, Jack happily hopped up onto the bar, and peeled his shirt from his body, earning himself thunderous whistles and catcalls. Staring at Jack's chest, Bianca grabbed Grace's hand and squeezed until her nails nearly drew blood.

Bianca walked behind the bar and Michael handed her the salt. She climbed on a stool and leaned over Jack with a devilish smirk on her face. Her long red hair draped over her shoulder, brushing along his chest. He winked at her and laughed as she leaned down and, starting at his bellybutton, licked a trail all the way up to his neck. Jack slapped the bar top as her tongue made its way up his chest. Michael and Ryan were howling behind the bar. By the time she finished, Jack's hands were clenching his normally perfectly styled hair as he tried to behave. She sprinkled the salt up the slick trail and placed the lime wedge between his teeth. She quickly whipped her hair up into a ponytail before lowering her lips back to his stomach where she licked the long salt trail up his body. Every so often, Jack would arch up off the bar as she seductively moved up his chest.

When she finally reached his neck, Michael handed her the shot. She downed it and hovered over him for a second before lowering herself on top of him to claim the juicy lime that waited in his lips. Jack reached around her and pulled the rest of her body onto the bar top with him. Wild screams and applause came from the crowd at Jack's bold move. Victoriously, Bianca sat up, the lime clenched in her teeth and a broad smile on her face. Michael guided her back down off the bar and then she held out her hand. Jack grasped it as he got off the bar and bowed to the now frenzied crowd, his hair sticking up in every direction.

Shit, shit, shit!

The whole body shot thing was hilarious when it was Meg and Jack, but now that it was Grace's turn, she was blushing as her heart roared to life in her chest. Meg and Bianca screamed her name, and Michael gave a flirtatious tap to the bar top while extending his hand out to her. She took a deep breath and took his hand as she climbed up on the bar. "Behave…" Grace said pointing at Michael. He teasingly crossed his heart like a good little boy, but the evil grin on his face told her he was anything but. She closed her eyes and slowly lowered herself back onto the cold bar.

Grace turned her head and saw Meg and Bianca flashing her a big thumbs-up. She felt her face flush at all the attention. Covering her eyes for a moment, Grace tried to calm herself down, but when she heard the crowd suddenly scream, she peeked out to find Michael standing over her on the bar top.

What the hell is he doing? Oh my God! Is he is going to do what I think he's going to do? Shoes, money, bragging rights! Shit, shit, shit!

He slowly lowered himself down onto all fours over her legs and looked like a panther about to pounce. Her arms were up over her head, her fingers clamped together as he started moving up her body. In her haste, Grace had forgotten to lift her shirt up and before she could do it herself, she felt Michael's warm fingers grazing the burning skin of her stomach as he slowly lifted the shirt up.

She kept her eyes on him the entire time. Even though she was completely dressed, the lustful way he looked at her made Grace feel completely naked. She watched him taking in every detail of her body as she lay helpless and shaking beneath him. His blue eyes twinkled before he lowered his head down to her stomach. She took a deep breath and waited for the moment when she would feel his tongue on her skin.

At first, Grace only felt his warm breath on the side of her abdomen, but then she felt his lips part as they touched her side and his warm tongue slid over her skin, causing Goosebumps to appear instantly. He laughed at the reaction his touch had on her and went back to the job at hand. He licked a small trail up the sensitive skin on the side of her abdomen. But then, to Grace's surprise, he continued crawling farther up her body until she felt his lips crash down on her exposed shoulder and he began licking another trail along her collarbone.

When he noticed her puzzled expression, he grinned and said, "I like a lot of salt."

"Sure you do," Grace said. *Shit, shoes, shit, money, shit, bragging rights—SHIT!* she screamed in her head as he took the salt out and began sprinkling it along her stomach and shoulder. The grains of salt that missed their mark slid off and landed on the bar top, tickling as they fell off her body.

"Ready?" he asked, leering at her as he held a small lime wedge between his thumb and index finger.

"Not in the slightest." She stuck her tongue out at him in protest, but he just shook his head and scolded her.

"Now, Grace, you'd better keep that sexy tongue to yourself or you can kiss the shoes goodbye. Behave." He placed the lime between her teeth and crawled back down to her abdomen. Grace watched Jack hand him the shot of tequila and say something that sounded like "Go get her, tiger" as he slapped him on the back, causing a bit of the tequila to spill from the shot glass and land in the middle of her stomach. Grace jumped when the cold liquid hit and she glared at Jack.

"No worries, Grace. My boy Mike will help you with that." Jack winked and wrapped his arm back around a giggling Bianca.

Setting the shot glass on the bar next to her shoulder, Michael ran his fingers through his hair and then lowered his lips to Grace's stomach, kissing her skin gently as the crowd went wild. He made his way to where the salt was piled and again she felt the moisture of his warm tongue slide over her skin. He pressed his tongue harder onto her skin this time, lapping up the salt. She felt it move slowly back and forth, gathering up the tiny grains. The crowd let out whistles of encouragement to Michael as the music blared on.

When he had collected all the salt from her stomach, he turned his attention to the drops of tequila that pooled on her. He sucked the cold liquid off Grace's belly, which tickled more than the licking had. Her hands, which had been locked above her head, came slapping down onto the bar top with a loud *whap*. Michael smirked and continued his way up to her shoulder to get the last pile of salt on her body.

He bowed his head to the side and, beginning at the edge of her shoulder, worked his way closer to her neck. Grace felt his teeth nip her skin occasionally when his tongue wasn't setting her skin on fire. It felt like the whole process had taken about twenty minutes, when in actuality it was probably closer to one minute, since the song was just now ending.

"You taste delicious, Grace," he whispered in her ear and Grace nearly lost it. He was so close and smelled exotic and spicy and all she wanted to do was concede the bet and wrap herself around him. She bit into the lime so hard, some of the juice ran into her mouth and a small bit ran down her cheek.

Michael, still kneeling over her, picked up the shot glass and raised it slightly to her, then threw his head back and poured the alcohol into his mouth. The crowed clapped and whistled as he leaned back over Grace, ready to claim his lime from her mouth. The lecherous grin on his face made Grace's heart thunder in her chest.

Keep your tongue in your mouth, Grace. Don't lose it now—you're almost done. So what if you have the sexiest man in the world straddling you. Shoes! Do it for the fucking shoes, Grace! she screamed in her head. She looked up and saw his darkened eyes coming closer. Grace couldn't take it anymore and closed her eyes, waiting for it to happen and praying that she could muster the self-control to make it through the next forty-five seconds.

Grace felt his warm breath on her face as he inched closer. His tongue touched her jaw as he licked the trail of lime juice that had run down the side of her face. Grace began repeatedly slapping the bar with her left hand as she tried to focus on something other than his tongue creeping closer to her mouth. She heard him murmur her name right before his mouth came down on top of hers to bite the lime. As soon as the wedge left her teeth, she pressed her lips together to make sure her tongue stayed put. Michael's lips, however, didn't make that any easier as he repeatedly kissed her, over and over and over, his tongue teasing against the seam of her lips and setting off a multitude of different emotions and desires in her.

She vaguely heard Maxwell congratulate the boys on a job well done before he thanked the lovely volunteers for helping give the boys their rewards. Grace's head was still spinning from the kisses with Michael when she opened her eyes to find his smiling face inches away.

"Did you like your surprise?" he asked as Grace watched him climb off the bar and hold a hand out so she could sit up.

"Yes, a little too much," she laughed as she hopped off the bar and into his awaiting arms. "Were you trying to give me a heart attack?" she asked. He simply smiled and shook his head from side to side. "I think I'm going to run to the bathroom and throw some cold water on my face." Her comment only made his smile grow wider.

"Go calm yourself. But just so we're clear, I'm not letting you out of my sight for the rest of the night," Michael said as he gave her waist a tight squeeze.

"That's what I was afraid of." Grace laughed as she moved away from him and headed quickly for the bathrooms.

She scurried to the back of the club and as the bathroom door closed behind her, Grace let out the loudest scream she could manage. It echoed off the walls as she tried to compose herself. She walked over to the sink and turned the cold water on high then watched it run into the basin as she gripped the sides of the sink for dear life. The door flew open and Grace looked up to see Meg and Bianca staring back at her, looking in no better shape than she was.

"What the... did you see? His mouth... and he said... and oh my God!" Grace screamed again before putting her head between her knees trying to catch her breath.

Meg came over and rubbed her back gently. "Grace, it's OK, you did a great job. You did it—you resisted his temptation, and by the way, just so you know, they are standing right outside the door so you may want to watch what you say—or scream." Meg stifled a laugh as the color drained from Grace's cheeks.

"Shit!" she yelled, scrambling to her feet.

Bianca laughed and hugged Grace tightly and whispered, "I'm right there with you, Grace. I licked Jack, for God's sake! He was shirtless and he tasted like heaven. I can't even breathe if I think about it."

Grace hugged her tighter and somehow it was extremely comforting to know Bianca was having the same inner struggle she was. After a few deep breaths, Grace went to the still-running sink, splashed the cold water onto her face, and then wiped it away with a towel. She threw open the bathroom door and found the smug trio standing in the hallway.

"Let's dance!" Grace grabbed Michael's hand and headed to the dance floor.

They spent the rest of the night dancing and laughing. Jack and Michael showed them some of their best break dancing moves which, again, were impressive. Ryan did his version of the robot until they all had tears in their eyes. Back to the table, they spent some time talking and laughing as they shared funny stories about one another.

At the stroke of midnight, Michael stood up and declared it time to go. Sad the night was over, everyone gathered their things and headed out to the cars. Ryan and Meg took Bianca and Jack with them leaving Michael and Grace alone in the car for their ride home.

"Did you have fun tonight?" he asked as they left the club.

"Of course. It was the best non-date of my entire life." Grace laughed as she held his hand, playing with his fingers.

"So, I get to feed you breakfast in the morning," he reminded her, a knowing grin on his face.

"Yeah, I wanted to ask you, how did you get Meg to agree to that? What did Ryan tell her?" Grace had been meaning to ask him that all night, but it slipped her mind until now.

"Well, I just said the reason for the 'meeting' was to help us with our Christmas shopping. I'm supposed to get ideas about what Jack and Ryan should get Meg and Bianca." He smirked proudly.

"Shopping? Very smart, Michael." Grace praised him as she ran her hand slowly down his arm.

"I thought so." He laughed then became serious. "Grace, do you trust me?"

She was startled by the question. "Of course I do. I let you lick me tonight, for goodness sake," she teased.

"OK, then do me a favor. Take a shower tonight." *Not a problem, a nice cold shower was already on my to-do list.* "And wear warm pajamas to bed. Can you do that for me?"

"They seem like reasonable requests. Odd, but reasonable, so, um, sure," Grace said cautiously trying to decipher the clues he had just given her.

He pulled up in front of the apartment, and before she jumped out of the car, he leaned over and gave her a kiss. "I'll see you bright and early. Keep your phone handy. I'll call you in the morning."

"Good night, Michael."

"Good night, Grace."

As she heard his car speed away, Grace skipped up to apartment door. When she stepped inside, Bianca and Meg were sitting on the couch waiting for her. "Hey," Meg said sweetly from the couch. Grace wandered over and sat down with them, laying her head on Bianca's shoulder.

"So, when is Michael picking you up tomorrow?" Meg asked softly.

"I have no idea. He said he'd call me. I'm exhausted so I'm going to jump in the shower and then go to sleep. I'll see you in the morning." She gave Bianca and Meg a kiss and sauntered off toward her room.

Bianca called from the couch, "Don't use all the cold water please." Grace laughed and closed her bedroom door.

❧

It was still pitch black in Grace's room when she heard her phone start singing. She sat up and grabbed it off the nightstand, only able to open one eye, the other still tightly closed.

"Who died?" she mumbled into the phone. Her comment caused muffled laughter to come from the deep voice on the other end.

"Grace, it's me. No one is dead. Can you please come to the door?" Grace heard Michael say in a hushed voice.

"What door? Where are you? Is this a dream?" she asked through a yawn. Nothing he was saying was making sense. Then she heard a banging noise in the phone and one coming from the kitchen.

"Come to the door, Grace. I'm here to pick you up for breakfast." Michael tried not to laugh at her in her haze. She glanced over at the clock; it was 4:45 a.m.

"Do you know what time it is? Are you insane?" Grace asked as she sprang out of bed and shuffled across the cold apartment floor toward the door. She stood on her toes, looked through the peep hole and then let out a shriek.

Standing outside were a wide awake Michael, Jack, and Ryan. All of them were too smiley and perky, given the obscene hour of the morning. "What the hell are you guys doing here?" Grace hissed in a panic through the door.

She could hear them laughing behind the thin piece of wood separating them.

"We're here to take you to breakfast," Michael said, still laughing.

"Huh?"

"Grace, can you please let us in before your neighbors call the police?" Ryan begged.

"Yeah, I'm freezing my nu—" Jack started in a loud voice but Grace whipped open the door before he could finish.

"Get in here." She was still confused how Bianca and Meg could possibly be sleeping through this ruckus. Jack and Ryan walked in and sat down on the couch like it was the middle of the day.

"What are you guys doing here at—" she glanced at the clock, "—4:47 in the morning?"

"I'm here to take you to breakfast. I have to return you by 10:30, but Meg and I never agreed on a start time for the meeting, so I decided to come extra early. Are you ready to go?" he asked calmly, like it was the middle of the afternoon. "By the way, nice hair."

"Bite me." Grace looked down to see that he was standing there in his pajamas too. He had on black flannel pants and a sweatshirt. "Nice pajamas." She laughed as she combed her fingers through her hair.

In the family room, Jack and Ryan picked up the video game controllers and were ready to start playing. "Jack, Ryan, before you do that, and trust me you will have plenty of time to play that while you wait for those two to get ready, do me a favor and go wake up my dear roommates? They will be so excited to see you here." Grace flashed them an evil grin as they jumped to their feet.

She pointed to one door and reminded them who slept where. "Meg," she said and Ryan headed that way. Jack grinned and walked to the other door, pausing briefly to look over his shoulder at Grace and wink before he opened the door.

"Don't suppose she sleeps naked or anything good like that, huh?" he asked with a twinkle in his eye.

"Sorry, lover boy, not when she's sleeping alone."

Michael laughed, but Jack had to think about it for a second and then did a small fist pump before going into her room. Michael wrapped his arms around Grace and hugged her tightly. "Hmm. I wanted to do this all night."

She snuggled her face against his chest. "Me too." Grace felt his lips gently brush the top of her head and then it happened: simultaneous screams.

"Argh!"

"What the hell are you doing here?"

Michael and Grace started laughing, not because of the screams, but because the first scream didn't come from Bianca; it came from Jack. Grace ran over to find Jack on his knees and Bianca gripping his wrist, which she had apparently spun behind his back in some sort of move she'd only seen before on *COPS*.

"God damn it! What are you, a fucking ninja?" Jack gasped from his knees. Bianca immediately let go of his wrist.

"Jack! Oh God, I thought you were a rapist or something. I just heard heavy breathing and smelled cologne. Hi…," she purred when he made his way to his feet. Grace rolled her eyes at Michael and they walked back to the living room where they were met by Meg, hands on her hips, and her sleeping mask still plastered across her forehead.

"Would you like to explain the early wake-up call?" She was furious, but Michael just smiled and explained that in their agreement, they had never established how early the breakfast meeting could begin. She looked wide-eyed at Michael who just grinned back at her.

"Very sneaky. Taking advantage of your little loopholes, are you?" Meg wagged an accusing finger at him. Michael didn't say anything; he simply took Grace's hand and pulled her in front of him as a human shield.

"It's a gift I have," he said sarcastically with a shrug. Grace had been trying not to laugh while Meg was mad, but she couldn't hold it in anymore.

Meg pointed to the couch across the room. "Sit," she commanded Ryan before going into her room to get ready.

"Actually, what she should have said is 'Get comfortable, Ryan,' because she takes a long ass time to get ready," Grace said with a laugh before a small voice came from Meg's room.

"Shut up, Grace! Or I'll tell Michael what I heard you say—or should I say scream—in your sleep the other night." Grace's face turned red. She had no idea what she'd said, but she remembered the vivid dream and definitely didn't want Michael to hear any of it. Jack snuck out of Bianca's room, rubbing his shoulder, and went over to the couch to join Ryan and wait.

"Give me a minute to brush my teeth and change and I'll be ready to go," Grace said as she turned to Michael, but he shook his head at her.

"Don't worry about changing, just come in your pajamas," he insisted. Grace looked at him in confusion, but shrugged and ran into her bathroom to quickly freshen up. A jolt of adrenaline ran through her body at the thought of nearly six hours with Michael, alone. She scrubbed her teeth, ran a quick brush through her hair, put some deodorant on, and dashed out of the bathroom to find Michael laying on her bed, smiling.

"Ready to go get some breakfast?" he asked sweetly.

Not really, I'd like you to stay right there…

"Sure, let's go."

❧

As they hopped into Michael's car, Grace asked, "So, where are we going to breakfast, in our pajamas, at five in the morning?"

He flashed a toothy smile. "My place."

That wasn't the response Grace was expecting, but the more she thought about it, the more she grinned. Grace leaned over and gave him a peck on the cheek. "You are brilliant."

"Of course I am." He picked up Grace's hand and kissed each of her fingertips. "So, let's get this out of the way now. Gift ideas for Meg and Bianca?"

She thought about it for a second and then an idea popped into her head. "For Bianca, have Jack try and get her tickets to the gallery opening for Marcus Frank. She used one of his paintings in the Conklin Building renovation last month and fell in love with his work. The opening is in Seattle, mid-January I think. It would score Jack some major points if he could swing that." Grace laughed and then began racking her brain about Meg. "For Meg, tell Ryan to drive her down to San Francisco some weekend so she can go to the boutiques and hunt for antiques. She'll be thrilled to explore all those little shops. Good enough? Is our meeting adjourned?" Grace laughed.

"Works for me." Michael laughed as they pulled in front of his place. He opened the door and led Grace up the front steps. Inside, his whole apartment smelled delicious. The aroma of bacon, sausage, and maple syrup wafted through the air. Grace stood in the kitchen in shock.

"What time did you wake up to start all of this?" she asked in amazement.

He shrugged and smiled. "I never really went to bed. I had kind of a difficult time getting to sleep last night, so I just stayed up and started a few things before we came to pick you up."

"You're unbelievable." She walked into the kitchen and picked up a spatula in an effort to help.

"No, no, no. You are my guest. Humor me." He pulled the spatula out of her hand. "Just tell me, how do you like your eggs?"

"Scrambled, with cheese if you have some." All of the talk about breakfast was making her hungry.

"That I can do. Now, follow me." He took her hand and led her out of the kitchen and through the family room and down a hall, which she assumed led to his bedroom. Grace stopped walking as they approached the door and gave him a suspicious look. He just laughed and gave her hand a tug, pulling Grace into his room.

"If you don't mind, I would like to serve you breakfast in bed." He held out his arm toward the inviting king sized bed that was in front of them. The navy blue comforter was neatly folded back, revealing the blue and white striped sheets beneath. A pile of fluffy pillows leaned against the headboard and a remote control to the stereo was sitting on the nightstand.

"Meg's going to kill you when she hears about this." Grace laughed as she kicked off her shoes and climbed into his bed. He tucked the comforter snugly around her waist and kissed her lips.

"I can handle Meg, don't you worry," he teased. He reached across her and laid the remote control in her lap. "I have a bunch of CDs loaded in there, see if you can find something you like. My only rule is that you don't leave this bed. Understand?" he said as his blue eyes sparkled in the dim lights. Grace nodded, and he dashed out the door to get everything ready.

Grace clicked on the stereo and quickly flipped through the songs. She found he had an eclectic taste in music, which was cool. She easily found something to listen to and as the music played, Grace snuggled down deeper under the covers, pulling them up to her chin. Lying there, still not believing he had managed to pull this whole thing off, Grace realized just how much the pillows and blankets all smelled like him. She buried her nose into one of the pillows and breathed deeply, feeling completely at home and relaxed.

A few minutes later, Michael came back with a tray full of food. He had fruit, bacon and sausage, scrambled eggs for her and eggs over easy for himself, pancakes, and toast. The tray was finished off by two glassed of orange juice. "Hungry?" he asked as he walked over to the bed.

"Actually yes, considering it's only 5:15 in the morning, I am." Grace quickly sat up against the headboard so he could set the tray across her lap. He slid into bed next to her looking absolutely victorious. "What are you smiling about?" she asked.

"Oh nothing, I've just been dying to get you into bed for weeks and I finally did it." Grace gave his shoulder a small, teasing shove.

"And neither of us lost our bets. Seriously, though, this is amazing," Grace said softly. The amount of effort he went through to make this happen was staggering. "Thank you," she said as she ran her hand down the side of his face.

"My pleasure," he whispered before he gently kissed her.

Breakfast was delicious, but what made it more wonderful was being so at ease with Michael. They finished breakfast in record time and the only time he left the bed for the remainder of the morning was to take the dishes into the kitchen. He quickly climbed back under the covers with Grace where they laughed and talked for hours. She had her arm draped across his chest and laid her head on his shoulder as he ran his hand up and down her back. They stayed like that, lost in a comfortable silence, for a long while.

"What classes are you going to be teaching next semester?" he asked as he played with a lock of her hair.

"One is called Major American Writers and the other is Literature of the Early 1900's," Grace said excitedly. "I even get to pick two of the books for the assigned readings."

"Choose wisely. You don't want the students mad at you from the get go," Michael teased, but she had to laugh because she'd been worrying about the same thing for a week.

"So how is the location search going for the bar?" Grace asked as she ran her fingers across his chest.

"Not bad. There are a few places we like. One is on High Street and it would be perfect, but I have a feeling it will be well out of our price range. We have a meeting with a developer next week. If they want too much, we'll just keep looking," he said encouragingly.

"Did you guys come up with a name for it yet?"

"No, not yet. I'm open to suggestions, so if you think of something, let me know." He lifted his head to check the clock.

"Don't say it," Grace grumbled as she nuzzled tightly against his chest.

"Sorry, sweetheart, but we do have to get going in ten minutes. Your 'mother' gave you a curfew." He laughed as he buried his lips into her hair, kissing her head, forehead and both cheeks, before settling down onto Grace's lips.

"Stupid Meg," she murmured as he kissed her. "Stupid bet."

In the silence of his room, wrapped in his arms, Grace thought about everything that had happened these last few weeks. How amazing Michael was, and how alive he made her feel when she was with him. Everything about him made her smile and she couldn't imagine her life without him anymore. His phone calls woke her up every morning and helped her sleep every night. She could barely remember what life had been like before him and didn't even want to try. All Grace knew was that she wanted to be with him, always. She looked up at his face, taking in his perfect features, when his eyes met hers.

I think love you, Michael, Grace whispered in her head. *I'm just too chicken to say it.*

She realized she was grinning like a mad woman and looked away before he could notice. Her heart sprung to life and she was filled with joy, finally knowing how she felt about him. Even though she wasn't ready to say it out loud, she knew with every fiber of her being that she loved Michael.

It was Michael's deep voice that pulled her out of her stupor. "Come on, my love. Time to get you home."

Chapter 14

Her head was still spinning as she walked into the apartment. As soon as she'd shut the door, Grace leaned back against the wood, slid down all the way to the floor, and sighed loudly. *I love Michael. Oh my God, I love Michael!* The words kept rolling through her head as her hands trembled in her lap. It took a second for her to notice that Meg and Bianca were standing over her calling her name.

"Earth to Grace! What's wrong with you?" Meg's voice suddenly became worried when she noticed Grace was shaking.

"Did he hurt you?" Bianca roared, ready to hunt Michael down and beat him to a bloody pulp. Grace looked from her enraged face to Meg's and shook her head no. With each movement of her head, she felt a smile growing bigger and bigger on her face.

"I love him." It felt so strange to say the words out loud, but as Grace heard them coming from her mouth, she knew without a doubt that they were true. Her voice grew stronger the second time she said it. "I love him."

After that, all she could see was a flurry of arms and squeals coming at her, wrapping around her body as Meg and Bianca threw themselves onto the floor with her.

"Grace, tell us everything," Meg begged.

"Can we get off the floor first?" Grace laughed, climbing to her feet and holding out a hand to each of them as she helped them off the floor. Then Grace ran and threw herself onto the couch.

Meg stood in front of her with her hands on her hips, grinning. "Spill it!" Bianca sat down next to her and folded her arms too, waiting for Grace to say something.

"Well, what do you want to know?" she asked coyly.

"Where did you go for breakfast? What did you talk about? And, oh, I don't know … you said you love him? Explain," Meg finally burst.

"He took me to his place for breakfast." Grace glanced up nervously at Meg who was turning purple.

"He took you where?" she hissed.

"His place, for breakfast … in bed." Grace mumbled the last part as quietly as she could, but when Bianca whistled, she knew it was going to be bad.

"Are you saying that you had breakfast in bed with him? That is so against the rules. Who has a breakfast meeting in bed?" Meg kept screaming "in bed" at the top of her lungs. Bianca snickered quietly next to Grace as she tried to do some damage control.

"Meg, it was nothing. You could have been sitting in the chair at his desk watching. Nothing happened except we ate and talked and I guess we snuggled a bit, but that isn't against the rules." Grace pled her case as best she could. When she saw Meg's jaw set, she decided to just move on, hoping that hearing the details would distract her.

Meg stood in silence, mulling the information over. "OK, that was romantic. He's good, I'll give him that. And technically, you stayed within the rules," she conceded as she sat down on the other side of Grace. She knew the big question was coming, she just didn't know which one of them would ask it.

"So, you love him?" Bianca asked, smirking.

Grace felt her face get hot as she nodded her head. "I do. I love him … so much. It sounds lame, I know, but it was just right, being there with him, in his arms. Nothing else mattered."

"Did you tell him?" Meg asked on the edge of her seat.

"No, not yet. I didn't want to scare him away, you know? It was a perfect morning, and I didn't want to mess that up by sounding like some deranged stalker," Grace laughed.

"I told Jack," Bianca whispered.

Now Bianca was the one pelted with flying arms and squeals in her ears.

"Tell us! Tell us!" Grace shouted as she clapped her hands. "Where did he take you this morning?"

"He took me to the Ritz Carlton for breakfast. It was spectacular. We had a quiet table in the corner overlooking the river. The food was to die for. It was their champagne brunch and there were lobster tails and caviar, oysters, Belgian waffles made as you watched, fresh fruits, crepes, prime rib, omelets, and you could even get the lobster tails in the omelets." Jack obviously was learning her tastes. "And Jack was wonderful. He was still Jack, and silly, but he was also sweet and thoughtful. He bought me flowers and held my chair out for me as I sat down and he held my hand through the entire meal." She sighed at the memory of her morning with Jack.

"So when did you tell him?" Grace asked.

"Well, we were done eating and he was staring at me with the cutest grin on his face. So I asked him what he was thinking, and he just blurted out, 'I was thinking that I love you.'" Her face turned red.

"He said it first?" Meg asked, in complete shock. Jack, the smooth operator, was the last one she would have pegged as a romantic.

"Yes. So, I leaned over and kissed his cheek and whispered in his ear, 'I love you too, Jack.' Lucky for us, we were in public or I'd have been all over him and out of the bet." She laughed as she toyed with the corner of a throw pillow.

"Bianca, that's so exciting! I'm happy for you two. You're so brave." Grace admired her so much for the way she just followed her heart and her feelings. She wished she could be more like Bianca at times, and this was one of them.

"Well, does anyone want to hear about my morning?" Meg asked, slightly hurt they weren't begging for her details.

"Yes, of course. Tell us everything," Grace insisted, as she and Bianca turned and gave her their complete attention.

"Well, after we got ready, Ryan put me in the car and *briefly* went back to his place to pack up a picnic basket and grab a few blankets because it was so cold this morning. When we got the car packed, we headed down to Washington Park. He pulled the picnic basket and huge blankets out of the back seat and we found a lovely place to bundle up watch the sun rise."

"Didn't you freeze? It wasn't exactly warm this morning," Bianca asked, astounded that Meg would risk freezing to death before sunrise for any man.

"Actually, I was quite warm in Ryan's arms, under the blankets." Meg giggled. "Then, after the spectacular sunrise, it warmed up and he spread out a lovely breakfast and a big thermos of hot chocolate for us to share. He even fed me strawberries." She swooned as she crashed into Grace's shoulder.

"He's just the most fantastic and interesting person. He wrote a poem which he shared after breakfast that just swept me off my feet," she gushed, her entire body conveying her excitement.

"A poem? Was it a love poem?" Bianca raised an interested eyebrow at Meg, who was twirling a piece of her blond hair in her fingers.

"Sure, he loves me," she beamed.

"And when did this happen? You've been holding out on us!" Grace raised her voice in surprise.

She sighed. "He told me a while ago."

"Days or a week?" Bianca pressed.

"Days."

"And you said?" Grace prompted.

"I told him I loved him too, of course. I already told him I was the woman of his dreams the second time I saw him. I was in love with him then; I just had to wait for him to figure it out," Meg said with a wink. Grace noticed that she was downright radiant as she talked about loving Ryan.

Nelly's song started playing so Grace hopped off the couch to pull the phone out of her pocket. Meg and Bianca laughed at her eagerness.

"She *must* be in love," Bianca muttered.

Grace glared at her over her shoulder then cupped her hand over her mouth to signal Bianca to be silent while she was on the phone with Michael.

"Hello."

"Hey. I just wanted to make sure Meg hadn't ripped you limb from limb for spending the morning in bed with me," he teased. Grace felt her cheeks turn red as her heart fluttered at the sound of his voice.

"No, I'm still alive, barely. I have a feeling she'll be watching you like a hawk for a while though, so you better behave." Grace laughed as Meg nodded her head in silent agreement from the couch.

"Put Meg on," he said.

Grace held the phone out to her, giggling as Meg winked and huffed into the phone. "Don't you 'hello, Meg' me, mister! Your sweet talking may work on Grace, but I'm a different story. You better get explaining or Grace is out of our bet," she pretended to fume. Bianca gave Grace a small poke which made her laugh more.

"No, no, no! You explain this: who has a breakfast meeting in bed?" Meg continued her interrogation brilliantly.

"What do you mean, you were done with business by then? What?" She pulled the phone away from her ear. "Grace, when did you discuss Christmas presents?"

"In the car on the way to his house," she said truthfully.

"That still doesn't make breakfast in bed within the rules, Michael," she scolded into the phone.

She rolled her eyes as he explained himself. "Yes, I have … no, I guess not. I'm watching you, though. I have my eyes all over you. One false move and … I didn't mean like that! … You're incorrigible. Here's Grace." Meg smiled and tossed the phone back over to Grace. She was pleased with how her intimidation of Michael went, flexing her muscles in a show of victory.

"Hello? Are you still there?" Grace asked, laughing.

"Yes, she doesn't scare me. Hey, I had another question I forgot to ask. When are you leaving to go to your mom's for Christmas?" *Shit, Susan. I had to go home.*

"Saturday. Bianca's coming with me and Meg's flying home to Boston. Why?"

"Well, I wanted to give you your Christmas present before I go. Actually we all do. Can we stop over tomorrow night and do a mini Christmas?" he asked hopefully.

Grace answered immediately. "Yes!" Meg and Bianca looked at her in confusion as she shouted into the phone with a bit too much excitement.

"Perfect! I'll let you go. You probably need a nap," he said sweetly.

"Goodbye, Michael."

"Goodbye, my love," he said softly into the phone before he hung up.

Grace held the phone, frozen in place. *My love? He said that before, at his place.* The realization finally hit her.

Bianca and Meg watched her clutch the phone to her chest for a second as she tried to process what he said. They became concerned when she didn't say anything for so long.

"Grace, what's wrong? Is Michael all right?" Meg asked, shaking her friend's shoulder slightly.

"Huh?" she asked, not having heard the question.

"What did he say?" Bianca prodded.

"My love …" Grace said softly.

"What?" they asked together, utterly lost with where this conversation was going.

"My love. H-he said 'goodbye…my love.' That's what he called me. He said it this morning too. He's never said that before." Grace stood there stunned, trying to put the pieces together in her head.

"He loves you," Bianca squealed with a huge smile on her face. Grace looked at her in disbelief.

Slowing the words down, Bianca tried again to get through to her friend. "He. Loves. You," she said clearly, enunciating every word. "Michael loves you. You don't call someone 'my love' if you aren't in love with them." Meg was forcefully nodding her head in agreement, too.

"No, he can't…It was just an expression," Grace murmured as she sat back down onto the couch.

"Why can't he? You love him. Why can't he love you? And don't you dare say you aren't worth his love or I'll give you a black eye," Meg shouted at her, holding her tiny fist in front of her chest.

"Grace, she's right. He loves you." Bianca held her shoulders as Grace shook her head no. She felt Bianca's hand grab her chin and lift it, forcing Grace's eyes to meet hers. "Don't question it; just accept it." She wiped the single tear that fell down Grace's cheek.

"He loves me?" Grace barely whispered. In that moment, she thought her heart would burst apart. There was a chance that Michael may actually feel the same way about her? For the first time in her life, Grace was in love, and if Bianca and Meg's guesses were right, he was in love with her, too.

Friday morning, the girls got an early start to the mall in search of the perfect Christmas gifts for the men in their lives. It took them hours and multiple returns before they each felt they had an acceptable gift and one that would convey the proper emotion with it. When they got home just after one o'clock, Grace turned on the television to check the weather. A huge storm was getting ready to slam into the east coast and Meg was getting worried about making it home for Christmas.

"You may want to call the airlines again and see if you can get out of here tonight," Grace told her as she watched the snowfall predictions for Saturday.

Meg spent the next hour on the phone with her parents and the airlines trying to change her flight, with no luck. She came into Grace's room and lay across the bed.

"There's no way I'm getting to Boston. Stupid snow," she said sadly as she crawled under the covers with Grace.

"Come to Spokane. Maybe my mom will try and set you up with the son of one of her garden club friends. It'll be fun!" Grace teased. "Seriously, come with us. It won't be the same without you."

"Fine, but I'm not kissing anyone just because I'm standing under mistletoe. I don't care whose son it is; they'd better keep their lips to themselves. You tell her that." Meg smiled as she hugged Grace. She hopped off the bed and went to repack for Spokane while Grace dragged herself out of bed to start the most hateful job of getting her own suitcase ready to go.

At 4:30, Bianca's phone started ringing. Grace could hear Jack's ring tone blaring in the family room. Bianca appeared at her door and gave it a little tap as Grace was putting the bow on Michael's Christmas present.

"What's up?"

Bianca's face was sad and she was still holding her cell phone. "That was Jack. They aren't going to be able to come tonight. They had to leave all of a sudden—something about the pipes at Michael's mom's house bursting, and they needed to go save the furniture and there's shitty cell phone service where she lives. They all went. I guess Ryan's flight to Chicago got canceled by the storm too," she groused.

"Well, shit." Grace didn't even try to hide her disappointment when she realized it would be almost a week until she saw Michael again. "Merry frickin' Christmas to us," Grace growled as she raised the glass of wine she had been drinking to Bianca, then rolled her eyes. Bianca shrugged her shoulders and sulked out of the room.

❧

Grace's alarm blared at eight a.m. and she was in no mood to listen to it. Michael didn't call the night before, the first time in weeks. She knew he was up to his eyeballs in a disaster at his mom's, but she couldn't help but be bummed. She checked the phone as she sat up in bed just to make sure she hadn't missed anything, but there were still no new messages.

She threw the covers off and headed out to the kitchen for some coffee and to wake up the other two. Bianca was already awake, lying on the couch and looking like hell. She had the thermometer in her mouth and a bucket next to her on the floor. Wadded up Kleenex were scattered on the floor at her feet.

"What the hell happened to you? You look like shit," Grace exclaimed as she put her hand on Bianca's blazing forehead.

"I love you too, Grace," she mumbled with the thermometer in her mouth. Meg stumbled out of her room and looked at Bianca's pitiful form on the couch.

"Good morning, Typhoid Mary," Meg said as she sat down on the couch at Bianca's feet.

"Such sympathy from my friends. It really is touching," Bianca said sarcastically as she held out the thermometer, which read 102 degrees.

"What are we going to do? We can't leave you here sick. We better wait and leave tomorrow. I'll call my mom and tell her we'll be a day late." Grace started walking toward the phone when Bianca stopped her.

"Grace, don't do that. I probably have what you had last week and that lasted three days. You guys can't stay here until I'm better; you'll miss everything. Just go, I'll be fine. I'm going to be sleeping the whole time anyway. That's what you did."

"But we can't leave you here alone. What if you get really sick?" Meg pleaded with her.

"Grace, Amanda's staying in town right? Can't I just call her if I need anything?" Bianca insisted. "Listen, I'm not going to ruin Christmas for all of us. Go to Spokane. Let Susan try and trap you under the mistletoe with the pimply, bad breathed, neighborhood boys and then come home and we'll celebrate Christmas again with the hot, sexy men that really matter. *That* would make me happy," Bianca said as she clutched the bucket as a precaution.

"I don't know about this, Bianca…" Grace was already beginning to feel guilty.

"I insist," Bianca said firmly.

As Grace looked at Meg for some help, she shrugged her shoulders and headed to her room to shower.

"If you're sure, Bianca, but we'll be calling constantly to check on you," Grace said as she gave her a small hug. She ran into her room to finish packing, and then made a quick trip to the grocery store to buy every kind of food known to man to help with the flu.

"What did you do?" Bianca asked in a groggy voice as she walked into the kitchen from her room, rubbing her eyes.

"I got some ginger ale, soup, pudding, bread for toast, hot chocolate, tea, and a ton of cold medicines that might help." Grace lined everything up on the counter for her to see.

Bianca just shook her head and smiled. "I'll be fine, Grace. I'm a grown woman. Love you guys. I'm going back to bed. Drive safely and call me when you guys get in." She gave a wave and shuffled back into her room. Meg came over and dropped her bag on the floor by the front door.

"Let's get this show on the road, Grace. Don't worry, she'll be fine. Amanda is going to come by and check on her tomorrow." They grabbed their bags and the pile of gifts, and headed out the door for Spokane.

Chapter 15

The drive through the mountains to Spokane was enjoyable with Meg in the car to help pass the time. They called Bianca once from the road to see if she was feeling any better. Their loving concern was met with a string of profanities for waking her up from a nap. The four and a half hour trip flew by, and soon Grace was pulling into a familiar, snow covered driveway.

Her parents' home sat in a small clearing that was surrounded on three sides by tall, mature pine trees that towered over the house. The two story house was white with black shutters, and as always, the yard was littered with thousands of Christmas lights. There was a sleigh, four reindeer, a giant inflated snowman and at least a dozen candy canes scattered across the lawn. Grace knew that in the evening, the driveway alone was so well lit that a commercial airliner could mistake it for and airport runway from the sky.

"Boy, you weren't kidding when you said your mom had a thing for Christmas, were you, Grace?" Meg gazed in awe out the car window to take in the crazed winter wonderland before her.

"My mom loves Christmas I think more than I ever did, even as a kid." Grace laughed as she turned off the car. Meg climbed out, and before she could shut the door, they heard Susan screeching from the front porch.

"Girls! You made it. Henry, get their bags." Seconds later, Grace's poor father came flying out the door with only his slippers on his feet to brave the snow and claim their bags, rather than face Susan's wrath.

"Can you tell she's a bit excited you girls are here and hopes to have you both engaged by Wednesday at the latest? Good luck." Henry kissed Grace on the head and pulled her into a hug. "You may want to remind her that you 'don't like boys' for a few more days."

"What did she do now?" Grace's eyes went wide with fear.

"I'm not at liberty to say." Henry shrugged his shoulders and dug his hands deeply into his pockets.

"Thanks a lot, Dad," she said sourly as she headed up the front walk. Meg was hot on her heels, giggling. "You won't think this is funny for long. Hi, Mom," Grace said as Susan crashed into her before she even made it up onto the front porch.

"My baby, my baby! I'm so glad you're here. We're going to have the most wonderful Christmas ever!" Susan hugged Grace like she hadn't seen her in years, even though she'd been home a month ago for Thanksgiving. "Meg!" Susan squeaked when she looked over Grace's shoulder to see the blond shivering as she waited to be let into the house.

Susan released her death grip on Grace and clung to Meg like she was a long lost daughter. "I'm so happy your flight was canceled. I mean, I'm sorry you can't see your family, but now we get to spend the holiday together. The more the merrier." She smiled and kissed Meg on the cheek.

Henry came up behind them, huffing from all the suitcases. "Ladies, are you here for a visit or are you planning on moving in?" He laughed as he balanced the bags in his arms and struggled his way through the door.

"I'll help you," Meg offered as she squirmed her way out of Susan's arms and grabbed the nearest suitcase.

"You girls go get settled. I had the guest room set up for Bianca, but now Meg can use it. Is there any chance Bianca might make it up?" Susan asked hopefully. Nothing made her happier than a house full of people.

"I don't know; we'll see how she's feeling in the morning," Grace said as she headed up the stairs behind Meg and Henry. "But if it's what I had last week, she'll be out of commission for a few days, so don't get your hopes up, Mom."

Henry led Meg down the long hallway of the second floor. Grace's room was at the end of the hall on the left. The guest room was just before it, so Henry stopped there first to drop off Meg's mountain of suitcases. Grace stuck her head into the room, grabbed her two small totes, and took them the one doorway further.

Her room was the same as it had been for the last ten years. The walls were a powder blue with navy curtains and bedspread. She laughed, remembering the fight she'd had years ago because her mother had thought it looked too much like a boy's room when Grace told her the colors she wanted to use. Grace laid the bags on top of her bed and tossed her overnight bag into the bathroom. Then she headed to the guest room to check on Meg.

The guest room was Susan's dream room. The walls were a pale pink and the curtains and bedding were green with subtle hints of pink. This was the way she thought Grace should have decorated her room, but since the color pink caused Grace to break out in hives, she conceded to letting the guest room be the 'girl' room she'd wanted. Meg, however, couldn't stop complimenting Susan on the decor of the room.

They quickly unpacked Meg's main suitcase. Grace found fresh towels for her bathroom and grabbed an extra pillow out of the hall closet to make sure Meg had everything she needed. As she put the last sweater into the dresser, Grace waved her over to the bed.

"What's up?" she asked as she lay down next to Grace, her chin in her hands.

"Before we go downstairs, we need to prepare," Grace said seriously.

"Prepare for what?" Her tone had confused and scared Meg.

"Susan. More specifically, the Spanish Inquisition she is about to put us through. We need to get our stories straight," Grace said as she pointed back and forth between the two of them.

Meg threw back her head and laughed. "Oh, Grace. Don't be silly."

"Listen, you need to trust me on this. We're still on our boycott of boys, understand? Let her think we are exploring our feminine options for the next few days. If not, then she's going to try and play matchmaker, and trust me when I tell you, she is the worst matchmaker in recorded history! She is the anti-cupid." Grace pulled a picture from her pocket and thrust it at Meg.

"What is this? Is this you? And who is that you are sitting next to? Is he wearing a … bib?" Meg asked, her eyes wide in disbelief

"Yes, that's me from Christmas last year. The guy's name is Arnold Fitzer and my mother thought we would make the 'cutest couple,'" Grace said, complete with air quotes. "I had to spend the entire evening with Bib Boy and hear all about his harmonica collection." Meg actually snorted, she was laughing so hard. "If you're lucky, he may stop over. I know Susan is still friends with his mom. Maybe she'll let you have a shot at him." Meg looked up in horror, but Grace kept rambling.

"I think the braces should be off by now, and I believe he went to speech therapy for the lisp." Meg let out a small scream as her hand flew to her mouth.

"So why don't we tell her about Michael and Ryan so she stops playing matchmaker?" Meg asked quickly, finally understanding Grace's need to deceive Susan and avoid her matchmaking at all costs.

"Do you really want to play twenty questions about Ryan only in the end to have Susan tell you she doesn't think he's good enough for you, and that she can find you a better guy right here in Spokane?" Grace held up the picture of Bib Boy again to remind her of the horrors that could await her at the hands of Grace's matchmaking mother. "Because that's what she has done every time I've tried telling her I have a boyfriend. We do not mention the names Michael, Ryan, or Jack while we're talking to her, deal?" Grace held out her pinkie to Meg with a serious look on her face. Meg glanced at the picture one more time before wrapping her pinkie tightly around Grace's.

"Deal," she said quietly. "I'm ripping down every piece of mistletoe in this house, too. There's no way I'm kissing him or any of his toadfish friends while I'm here." Meg climbed off the bed and headed out the door with Grace right behind her.

Susan was down in the kitchen, making sandwiches. "Hey, girls, sit down at the table and I'll fix you something to eat." She slid a turkey sandwich in front of each of them, along with a glass of soda, and sat down at the table with them, grinning from ear to ear.

"So, how's your silly boycott going?" she asked as she popped a potato chip into her mouth.

"Fine," Grace mumbled giving a quick glance to Meg who was concentrating very hard on her glass of soda to avoid Susan's stare.

"I, um, talked to Mrs. Sullivan yesterday," Susan said, trying to sound casual, but Grace knew she had some bomb she was getting ready to drop, "and she said when Liam came home the other day, he mentioned that he ran into you in Portland."

Crap! Stupid Liam! How much did he tell her? Did he mention Michael? I wonder if he told his mommy about rubbing his penis on my leg!

"Oh?" Grace wisely kept her answers brief until she found out how much Susan already knew. Meg watched silently as Grace tried to outmaneuver her mother. Locked in a stalemate of sorts, Susan sighed, fully aware that Grace was withholding information from her.

"Yes, he said he met you at a bar, and that you were with your two girl-friends." She threw out her first bit of information.

OK, no big deal. Meg and I can corroborate the story.

"Oh, yeah. Meg, you remember Liam, don't you?" Grace asked with a smirk on her face. Meg bit her lip to keep from laughing.

"Yes, he was quite a dancer, as I recall."

Grace casually looked back across the table to Susan for her next question.

"Funny you should mention dancing, Meg, because he also said that while he was dancing with Grace, some guy threw her over his shoulder and dragged her off the dance floor. Apparently he also threatened Liam if he ever looked at Grace again. Do you remember that part, too?" Susan asked in an overly sweet voice, her motherly eyes staring into Grace's soul, waiting for the slightest sign of weakness. Grace felt Meg give her a small kick under the table to snap her out of it.

"Oh that, yeah! That was funny. Meg, remember when 'M' did that? It was all a joke. I'm sorry if Liam thought he was serious. He was just messing around." Grace started laughing and gave Meg a nudge with her elbow to signal her to join in.

"Oh, that was too funny. Gosh, Liam thought he was serious?" Meg giggled for a second and then took a large gulp of soda.

"M? Who is this M character? Is he someone you're seeing?" Susan asked hopefully.

"No, mom, remember? We're a 'No Man Zone'—it's girls only for another week and a half. M is just a friend of mine. And for your information, he's not sleeping with girls anytime soon!" Grace blurted out, taking the elaborate lie to a whole new level. Meg started coughing, apparently choking on a piece of ice.

"He's gay?" Susan asked as more of statement that question.

You mean cheerful and merry? Yes, he's gay, Mom…

"Absolutely. He's helping us… explore all our dating options. Because of him, we met Vicki and her partner. Vicki's great, Mom, she has fourteen piercings all over her body," Grace revealed, still not knowing how she was keeping a straight face, especially as Susan's eyes began to bug out of her head.

"Actually, Grace, she has eighteen, but you can only *see* twelve," Meg added a wink to make sure Susan got a good idea of where the others might be located. Her comment added some support to their carefully built lie. "And she wears the coolest leather biker boots too."

"Oh." Susan scowled, mulling over the line of crap they'd just given her. "Well, did you give Liam the number to that pizza place by accident or on purpose?" she countered, already sensing the answer.

"Mom, he was … it was … I'm not …" Grace stammered, flabbergasted that Liam ran home and told his mother that bit of info.

What a baby.

"Mom, the guy looked like someone being electrocuted on the dance floor. He was vibrating all over the place, and I think his mom may want to get his hearing checked because I don't think he ever came close to dancing on the beat. If it's not his hearing, then he must be having seizures. Either way, he needs medical attention."

Meg finally exploded with giggles. "If Grace ended up with him as a husband, Susan, your grandchildren would be … well, I'm sorry to say, dorks."

Grace completely lost her composure and burst out laughing when she saw Susan's face as Meg called her future grandchildren dorks. Her mother's mouth was hanging open and her eyes were huge. As she looked back and forth between the two of them a light bulb suddenly went off in her head. Susan's jaw snapped shut and a wide smile spread across her face as she leaned over the table.

"And what kind of grandchildren would I have if Grace married this guy named M?"

Damn my observant mother. Grace glanced over at Meg, who looked like she'd just seen a ghost. Grace gave her friend's chair a kick to wake her from her stupor.

"Wh- what did you say?" Meg asked, still baffled about how to respond. Susan was smiling broadly now, feeling Meg was about to crack.

"I said, dear, what kind of grandchildren would I have if Grace married M?"

"I never really thought about it before. I guess … tall?" Meg replied innocently as she batted her eyelashes. It was such a perfectly generic answer that it threw Susan off the scent of a relationship completely.

"Well, I guess tall is better than dorky. This could get awkward when Dad and I go to the Sullivan's tomorrow." Susan cleared the plates from the table, lightly laughing.

The rest of the evening was spent putting the remaining decorations up throughout the house. There were lights to wrap around the banisters and popcorn garlands to be made. Henry and Grace worked on setting up the train under the tree while Meg and Susan finished boxing up the last batch of Christmas cookies. By eleven o'clock, Henry and Susan were watching the news, and Meg and Grace were exhausted so they decided to go to bed. Grace said a quick good night to Meg in the hall and headed to her room.

In the pitch black bedroom, she noticed that her cell phone was on the nightstand, blinking. She threw on the light and quickly snatched it up. There were two missed calls and one new message. When she saw who the message was from, her heart dropped knowing she'd missed Michael's call. She quickly found the message he left.

Grace,

I'm sorry for dashing out on you yesterday and not calling. My mom's house is a disaster and we have been dragging boxes and trying to fix pipes since we got here. I miss you, I miss talking to you. And right now, I hate all indoor plumbing. I'll try and call you tomorrow if my phone cooperates.

Good night, sweetheart.

Michael

Grace had just finished reading it for the second time when she heard a tap on the door. "Come in," she said absently, still upset she had missed his call. Meg's head poked through the doorway.

"Did you get one too?" she asked with a small pout, as she held out the phone in her hand. Grace nodded her head in sad agreement.

"Did you call Bianca?" Grace asked.

"Yeah, she still sounds terrible. Amanda will check on her in the morning. Don't worry," Meg said with a wave as she headed back out the door. "See you in the morning."

"Good night."

Once she was gone, Grace opened the phone and read his message one more time and then sent a quick note back.

Michael

Sorry about the pipes. I hope everything is OK at your mom's. My parents' house is the usual torture.

I miss you too—a lot. I'll keep my phone on me tomorrow, just in case.

Good night.

Grace

"I love you," she whispered to the screen before she hit the 'send' button. Grace laid the phone back on the nightstand beside her bed. As her head hit the pillow, she hoped somehow tomorrow she would get to hear Michael's voice. Grace lay in bed and listened to the hum as the furnace turned on for a few minutes before she fell fast asleep.

⌒)

Grace awoke to the rich smell of coffee and the clanking of dishes downstairs. She glanced at the clock and was surprised to see it was already after ten. She hopped out of bed, snatched her phone, and ran next door to Meg's room to see if she was still asleep. Grace tapped on the door and opened it only to find her friend still curled up in a ball under the thick green comforter.

"Good morning," Grace said softly as she sat down on the bed, rubbing Meg's back to help wake her up.

"Ryan?" Meg murmured as she started to wake up. Grace laughed.

"Sorry, it's just Grace."

Meg's eyes opened and she rolled over and stretched. "Damn, I was hoping…" she laughed as she climbed out of bed. "Good morning. Bless Susan for letting us sleep in today."

"I'm going to shower, but I was hoping I could ask for a favor." Grace smiled as she bounced on the edge of the bed.

"Sure, what do you need?" Meg asked with a smirk.

"Would you babysit my phone, and if he calls, come get me?" Grace asked in a super sweet voice, all the while blushing, because she couldn't believe she was asking her to do that.

"Of course. As long as you return the favor when you're done showering," Meg said with a laugh and a hug. "We're quite a pair."

Unfortunately, Grace and Meg showered and the only call either of them got was from Amanda who reported Bianca looked a bit better and that she got her to eat some toast and orange juice before she left the apartment. When they were showered and dressed, with their phones safely tucked into their pockets, they bounded downstairs together, finding Henry in the kitchen having a cup of coffee and reading the newspaper.

"Here they are. Good…morning, ladies," Henry said with a glance to his watch to make sure he could still say morning.

"Good morning," they said in unison as they headed to the coffee and crumb cake that was sitting on the counter.

"So, where's Mom?" Grace asked as she joined Henry at the table, Meg sat down beside her.

"She's out running an errand. Dropping towels off or something," Henry said absently as he buried his nose deeper into the sports page.

Grace and Meg ate their breakfast and were half way through the crossword puzzle from the paper when Susan came home, her arms full of groceries. "Girls, girls, girls," she said with a smile as she set the bags on the counter.

Uh-oh, she ran into someone at the grocery store.

"You'll never guess who I saw today," she started as she began putting the groceries away.

Henry shook his head knowingly and whispered "It starts…" before heading out to the family room.

"Well, actually, you'll never guess, but that's beside the point. Wait until you see who's coming over later. And you owe me! I found you some men." The joy in her voice terrified both of the girls. Meg grabbed Grace's hand as visions of Bib Boy danced in her head. *If only she knew about all the other ones. She would be running and screaming down the street,* Grace thought to herself as she lowered her head and readied herself for the fight that was about to start.

"Mom, we aren't interested in being set up right now," Grace said through her clenched teeth.

"Oh, come on, Grace! They're cute with a capital C," she said, grinning. "You just might change your mind about this silly boycott thing."

"No, Mom, no set ups. Do you understand me? Or I will do something drastic!" Grace glared at Susan as she slouched against the counter, sensing defeat. She knew Susan remembered vividly the year she'd invited the boy who was named the state Math Olympics champion in the hopes of getting Grace her first kiss. In protest to the set up, Grace had dyed her hair blue and scared him and everyone else away. Grace glanced over at Susan defiantly and looped her arm in Meg's, and in a show of feminine affection, bent to rest her head on Meg's shoulder like they were a happy couple and sighed blissfully. Susan's eyes narrowed but then she threw in the towel, knowing her stubborn daughter wouldn't back down.

"Fine, be alone for the rest of your life, Grace. I'm just trying to help you find love," she snarled as she stormed from the kitchen.

"Already found it, Mom," Grace whispered to Meg who was laughing with her head down on the table.

The rest of the afternoon, they avoided Susan, who was still fuming. Grace took Meg on a tour of Spokane. Then Meg wanted to get a gift for Grace's parents to thank them for letting her stay with them for the holiday, so they did some quick shopping. A few hours later they returned home, grumpy, not having heard from either Michael or Ryan all day. When they walked in the door, they found Susan in the dining room, tangled up in a wad of red ribbon, cursing.

"Mom? Need some help?" Grace asked with a laugh as she started untangling her mother's arm.

"Grace, Meg, you're back. Oh, thank goodness. I have all these things left to wrap for my friends and you know how bad I am with tape, and people are coming over tonight." Susan looked helplessly at Grace and held out the scissors and gift wrap.

"Just leave it to us; we can wrap them for you!" Meg offered happily. She was anxious to get back into Susan's good graces after the showdown earlier.

"Thanks, girls. I need this one done first, if you don't mind." She threw a green sweater at Meg's head and ran out of the room. Grace shrugged her shoulders and they dug into the pile of gifts, wrapping like department store professionals. They had an elaborate system worked out. Grace was the paper person while Meg was the ribbon decorator and label master. In a matter of twenty minutes, they had finished the large pile Susan placed before them, plus a few extras she threw in along the way.

"All done, Mom!" Grace shouted into the kitchen where her mother was frantically making something to eat.

"You girls are lifesavers! Thank you," she yelled from the other room as dishes clanked. "Go relax. I've got everything under control." Of course the sounds coming from the kitchen sounded like they were anything but in control.

"I'm going to go upstairs and try to call Ryan," Meg said as Grace made herself comfortable on the family room couch.

"Go ahead. I'm just going to plant myself here and listen to some music until we have to hide from her guests." Grace laughed as Meg headed up the stairs. She lay down on the couch and turned on the stereo. Her eyes closed and she found herself wondering about Michael, what he was doing and whether or not he missed her. She imagined how it would feel to be in his arms or to hear his voice. The smell of his pillow filled her memory as she imagined how it would be to kiss his incredibly warm lips again. Grace even debated sending him a text message, but thought it might be a bit too desperate, as Meg would put it.

If she gets hold if Ryan, then I'll try and call him, Grace thought, a dull ache in her chest from missing Michael. She took her phone out of her pocket for the tenth time and checked for a message, only to find she didn't even have a signal. Susan flitted into the room and started placing small bowls of snacks on the end table, a sure sign someone was arriving soon.

"So, who's coming now, Mom?" Grace asked. Of course her real question was "Who's coming and how quickly do I need to find a place to hide?"

"A friend of mine. She's a sweetheart, and she's bringing—" But her mother never got to finish because the doorbell rang and she immediately rushed over to the door. Grace could hear her laughing as she greeted her guest in the foyer. The music from the stereo made Grace miss out on most of the conversation, but she could hear other voices now.

Great, a group of people I need to hide from, Grace thought as she sat up on the couch and ran her fingers through her hair to make herself slightly more presentable. She heard the voices growing louder as they approached.

"I hope you called the Realtor and told her about all the trouble you're having, Liz," Susan said sternly.

"Don't worry. We've been on the phone all weekend with her and a number of handymen. These guys saved me, I have to say." Grace heard a female voice grow louder as heels clicked on the wood floor.

"Come in, please. Just set your coats down. I want you to all to meet my daughter. She's home for the holiday." Susan and a beautiful woman with chocolate brown hair stepped into the room, arm in arm. "Liz, this is my daughter Grace. Grace, this is my dear friend Liz."

Grace gave an awkward wave from her place on the couch. "Hello, nice to meet you." Grace smiled and couldn't help but notice her mother was beaming. *I've never met her before,* Grace thought to herself as she watched Liz and Susan put their heads together and whisper back and forth. Susan threw back her head and laughed.

"No, sorry, Liz. I forgot to mention, my daughter here is apparently trying her hand at being a lesbian," Susan said as she nodded her head skeptically in her daughter's direction. Grace's face turned bright red at Susan's comment. Liz however raised an eyebrow in surprise and smiled as she turned and reached her arm behind her.

"Well, then, she just *has* to meet my newly gay son. Come here, Michael," Liz hissed as she pulled a handful of a gray shirt through the doorway, and a very embarrassed Michael stumbled into the family room, his eyes glued down on his shoes.

Grace was certain she was hallucinating. He couldn't be here, in her living room. He was a figment of her very active and very desperate imagination. She was losing it. Grace slowly stood up, but the hallucination didn't move or look up at her from his position in the doorway, instead he fidgeted nervously in front of her.

"Michael?" she said softly in disbelief, still unsure if he was real.

His head shot up at the sound of her voice, and his look of embarrassment turned to complete joy in a fraction of a second. "Grace?" he said in astonishment, his blue eyes dancing.

Grace didn't remember making the decision to do it, but the next thing she knew, she was on her feet and catapulting herself into Michael's arms. Her arms flew around his neck, and he stumbled back slightly from the force with which she crashed into him. Grace felt his arms wrap tightly around her as her feet left the floor and he swung her around.

She felt her feet slowly touch the ground, and only then did she look up into his gorgeous face. He looked just as astounded and confused as Grace felt.

"What are you doing here?" they said at the same time.

A voice from the doorway said suspiciously, "I take it you two know each other?"

Shit! Susan! God, how am I going to pull this one off?

She hid behind Michael's chest and said very softly, "Please go along with whatever I say. She will drive us crazy for the next few days otherwise." He smiled and winked, letting Grace know he would follow her lead. She moved around him to face their smirking mothers.

"Sure, we know each other. Mom, this is my friend 'M' I was telling you about earlier," Grace said casually pointing her thumb in his direction. Michael raised his hand and waved, grinning.

"And where did you two meet?" Liz asked, staring intently at her son now.

"Um, at the bar," Michael fumbled, not knowing what Grace had told Susan already. Behind Susan, Grace saw a tall blond figure in the doorway.

"Ryan?"

He poked his head into the room, his hair slicked back into a ponytail, and smiled. Grace couldn't contain her excitement.

"Go upstairs, first door on the left." She pointed behind him to the stairs so he could go surprise Meg. He saluted, then turned on his heel and Grace heard his heavy footsteps as he made his way up the stairs. Susan and Liz just looked at each other in confusion.

"Ryan and Meg know each other too," Grace said, trying to make it sound like no big deal. Of course the scream and crashing noise from upstairs made that a tad bit more difficult. Michael chuckled softly next to her.

"You have no idea who we're dealing with here!" Grace hissed through her clenched teeth.

"I think I do. Our mothers seem very much alike, don't you think?" he muttered, barely moving his lips.

"Shit, we're so screwed," Grace whispered, shaking her head. Susan and Liz continued to examine them as they stood nervously side by side in the family room.

Grace didn't dare glance over at Michael while facing her mother or it would be all over; she would know without a doubt that Grace was completely in love with him. She had always been able to read Grace like a book, and since she hadn't been able to tell Michael how she felt yet, she didn't want her mother spilling the beans.

From what Michael had said, his mom was going to be just as difficult to fool. Their mothers whispered something between them, and then announced they were going to the kitchen.

"Well, you two kids chat. I'm going to get Liz some coffee and a bite to eat." Grace could hear them talking and laughing as they walked away. "Is Mike coming over too?" Susan asked and Grace heard Liz mention something about a malfunctioning water pump as their voices drifted out of earshot. Grace waited one more second before turning to Michael just to make sure they were, in fact, gone.

Before she could look at him, she felt Michael's arms clasp around her waist, and Grace found herself being pulled tightly against his chest. "Hello, beautiful," he murmured into her ear as he kissed the side of her face. Grace felt her heart pounding in her chest.

"Hello there. How in the world are you here with me now?" she asked as she ran her hands up and down his back, still not completely believing he was standing in front of her.

"I'm not sure myself. The pipes burst at my parents' new house, so we came up here to help my mom move all the stuff out of the basement because it was filling up with water. My dad did what he could; but for the past two days, we've been moving furniture, boxes, and learning all there is to know about plumbing, pipes, and water heaters—and swearing a lot." He laughed.

"But I thought you said you grew up in Salt Lake City?" Grace laced her fingers in his and held on tightly to his hand.

"I did, but just before Thanksgiving, she and my dad announced they were moving to a small town just outside of Spokane. My dad got a job offer and mom was all excited because she was going to get to live near an old friend of hers. I guess that's where your mom comes in," he said as he smiled down at Grace and brushed the hair out of her face.

Grace was so happy she couldn't contain it anymore. Once again, she wrapped her arms around his neck and found herself nearly strangling him. "I missed you so much! And now, we get to spent Christmas together," she squealed. Releasing his neck, she slid down his chest, grabbed his hands and started pulling him toward the kitchen. "Come here."

Cautiously, she poked her head into the kitchen where Susan and Liz were having a glass of eggnog and a bite to eat. They didn't stop their conversation while Grace hid in the doorway with Michael.

"Mom, Michael and I will be upstairs if you need us." Grace turned to walk out, but Susan caught her.

"Grace, do you think that it's appropriate for you to have a young man up in your room … alone?" she said, giggling. Liz was doing her best to contain her laughter as well.

"Get a grip, Mom. Michael and I are *friends*. Got it?"

Susan just continued to smirk. "Whatever you say, Grace." Susan rolled her eyes as Grace stormed out of the room.

Hand in hand, Grace and Michael went upstairs. She was going to stop in Meg's room first, but instead, she pulled Michael to the end of the hall and into her room where they could be alone.

As Grace gently closed the door behind them, she felt herself being pushed back against it and Michael's lips were all over her neck and ear. She heard him murmur 'loophole' in between kisses. Trying to stay upright as her heart raced in her chest, she held on to the sides of Michael's shirt as his kisses trailed up and down her neck and finally stopped on her lips.

Until their lips touched, she didn't realize exactly know much she had missed him. Grace felt every part of her body react to his touch, aching to be closer to him. His chest crashed into hers, causing the door to bang slightly behind her back. Much too soon, Michael pulled away from her lips, leaving her breathless and weak-kneed.

"I told you I missed you. You're just lucky I controlled myself in front of our mothers." He laughed as he pulled Grace away from the door.

"Susan would have loved to have seen that," Grace replied, still trying to clear her head.

He released her hand and turned to inspect her bedroom. Immediately, he walked over to the pictures that were sitting in frames on the dresser. He picked up each one and examined them, occasionally asking Grace questions, like when it was taken or how old she was in the picture.

Grace sat down on her bed, her legs crossed as she sat back and watched the man she loved wander through her room, looking at all of her childhood treasures. When he came across her prom picture, he let out a chuckle.

"Who's the stiff?" he asked, pointing to her date, who wasn't exactly smiling in the picture. As she recalled, he was trying to look tough.

"His name was Bill and he was on the chess team." Grace mumbled the last part into her sleeve.

Michael grinned and took a few steps closer. "He was on the what?" His eyes were twinkling as he moved closer to her.

Grace playfully clamped her hands over her mouth to show she had no intention of repeating what she'd just admitted. He jumped on her and started tickling Grace's sides. She began to thrash around under him on the bed, laughing hysterically.

When she could take his torture no longer, she gasped, "Chess team. The guy was on the chess team, OK?" Michael froze above her and started laughing until he had tears in his eyes. She gave him a smack on the arm and pushed him off the bed, causing him to land on the floor with a loud thud. A minute later there was a knock on the bedroom door.

"What are you two up to in here? Did I win some shoes?" Meg sang as she pushed the door open, Ryan at her side.

Michael was still on the floor laughing, holding the prom picture up to them and managing to choke out "Guy...chess club...dork." Meg took the picture from his hand and after examining it herself, she and Ryan joined Michael in laughter.

"If you guys are done mocking my childhood memories, I'm going down-stairs to watch a movie," Grace said with her hands planted firmly on her hips. She started to storm towards the door when Michael threw himself in front of it, blocking her escape. "Move, Michael."

"I'm sorry I laughed at your dork—I mean date," he said with the cutest, dimpled grin on his face. When he smiled at Grace like that, she couldn't stay mad at him. All she could think about was kissing him, so she did.

"Wait!" Grace ripped her lips away from his, a light bulb suddenly going off in her head. "Where the heck is Jack?" Grace and Meg looked at each other, their eyes huge as they both had the same thought.

"We got a call this morning from The Vault that they needed someone to come in last minute and cover the holiday. Derek broke his leg, apparently. We drew straws and Jack lost. He just left for Portland a few hours ago. I doubt he's even home yet, why?" Ryan asked, still confused by the incredulous looks Grace and Meg were exchanging.

"It's probably nothing, but Bianca is home sick, and alone," Meg said suspiciously. "Maybe we'll have Amanda make a surprise visit over to the house tomorrow." Grace nodded in agreement and actually found herself a little excited. If someone was knocked out now, maybe *no one* would last until New Year's.

Looking for something to do, they all decided to watch a movie while Liz and Susan continued their visit. Downstairs, Grace and Michael lay across one of the L-shaped couches and Ryan and Meg took the other. Grace threatened to make everyone suffer through *The Sound of Music* if they didn't stop bringing up her prom date. Eventually they backed off so she let Ryan and Michael pick the movie. Grace set up the television while Meg braved going into the kitchen and facing the gossiping Susan and Liz. As the opening credits of the movie started, she came back into the room with two huge bowls of popcorn and Ryan trailing behind her, laughing.

"How bad was it?" Grace fearfully peeked up from the safety of Michael's arms.

"They're on to you, my friends. You better watch out." Ryan laughed as he handed a bowl of popcorn to them, then grabbed Meg, pulling her onto the other couch.

Grace nervously glanced at Michael. "Do you think you could kiss Ryan or something to throw them off the trail? Maybe you two should sit together on the couch and snuggle—that might help too," she offered in a near panic as she started to stand up, but Michael didn't let her get very far.

"I'm *not* lying on this couch with anyone other than you, and I'm most definitely not kissing anyone other than you," he said as he laid back and pulled her against his chest.

"That's getting pretty close to a rule violation over there." Meg glanced from the adjoining couch and scowled.

"Stupid rules," Michael groused as he turned onto his side, holding Grace in front of him. She gave him a kiss then turned over so she was facing the TV, her back pressed tightly against his chest. He grabbed the blanket from behind the couch and tossed it over them, earning another dirty look from Meg.

"What?" he asked innocently as he laid back down, pulling the blanket up to Grace's shoulders.

"If I see that blanket moving in the wrong places, you two are in trouble. You may want to keep your hands visible, just to be safe," she advised, glaring at Michael.

He rolled his eyes at her. "Just watch the movie, Meg. Just watch the movie."

Meg huffed and laid her head against Ryan's chest as they snacked on the huge bowl of popcorn in front of them. Grace set their bowl on the ground since there was nowhere to put it with them snuggled up on the couch.

Susan and Liz, not so subtly, cruised through the room just after the movie started. The smiles on their faces were gigantic when they found Grace and Michael in each other's arms. They didn't dare say a word and Grace kept her eyes locked on the television, trying to ignore them. On their way out of the room, they turned off the lights, probably trying to make it dark and more romantic, knowing them.

Grace was watching James Bond flirt with some scantily clad woman when she felt Michael's hand, which was under the blanket, stealthily playing with the bottom of her shirt. He lifted her shirt up slightly and started slowly running his fingers across the exposed section of her stomach. She wasn't sure if he was trying to drive her crazy with the leisurely pace of his movements or if it was to make sure his activities would go undetected by their watchdog, Meg. Whatever the reason, Grace gave him a little nudge with her foot to try and get him to stop, because her resistance was beginning to crumble. Of course, it had the opposite effect.

The next thing Grace knew, Michael reached up and brushed her hair back behind her ear, saying something about it being in his face, loud enough for Meg to hear. With the side of Grace's neck fully exposed, she felt his warm breath flowing across her skin. Every breath he took, every time he exhaled, caused a delicious tickle from the nape of her neck to her ear, causing her entire body to come alive.

Again, she tried to nudge him with her foot, but he whispered "What?" sweetly in her ear. "I'm not doing anything."

Grace tried to pay attention to the movie and the constant barrage of objects that were being blown up on the screen, but all she could think about was Michael lying behind her and the feel of his hard body pressed against hers.

A while later, he began round two of his playful assault. This time he decided see how far he could hike her shirt up her stomach before she would panic and yank it back down. Grace tried to ignore him and see just how far he was willing to take this little game of his, but when she felt his fingers graze over her bra, Grace elbowed him in the gut. Instead of being apologetic, he shamelessly snickered behind her.

Fine, two can play this game.

He was easy to tease because he was a man, and Grace found she didn't have to do much to get him worked up. A little incidental contact in all the right places and he was done. Grace pretended to stretch, and as she did, she made sure to rub her hip and rear firmly across his groin. Immediately, Michael jumped, and sank as far back into the couch as possible. Grace looked over her shoulder and smiled at him.

"Sorry," Grace whispered, but he could tell from the look on her face that she was anything but sorry. He gave her a warning look, but she quickly shrugged it off and turned back to the movie. She waited another minute before she sat up, pretending the blanket had come off her feet. She innocently moved the blanket to cover their feet again but as she laid back down, Grace carefully tucked the blanket around Michael's legs, thighs and hip, causing her hands to come in close contact with his rear, giving it a little squeeze before laying back down, snuggling closer to him than ever.

Michael let out a playful growl when Grace laid her head back on the pillow they were sharing. She heard him murmur "Cheater" into her hair. Grace proudly smiled at her successful revenge.

As time passed, she could actually *feel* her plan working when she occasionally would shift her hips, causing more rubbing and contact with his now very stimulated groin.

"Grace," she heard him whisper. "Truce?" he whimpered as he pulled his hand out from under her shirt.

Grace moved her body a few inches away from him as a sign of her acceptance of his truce, allowing him room to breathe, settle himself, and avoid the constant contact with her ass which he was apparently enjoying way too much.

Thank goodness he caved, she thought as she closed her eyes in relief, trying not to think too much about the dangerous game they had started to play. *Shoes, Grace. Stupid, expensive shoes, Grace.*

Michael must have been thinking the same thing because he leaned forward and whispered softly, "How much are these shoes you want, anyway?"

Grace rolled onto her back and looked into his stunning baby blues and said, "You can buy shoes, but you can't buy eternal bragging rights, Michael." Then she gave him a kiss on the tip of his nose and went back to watching the movie.

"Bragging rights are overrated, if you ask me," he muttered softly, enveloping Grace in his arms again.

The movie dragged on, and when it finally ended, Ryan started the next one. Grace yawned and snuggled closer to Michael, the effects of her long day finally catching up with her. She could feel herself getting really sleepy, so she nestled in the comfort of Michael's arms, knowing she would be asleep in minutes.

Michael yawned as well and kissed her head. That was the last thing Grace remembered before she drifted off to sleep.

Chapter 16

Meg had fallen asleep on Ryan, but when she felt his chest shaking underneath her head, she immediately woke up. Before she could even open her eyes, Meg realized he was laughing at something. She pushed herself up off of his chest. "Ry?"

He looked down and kissed the top of her head. "Shh, sleepyhead. Don't wake them up. This is too funny," he whispered, pointing over to Michael and Grace, who were both sound asleep.

They looked adorable together, snuggled up tight under the blanket. Michael had his arm wrapped around Grace's waist and she had rolled onto her back, their faces only inches apart on the pillow, Grace's hand clutching the front of Michael's shirt. Meg was smiling at the sight of them together when then the talking started.

"Avocados ... I need three," Grace mumbled.

A few seconds later, Michael answered her. "I only have two."

Meg bit her lip to control her giggling while Ryan continued to shake with laughter.

"They've been doing this for a half hour. A few minutes ago, they were talking about pine cones. Just give them some time and they'll do it again," he said, pointing back in their direction.

"I know Grace talks in her sleep, but Michael too?" Meg said in amazement, waiting for the odd conversation to continue.

"Grace," Michael whispered.

"Hmmm. Michael," Grace responded to her name.

"They do that all the time." Ryan laughed.

"I need more socks," Michael moaned.

"OK, here," Grace replied.

Their silly conversations continued on and off for another ten minutes. Meg grabbed the camera so she could snap a picture of the two of them. As she lined up her shot, that's when she heard it.

"I love you, Michael," Grace said as clear as day.

Meg froze and looked at Ryan, who had a similar expression of shock on his face. They both held their breath and waited to hear Michael's response.

"I love you too, Grace," he said as pulled her tighter to him.

"Oh, Ry," Meg sighed. "Do you think they've told each other yet?"

Ryan laughed. "Not while they were awake."

Meg got up off the couch and snapped a picture of the two love birds, forever memorializing the moment when they first admitted their love to each other—even if it happened while they were asleep. The flash of the camera made them start to stir. Meg dashed back over to the couch with Ryan and gave him a kiss.

"I love you."

"I love you too, Meg. More than you know."

Vaguely aware of the noises around her, Grace opened one eye to find Michael's face right next to hers on the pillow. His arm was wrapped tightly around her while they stayed toasty warm under the blanket. Grace glanced over at Meg who gave her a strange smirk from across the room with Ryan. She looked back at Michael who was now beginning to wake up. She brushed his bangs out of his face, and kissed each eye lid.

"Wake up. All we need is our moms finding us sleeping together. They'll have the church picked out by morning," Grace teased.

His eyes opened and he smiled. "I'm comfy here; I'm not moving. Let them find us," he said as he nuzzled Grace's neck.

"Boys! We need to get going," Liz said loudly from the next room. Both Grace and Michael shot up off of the couch and stood next to each other, but with a safe distance between them as to not call too much attention to themselves.

Grace quickly ran her fingers through her hair before Liz and Susan turned the corner.

"How was the movie?" Susan asked, her eyes darting back and forth between the two of them, looking for any evidence of a romance between them.

"Good. I fell asleep for a bit." Grace yawned as she stretched.

"Well, you two did look rather ... comfortable there on the couch," Liz said, making the same face Michael made when he was being coy.

"Come on, Mom. We've bothered the Parks enough for one day. Let's go see how much damage Dad's done to the house by now." Michael laughed as he gently moved his mother toward the door before she could say anything more. He glanced back at Grace and mouthed "I'll call you" and gave her a wink that, of course, Susan noticed.

The door no sooner shut behind the three of them before Susan pounced. "Grace Park, you'd better start telling me what the heck is going on between you and Michael. And for the record, that man is most definitely not gay. He, he's ... I think, he's in ... lo—"

"Dad! Help." Grace screamed, interrupting her mother's comments that were getting way too accurate.

Henry came into the kitchen, joining Susan in the doorway, and before she could say another word, he planted a big kiss on her, complete with a dip and everything. Susan stood there stunned for a second by her husband's amorous behavior, until Henry pointed over her head at the mistletoe and grinned. She blushed and followed him into the other room, completely distracted from her previous chain of thought.

"I'm going to bed after all this excitement," Meg said as she danced up the stairs.

"I'll be right there. I'm going to clean up the family room." When Grace turned to grab the bowls of popcorn, she heard a soft knock on the door. "I got it," she called to Henry and Susan who were already on their way upstairs.

She peeked out the window and was surprised to find Michael standing on the porch. "Miss me already?" Grace teased as she opened the door. He stepped inside and closed it behind him.

"No, I forgot something," he said as he glanced in the other room.

"What?" Grace asked. She hadn't noticed his phone or anything lying around when she started her cleaning. She looked up at the grin on his face and waited for his answer.

"This," he whispered as he leaned over and took her face into his hands, placing a gentle kiss on her lips that caught her so off guard, it nearly made her knees buckle. "Good night, sweetheart," he whispered as he turned and walked back out the door, chuckling.

Grace stayed a second, frozen in the doorway, looking just as stunned as her mother had a moment ago. When she heard the horn honk as he drove away, it broke Grace from her trance. She waved and then slowly closed the door.

℘

The next morning, Grace woke up to find Meg already downstairs chatting away with Susan over some donuts. "Good morning," she grumbled as she reached for the coffee pot. "So what's the plan for today?" Grace paused and plucked a donut from the box, then took a bite.

"It's Christmas Eve, silly. There will be a houseful of people here tonight, you know that." Susan laughed. Christmas Eve meant Susan's annual Open House, also known as the longest evening of Grace's year. This was the night when the who's who of Spokane would parade through the house for some food and eggnog. Grace's old teachers, neighbors, people from high school, and basically, anyone she would hope to never cross paths with again would be sitting in her home, and she'd have to get them refreshments and make irritating, meaningless small talk.

"We have to go shopping," Meg gasped, breaking Grace out of her sulking. She was on her feet and quickly rinsing her dishes in the sink before Grace could even respond.

"Why in the world do we have to shop now?" Grace grumbled, snatching another donut out of the box before Meg put it back on the counter.

"Do you have a Christmas gift for *everyone* on your list?"

Grace began to check off the names in her head: Meg, Susan, Henry, Michael … Uh-oh. Michael's gift was sitting in the apartment back in Portland. "You're right. Mom, will you be OK without us for a bit? We'll go fast, I promise." Grace chugged her coffee and shoved the donut into her mouth as she ran up the stairs. They didn't waste time showering. Instead, they simply threw baseball hats on their heads and flew out the door.

Grace called Michael from the car, explaining that they had to run out and do some last minute shopping. It sounded like he and Ryan were doing the same thing. Not surprisingly, he informed Grace that they were invited back over to her parents house tonight and that Liz had offered to come early to 'help set up.' With a grin on her face, Grace told him they'd see him back at the house and, for the first time in years, she was actually looking forward to one of Susan's parties.

Two hours later, an exhausted Grace and Meg returned home with great gifts for Michael and Ryan. Meg, of course, went with a sentimental gift. Grace, however, went for a gift that she hoped would be useful and make him smile. They hurried upstairs to wrap their purchases and then showered so they would be ready to help Susan if she needed them. It was just before noon when the girls reappeared in the kitchen.

"Put us to work," Grace said, rolling up her sleeves. But Susan just laughed and waved them away. "I won't be needing you. I have some helpers of my own coming this year," she said with a grin. Right on cue, the doorbell rang.

Grace opened the door and squealed at the sight before her. "Aunt Evelyn, Uncle Frank!" She screamed as she rushed out onto the porch to hug them. "Come in!"

"Grace, you get more beautiful every time we see you," Aunt Evelyn said sweetly as Grace slid her coat off her shoulders and hung it in the closet. "You are absolutely glowing, child."

"Thank you," Grace said shyly, trying not to make eye contact with her aunt. Evelyn was even more observant than Susan, if that were possible. There would be no hiding the source of her glow once Michael arrived.

"How are things at the hospital, Uncle Frank?" Grace asked as he put his arm around her and together they walked inside to where Henry was hiding out in the family room.

"Same as always: busy." He grinned.

Grace wasn't blood related to Evelyn and Frank, but she still referred to them as her aunt and uncle because they were like family; she had known them since she was a little girl. Her parents met them at a charity fund raiser years ago and they'd become fast friends. Since then, they'd always spent the holidays with Grace's family if they were in town.

Frank was an ophthalmologist at one of the area hospitals and they were very well off. They lived in a huge house on ten acres, up in the mountains. They were very kind and two of the most breathtakingly beautiful people on the planet. Susan was always commenting on how they looked younger and younger every time she saw them, and Grace had to agree. It had been at least two years since she'd seen them, but they looked exactly the same.

Grace went back into the kitchen and found Evelyn and Susan up to their elbows in potatoes and peelers. "Aunt Evelyn, did you meet my roommate, Meg?"

"Very nice to meet you, dear. How are you enjoying Spokane so far?" Evelyn asked with a kind smile.

"I'm having a wonderful time but the mountains are wreaking havoc on my cell phone reception. Are you sure we can't help with something?" Meg asked as she looked at the pile of potatoes before the two older women, but both of them smiled and waved the girls off.

Meg took a seat at the counter and was telling Evelyn about some of the quirky clients she had designed for when the doorbell rang again. When Susan and Evelyn exchanged a knowing smirk, Grace knew who it was before she even opened the door.

"I'll get it…" she said loudly in her mother's direction. Grace took a deep breath and opened the door.

Liz and her husband, Michael Sr., were standing on the porch, with Michael and Ryan a few steps behind. "Hello, dear," Liz said as Grace opened the door. She gave Grace a tight hug as she walked through the door and right into the kitchen where she was welcomed by Susan's happy laughter.

Mr. Andris, Michael, and Ryan stepped inside, but they stayed in the foyer with Grace rather than bravely follow Liz when they heard the women chattering in the kitchen.

"May I take your coats?" Grace held her arms out, but both Michael and Mr. Andris shook their heads. Michael took his father's and Ryan's jackets and hung them in the closet himself.

"You must be the lovely Grace. I've heard so much about you. Actually my wife hasn't stopped talking about you … *and my son* since she came home last night," Mr. Andris said with a laugh. Grace's face turned bright red, just imagining what Liz might have said about her.

"Oh, goodness. Sorry, Mr. Andris. She and my mother, I think, misunderstood some things yesterday," Grace tried to explain as Michael watched her dying of embarrassment before his father.

"First of all, call me Michael. That should be easy for you to remember," he said with a sly glance at his son, who was beaming. Mr. Andris watched Michael stare at Grace for a moment. "Secondly, I don't think my wife and Susan were too far off." He gave Michael a fatherly pat on the back and strolled off to find Henry and Frank. Ryan headed into the kitchen where Grace could hear Meg introducing him to Evelyn.

While everyone else was occupied, Michael came over and swept Grace into his arms. "Hello, beautiful," he said in that silky voice that made her heart race.

"Hey, you," she replied as she laid her hand on his cheek. He had just bent down to place a small kiss on her lips when they heard a noise.

"Eh-hem!" came a voice from behind Grace. She jumped and landed as far away from Michael as possible only to find Meg and Ryan, grinning from ear to ear.

"What? Is it 'scare the living crap out of Grace' day or something?" Grace grabbed her heart as it thumped wildly in her chest.

"Evelyn would like to meet your 'friend,' as they keep referring to Michael. I'd get it over with before the three of them have any more time to gossip. But you may want to wipe that bit of gloss off your lips, Michael," Meg teased as she pointed at his face.

Michael quickly wiped his mouth with the back of his hand, smiled at Meg, and bravely headed off into the kitchen.

Please, God, just let them behave, Grace prayed as she stood next to Michael in the doorway of the kitchen. "Aunt Evelyn, this is Michael. Michael, this is my Aunt Evelyn, and you remember my obnoxious mother from yesterday." Grace glared at Susan, who looked like the cat that swallowed the canary as she sat on her barstool across the kitchen.

"Michael, it's so lovely to meet you," Evelyn said as she shook his hand, her eyes never leaving his face except to glance in Grace's direction, which instantly made her stomach flip with nerves. "I can see why she's so taken with you," Evelyn whispered quietly enough for only Grace and Michael to hear. Then with a wink, she returned to her friends at the other end of the kitchen.

Well, that was relatively painless, Grace thought, and then it happened...

"Oh, Grace, before you and Michael leave, will you both do me a favor?" Susan asked as she kneaded the bread dough on the counter.

"Sure, Susan, what can we do for you?" Michael asked, eager to score points and help out where needed.

An evil grin danced across her face. "Look up." She pointed a dough-covered finger over their heads. There, perched in the doorway, was a freshly hung piece of the most annoying, parasitic, green plant known to mankind, or at least to Grace: mistletoe.

"Damn it," she groused as she banged the back of her head on the door jamb repeatedly.

Michael, however, must have found the whole thing amusing, because he was grinning. He grabbed Grace by the waist with such force that not only did it make *her* gasp, but also the other three women who were staring at them from the other side of the kitchen.

With a sinful smile, he placed his hand on Grace's cheek. He slid his hand down across her shoulder, slowly leaving a fiery trail with his fingers as he worked his way down her arm, her elbow, her wrist, before finally resting at her fingertips.

Grace was holding her breath, not sure what was going to happen next. She heard a small squeak from their audience, as they too held their breath in anticipation. He winked and then lifted Grace's now completely limp hand to his lips, gave it a tender kiss, and then placed it back at her side.

"Ladies," Michael said with a nod of his head, then placed his hand on the small of Grace's back and led her out of the doorway.

Even in her breathless state, she heard the kitchen erupt into girly squeals. Grace flopped into a nearby chair and sighed. "Great. Now I think my mom and my aunt have a crush on you too."

Michael laughed out loud, unaware of the effect his little display had had on them—or Grace.

"Come on, let's find Meg and Ryan and get out of here," he said with a smile. They headed upstairs, only to find their friends flipping through old photo albums in the guest room.

"Let's get out of here. I need to hide from my mother for a while." Grace laughed as she snatched the album of her toddler years from Meg's prying hands.

"What do you want to do?" Ryan asked curiously.

Then it hit her—the only thing to do on a snowy day. "Let's go sledding!" Grace squealed as she ran off to put on warmer clothes.

⌒

They bundled up, borrowing some clothes from Henry's dresser for Michael and Ryan, and came bounding down the stairs like a herd of elephants.

"Bye, Mom. Going sledding!" Grace shouted as they ran past the kitchen.

Susan just shook her head and laughed. "Haven't heard that one for a few years. Have fun, kids! And don't be too long. Our guests will be arriving soon," she yelled out the door after them.

Grabbing a bunch of inflatable tubes from the garage, they headed out into the woods for an afternoon of fun.

The snow was perfect for sledding. Grace led the gang to the hill that she used to spend hours on every weekend as a kid. Somehow, the hill didn't seem as big and daunting as she had remembered it; but then again, it had been ten years and she was a bit bigger and older now.

Michael and Ryan constructed huge snow ramps so they could hit them at full speed and make their sleds sail through the air, landing with a thud yards away from where they left the ground. Michael, of course, won every race, but Grace won the distance contest. By the time they wandered back to the house, there were new cars in the driveway.

Grace looked back at everyone. "It starts." She waved her hands at the festively illuminated house.

They managed to sneak in without Susan seeing them. Henry caught them on the stairs and told them to hurry up and shower and then get back downstairs as soon as possible or Susan would come looking for them.

Everyone's clothes were soaked, so Grace suggested Michael and Ryan jump in the showers first and she'd dry their clothes while they were doing that. Then the guys could go downstairs and mingle while she and Meg got ready.

Grace found a towel for Michael in the linen closet and sat on her bed while he went into the bathroom to shower. She heard the water turn on and tried to busy herself instead of sitting there, imagining the very naked—very yummy—man who was on the other side of her bathroom door.

As she dug through her dresser, looking for something to wear tonight, Grace heard the creak of the bathroom door open behind her. She was expecting him to fling the clothes out onto the floor. But when she didn't hear anything hit the ground, she turned to find Michael standing in the doorway, with just a towel wrapped around his waist and a pile of clothes in his arms.

Stay right where you are, Grace! Not another step! she screamed in her head.

"Toss them on the floor, I'll get them in a second," Grace said breathlessly, turning her attention away from his god-like form and back into the dresser drawers, trying to ignore the way her stomach was wildly fluttering. *Breathe and don't look at him. Don't look at him!*

"I can't just throw them on the floor. Here."

She could see him walking closer out of the corner of her eye and panic started to set in. *Shoes… something and something else… shoes and a bunch of crap that doesn't matter… shoes and… Oh, who cares about shoes, really?*

Grace looked up into his playful eyes and felt all her willpower fading away with each step he took toward her. He stopped inches away, his smoldering eyes making her heart thump wildly in her chest.

Chapter 17

Grace scurried out of her bedroom, her face still flushed from seeing Michael, nearly naked, pre-shower. With a shaking hand, she knocked on Meg's door and, after an extended pause, it opened a crack, just enough for Meg to stick Ryan's clothes out. All Grace saw was Meg's bare, pale arm as she dropped them into her arms.

"Thanks," Meg's muffled voice said as she quickly slammed the door shut.

Weird, she thought to herself.

She tossed the pile of clothes into the dryer and turned it on high. Shamelessly, Grace hid in the laundry room, hoping to remain undetected by Susan and her loony guests. As she watched the timer countdown to zero, she opened the door and took the warm pile of clothes out, spreading them out on top of the dryer before it could chime and give away her location.

Grace easily sorted through the shirts and pants, but then she was faced with a major dilemma, who wore the boxers and who wore the boxer briefs. As she stood in the laundry room, she held the identically sized men's undergarments in her hands, giggling as she tried to imagine whose ass went in which pair.

For some reason, Ryan struck her as more of a boxers guy so that was her best guess, but she figured she'd ask before handing the clothes back to Meg. That was if she stuck more than her hand out of the door this time.

Meg ushered Grace into her room and took Ryan's clothes from the pile in her arms. He confirmed the boxers were his when he stuck his head out of the bathroom door. Grace quickly exited the room before she saw more of Ryan than she had intended.

Before Grace walked in her own room, she gave a quick knock on the door, not wanting to walk in on Michael in any state of undress. Cautiously, she pushed open the door and glanced around the room, but he was nowhere to be found.

Where the hell could he have gone with no clothes?

"Michael?" she called softly.

The bathroom door flew open revealing Michael in her baby blue bathrobe with tiny yellow rubber duckies printed all over it.

"You look very manly." Grace laughed and whipped out her phone to snap a picture of him in his hilarious outfit.

"Ha ha. If you want to see manly, I'll show you manly, Grace," he threatened as he started to loosen the belt on the robe.

The devilishly naughty part of her wanted to call his bluff and let him drop the robe and show her the goods, but the sensible side of Grace kicked in. *If he does that, it is all over, and the point of no return will be upon us.* Her face turned red at the thought of being flashed by the perfect specimen of a man before her. With her heart racing, and before he could intentionally or unintentionally have a wardrobe malfunction, Grace thrust his clothes at him, hoping he wouldn't see how much her hands were trembling.

She gave him everything but his underwear. "Here you go. Somehow I just knew you were the boxer briefs kind of guy," Grace teased as she playfully dangled his underwear from her finger.

He snatched it out of her hand and closed the bathroom door with a bang as he pretended to be upset. A minute later, Michael emerged from the bathroom, clean, dressed, and smelling like soap. Grace was lying across her bed when he came out and she couldn't help but smile at the sight of him.

"You clean up pretty nice, Mr. Andris."

"Thanks, Miss Park, glad to hear you approve. I'm going to go downstairs and flirt with your mom and aunt for a while. I'll see you in a few. Oh, by the way," he said as he opened the bedroom door, "I left something for you in the bathroom." And with a wink and a dimpled smile, he was gone.

Grace climbed off the bed and took her pile of clean clothes into the bathroom so she could shower. When she opened the door, she couldn't help but smile. Lying on the counter were Michael's neatly folded boxer briefs.

Damn that man and his naked ass. Grace laughed as she undressed and turned on the shower.

She quickly showered, lathering her hair and wondering what Susan was doing to poor Michael, or worse, how she was introducing him to her guests.

With newfound energy, Grace quickly washed herself and got dressed. Feeling rebellious, she decided to follow Michael's lead and left her forest green silk panties sitting on top of his boxer briefs on the bathroom counter. She slid into a pair of plain black slacks and a form fitting green blouse with a deep V-neck. She took a quick look in the mirror at her outfit and smiled.

Before Grace left the bathroom, she gave her hair one last fluff, threw on a quick spray of perfume, and headed to check on Meg. She tapped on her door and found Meg dressed and sending Bianca a quick text to check on her—and Jack.

The two women headed downstairs to join the party. As they got to the last step, Grace could hear the ladies chattering in the kitchen and assumed the men had congregated in the family room to watch television. The girls walked into the kitchen to see who was there. Six women were huddled around the punch bowl, laughing, as Grace stuck her head in the room.

"Grace, Meg!" Susan called them over, wanting them to meet all of her friends.

They spent the next fifteen minutes talking with the wife of Grace's old dentist, a girl from high school she completely detested, and the wife of one of the new deputies at the police station.

Meanwhile, Meg sucked down a glass of wine. Her head, Grace was certain, was spinning from all the local gossip.

"Mom, we're going to go, um, say hello to everyone else." Grace carefully slipped from the gaggle of women and generously refilled both of their wine glasses.

Meg mouthed a silent "thank you" as they headed out of the kitchen. In the foyer, they sat down at the bottom of the staircase and drank their wine in relative peace and quiet.

"This is going to be a long evening, isn't it?" Meg asked nervously.

Grace solemnly nodded her head.

"She has plenty of liquor, right?" Meg asked with a playful smile.

"Yes. If we're lucky, we can drink ourselves silly by ten, and then we won't remember a thing—no matter how bad it gets." Grace laughed as she stood up, feeling the need to check on the guys in the family room.

Meg walked in first and found an open seat next to Ryan. Grace stood in the doorway for a minute and watched the two of them whispering back and forth. Meg laughed at something Ryan was saying and laid her head sweetly on his chest.

They just fit together, Grace thought with a smile.

She continued looking around the room until she spotted Michael. He was sitting on the couch with Uncle Frank, deep in conversation. She couldn't hear what they were talking about, but instead watched Michael gesture with his hands to demonstrate something to her uncle, and then Frank laughed out loud. Frank must have begun telling Michael something interesting because she saw him lean forward with a serious look on his face.

Michael's hair looked darker in the dim lights of the family room, but his pale blue eyes shone like always. Grace wasn't sure how long she had been watching him when felt someone come up behind her and gently put a hand on her shoulder.

"You love him, don't you?" Evelyn whispered as she brushed her hand down the back of Grace's long hair.

"More than I ever thought I could love someone, Aunt Evelyn. He's just so … amazing," she said, never taking her eyes off of Michael.

"He loves you too, you know," she whispered in Grace's ear. She turned her head and found Evelyn's eyes were warm and loving as she nodded her head knowingly before she went and joined her husband on the couch. Michael looked up, finally noticing Grace standing in the doorway, and hurried over.

"Don't you look gorgeous," he said as his eyes raked over her body, making Grace's skin tingle. "Did you like the present I left in your bathroom?" He smirked, giving a slight tug on his belt loop.

"As a matter of fact I did, and I was inspired to follow your lead." Grace softly ran her hand over her hip, making Michael draw a quick breath in surprise. "Come on, there's got to be an empty room in this house somewhere."

Grace took his hand and they navigated their way through the family room to their final destination, the completely empty living room. "Peace at last," Grace murmured as she fell onto the couch.

Michael stood near the piano and smiled. "Are you having fun yet?" he asked as the doorbell rang, signaling the arrival of even more freeloaders in Grace's home.

She let out an annoyed groan in the direction of the front door and threw her arm over her eyes. "Wake me up when they leave, please."

Grace heard his footsteps followed by the soft tinkling of a single piano key. She moved her arm to find Michael sitting at the piano bench, smiling, while he messed with the keys.

"Do you play?" he asked, looking over the top of the piano at her.

"Sure, I'll show you what I learned after two solid years of piano lessons." She took her place beside him, sat up straight as her teacher had always taught her to do, and cracked her knuckles loudly, before finally placing her fingers on the keys.

Michael raised an interested eyebrow at her elaborate preparations and waited for the show to begin. Grace then broke into the most horrible version of "Jingle Bells" ever played by a human who still possessed all ten of their fingers.

Michael's face was priceless. He sat stoically beside her, trying his hardest not to laugh for fear of hurting her feelings. Grace saw him biting his lower lip with each sharp note she hit, like it was somehow causing him physical pain as she played completely out of tune.

Keeping a straight face, Grace turned to him and asked eagerly, "What did you think?"

"It, um, it was... It was really..." he struggled to find a tactful word to describe how bad it actually was, but he was saved when Susan came into the room.

"Grace, that was horrible! And you had lessons for years. Mrs. Wonters is probably rolling over in her grave at that." Susan laughed as Grace clutched her chest and faked being offended.

"Michael liked it, didn't you?" she asked as she turned to him, unleashing her big, brown baby doll eyes on him.

"It was lovely. I doubt I could have done much better," Michael said, gently patting her hand.

His mother couldn't resist jumping into the conversation. "You might have been able to do better, but I guess we'll never know now, will we? Had you continued with your piano lessons instead of taking up the electric guitar the summer you turned twelve, who knows how good you could have become?" Liz gave her son a quick swat to the back of his head. He rolled his eyes at his mother and turned back to the piano, running his fingers lightly over the keys.

"Do you remember anything?" Grace asked as he plucked away at random keys.

"A little," he said as he placed his fingers on the keys and began to play out of key. Liz couldn't stand it a second longer and tapped him on the shoulder. Michael stood up, allowing his mother to take his place on the bench beside

Grace. As she played the opening chords to "The First Noel," Michael stood beside the piano and began to hum with the music.

Grace watched in amazement as Liz played and, after some prodding from his mother, Michael began to sing along in perfect tune. He sang "The First Noel" and, without pausing, they smoothly transitioned into "Silent Night," followed by "O Holy Night."

The entire time he sang, a peace and tranquility seemed to wash over him. As he smiled at Grace, his face was completely relaxed, showing no sign of stress or even concentration, only joy. He was as beautiful as the music itself. By the second song, the other guests had crowded into the small room to hear him sing. When the final note hung in the air, the room erupted into applause.

Grace placed her hand over his. "Michael, that was phenomenal."

"Thank you," he whispered as he leaned over and touched his head to hers, embarrassed by the attention from the people around him.

The crowd of admirers descended, and as they began their flurry of compliments, Grace stepped to the side, leaving him to their praises.

"Thank you very much," she heard him say, flashing a shy smile, his cheeks red.

The room began to feel much too small for Grace. She weaved her way through the room, listening to Liz discussing Michael's years of success in choir during high school.

Grace smiled at the faces she passed by as she retreated to the kitchen for some much needed time to herself.

While she sat on the kitchen counter, watching her legs swing back and forth, her head was spinning. She had just witnessed something so beautiful she couldn't even put it into words. He was simply an extraordinary man.

Grace already knew she loved Michael. But with every day that passed, she continued to find out something new about him—something that made her fall even more deeply in love with him even though she hadn't even told him yet. Plus, she only had inklings about how he actually felt about her. The voice in her head began whispering doubts and reminding her how boring she was in comparison to other women.

Before she could allow her demons to consume her, Grace heard footsteps on the kitchen floor.

"There you are. I was wondering where you ran off to." Michael made his way across the kitchen to her.

"Michael, that was beyond impressive," Grace stammered, dropping her eyes. "It was…breathtaking." The footsteps stopped and she could see his shoes on the floor directly in front of her.

"The only breathtaking thing around here is you, Grace." He lifted her chin and his darkened eyes bore into her, making her feel the intensity of the feelings that were behind them. He put his hands on her knees and ran them softly, intoxicatingly up and down her thighs.

This is it, Grace told herself. *I need to tell him. I want to tell him. It's now or never.*

She took a deep breath, trying to collect herself and work up the nerve to actually say the words. She opened her mouth and her mind went blank. The well-thought-out speech she had come up with to profess her love to him left her head, and instead, she started rambling. "Michael, I need to tell you something, and I don't want you to think I'm nuts or anything, but I know how I feel even if I've never felt this way before about anyone, but I'm sure, trust me, and I just want you to know that I…love you. And I know I haven't known you very long, and it seems fast, but—"

Grace didn't get another word out because Michael's finger flew over her lips and stopped her babbling. He moved even closer, now standing firmly between her legs. His face was directly in front of hers, their noses nearly touching.

"Did you just say that you loved me?" he asked with a brilliant smile on his face.

His finger was still pressed to her lips, so instead of answering, she slowly nodded her head up and down.

The next thing Grace knew, she was in his arms. It was as though she were flying as they spun around the center of the kitchen. He threw back his head as his deep laughter filled the room.

At least my declaration seems to amuse him.

Moments later, he hugged Grace tightly then placed her safely back up on the counter where she had been sitting earlier. He took her hands in his and looked deeply into her eyes.

"Grace, I love you too." He raised her hand, pressing his warm lips to the center of her palm. "I've loved you, I think, since the first time I heard your voice, when you told Jack to go take a hike." He kissed the other hand. "Then each time I saw you after that, I just fell deeper, more helplessly, in love with you. The morning we spent in bed was when it hit me. When I had you in my arms, I realized that I love you. I knew, right then and there, that I could never stand to let you go."

Even though she was shocked by his words, she completely understood everything he was saying. Grace felt the exact same way. Her overwhelming emotions started to get the best of her and tears of joy filled her eyes.

"My love," Grace whispered.

He tilted his head to the side, his eyebrows furrowed together slightly, not sure as to what her muttering meant.

"You started calling me 'my love' after breakfast that day," Grace clarified, wiping a tear from her cheek.

"You noticed?" he asked with a sheepish grin. "And here I thought I was being clever, telling you, without really saying the words."

He wrapped his arms around her waist and pulled her closer. Being up on the counter, they were eye to eye so Grace decided to take her second leap of faith and do the other thing she had been putting off for far too long.

"I love you," she said intensely as she put her hands on the sides of his face and gazed lovingly into his eyes.

"I love you too," he said as he leaned in, making their faces less than an inch apart.

Grace didn't give him any warning that she was going to use her free kiss; she just let things happen on their own.

The kiss started gently, as all the others had. But when she parted her lips against his and her tongue grazed his lower lip, he responded immediately, parting his lips as well, allowing her tongue to explore his mouth for the first time.

The chemistry between them was explosive. His hands moved to her hips and he pulled her to the very edge of the counter. Grace wrapped her legs around his waist and pulled him closer to her, not wanting any space to separate their bodies.

Her hands left his face and secured themselves tightly in his hair, causing him to let out a small moan which only made her more excited. Their lips continued to move together, and Grace couldn't stop kissing his incredibly soft lips, even if it meant not breathing. The taste of him, the fire between them was indescribable. Michael allowed her to begin the kiss, but from that point on, he controlled every part of her.

He was all that mattered: his lips on hers, their bodies pressed together, the warm feeling that was filling Grace's body as he touched her. Every cell in her body craved him. This kiss was everything she had hoped it would be and, at the same time, everything she feared it would be, because Grace didn't know if she could stop herself.

How am I going to do this and then have to wait another seven days to be with him like this again? In her head, Grace wondered if they could slip into the laundry room undetected and see where things went from there.

His hands ran up and down the sides of her body as she continued kissing him. Grace felt his fingers lift the bottom of her shirt like he had done under the blanket the night before, except this time she didn't want him to stop. She kissed him even more voraciously and his hands flew up into her hair, clutching it tightly in his fists.

Using all the will power she possessed in her body, Grace finally broke the kiss and pressed her forehead to his as they looked at each other, panting like they had just run a marathon.

"Impressive," Grace whispered.

"Exquisite." Michael smiled back at her.

They were allowed a moment to savor what had just happened between them; then they heard a giggle. "Well, I guess they aren't gay anymore, Liz," Susan said loudly from the direction of the kitchen doorway.

Liz started snickering next to her. "I always knew they were full of shit."

"Kids, as happy as I am that you are enjoying each other's company, we do need to make Christmas dinner on that counter tomorrow, so if you could move this to a surface we won't be preparing food on—or eating on—tomorrow, I would greatly appreciate it. Other than that, carry on!"

Grace and Michael started laughing the moment Susan and Liz left the kitchen. Grace finally caught her breath and told Michael, "I was going to ask you to meet me in the laundry room, but now, I think the moment has passed."

"Your mom did give us permission, you know," Michael said with a devilish grin, as he nodded his head toward the door.

"You know they're out there telling everyone they caught us. We have about ten seconds until Meg finds out and comes screaming through that door." Grace counted back from ten in her head and then pointed across the room.

"Grace!" A small object rocketed into the kitchen and tried to yank her off the counter, but Michael held on tight, refusing to let Grace go.

"Michael Andris, you let go of my friend right now," Meg said with a ferocious growl. "We have important girl things to discuss, and from what I hear, she has a rather juicy story to tell," she said as she stomped her foot on the floor.

"I better get this over with," Grace groaned, but Michael still refused to release her. He raised his eyebrows, as if waiting for her to say the magic words. "I love you," Grace whispered against his lips and he finally released his grasp. Meg giggled as Grace hopped down.

"I love you, too." Michael smiled as he leaned against the kitchen counter and watched them walk away.

They turned the corner and Meg grabbed her wrist, dragging Grace upstairs to her room and slamming the door shut behind them. "You finally told him, didn't you? Well, you told him yesterday, but I doubt he remembers—"

Grace interrupted Meg's excited squeals and ramblings. "What did I tell him yesterday?" Grace asked sharply.

Meg settled herself and smiled back at her friend. "You said 'I love you' in your sleep when you two were on the couch, and he said he loved you back. Apparently, he talks in his sleep, too. Ryan and I thought it was very cute." Meg fished in her pocket for her cell phone. "Don't say another word. We need to get Bianca on the line so she can hear this."

Grace waited quietly as Meg dialed, knowing she still wore a goofy grin on her face, but she didn't care. Her heart was thundering in her chest and in her head she kept hearing Michael tell her he loved her too. Meg set the phone to speaker and let it ring out loud. On the fifth ring, they started to look at each other with concern, but then they finally heard the phone open and clank onto the floor.

"Hel—shit, wrong one…Hello?" Bianca called out as they heard the squeaks of her rolling around on her bed, trying to find the phone.

"Hey, Bianca! How are you feeling?" Meg asked.

"Oh, hey, guys. I'm doing OK. How's everything there?" They smiled in relief at each other; Bianca finally sounded better.

"Things here are great. Our little Grace has something to share," Meg said in a proud and motherly voice.

"Eek! You kissed him, didn't you?" Bianca screeched into the phone. "Tell me, tell me! You didn't tell Meg about it yet, did you?" Bianca accused as they heard a loud thud on the phone.

"What was that?" Grace asked. She heard Bianca scrambling.

"It was a pile of magazines I had laying on the bed. Sorry, my foot just knocked them off. OK, back to the kiss. So…"

"Well, he had just sung beautifully while his mom played the piano, and I went into the kitchen to clear my head. He looked so gorgeous standing there beside the piano…but anyway, I was up on the kitchen counter and he came in looking for me. I don't know what came over me, but I decided I had to tell him I loved him. And when I said the words, he grabbed me off the counter and swung me around the kitchen, laughing."

Meg and Bianca both sighed as they visualized the scene. Grace heard a smack over the phone.

"Bianca? Are you OK?" Meg said, looking extremely suspicious.

Again, Bianca stumbled over her words. "Sorry, there was this pesky *fly* bothering me so I smacked it—or tried to anyway, but it was too fast. Anyway, get to the kiss, Grace."

"Well, he set me back up on the counter and told me he loved me too. It was the most amazing moment of my life. I took his face in my hands and kissed him. When he realized what I was doing, he was, let's just say, very eager to make me happy. He is such a great kisser. I felt it all the way down to my toes." Grace sighed, thinking back to the kitchen. "And I really thought I was going to lose the bet right then and there in my mom's kitchen. Actually, I was going to take him into the laundry room until—" Grace stopped because she heard quiet snickering in the background with Bianca.

Meg signaled for her to go on with the story while she silently slipped out of the room.

"Until?" Bianca asked.

"Sorry, until I decided to end the kiss. I was still thinking about sneaking off with him when our mothers caught us," Grace said sheepishly.

"Your moms walked in on you getting all hot and heavy on the kitchen counter?" Bianca gasped, and then started giggling. "Oh, Grace, I bet you turned a new shade of red."

"Yeah, it was great." Meg returned to the room silently, with Michael and Ryan in tow. Ryan had his phone in his hand and was getting ready to dial. "After she announced she didn't think we were gay anymore, she gave us her blessing to do it on any surface in the house that we wouldn't be eating on tomorrow." While Grace finished her story, she watched Ryan press a series of digits and tuck the phone to his ear.

"Oh my gosh, Grace. That is just—" As Bianca was laughing, they all heard it—and Bianca did too because she suddenly fell silent. The only sound on her end was the phone ringing in the background and a ruckus as someone tried to answer it.

"Bianca, is that a phone ringing? Whose phone is it?" Grace asked, somehow managing not to laugh.

"Um, yeah. Well, I guess…" she stammered. Then they heard a deep male voice growl in the background.

"What do you want, Ryan? I'm at work," Jack spat into the phone. Michael and Ryan nearly burst out laughing and quietly left the room with their phone to interrogate Jack.

Grace and Meg waited a second to let Bianca finish swearing and throwing things at Jack before they started teasing her. "So, Bianca, is there anything *you'd* like to tell us?" Grace teased, giggling uncontrollably.

"Yes. I'm out. Jack was spectacular! Amazing! The best sex ever! My God, he's an animal in bed. And it was well worth losing that damn pair of shoes. Enjoy another week of cold showers, ladies, and now, I'm going to have hot, sweaty sex—again!" And without another word of explanation, she hung up.

Grace and Meg rolled around on the bed laughing until their sides hurt. When they finally caught their breath, they looked at each other and smiled. Grace extended her hand to Meg, saying as they shook, "And then there were two…"

Chapter 18

*G*race and Meg followed the roaring laughter into her room, where they found Michael and Ryan clutching their sides, the cell phone still in Ryan's hand.

"What did Jack say? We want details," Meg begged as she ran across the room to Ryan. Michael was wiping his eyes when Grace sat down on his lap in the rocking chair, gasping for breath.

"He didn't get to say very much other than they had sex and he enjoyed himself immensely, but then our conversation with him was interrupted by Bianca whispering very dirty things that we probably weren't supposed to hear. Then we heard the phone dropping to the floor." Michael managed to get part of the story out, but was interrupted by Ryan.

"And then, there was a lot of moaning." The two of them exploded into laughter again while Grace and Meg stared at the phone in Ryan's hand.

"Are they still on the line?" Grace asked in horror. Michael nodded his head and held his sides.

Meg whipped the phone from Ryan's hand, pressed her ear to it, and immediately started blushing. "Oh my…" She quickly snapped the phone shut and shook her head from side to side. "Well, she certainly sounds like she's enjoying herself."

After laughing for who knows how long, they all decided to return to the party and see how many people were gathered downstairs now. Meg and Ryan walked out the door first, and as Grace was about to follow behind them, Michael caught her arm and held her back.

"What's wrong?" she asked as she looked into his eyes, puzzled.

"Nothing. Everything's perfect." He leaned in and kissed her gently on the lips. "I love you," he whispered as he took Grace's hand and led her out the door, making her heart flutter.

"I love you, too."

When they finally made it downstairs, it looked like the crowd had tripled. Susan found them and began making introductions. Grace politely made conversation with Susan's guests while Michael charmed all the ladies in the room.

The best moment of the evening was when the Sullivans arrived. Grace saw her parents chatting with Mr. and Mrs. Sullivan and pointed them out to Michael. He snickered something about the apple not falling too far from the tree when he got a look at the portly Mr. Sullivan.

"Did their creepy son come too?" Michael whispered in Grace's ear as she sat on his lap in the recliner. She glanced into the foyer but didn't see him.

"He's not out there. We just might be safe." Grace laughed. "I'm going to go get some punch. Do you want anything?" Michael shook his head no and flashed one of his heart stopping smiles before she turned to walk away.

Grace had almost reached the punchbowl when someone bumped into her near the doorway to the dining room. "Oh, sorry," she mumbled. When she looked up, Grace found herself standing chest to chest with Liam Sullivan, who was beaming with excitement.

"Grace, there you are. I was looking for you." She felt his arms wrap around and pull her into a hug that was way too close for comfort. Grace shuddered in disgust.

"Liam, I didn't know you were here." She looked around frantically for help, but couldn't find anyone near. For a split second, Grace considered screaming but decided that would be considered rude and she'd catch hell from her mother. So instead, she opted for mind-numbing small talk while she waited for the first chance to run for her life. "How've you been?"

"Good. You know," he spoke in a very low voice, "I've been thinking about you ever since our dance last week."

At that moment, Grace threw up in her mouth a little bit. "Um, great. Hey, I'm sorry, but my mom needs some help," she muttered as she tried to wiggle away from him. But he put an arm on either side of her, trapping her against the wall. He snickered and pointed up over his head.

"Look, mistletoe," he said smugly as he inched closer to her.

If you think I'm kissing your vile face, you're actually dumber than you look.

Grace took a deep breath to object when she heard the deep voice of her hero. "Sweetheart, there you are."

Joy radiated from her when she realized she was saved from the slimy clutches of Liam. "Do you remember Michael?" Grace said casually as Michael glowered at Liam, who was looking more frightened by the second. Liam didn't speak; he simply nodded his head and dropped his arms from her sides.

"Liam, funny running into you again. Especially when you're so close to Grace. I thought we had an understanding." Michael folded his arms across his chest and scowled until Liam took a large step back from Grace.

Pleased with Liam's obedience, Michael turned to Grace with a wicked look on his face. "It looks like we've found ourselves trapped under the mistletoe again, sweetheart." He possessively pulled Grace into his embrace and felt her body mold against his. Liam moved aside, but continued gaping at their little performance.

Michael held Grace in his arms and bent over her, whispering "I love you" as he pressed his lips to hers in a rather dramatic fashion. Grace's dark hair cascaded over his arm as he dipped her back similar to the way Henry had kissed Susan the night before.

Behave, Grace, behave! she screamed in her head when she felt his soft lips moving against hers. All she could think about was kissing him without abandon like she had earlier in the kitchen.

He must have felt her inner struggle and broke the kiss before she did anything stupid. Grace fell back against the wall, breathing heavily with her fingers reverently touching her lips. It took her a few seconds before she even remembered Liam was standing there.

Michael reached up and roughly pulled down the mistletoe, stuffing it into Liam's front pocket. With a voice full of menace, he said, "Don't ever get that close to her again. Do we understand each other?" Liam nodded his head and stumbled backward as he made a hasty retreat.

Michael smiled triumphantly. "I'm not letting you out of my sight for a single second." Wrapping his arm around her shoulders, he led her over to the punch bowl so he could make sure she got something to drink without being accosted again.

The rest of the evening, Michael stayed true to his promise and never left Grace's side. They mingled with guests and listened to endless stories from people they would never see again, but they did it together. Michael was charming with the ladies while Grace enchanted the gentlemen in the room. Susan beamed with pride as she watched the two of them interact; the bond between them at times was palpable.

Meg and Ryan spent a great deal of time visiting with Aunt Evelyn and Uncle Frank. Every time Grace looked their way, they were huddled together laughing. It made her happy to see the important people in her life all getting along so well.

Around eleven-thirty, the last of the guests finally left. The only people who remained at the house were Michael's parents and Uncle Frank and Aunt Evelyn. Grace collapsed onto the couch and snuggled up beside Michael. He put his arm around her shoulders and pulled her close. Content, Grace closed her eyes and laid her head against his chest while he hummed softly in her ear.

"Michael, honey, we need to go," Grace heard Liz's voice call from the other room. She grabbed a handful of his shirt and held it tightly in her fist.

Michael started laughing. "Sorry, sweetheart, I need to get going."

"Stay with me," she whispered into his chest. "Please."

The thought of him leaving was unbearable after everything that happened between them this evening. He'd admitted he loved her, and Grace couldn't stop thinking about the fiery kiss they had shared. Her heart started racing just remembering the feel of his mouth on hers and the way it felt when her body was wrapped around his in a very intimate embrace. She opened her eyes to see a smile on his face.

"I have to go. I'm sorry. Believe me, there's nothing I'd rather do than stay with you. You have no idea how difficult it's going to be for me to walk out that door," he said as his lips grazed her cheek.

"Michael," his dad said as he stuck his head into the room. He grinned when he saw them huddled together and stepped out. "I'll give you a minute…"

Knowing it was time, Grace sighed and released her grip on his shirt. "You have to go." She pouted like a child until he took her face in his hands and rubbed his thumbs over the apples of her cheeks.

"I have to leave for a while, but I'll be back soon. Sleep well. I love you more than you could ever know, Grace." The tenderness in his voice brought tears to her eyes.

"Good night, Michael. I love you, too." Grace gave him one last hug before he headed off after his parents. Ryan met him in the foyer and the two of them said a quick goodbye to Susan and Henry before they closed the front door behind them.

Meg sulked into the room and sat down on the couch beside Grace. Her tiny head fell onto Grace's shoulder. "I miss Ryan," she sighed in a sad voice. They both giggled as they heard a horn beep in the distance as the car pulled out of the driveway.

"I know. I asked Michael to stay. You almost had yourself some shoes." Grace chuckled as she stood up and started throwing plates and cups into the nearby trashcan. Meg came over to help.

"I'm glad you told him you loved him, Grace." Meg smiled and patted her friend on the back.

"Believe it or not, I am too. Now, let's get this cleaned up. We need to call Bianca and find out what the hell she's been doing while we've been gone!"

"I think we know exactly what she's been doing, and with whom," Meg said smugly. "You forget—I heard some of it."

With the proper motivation, the girls began their clean-up effort. In no time, they'd finished most of the family room and headed to the dining room.

A half hour later, when the final traces of the evening's freeloaders were gone, the house looked presentable once again. Susan dragged herself up to bed, exhausted from her long day. Before she left, she did get in one parting shot at Grace when she mentioned that the laundry room was a much better location for a romantic rendezvous if Grace and Michael felt the need to be alone again.

In reply, Grace told her to back off and that if she emails her one bridal Web site, she'll never speak to her again or she'll get married at a drive-through chapel in Vegas with Elvis as the minister. Susan rolled her eyes at her daughter and wished them both a good night.

Grace and Meg were the last two up to bed. In Meg's room, they dove onto the bed and called Bianca.

"Hello?" Bianca's sleepy voice answered the phone.

"Bianca Angelique Quinn, you have some explaining to do," Meg said sternly.

She started laughing, knowing she was completely busted. "Hang on; let me go in the other room. He's snoring." They could hear the fumbling of the phone as it moved closer to the loud, deep snores. Jack sounded more like an angry bear than a man when he slept. Meg and Grace laughed, wondering how

Bianca could get any sleep with him around. Then they heard the squeak of a door opening, and Grace could tell from the echo that Bianca was sneaking into the bathroom.

"OK, what do you want to know?" Grace could almost see Bianca bracing herself for their questions, twisting her long red hair around her fingers like she always did when she was nervous.

"Were you ever really sick?" Grace decided to start with an easy one.

"No," she said quietly.

"What? How did you fake the fever?" Meg asked in shock. Grace had felt her head multiple times before they left, and she was blazing hot each time.

"I had a heating pad under the blanket," she confessed, chuckling slightly. "It always worked like a charm when I was a kid trying to get out of school."

"And did Jack know you were going to fake an illness to stay behind?" Meg asked suspiciously.

"It was all his idea. I wasn't going to go to Spokane at all; we were going to spend Christmas together. It was always the plan for me to fake being sick, and Jack was going to pretend to get a call from work saying they needed someone last minute to stay and work the holiday before he left with Michael. Then his mom's pipes broke, and he had to go up early to help them. The call he got from 'work' while he was up there was actually me."

"How did we miss all this?" Meg said to Grace with a bewildered look on her face.

"It was easy, actually. You were distracted by your flight getting canceled, and Grace was … well, in love. It made this much easier than I ever expected." Bianca laughed, relieved to finally come clean.

"So," Grace said, giggling. "What have you two been up to?"

"Honestly, we haven't left bed except to eat and shower for the last two days. And he has the sexiest tattoo across his back and another one on his hip that's amazing."

"A man with tattoos and facial hair?" Meg giggled. "Who are you and what have you done with Bianca?"

"I'm sold. I was wrong. Everything about the man just screams sexy." The purr of her voice when she talked about Jack told Meg and Grace just how important he was to her. So many things had changed for them, for the better.

"Well, it certainly sounded like you were having fun before," Meg teased. "Did Jack realize he didn't hang up the phone when he was talking to Ryan?

Because we got to listen in on your latest sexcapade, you know." They both burst out laughing.

"He did what? What did you hear?" she screamed. They heard a loud noise that sounded like a door crashing into the wall.

She must have flipped the light on because then Jack yelled, "Hey, I can't see! I'm blind, Bianca. What the hell are you doing?"

"Where's your phone?" she hissed at him.

"Um, I don't know. I had it, but I kinda dropped it when you did that thing with your tongue," he said in a very husky voice. Grace and Meg giggled as they continued to listen in on the others' conversation.

"Jack, Meg and Grace are on the phone, so please shut up. You didn't hang up your phone before, and our sexually repressed friends were listening to us having sex," she yelled.

"Good, maybe Mike and Ryan learned a thing or two. You girls better thank me when you see me again!" Jack yelled in the background. Grace had tears running down her face from laughing as Jack carried on.

"Here it is, you idiot."

They heard a crash, and Jack started yelling. "OK, girls, I'm gonna go," Bianca said with a giggle. "Tell Michael and Ryan they're assholes for listening, and I plan on smacking them the next time I see them. I love you two. Don't do anything I wouldn't do!"

"From what I heard before, there isn't much on that list," Meg squealed into the phone. Just before she snapped it shut, she added, "We love you too, have fun! Bye, Jack, you hot, sexy, beast!"

They rolled off the bed and laughed on the floor until they were gasping for breath. Finally, when their sides hurt so badly they couldn't stand up, they were ready for bed. Grace hugged Meg, and they made an agreement that whoever woke up first would wake up the other person. It was Christmas morning, after all, and there were presents to be opened.

Grace went into her bathroom and found Michael's underwear still sitting on her sink with her silk panties on top of them. She brushed her teeth and got dressed for bed. Having spent the whole evening being daring and going commando, her more conservative side was ready to put some underwear back on. She glanced back down at Michael's and decided to wear them instead of a pair of shorts to bed along with a T-shirt. She slipped under her thick comforter and grabbed her phone to send a message to Michael.

I'm going to bed. Just wanted to say good night.
I love you.
Grace
PS: I'm wearing your underwear. I look pretty cute in them, if I do say so myself.
Too bad you're not here to see it. Oh well.

Grace chuckled as she closed the phone, imagining his face when he read the message. *That will teach him to go home,* she laughed to herself. Reaching over, she flipped off the light beside her bed and snuggled down under the covers, waiting for the bed to warm up.

It was impossible to sleep. Every time she closed her eyes, Grace saw Michael's face, or she would remember the deliciously rich scent of his cologne or the feel of his lips on hers and it was just too much. Luckily, she didn't know his mom's address or she probably would have made a fool of herself and driven over there in the middle of the night and crawled in his bedroom window just to see him.

God, I'm pathetic, Grace was thinking when she heard the familiar jingle of her phone receiving a message.

Are you trying to kill me tonight?
First you ask me to stay with you, and then you tell me you're lying in bed, wearing my underwear.
I'm only human.
I would say good night, but I'm getting out of bed to take a nice cold shower.
I love you, too.
Michael

Grace was still giggling at his reply when the phone started ringing.

"Hey, there. How was the shower?" she laughed quietly into the phone.

"Lonely," he murmured.

"I'm sorry. Only one hundred sixty-seven hours, if that makes you feel any better."

"It doesn't." He laughed. "Hey, I forgot to ask you something tonight."

"What?"

"I wanted to see if you would be my date for New Year's Day," he said sweetly.

"Why, I would *love* to be your New Year's Day date. What time will you be picking me up?" Grace said coyly, playing along with his game.

"Well, I'd like to get an early start to our date, so I'll get you at the stroke of midnight. How does that sound?"

"Sounds like a plan. Of course, I'll be out with my girlfriends celebrating New Year's Eve, so it might not be a bad idea to go to the same place so we can meet up and leave from there." Grace was grinning from ear to ear at the thought of actually going on a date with Michael, alone, without any crazy bets hanging over their heads.

"Great idea. OK, I'm going to try and get some sleep, but I'm finding myself a bit distracted this evening."

"Me too," Grace said quietly. "Good night, Michael."

"Good night, sweetheart. I'll see you tomorrow."

The next morning, the first thing Grace remembered hearing was the creaking sound of her bedroom door opening then quiet footsteps moving across the floor. She was facing the window and Grace opened one eye to peek at the clock. It was 7:00 a.m. and the sun was just starting to rise outside her window. She buried her head under the pillow and groaned.

"Meg, we are not eight years old. Don't you think seven o'clock is a bit early?"

She said something, but with the pillow over Grace's head, Meg's words were muffled and lost.

"Just get in bed and lay down for a little bit. I'm not ready to go downstairs and face Susan and her questions about Michael again." Meg lifted the covers next to Grace, pausing before she climbed into bed and began gently rubbing her back.

As Grace tried to fall back to sleep, she rolled all the way onto her stomach and her bare leg brushed against Meg's flannel pajama bottoms. *Wait, Meg doesn't wear flannel—ever.* "This isn't Meg in bed with me is it?" Grace said, mortified. The bed was shaking from laughter, confirming her suspicions. "Michael!" she shrieked as quietly as she could, flipping over to find his beautiful face propped up on the pillow beside her. His hair was still messy, like he had just rolled out of bed himself.

"Merry Christmas!" he said happily as Grace bolted upright in the bed, holding the sheet to her chest.

"What the hell are you doing here? How did you get in? Who told you to come up here?" Grace paused for a second then growled, "Susan..." She muttered her mother's name like it was a dirty word.

"Actually, she's the answer to all those questions. She and my mom decided last night that you all were going to come to my house for breakfast. She and your dad are off getting ready, and Ryan is waking up Meg." He pointed his thumb in the direction of Meg's room when they heard her scream. "See? Now Meg's awake too." His smile made her melt completely into his arms and savor the feel of his body against hers. Everything was perfect until there was a knock on the door, and Susan stuck her head in.

"Merry Christmas, you two love birds!! Hurry up, we need to go." She stood in the doorway in her green flannel Christmas tree pajamas.

"Um, hi, Mom. This isn't what it looks like, and are you going to put on some real clothes before we go to the Andrises'?" Grace asked as she tucked the cover around herself to hide Michael's underwear she was currently wearing.

"No, we're supposed to come over in our pajamas. Liz's orders. Come on, get up! And don't worry, I didn't see anything," she said in a sing song voice as she closed the door.

Grace glanced over at Michael, who was highly amused by the whole exchange. "Don't encourage her. I'm telling you, don't encourage her," she warned as she put her elbow on the pillow and propped her head up in her hand next to him. He mirrored Grace's body position and gave her a sexy smile that sent her heart flying. "Michael, whatever you're thinking, stop it."

"What?" he asked innocently as he leaned over and she felt his lips not-so-innocently running along the side of her neck. He gently pulled the collar of Grace's T-shirt to the side so he could kiss her collarbone. Grace's head fell back as she enjoyed the sensation as he nipped at her skin. His free hand wrapped around her side and rested on the small of her back so he could hold her close.

"I missed you last night," he whispered as his lips moved across her cheek. "You have no idea how much."

Grace, this is trouble. You are getting close to the point of no return here. But then again, would that really be such a bad thing?

Her internal argument raged on until she heard Susan yell from downstairs, "Grace!" In her attempt to hurry, Grace stumbled backwards out of the bed. Michael flung himself across the mattress, trying to catch her before she hit the floor, but missed.

His arms dangled over the side of the bed as his cobalt eyes ran themselves all over her exposed body. She didn't realize what he was staring at until he muttered, "You really do look unbelievable in my underwear." His voice was thick with desire as he started to advance toward her.

Her skin began to tingle as his eyes lingered, devouring the sight of her long, bare legs. When he tried to reach out and touch her, she snapped. "Freeze, Andris! I need to throw some pants on. Don't you take another step." Grace held up a shaking finger in warning to him. He sat up on the bed and sulked, but Grace could feel his keen eyes still examining her body as she went to the dresser in search of more appropriate clothes.

From the top drawer she pulled out a pair of red and black plaid pajama pants, and slipped them on over what she was currently wearing. He fell back onto the bed and groaned, "You're going to keep them on?"

His body was completely sprawled out across the bed as Grace leaned down to kiss his cheek. "Yes, I am. And you know you love it." Before she could scoot away, his arms grabbed her and pulled her over onto the bed beside him.

"You know we could always just stay here." His tongue began running along her jaw as he slowly worked his way to her mouth.

"Grace Marie Park!" Susan hollered from the bottom of the stairs. "Michael Alexander Andris! Get down here!"

She pointed at Michael and laughed. "Ooh, you're in trouble." She jumped off the bed and ran to the door.

"I'm coming, Mom, sorry. It's all Michael's fault." Grace glanced back and stuck her tongue out at him, but he had sprung to his feet and started chasing her down the stairs amidst her squeals of laughter.

Susan stood at the bottom of the stairs, tapping her foot, trying to look intimidating, but a faint smile came over her face when Michael wrapped his arm around Grace's shoulders.

"Sorry, Mom," they said together. She rolled her eyes and headed out the door with Henry.

Meg was standing off to the side in her silk pajamas, looking very excited but unsure of her wardrobe. She kept fidgeting with her pajamas and running her fingers through her blond hair. Meg was most comfortable when she was showered and dressed to the nines.

"Don't worry, you look beautiful, Meg." Grace skipped past her to the Christmas tree. She quickly grabbed all of her gifts: one for her parents, one for Meg, and one for Michael, who eyed the presents curiously.

"Mr. Nosy, don't worry about which one is yours. Just get in the car. You'll find out soon enough."

⌇

The Andrises' house was about twenty minutes away and sat a little higher up in the mountains. It was a beautiful red brick colonial with black shutters, complete with white pillars on either side of the front door. A single candle illuminated each of the windows of the house, and perched on the roof of the garage was an enormous lighted Santa, sleigh, and four glowing reindeer.

"Merry Christmas!" Liz cried as they approached the front door. She was dressed in green plaid pajamas that matched Mr. Andris's exactly. Grace glanced down at Michael and found him wearing the exact same plaid bottoms, but with a solid green shirt. She had to bite her lip to keep from laughing.

"One day a year I wear them because it makes her happy if we all match. Tell anyone and I will scan your prom picture and make T-shirts. Do we understand each other?" His cheeks turned pink from embarrassment.

"I think it's adorable, and very thoughtful." With a quick wink at Michael, she went over and hugged Liz and Michael's father. "Merry Christmas, and thanks for sending the human alarm clock after us." Grace gave a nod in Michael's direction.

Liz stole a quick look at her son, her eyes twinkling. "He's the one that woke *us* up so early this morning. It was like he was five years old all over again." Liz leaned in, grinning and said, "I think he missed you."

"That's enough, Mother." Michael scowled as he placed a hand on Grace's back, leading her out of the foyer and far away from Liz.

They wandered into the kitchen where Ryan was flipping pancakes into the air and Meg was catching them on a plate. Michael started to work on the bacon and sausage when he handed Grace a box of eggs. "Get scrambling, girl." They all worked side by side, watching Meg run around chasing Ryan's flying pancakes and trying not to get hit by the airborne flapjacks when one sailed out of control.

Breakfast was delicious. Both families gathered around the dining room table and spent the next hour listening to stories about Liz and Susan from their college days and all the trouble they'd gotten into. A few times, Grace covered her ears because she was learning more about her mother than she ever wanted to know. More than once, Michael also cringed at hearing about his mom and the frat boys back in the day.

When the last plate was loaded into the dishwasher, Liz gathered everyone around the Christmas tree to exchange gifts. Grace and Michael sat next to Meg and Ryan on one side of the tree while their parents sat on the other.

"I want my gifts first," Meg demanded. Patience never was her strong suit. Grace dug around under the tree and found a large, rectangular box with penguin wrapping paper and handed it to Meg, grinning madly. "That smile has me worried," Meg said hesitantly as she started tearing the paper off the gift. She opened the box and stared at the contents with a confused look on her face. Her nose wrinkled like she smelled something bad as she began inspecting what was inside.

"Sweatpants? You got me sweatpants?" She sneered as she looked at the tags. "Are you serious? I don't wear sweats, ever. Heck, I don't even like to sweat!" Grace started hyperventilating, she was laughing so hard. "And a sweatshirt—size large? What are these, new fat clothes? Are you trying to tell me something?" She was glaring at Grace for explanation.

"Remember a few weeks ago, when you asked me to go outside my comfort zone, and I agreed, under the condition that I got to push you out of your comfort zone just once? Well, Bianca went to a football game as her payment, and I decided that you would get to wear whatever I picked out for you for one day, and I picked bland clothes."

"Wait a minute, I ask you to go outside your comfort zone and you get … this!" She waved her hands, motioning to Michael. "A totally hot guy that you fall madly in love with!" Grace heard Susan and Liz screeching on the other side of the tree. "And I get *this*?" She thrust the pair of gray sweatpants into the air.

Michael was slapping the floor with his hand he was laughing so hard. Ryan was trying his hardest not to laugh at Meg, but was failing miserably so he buried his face in his hands.

"Come on, Meg, it's just us and we all love you. You'll look cute. If anyone can pull off gray sweats, it's you." Grace unleashed her big brown eyes on Meg. "For me?"

"I hate you!" she spat as she marched off to the bathroom to change.

When she was out of earshot, everyone burst into hysterics. Meg was gone much longer than Grace thought she should be, and part of her was worried she was shimmying out the bathroom window, trying to escape. But they continued opening gifts, anxiously awaiting her return. Ryan went next and gave Michael a bunch of CDs while Michael gave Ryan a set of DVDs on World War II. Both of them were examining their gifts when Meg returned.

As she stood in the doorway, Grace almost didn't recognize the clothes she was wearing. It looked like she had been attacked by Edward Scissorhands. The sweatshirt was cut so that it was now sleeveless and hung fashionably off her shoulder, exposing the white tank top underneath. The sweat pants were rolled up to her mid calf and somehow she'd made them very form fitting. To get around the bland color, she took a marker to certain sections of it, making a gorgeous tie dyed effect and bringing in the brightness she was known for in her clothing choices. Even though Meg would never agree, Grace thought she looked cute.

"Happy?" Meg scowled.

Ryan saved the day by whispering something in her ear that made her grin bigger than Grace had ever seen before. She threw her arms around his neck, and as she hugged him tight, her entire attitude changed on a dime.

"OK, where were we before I was forced to dress like a bland hobo?" She reached under the tree and found a box wrapped in red paper. Meg held it out to Grace to give it to her, but not before she stuck her tongue out at her one more time and smiled to let her know she was forgiven.

Taking the package from her hands, Grace gingerly removed the paper. Inside was a first edition copy of *To Kill a Mockingbird*, her favorite novel. "Meg, this is fantastic!" Grace wailed as she tackled Meg.

"I bet you feel pretty bad for doing this to me now, don't you?" she teased as she tugged on her sweatpants. Grace searched behind herself and pulled out a small wrapped box then handed it to Meg.

"Here's your other gift," she said as Meg's face broke into a smile, realizing the sweats weren't her only gift.

Inside the box was a charm bracelet that she had admired once when they were shopping. Grace added a few charms, some to make her laugh, but each representing an important person in her life. There was a high heeled shoe, a tiny Seattle Seahawk, and a book. She even found an 'R' charm which was hanging beside the shoe.

"I love it!" Her body crashed into Grace, knocking her to the floor. She climbed off of her friend and ran over to Ryan to show him all the charms. He smiled proudly when he saw the gorgeous script 'R.'

"Would you like your gift now?" Michael asked, his smooth voice making Grace's heartbeat speed up in anticipation. There was a twinkle in his eye as he waited for her answer.

"Sure."

As he handed Grace her present, she tried to rack her brain and guess what it could possibly be. The package was a long, rectangular box, a bit deeper than a normal box, but not large and not very heavy. Grace gave it a playful shake before she started to carefully rip the gold paper off the box. With trembling hands, she lifted the lid, and what she found inside took her breath away.

"Do you like it?" Michael asked anxiously as he awaited her reaction.

"Oh, Michael, it's beautiful." Grace gingerly picked up the fabric to reveal the most exquisite black dress she had ever seen.

"I wanted you to have something beautiful to wear with your new shoes on our first date."

His silky voice stirred something deep down inside her. Grace imagined how she would look in this dress and a second later, imagined how it would feel to have Michael take this dress off her and carry her to his bed. She gave her head a shake to bring her out of her vivid fantasy.

With a confident grin on his face, Michael watched Grace stare at the dress, hypnotized by it. It was so beautiful she couldn't stop looking at it or touching it. She stood up and held it up against her body while Meg jumped to her feet and started clapping her hands together, giving her seal of approval. Liz and Susan came over to admire the dress as well.

"Michael, it's spectacular. You'd better take her someplace wonderful," Liz advised her son, while Susan nodded her head in agreement. They gawked a minute longer, then instructed Grace to put it away before it got dirty.

Still smiling, Grace carefully placed it back into the box. "Thank you so much. I absolutely love it, and I love you." She brushed his hair out of his eyes and ran her fingers down the side of his face before placing a tender kiss on his lips. As she rested her forehead on his, Grace smirked. "Would you like your present now?"

"Absolutely!" he said as Grace reached for the box wrapped in the cranberry colored paper. She placed it in his lap and sat at his feet to watch while he opened it. He looked down and raised a suspicious eyebrow at the excited grin on her face. As soon as his fingers broke through the paper and peeled back, revealing the gift underneath, he started laughing. His reaction was music to Grace's ears and she could no longer contain her excitement.

"Do you like them? I thought they might come in handy." With a teasing grin, she reached into the box and pulled out one of the running shoes and dangled it on her finger. "Maybe you'd like to work on your stamina over the next few days." She was still giggling when he snatched the shoe off her finger and stuffed it back into the box with a smile on his face.

He coyly crooked his finger at Grace, calling her closer. His eyes were so full of fire and desire that she felt the butterflies swarm in her stomach as she inched in his direction. "So, worried about my stamina, are you?" He asked the question so softly that Grace was the only one who could hear him. "You know, I'll admit that when I run, I don't have the greatest stamina. However, in *other* activities, my endurance is rather … phenomenal. I'll have to show you sometime."

Grace rocked back on her heels, completely speechless, her mouth dangling open. *Screw the shoes, Grace!*

Michael was grinning proudly at her flabbergasted expression. She could feel the blood coursing through her veins as her body responded to not only his words but the expression on his face. She also became very aware of his lips and just how sexy they looked curled up in that smirk of his. Grace couldn't take her eyes off of him, and she could see the same yearning and fire in his eyes. He reached down, picked up her hand, and kissed the inside of her wrist gently. Her entire arm began to tingle under his touch.

"Michael…" Trying to warn him not to push things too far, Grace nodded toward their parents who were on the other side of the room and Meg who was watching them like a hawk.

"Thank you for the gift. I'll put them to good use. I promise," he said with a wink, and then returned her trembling hand to her lap.

"Meg, give Ryan his gift," Grace awkwardly called out, trying to distract herself from the fact that Michael was now caressing her hair, making her shiver with excitement.

He chuckled softly behind her. "What's got you so worked up, sweetheart?" Grace turned and smirked as she pointed directly at his face. Extremely pleased with himself and not even trying to hide it, he sat back and laughed.

Everyone watched as Meg gave Ryan a beautiful, hand carved mahogany box, which could be used for storing his important papers, mementos, or letters.

When he opened it, Grace could see a few pink envelopes peeking out that Meg must have slipped inside.

The antique shop, where they bought it, said they thought it was from the mid 1800's and as soon as Meg saw it, she knew Ryan would love it. He ran his fingers across the carvings on the top of the box a few times, admiring the craftsmanship that had gone into making it. He scooped Meg up in his arms and hugged her tightly and again whispered things privately in her ear.

Ryan sat Meg on his lap as he handed her a beautiful box, covered in silver paper with an enormous red bow tied on top. She carefully slid the ribbon off and ripped the paper from the box. Opening the box a crack and squealing, Meg pulled out three thick, bound journals.

Meg had been writing in her journals every night since she was ten years old, recording her thoughts and experiences, documenting every day in her life. Grace knew someday she hoped to share them with her daughter and show her how she had been feeling at some of the most important times in her life—her first love, the boy who broke her heart, examples of true friendship and love.

Grace watched her caress the leather covers as Ryan pointed to the one with the darkest cover. Meg placed it in her lap, opening it to the first page. Her eyes immediately filled with tears as she started reading. Her eyes darted across the page, taking in every word, and then she collapsed back into Ryan's arms and buried her tear-stained face into his chest.

Taking Michael by the hand, Grace and he went and joined their parents, giving Meg and Ryan a moment alone.

"So what did you get, Mom?" Grace asked Susan, who was clutching a box in her arms and grinning.

"Well, Liz and I got each other gift certificates to the salon, so we can get our hair and nails done one afternoon. And Daddy got me the Food Saver food vacuum!" She was giddy over the crazy machine in her hands.

"Very romantic, Dad."

"Hey, she's been asking for that crazy thing since she saw it on television last month. And she looks rather happy to me." Henry wrapped his arm around Susan and kissed the top of her head. "Now just think how much fun you can have when I come back from fishing, honey."

Liz showed off the new mixer Michael's father had given her. It was a pale blue and matched the small flowers on the wallpaper in her kitchen. She was as pleased as Susan with her gift and asked Michael to carry it into the kitchen for her. Henry and Michael Sr. followed, wanting to get another cup of coffee.

"Grace, I have something for you, dear," Liz said softly as she held out a present with a warm smile on her face. She patted the couch next to her, hoping Grace would sit down.

"I'm sorry, Liz. I feel terrible. I didn't get you anything," Grace said with embarrassment.

"You have given me the best gift of all: you make Michael happy." She glanced toward the kitchen, where they could hear the men arguing about who was going to climb on the roof and take down the giant Santa, and smiled. "All I have ever wanted was for him to be happy and to find true love." She placed her hand on Grace's knee, her eyes glistening with tears. "He found that with you, Grace, and I couldn't be happier. You're such a lovely young lady. I can see in your eyes how much you love him. It radiates off of you when you look at him. He's happier than I have ever seen him, chipper and smiling for no reason. That's all because of you."

By the time Liz finished speaking, Grace had been trying to hold back her tears, but a few escaped and streamed down her cheek. Liz motioned to the gift, and Grace started to rip the paper, her heart pounding. Meg came over, interested to see what would be inside. When she took the lid off, Grace nearly dropped the box in shock.

Sitting on her lap was an ornate, antique silver picture frame that held two photos. One was the picture that Meg must have taken the night Grace and Michael fell asleep on the couch. She was on her back, clutching the front of Michael's shirt in her hand and he was huddled next to her, his arm draped across her stomach, his face right beside to hers.

"That was the picture I took, right after you told him you loved him, Grace," Meg said quietly. Grace's tear-filled eyes looked up at her friend as she mouthed a silent "thank you," because she was too overwhelmed to speak. Her eyes then moved to the adjacent photo.

It was a very sweet picture. There were two small children who couldn't have been more than two years old, lying on a couch sound asleep. The little boy was lying on his back and the little girl had her head resting on his stomach, her dark hair spread over his chest as she slept. Grace looked up at Susan, confused.

"Is that me?" she asked pointing to the little girl. The face was half hidden in the boy's shirt, but she looked familiar. Susan nodded her head yes, and Grace noticed her eyes were full of tears too. She glanced back at the picture and looked at the little boy. "Then who is this?" Grace looked Liz, who was staring off in the distance. She followed Liz's eyes over to Michael, who was standing in the doorway, watching them quietly.

"Michael?" Grace asked in disbelief.

"This was taken just before they moved to Salt Lake City. When Meg showed me the picture she took of you guys the other night, I called Liz to see if she still had a copy of this one," Susan said softly, stroking her hair.

"Thank you; it's the most precious thing." That was all Grace managed to squeak out before she started crying, as she clutched the photo against her chest, holding onto it for dear life.

$$Chapter\ 19$$

Michael watched from the doorway as Grace held the picture in her arms. Susan and Liz reminisced about the day it was taken. They had gone to the local park for a picnic, but instead of eating, Grace and Michael had discovered a playground to explore. They'd spent the afternoon running, climbing, and going down the slide. By the time they made their way back to the house, Michael was sound asleep, so Liz laid him on the couch for a nap. Grace apparently crawled up there a few minutes later and fell asleep, too.

After they shared the story behind the picture, Susan and Liz excused themselves into the kitchen. Meg mumbled something about going to find Ryan, and then she too disappeared. With the room empty, Michael walked over to the couch where Grace was sitting, and joined her.

"May I?" he asked as he took the frame from her hand. Grace watched him tilt his head to the side as he inspected the picture. He ran his finger delicately across the little girl's hair in the photo, a small smile on his face. He seemed to be taking in every detail of it, holding the frame close to his face occasionally to get a better look at something. "You were a very cute little girl," he said softly, his voice thick with emotion.

Grace took the picture from his hand and pointed at his sleeping, toddler face. "And you were adorable. Just look at all the curls you had." She looped her finger through a wavy piece of hair that had fallen into his eyes and pushed it to the side, then let her hand rest on his cheek. "Did you know about this?" she asked softly.

He shook his head, his eyes going back to the picture for a second. "I found out when you did. My mom was looking through her old photo albums, but I just thought that she was being nostalgic because it was Christmas." He shrugged his shoulders, and again turned his attention back to the pictures, searching them as if trying to remember something. "I've seen this picture so many times, but I never knew who she was," he whispered so softly Grace didn't know if he meant for her to hear.

"I will treasure this always." Collapsing against his chest, Grace clutched the picture in her hands.

❧

The day went on with typical Christmas fanfare. Grace was still affected by her emotional gift from Liz. She had looked at the picture at least twenty times since opening it. Every time she saw Michael's baby face, complete with dimples, her heart melted a little more. As she stood in the kitchen, Meg caught her peeking at it again and laughed.

"Do you believe me yet?"

"Believe you about what?" Grace asked only to be met by the smug look on Meg's face.

"About this," she said, tapping her finger on the frame. "That the two of you are meant to be."

More than anything, Grace wanted to believe her, but in the back of her mind, her insecurities flared. "I don't know." As much as she tried to bury the voices and the doubt, they were still there, screaming in her head. Reminding her that she really didn't deserve someone like Michael.

"He loves you, Grace. It's written all over his face. Every time you walk into the room, he absolutely glows," Meg said with certainty. Grace, however, was hesitant to believe it. "Surely you can't be questioning how he feels about you?"

"No, I know he loves me. I just..." Her mind was racing for the words to make Meg understand. "I guess I just don't understand *why* he loves me." Grace looked back down at the picture, letting her hair cover her face so she could hide.

From behind her, Grace heard the kindest, most gentle voice offering a very simple answer to her complex question. "I love you because you're brilliant and funny, clever and silly, beautiful and honest, loyal and trusting, thoughtful and kind." Michael gently spun her around to face him so she could see the sincerity on his face. He lifted her chin and looked into Grace's tear-filled eyes as he continued. "I love you because you are the most amazing woman I have ever met, and I will love you forever." There was no doubt or uncertainty in his voice, only love.

His thumb feathered across her cheek as he slowly wiped away the glistening trail of tears. "I love you," he whispered. If the look on his face wasn't enough to convince her, the intensity of his eyes told her that every word he spoke was true.

"I love you, too. More than I ever imagined I could love someone." Grace stood on her tiptoes to kiss his now smiling lips. "Only one hundred fifty-six more hours," she whispered while her lips were still touching his.

He made a playful growl then buried his face in Grace's hair. After they spent a few moments in each other's arms, Michael sighed. "Now I'm off to find Ryan. We have a Christmas dinner to cook." He gave Grace's hand a reassuring squeeze before he disappeared out of the kitchen. A minute after he left, there was a ruckus in the other room. Grace heard Michael and Ryan arguing about who got to drive the girls home.

"Feel better?" Meg asked gently. Grace nodded her head, still smiling. "Good. Be happy, Grace, you deserve this." She hugged her friend as tightly as her tiny arms could. When Grace wrapped her arms around Meg to give her a hug, her fingers got tangled in the shredded sweatshirt that Meg was still wearing.

Laughing, Grace said, "Come on. Let's get you home, out of these ugly rags, and into something more Meg-worthy."

Michael and Ryan dropped them off at Grace's parent's house so they could get dressed and help Susan get dinner started. They showered and Meg made a call to her parents while Grace made a quick call to Bianca and Jack to wish them a Merry Christmas. Then they headed off to the kitchen, the smell of turkey starting to fill the house.

"Give us a job, Mom."

Susan looked up from peeling potatoes long enough to say, "Go set the table, girls. There will be ten of us this year. The dishes are in the hutch. Use the red table cloth and the green napkins."

"We've got it under control, Mom. Don't worry." Flitting about the dining room, Grace and Meg placed the extra leaf in the table, making it large enough to accommodate all their guests. Meg folded the napkins into elaborate shapes, something her mom had taught her when she was little. When they were done, the table looked like it should have been on the cover of a magazine.

The rest of the afternoon was spent in the kitchen. Meg was on cookie duty, making elegant trays for the dessert table. Grace was put in charge of the salad and the cheese tray. When Aunt Evelyn arrived, she and Susan went on turkey watch, nervously peering into the oven window every few minutes, hoping the bird wouldn't be late and hold up dinner.

The sound of crunching tires on the driveway sent Grace racing to the window. "They're here," she squealed, dropping the bowl she was washing into the soapy water, sending suds into the air.

"Someone's a little excited …" She could hear Evelyn giggle as she cleaned up the bubbles that had spilled over the edge of the sink and onto the floor with Grace's exuberant exit.

Grace smoothed her hair and brushed off her apron before opening the door. Michael was standing on the porch, smiling, while the rest of his family was still yards behind him, laughing. Ryan was right beside him, peering over Grace's shoulder in search of Meg.

"I haven't seen him move that fast in a while," Michael Sr. snickered to Liz, who couldn't help but smile when she saw that Michael already had Grace in his arms.

"Leave him alone, dear. He's in love. You used to be that excited to see me too, many moons ago," Liz teased as Grace said hello and led them all into the house. Michael collected their coats and graciously hung them in the front closet.

"Gentlemen, I find it best to stay away from the kitchen at this point in the dinner preparation, for the good of my marriage," Henry joked. "Susan gets a little nuts right now. The turkey never cooperates. Frank and I are hiding out here watching the game; you're welcome to join us." He held out his arm, ushering them into the family room.

The turkey was only a half hour late this year; it was the closest Susan had ever been to serving dinner on time. The rest of the food was fabulous and the company was even better. Michael and Ryan told everyone about their plans for the bar, including what locations they were currently looking into as possible sites. Grace watched Uncle Frank and Michael put their heads together and discuss the merits of one location over another when marketing the bar. Henry kept everyone laughing with stories from his latest fishing trip, including the one about the legendary twenty-pound black fin trout that he swears was on his line—twice, but each time, the line broke and the fish escaped.

Christmas with Michael was magical. There was no other way to explain it. Meg and Ryan were off whispering together on the couch while Michael pecked away at the keys on the piano. Grace listened in awe as his voice would perfectly match the tone of the keys he touched, creating the most magnificent melody. When his fingers would pause, not knowing where the next key was, his voice would continue, filling in the blanks with more of his entrancing composition. After only a few notes, she recognized it as the tune she frequently heard him humming to himself.

They left much sooner than she would have liked. Liz needed the rest of the ruined basement carpet torn up before they headed back to Portland the following day. Grace and Meg offered to come over and help, but the boys wouldn't hear of it. They were, however, more than willing to ride back to Portland with the girls when Grace offered. With Jack taking the car when he 'went back to work,' they were trapped in Spokane. It was either ride back with the girls, or Michael's father was going to have to make the long trip. When they agreed to ride back together, Michael's dad was able to stay home and help Liz with the rest of the basement clean up, and Susan felt better knowing that Grace and Meg wouldn't be driving all that way by themselves.

The following afternoon, just after lunch, the girls said their goodbyes to Grace's parents. The snow fell gently on the lawn as Meg thanked them profusely for their hospitality. Susan told her she was welcome to come back anytime, the sooner the better. Henry jammed their bags into the trunk, trying to make sure there was some room for Michael's and Ryan's things as well. Henry made sure they had maps, their cell phones, and a blanket in case they broke down. Grace flashed her AAA card at him and rolled her eyes, telling him they would be fine and making some smart comment about not being sixteen years old anymore.

After he closed the trunk, he gave Grace a hug and kissed the top of her head. "I love you, baby. You girls be careful on the way home. If you get tired, let Michael drive, please. Don't be stubborn." Grace responded with another eye roll which made her father laugh. "Can I tell you a secret?" Henry asked in a hushed voice. She leaned in closer so she wouldn't miss it. "Your taste in men is almost as good as your mother's."

"Dad, you're a dork," she said as she nudged his shoulder, trying to look annoyed. But really, Grace was about to jump out of her skin with excitement because Henry liked Michael—a lot. "I love you both. We'll call you when we get in." After hugging her parents, she jumped into the car where Meg was already bouncing with excitement. The girls waved as they pulled out of the driveway and headed toward the Andrises' house.

Michael and Ryan were packed and standing on the porch waiting when they pulled into the driveway. Grace turned off the car and started laughing. "Is Liz ready to get rid of you two already? Why are you standing on the porch like you've been thrown out of the house?"

Michael smirked. "You haven't bothered to look at the weather, have you?" Grace shrugged with a questioning look on her face. "There's a storm coming; we need to get moving. Come on." He threw the bags in the overcrowded trunk and had to use considerable force to shut it. Grace ran into the house quickly so she could say goodbye to Liz and Michael Sr. They both gave her a big hug and wished them a safe trip, insisting they call when they made it home.

Liz pulled Grace into one last hug and whispered, "Take good care of my baby for me." Then she kissed her on the cheek and shooed her out the door.

"I will, I promise." Waving, Grace ran out to the car. Michael was already inside, sitting impatiently behind the wheel.

"What the hell do you think you are doing?" Grace asked as she ripped open the driver's side door.

"I'm driving. Get in," he directed. Grace, however, perched her hands to her hips and glared. "Please, be reasonable. I'll get us home faster."

She was about to throw a handful of snow directly into his face, when Meg saved him. "Come on, Grace, let the big baby drive, and you can be in charge of the radio. Let's get this road trip started." There was no mistaking the triumphant smirk on Michael's face when Meg jumped to his aid.

"Fine." She slammed the passenger side door as she fastened her seat belt. "Quit smiling at me; I'm mad at you." Her arms were crossed tightly over her chest when he started the car, but before pulling out of the driveway, Grace could see him grinning at her out of the corner of her eye. She tried to ignore him, but it wasn't working. All she could think about was how soft his lips were and how badly she wanted to lace her fingers into his hair and kiss that smug smile off his face.

"I thought you were going to get us home fast. So far we've been in the car for five minutes and gone nowhere!" she teased, as he threw the car into reverse and started flying down the snowy driveway. As soon as they hit the road, she asked the questions that always annoyed the hell out of Henry whenever they were in the car. "Are we there yet? How much longer until we get there? I think I need to pee."

Meg groaned from the backseat. "Are we going to have to listen to you two bicker for the next five hours?"

"The way Michael's driving, it may take more like seven now," Ryan said as he glanced over Michael's shoulder at the speedometer.

"Um, I hate to break it to all of you, but it's snowing. I'd prefer we make it back in one piece if you don't mind," Michael retorted as he reached over and took Grace's hand in his, giving it a squeeze.

They spent the next few hours talking and laughing. Michael was really funny and a great storyteller. He remembered every little detail of things that happened, much to Ryan's chagrin. He told Meg, in great detail, a hilarious story involving Ryan, a girl, and a night of karaoke where he tried to get a girl's attention by singing numerous sappy love songs after way too much beer.

"How'd that work out for you, honey?" Meg asked, patting him on the chest.

"Obviously you've never heard him sing." Michael chuckled from the front seat.

"Thanks, Mike."

"Am I lying?" Michael peeked back at his friend in the rear view mirror, eyebrows raised.

Ryan shrugged unapologetically and looked down at Meg. "I ended up getting a pitcher of beer poured on my head."

"Poor baby." Meg nuzzled her cheek against his chest. "Too bad. The bimbo's loss is my gain."

The snow began coming down harder the father into the mountains they traveled. What had started as occasional snowflakes fluttering through the sky changed into a fine, powdery snow that began to fall hard and fast. Giant snowplows tried to keep up with the weather, but it was apparent it was becoming a losing battle. When the girls mentioned they were hungry and wanted to eat, Michael found a more populated exit and stopped, eager to take a break from driving as well.

While they were inside the dinky restaurant, the weather went from bad to worse. The people at the table next to them had been driving up from Portland, and they said the roads were horrible about thirty miles farther south, toward the next section of mountains. There was a television that was giving weather updates every few minutes. The weatherman in his dark blue suit managed a smile as he broke the grave news that people in the city should expect a foot of snow to fall in the next few hours, that total was doubled for the mountain regions. The foursome was still at least two hundred miles away from Portland.

Grace nervously glanced out the window and watched the huge white snowflakes, now falling so fast she couldn't see across the street.

Michael took out his phone and called Jack to find out what was going on at home. Jack told him the news stations were reporting a number of accidents on the side roads, and that there was a huge pileup on the icy highway they were currently traveling on that had traffic backed up for miles. They were recommending people stay off the roads, if at all possible. Jack estimated they had only about another hour before they too would be in the heart of the storm.

Michael and Ryan began trying to figure out what the best course of action was. They both looked extremely concerned as they finished their discussion. "Ladies, how would you feel about stopping for the night?" Ryan asked, with his brow still furrowed, not sure how the girls would react to the suggestion. "We would need to go a little farther west, but I know there are some ski resorts that hopefully we can get to before this storm gets much worse. I don't want us to get stuck in the mountains during the worst of it."

Grace looked over at Meg and shrugged. "It's fine with me. Do you care?" The huge grin on her face was answer enough. "We'd better make a reservation, though; I'm sure rooms are going to be tough to find."

"Then we'd better get out of here. The only thing at this exit is this diner and a gas station," Ryan said as he tapped his fingers nervously on the top of the table. Not wanting to waste another minute, he quickly paid the waitress, and they took off in the car, trying to get through the mountains before the worst of the storm hit.

As they carefully made their way onto the highway, Grace took out her phone and was never so thankful for cell phone service in her life. She quickly called Susan for help.

"Hello?"

"Hi, Mom. Hey, I need your help with something."

"What do you need, baby? Where are you anyway?" The concern in her voice was obvious. Grace imagined her mother had been glued to her television, watching the weather updates and worrying.

"We're fine, Mom, don't worry. But the snow's getting really bad. Michael and Ryan think it might be dangerous to keep driving, so I think we're going to stop and spend the night."

Michael raised his eyebrows, waiting for Susan's reaction, while Meg giggled from the backseat.

"I think that's a good idea. Things are getting really nasty from what the news is saying. Oh, I'm so glad you girls aren't by yourselves. Now, how can I help?" Susan sounded genuinely relieved to hear they weren't going to brave the snow and dangerous highway much longer.

"Can you get on the computer and quickly find us a hotel and make a reservation?" she asked, knowing Susan was a whiz with online shopping and reservations. "Ryan thinks there might be some ski resorts in the area."

Susan jotted down the exit number they'd just stopped at and began searching for lodging in the area. "Give me a second. I'm searching hotels," Susan said as Grace heard her fingers pecking away at the keyboard.

The first place Susan called was booked for the night. Because of the weather, they even had people sleeping in the dining room of their restaurant as they were booked to overcapacity. Grace passed the information on to the rest of the group and watched their expressions grow more concerned. Michael cursed and clutched the wheel tighter as the snowfall picked up in intensity.

Reaching across the car, Grace gently rubbed Michael's back, trying to relieve some of the building stress in his muscles. He glanced over at her and smiled appreciatively.

"Grace, you're on Route 12 outside of Yakima, right?" Susan's voice crackled through the phone.

"Yeah, about five miles or so, why?" She pressed her finger in her other ear so she could hear her mother better with the sketchy connection.

"I found a place—Crystal Mountain. It's about twenty minutes off the highway you're on, but they have a few rooms left. How many am I booking?"

"Um, just get one if it has two beds. If not, I guess we need two rooms," Grace said to Susan as Meg nodded her head in agreement.

Susan managed to book a room with two queen sized beds in Michael's name at the ski resort. Michael continued along the highway, wanting to be out of the mountains as soon as possible. The roads grew more treacherous the further they traveled. Their jovial mood from earlier was forgotten as Michael concentrated on the snow-covered road in front of him. Grace sighed in relief that he and Ryan were with them; otherwise, she would have been the one driving through this mess.

Shortly after three o'clock, they pulled up to the resort, and by then the snow was falling so hard they had trouble seeing the lights of the lodge in the distance. Grace was never so happy to see a hotel overhang as she was then.

Michael parked the car and helped the girls dig through the trunk to find their bags. Unfortunately, everything was jammed in so tightly they couldn't really reach all the bags, so Grace ended up grabbing a random tote and headed into the hotel after Meg. She and Ryan were sitting on a brown leather couch in the lobby while Grace and Michael went to the front desk to get the room keys.

"We have a reservation under the name Andris," Michael said smoothly to the woman behind the front desk. She was in her mid-thirties, if Grace had to guess, and she looked thrilled by his polite attention. She grinned and fumbled around with her computer for a second.

"Oh yes, here it is. One room with two beds. Let me see what we have available." She continued talking to herself on and off as she pecked away at the buttons on the keyboard. Grace couldn't help but look around the room and take in beauty of the hotel.

The lobby was filled with rich shades of brown and yellow painted on the walls with rustic details and trim throughout to give it that ambiance of a distinguished lodge feel. The wood floor was freshly polished and the deep brown of the lobby desk made the hotel feel very warm and inviting. Off in the corner, a large fire raged in the fireplace, throwing soft light and shadows throughout the lobby.

"I'm sorry. It seems that because of the storm and the driving conditions, the previous guest is refusing to vacate that room. All we have left are rooms with one king-sized bed. Would you like two of those instead?" she asked, her eyes glancing over to where Meg and Ryan were sitting.

"That would be fine, as long as they're close to each other, please." Michael shamelessly flashed his dimples which made the woman blush. Grace internally rolled her eyes at his flirtatious attempt to manipulate the poor woman.

"The only two rooms I have are luckily across the hall from each other, but they're our deluxe rooms and are more expensive," she started to explain, but Michael cut her off and slipped her his credit card.

"We'll take them." Grace's eyes grew huge when she saw how much the rooms would cost, but Michael turned to her with love in his eyes. "I'm not getting back on that road, and an evening with you is worth every cent." He kissed the tip of her nose and signed his name across the piece of paper the woman handed him.

"Here are your keys," she said, extending one key to Michael and the other to Grace. "And these are for your friends." She handed a pair of keys in an envelope to Michael and nodded in the direction of Meg and Ryan. "I'll call Mark to help you with your bags."

Michael held up his key to Grace's; both were for room 315. "Looks like we're roomies," he said as he ran his fingers down her cheek and along her jaw line. The twinkle in his blue eyes was making her knees wobble and her stomach flip, so she leaned back against one of the wooden columns in the lobby for support. Michael took step closer, nearly pinning Grace against the pole. "Maybe you can help me get ready for bed." Her face turned bright red because she had been thinking the same thing, but she would never admit that to him. She turned her head to the side and the next thing Grace knew, his mouth was right at her ear. "Or I can help get you *into* bed, whichever you prefer." His tongue gently ran along her earlobe, making her shiver.

"Ryan," Grace managed to croak out, completely distracted by Michael and his attempt to seduce her, "take this before I do something I most certainly will not regret." She held her key out in her trembling hand and tossed it into his lap.

Michael dramatically put his hand over his heart. "I'm hurt that you don't want to spend the night with me, Grace."

"It'll hurt more to be out six hundred bucks and a kick ass pair of shoes, Mr. Andris. Trust me."

Meg stifled a giggle and gave Ryan a playful nudge. "Go on, Ryan, help save Grace from herself. You know how hard it is for a girl to resist the advances of a sexy man who is hell bent on trying to seduce her."

Ryan laughed as he tucked the key into his pocket and helped Meg up off the couch. She went over to Grace and gave her one of the keys from her envelope to room 314, their new home for the evening.

"Can I help you with your bags?" a deep voice asked from behind them. Grace turned to find an average looking guy who was about their age dressed in a maroon hotel uniform with black pants. He was much shorter than Michael and Ryan, but stocky. His hair was on the longer side but gelled back to keep it off his face. There was a colorful tattoo peeking out from under the collar of his shirt.

"My name is Mark. What's yours?" he asked as he held his hand out to Grace.

Innocently, she went to shake his hand and was disgusted when he kissed it instead. *That's creepy,* she thought to herself as she wiped it against her jeans. "Um, I'm Grace." She glanced over at Michael who had crossed his arms as he stood scowling at Mark.

"And you are?" he asked smoothly as he turned his attention to Meg, ignoring the men completely.

"Hi. I'm Meg." She gave him a small wave, which he returned with a wink. Ryan's mouth fell open slightly at Mark's apparent death wish. He and Michael exchanged a look that asked "Can you believe this guy?"

Happy to know the girls' names and paying no attention to Michael and Ryan, Mark loaded the bags onto the cart and started walking down the hall. "Follow me, ladies."

Michael and Ryan eyed at him suspiciously. In a show of male possession, Michael wrapped his arm around Grace's shoulders while Ryan took Meg's hand and pulled her as far away from Mark as possible. Grudgingly, they followed the smarmy hotel employee into the elevator, off to find their rooms for the night.

With five adults on the elevator, plus their bags, things were rather cramped inside. Michael and Ryan both placed themselves between Mark and the girls. Grace's back was pressed up against the chilly wall of the elevator as Michael's chest pressed against hers, the close proximity causing delicious friction between their bodies.

Grace couldn't help but wonder as Michael's hand settled low on her back and the sexual attraction between them increased if, by morning, the whole boycott could be over and someone might be crowned the winner. But who would it be? As Michael's fingers mischievously toyed with the neckline of her T-shirt, it was anybody's guess.

Chapter 20

The ride to the third floor was the most uncomfortable two minutes of Grace's life. Mark continued to make small talk with her and Meg, leaving the guys fuming. They, in return, spent the entire time giving him the dirtiest looks the girls had ever seen on their faces. Michael's hands fisted at his sides every time Mark would try and "accidentally" brush his shoulder against Grace. In a completely twisted way, Grace found Michael's jealous streak incredibly sexy.

Finally the doors to the elevator opened and they poured out of the cramped space onto the third floor. Mark led them to the left down a long carpeted corridor. About halfway down the hall, he stopped and pointed to a door. "Room 315, gentlemen." Swiftly he dropped their bags on the floor beside the door then turned his attention back to the girls.

"May I?" he asked, brazenly reaching for the room key in Meg's hand. She was so stunned all she could do was watch as he snatched the tiny piece of plastic from her grasp. He slid the key into the lock, waited for the green light, and then turned the handle. "Come in, ladies. I'll give you a tour of your room and show you where everything is."

Not knowing what to do or how to escape when he extended his arm and ushered the girls into the room, they warily followed. Grace glanced over her shoulder to find a furious Michael standing in the hallway with his hands firmly planted on his hips, and Ryan looked no better. She tried to give them a reassuring smile, but it didn't seem to help.

"So, ladies," Mark said as he let the door fall shut behind them, stopping the cart near the closet to unload the bags. "Welcome to Crystal Mountain. You have a beautiful view of the slopes." He pulled the curtains open to reveal the snow-covered landscape outside. It was a spectacular view of the area, with the dark lines of the ski lift marking the route the skiers followed on the mountain.

"Here's your television," he waved his hand at the armoire, and then sat on the bed and reached into the drawer of the nightstand, "and your remote." He ran his hand across the comforter and purred, "And your bed . . ."

The two women gave each other a shocked look. "Um . . . thanks. I think we've got it from here," Grace muttered, trying to cut the show short and get him to leave.

He winked but refused to be dismissed so easily. "Wait! I didn't show you the best part of this room yet." He leaped off the bed and walked into the bathroom. Willing to do anything to make him go away, they both followed, figuring the sooner he finished his little tour, the sooner he'd leave.

"The shower has a rainfall feature and six body jets, three on each side. The shower stall itself is also extra large. There's room for two . . . or even three," he said with his eyebrows raised as he again eyed Meg.

He pointed to the counter. "You also have all kinds of shampoos, soaps, and lotions at your disposal. And here is my favorite part," he said as he turned to the oversized tub in the corner, "the Jacuzzi." He ran his hand slowly and seductively across the smooth marble surface.

A loud thumping on the door interrupted them from the creepiest room tour of their lives. "Grace! Open up. Is that little twerp gone yet?" Michael yelled from the other side of the door. He was still smirking when she opened the door and mouthed "Thank you!" to him. His smile faded when he saw Mark over her shoulder. "Oh, I guess he's still here, isn't he?" Michael said without missing a beat. He strode into the room and protectively grabbed Grace's hand, pulling her to his side. "Thank you, but this tour is officially over. They can figure things out on their own; they're quite intelligent women." He didn't even try to hide the hostility in his voice.

Mark gave Michael a dirty look for interrupting, but refused to be distracted from his agenda. "Ladies, if you need *anything*, please call me. I would be happy to take care of you."

Ryan walked into the room just then to hear the end of what Mark was saying. He held his hand up to the shorter man, doing his best to look ominous. "No need to worry about them," he paused to read his name tag for effect, "Mark." He spat the name like it was a curse. "My friend and I will take care of anything these ladies may need." He snaked his arms around Meg's waist and kissed her neck. "And I mean *anything* they may need." Meg giggled as Ryan continued to kiss her in front of their audience.

With one arm, Michael held open the door to the girl's room and waited for Mark to take the hint. When he finally gave up and walked past Grace, his hand brushed against hers and she felt him slip a small piece of paper into it. Once Mark was safely in the hall, Michael slammed the door shut. "What the hell was that all about?"

Grace opened her hand and showed Michael the piece of paper Mark had given her. Meg started laughing. "He did *not* just give you his phone number."

Without even looking at it, Michael shredded the paper into pieces, swearing under his breath.

"Looks like you might have a little competition there for Grace's affections, Michael," Meg teased.

"Oh, I don't know about that, Meg. You're the one he was looking at when he was talking about how many people could fit into the shower," Grace shot back.

Ryan just shook his head back and forth. "Neither of you is to go anywhere in this place alone. Do you understand me?" He pointed to both of them. "If you leave this room, one of us needs to be with you." He looked over at Michael, who was nodding his head in agreement.

Grace went over and kissed Michael's cheek. "You can be my personal bodyguard, how does that sound?" She tried to defuse the tense situation with a little humor and put his mind at ease.

He looked at her seriously for a second and then a smile appeared on his face. "I would love to guard your body tonight, Grace. What a great suggestion." He smirked as he raised her hand, kissing the top of it, while never taking his eyes off of her. "Now, why don't you ladies unpack, get settled, and we'll meet up in a while and check this place out." He paused before he opened the door. "And please keep this double-locked."

Meg saluted them, and as soon as they closed the door, she fumbled loudly with the locks and hollered, "We're all locked in!" Grace could hear them chuckling until they disappeared inside their room.

Sifting through the closet, Grace handed Meg her black suitcase with the hot pink polka dots, and tossed her own blue and green plain bag onto the bed to sort through it and see what she had to wear. As she unzipped the lid, she paused in confusion. "Meg? Why are your clothes in my suitcase?"

From across the room, Meg was grinning sheepishly. "Well, you remember all that stuff I bought on our shopping trip? Funny thing, I didn't have enough room in my suitcases for it, so I kind of repacked your bags for you."

"What did you do to my clothes?" Grace shrieked, digging to the bottom of the bag, only to find it completely filled with Meg's size zero purchases.

"I needed more room so I consolidated your three bags into two and used the extra one for my stuff." Meg continued to look wide-eyed and innocent at Grace.

"And you didn't think it was important to tell me that when we were picking what bags to grab out of the car?" Grace continued looking through the bag, hoping that one piece of her clothing had made it into the hotel. The thought of wearing the same jeans and T-shirt all night was not a pleasant one.

"But I have no pajamas, nothing to sleep in tonight, just my jeans … unless I want to try and squeeze my butt into these." In her hand, she twirled a pair of extra small red silk boy shorts of Meg's she had found in the suitcase with a matching silk camisole. "If I don't move or breathe all night, I should be fine," Grace said sarcastically.

"Sorry," Meg offered. "In my defense, I had no idea we'd be stranded in a hotel. You'll have to blame the weather." She was digging through her bag to see if anything of hers might fit Grace.

"My bra is in the car," Grace groaned. Meg cocked an eyebrow suspiciously. "You know I hate wearing one on long car rides."

"I was gonna say, I know I dozed off, but it wasn't for that long. Michael better not have helped you out of it, either, because that would definitely be against one of our crazy rules." Meg shook her head and laughed.

"Have I told you lately that you're insane?" The snow continued to plummet from the sky with stunning intensity. The snow drifts looked at least two feet taller than they had been when they pulled into the parking lot. "I better go get it." Grabbing her jacket, Grace headed for the door when Meg stopped her.

"Are you crazy? The snow is three feet deep. Leave it alone, you'll be fine. I think you'll cause far more of a ruckus if you go down to the valet stand, in a snowstorm—braless—and ask them to retrieve the car so you can grab your undergarments off the front seat. Plus, Michael will kill you if you leave this room without him."

Not in the mood to trudge through waist deep snow, Grace zipped up her useless suitcase and stomped across the room, putting it into the closet before hurling herself onto the bed. Unfortunately there was nothing good to watch on television to help pass the time. Most of the local channels were all trying to outdo one another with their coverage of the storm.

"I'm going to try out the Jacuzzi!" Meg squealed when she finished unpacking her bag. She rounded up her iPod and a change of clothes before she dashed off into the bathroom. There was a loud rush of water as the tub began to fill. Bored, Grace looked around the room for something to amuse her. On the dresser was a tall pink ice bucket. She grabbed it and decided to go for a quick walk and get some ice.

As she passed the bathroom, the water shut off and the low hum of the Jacuzzi jets came from inside. Meg must have had her iPod on because when Grace tapped on the door there was no answer but she could hear her singing.

"I'm going to get ice," Grace said loudly to the closed door.

"What?" Meg yelled.

Grace stuck her head in the door and pointed to her ear buds, signaling for her to take them out. "I'm going to get ice."

"Call Michael," Meg said sternly.

"I'm perfectly capable of getting ice on my own, thank you."

"Grace!" Meg bellowed. "You get on the phone and call Michael right now. If you step foot outside this room—"

"Fine, I'll call. Just stop yelling." Her fingers pecked away at the buttons on the phone as she dialed nine, then their room number.

On the second ring, Ryan answered. "Hello?"

"It's Grace. Your lunatic girlfriend won't let me get ice alone. Apparently, I need a police escort. Are you or Michael available to make sure I'm not murdered and stuffed into the ice machine?"

Ryan chuckled. "I'll meet you in the hallway."

"I'm going to get ice with Ryan ... *alone*, and we may just be in love by the time we get back!" Grace snarled into the bathroom door, hoping to annoy Meg.

"Have fun." She dismissed Grace with a giggle and a wave and went back to singing at the top of her lungs.

When she opened the door to their room, Grace found Ryan leaning against the wall in the hallway. "What in the world are you two watching in there?" Ryan asked just as Meg tried to hit a high note that sounded more like a dying cat. Grace smiled and headed down the hallway in search of ice.

"That, Ryan, is the woman you love. She loves to sing, but doesn't do it well. She wants to try out for one of those reality singing shows someday. See? You had no idea what you were getting yourself into, did you?" They turned the corner into the tiny alcove that housed the ice, vending, and soda machines. "I wonder where the ax murderers are hiding," Grace said sarcastically as she glanced over her shoulder while Ryan filled the buckets with ice.

"Very funny. I know it sounds overly protective, but too bad. We're not about to let anything happen to the two of you on our watch, and that guy was weird. Humor us, OK?" He put his hands on her shoulders and marched her back down the hall.

"So what's Michael doing? Why did he make you come down here with me?" She tried to keep her tone casual as she chomped on a piece of ice from her bucket.

Of course, Ryan wasn't fooled. He smirked and pointed at his door. "His back was bothering him from the driving so he's in the Jacuzzi." His eyes glanced over toward the girl's door. "What's Meg up to?"

"She's in the tub too." A sinister grin spread across Ryan's face as he looked intently at the door to Grace's room. Having the same thought, she handed him the ice bucket and punched him in the shoulder. "If you sneak up on her, you better plug your ears because I promise you, she's a screamer." Grace crept across the hall and quietly opened the door to the guys' room.

"Yeah, I know." Ryan laughed as he slipped behind the door across the hall.

Grace let the door to the guys' room fall shut on its own. She could hear the sound of water gently splashing, probably as Michael shifted around in the tub.

What the hell are you doing, Grace? You go through that door and you will be in a small, confined room with a very wet and naked Michael. That could be a really bad idea, she told herself as she paced the room. *Are you serious? Who the hell cares? Get your ass in there, girl.*

Listening to her less than angelic side, she put her hand over her eyes and walked through the bathroom door. She peeked down at the small piece of the floor she could see under her hand and found his clothes lying on the bathroom floor. Grace quickly grabbed the button-down shirt he had been wearing in the car and carried it with her as she blindly staggered over to the counter that she knew was directly across from the tub.

"Hi," she said casually, trying not to think about the fact that he was totally naked only a few feet away. Her heart started to pound in her chest the more she thought about it.

There was a big splash of water as Michael realized someone was in the bathroom with him. The hum of the jets and the bubbling water had made her entrance rather stealthy. "Oh, it's you. Thank God! I thought it was Ryan, which would have been really awkward." His laughter echoed through the bathroom. "Um, why do you have your face covered?"

Her mind started spinning out of control. *Does that mean he wants me to look at him? What if I see him naked? That wouldn't be good. It would actually be phenomenal, amazing, life-alteringly great.* But, then again, she knew she'd lose the bet.

"I'm trying to give you your privacy. I just wanted to say hi, and maybe steal your shirt if you don't mind. Meg repacked my suitcase and didn't tell me so when I grabbed a bag from the car, it had all her stuff in it, and I don't want to go out in the snow for my clothes, and oh yeah, I'm not wearing a bra." Grace had a verbal explosion of nerves.

"Please take your hand off your face so I can see you when you're talking to me. Relax, there are a bunch of bubbles in here, you won't see anything." She could hear the laughter in his voice as it dropped to a husky rumble. "Unless you want to …"

"Keep your penis covered, Michael. Do we understand each other?" Grace warned before she slowly removed her hand from her face.

"I promise. As long as you keep your breasts covered, we should be fine." Not trusting him fully, Grace peeked carefully between her fingers to find him sitting in the tub, the jets causing the water to bubble and move around him, making the water extremely blurry and keeping all his bits covered. His chin was resting on his hand along the edge of the tub; his piercing blue eyes raked over Grace's body, taking her breath away. He sat up and ran his hand through his already wet hair; then he held his arm out to the bubbling water. "Care to join me?"

Grace closed her eyes and prayed for strength when she heard the seductive tone of his voice. "Michael, you need to behave, please," she pleaded with him. She took a deep breath before she opened her eyes, only to find him holding his hand out to her, beckoning her to come closer. *You have no other clothes; do not jump into that tub, Grace! Don't do it...* She took his hand and knelt next to the tub, their fingers intertwined as she sat facing him, occasionally getting splashed by the thrashing waves created by the Jacuzzi jets.

"So, how many more hours now?" he asked casually, like he wasn't sitting there completely naked as he gently kissed each of the fingers on her hand and began to move his lips higher up her arm.

"One hundred twenty-five, but who's counting?" She made a feeble attempt to feign indifference, but if he only knew how many times in the last few days Grace had glanced at her watch to calculate how much time was left in the bet, she'd be mortified. When he lowered her hand she let it dangle in the warm bubbling water, making sure to keep her eyes on his face and not let them drift down and look into the water.

"So what were you saying about your clothes?" he asked, breaking Grace out of her trance.

"Meg decided to unpack my bag to make room for all the things she bought, so she crammed all my clothes into two suitcases and filled the third with her extra stuff. When we got out of the car, I grabbed the one with her stuff in it. Now I have no clothes, so I may need to borrow a shirt of yours later, if you don't mind. I might steal this one now, if that's OK?" The black button-down shirt that she'd picked up off the floor was still in her hand.

"You can take whatever you need. Everything in my suitcase is clean." He waved his arm toward the bathroom door, smiling. Grace also remembered that he had made it very clear back in Spokane he enjoyed seeing her in his clothes.

"Thanks. I'm going to leave and give you some privacy. I'll stop over later and grab a T-shirt from you." Grace stood up to leave but from such an angle, she could make out the outlines of his long legs in the water. She followed them up toward his body, and then slapped her hand over her eyes. She could hear Michael laughing at her bizarre behavior.

"Grace, sweetheart, did you peek?" His hand rubbed her leg while she stood next to the tub.

"I'm sorry...Oh, just...Never mind. I need to go. Now." Flustered, Grace leaned down, her eyes still closed tightly, and blindly went to kiss him goodbye. She felt two very wet, warm hands on her face that pulled her toward him.

"Open your eyes, Grace," he whispered softly. She could feel his breath on her lips and she knew when she dared to open her eyes they would be face to face. Stretching out, she put her arms onto either side of the tub to keep herself from falling in. When her eyes finally opened, his lust-filled eyes greeted her. "I love you." Three simple words that set her body on fire. Three simple words that melted her heart.

Then he kissed her.

The warmth of his lips traveled down to her chest, making her body tingle from head to toe. Grace tightened her grip on the tub, trying to control herself, but her resolve was wavering with every second that passed. The steam from the tub began to rapidly warm her body as he kissed her longer and harder than he had in a few days. By the time he pulled away, her heart was flying in her chest. "OK, now you may go." The slow, sensual curve of his lips was intoxicating.

Grace needed space and distance so she could think straight. She rolled her eyes and stood up, once again shielding her eyes. There was a gasp from Michael then she felt a cool sensation on her chest. She looked down to see the front of her shirt had draped into the water when she was leaning over the tub, kissing Michael. The cooler air away from the tub and the transparency of her wet shirt left little to the imagination as Michael sat there, open mouthed, staring at her breasts and now highly visible nipples. Quickly wrapping her arms across her chest, Grace turned bright red.

"Oops." Her eloquence reduced to scrambled babbling, that was all she could manage to make come out of her mouth as she stood there mortified. She glanced down at Michael, who was doing his best not to laugh, biting his lip and trying to breathe slowly, but the twinkle in his eyes gave him away. "Do you find this funny, Michael?"

"Funny, no. I find it absolutely hilarious!" And all the laugher he had been trying to contain came spilling out of him, echoing off the bathroom walls.

Funny? You want funny, Mr. Sexy Guy in the Jacuzzi looking all hot and laughing at my accidental wet T-shirt contest? We'll see who's laughing now. Grace glared at him as she picked up his black shirt off the floor and held it between her knees. She turned her back to him, raised her shirt slowly over her head, and glanced back over her shoulder at him as she held the damp shirt in her hand. Michael sat in the tub, stunned at the sight of her completely bare back as she balled up the shirt and chucked it into his face. She bent over and grabbed his shirt, sliding her arms into the sleeves, and pulling it up onto her shoulders. Still completely unbuttoned but with her breasts mostly covered, Grace turned to face him.

"Too bad you're in the tub; I was going to ask you to help button me," Grace said with a sexy little pout.

Before she knew what was happening, Michael stood up in the tub. Her eyes immediately flew to his, never breaking his gaze as he stalked, dripping wet, closer and closer to her. He stopped in front of her and ran his fingers through his hair, which for some reason made Grace gasp out loud. The combination of the water beading and dripping down his creamy skin, along with the knowledge that he was completely naked while within touching distance made her knees wobble.

"I wasn't expecting this reaction. Y-you do know you're naked, right?" Grace asked, her voice trembling uncontrollably.

"Yep." A single word was all he muttered, his eyes telegraphing his intense desire.

"And you aren't at all embarrassed?" With everything in her, Grace forced herself to stay calm as his hands stretched out and touched the exposed section of flesh between her breasts. Her body trembled uncontrollably at his touch and the pleasure it promised. He gently took the two sides of the shirt and began leisurely buttoning them together.

"Not at all," he said as he glanced back and forth from the buttons to her eyes, the smug grin never leaving his face. Grace dared to take a moment and admire the way the water glistened on his shoulders, accentuating his thick muscles. Her hands were clenched into fists at her side, fighting the urge to run her fingers down the length of his muscular arm.

"Well, that's OK. I think I'm flustered enough for the both of us," Grace said breathlessly as she leaned against the bathroom door, feeling lightheaded. Michael took another step toward her, finishing the last button, then standing confident and sexy in front of her.

"Are you feeling all right, sweetheart? You look a little flushed. Maybe you should come lay down … with me." Grace froze. All bodily functions shut down; she couldn't breathe, move, or speak. She just stared at him as he inched his face closer to hers. "What do you say?" he whispered as he wrapped his arms around her waist, pulling her up against his wet, naked body and began kissing her neck.

"Michael … I, um … wow …" There was no way for her to stop her incoherent muttering as his warm lips continued kissing her neck and shoulders.

Screw the bet, she thought as Michael nibbled relentlessly on her earlobe.

<h1 style="text-align:center">Chapter 21</h1>

*I*s that a yes?" he asked as Grace felt his hands slide down her back and come to rest firmly on the curve of her hips. He pushed her back into the door, their bodies crashing together creating an unforgettably wonderful friction between them. It was then that she realized he was just as aroused as she was.

"Oh, Michael." The words came out of her mouth as a deep throaty moan. Not only did she not want to fight him any longer, she didn't even think it was possible. She wanted him with every fiber of her being and was ready to lose the bet just to spend one night with him.

His head immediately raised, his ice blue eyes locking on her. "Grace, I love you," he whispered as she knotted her fingers deep into his wet hair. Her feet left the ground as he picked her up allowing her legs to wrap tightly around his waist. The moment that they had been waiting weeks for was ruined by a loud slamming sound.

"Grace? Michael? Where the hell are you?" Ryan called from the other side of the door. "Oh, wait, never mind. I'll leave. I'm not here. Carry on. Forget you heard me."

Michael let out a groan at the sound of Ryan's voice. Grace slid down his body, making Michael stagger back from the contact with his aroused groin. When her feet hit the floor, she leaned back against the door, gasping for breath.

"It's fine, Ryan. We're just … talking in here," Grace stammered as she kicked the bathroom door with her heel in frustration. For a few seconds, she buried her face into her hands, desperately trying to pull herself together. When she finally looked up, Michael had a white bath towel wrapped low around his waist. The beads of water were still slipping down his chest, leaving slick trails of moisture down to his chiseled abs.

Michael put plenty of distance between them, while they both tried to regain their composure. "It's all your fault, you know," he said as he pointed an accusing finger in Grace's direction. She opened her mouth to set him straight but he continued before she could speak. "I told you to keep your breasts covered. But then you go and get your shirt wet. Then, as if that isn't bad enough, you take the damn thing off right in front of me," he said, gesturing his hand in the air. "What's a guy supposed to do?"

As the events of the last few minutes began to sink in, Grace started giggling, unable to stop. She slid down the door laughing.

Ryan decided to throw in his snarky two cents. "Hey, I don't want to criticize your technique, Mike, but I don't think it's normal for your lady to be laughing at you like that. You may want to try something different. She should be doing more moaning than laughing if you're doing it right."

"Shut it, Ryan. We aren't doing anything," Michael yelled at the door, then dropped his voice and added with a wink for Grace's ears only, "anymore." He leaned back against the counter top, pouting.

Grace got up and cautiously, walked over and gave him a kiss. "So close." She grinned and patted the palm of her hand against the side of his face. "Better luck next time, lover boy." Heading for the door, she paused with her hand on the knob. "And thanks for the shirt." She pulled the collar up to her nose and took a deep breath. "Mmm, it still smells like you. Yummy," she purred, rubbing the material against her body. As she walked out the door, she could hear Michael cursing, followed by the shower turning on.

"Hello, there." Ryan leaned against the wall with his arms folded across his chest and a huge grin on his face.

Stuck in the awkward moment with absolutely no defense, Grace fluffed her hair around her face to help hide her embarrassment. "Stop looking at me like that. Nothing happened."

He eyed her suspiciously, but hearing the twinge of disappointment in her voice, he knew she was telling him the truth. "It's not me I'd be worried about explaining your wardrobe choice to." He gave his thumb a point toward the doorway where Meg stood, silent but looking like she just might burst.

"He better not be using up all the hot water. I need a shower." Ryan tried to change the subject, but Meg continued to stare at Grace with her mouth open.

"Oh, you have nothing to worry about. There will still be plenty of warm water. I'm pretty sure right now he's got the water on the icy side." Ryan laughed out loud when they heard Michael's yelp from the bathroom as he stepped into the frigid shower.

Meg gave a sharp tug on Grace's arm and pulled her out of their room, dragging her across the hall. "Is there something you'd like to tell me?"

"No," Grace said, refusing to make eye contact with her. There was no way she wanted to admit what just happened, or almost happened, in the bathroom with Michael. She felt her cheeks burn with embarrassment at the memory of her legs wrapped around his waist and the enormous bulge... "I have no idea what you're talking about, Meg."

"OK, let's start with: Why are you in Michael's shirt? What happened to *your* shirt? Why are the buttons all done wrong? And why the hell is the front of you all wet?" She sat silently next to Grace on the bed, patiently waiting for answers.

"I'm wearing his shirt because mine got wet, accidentally, so I borrowed his." Meg raised her eyebrow at Grace, indicating she should continue her explanation. Instead of clarifying, though, Grace kept on talking. "My shirt's in their Jacuzzi; I threw it at Michael." She didn't dare look Meg in the face. "As for the buttons, I guess he wasn't paying attention." Grace mumbled the "he" as softly as she could, but Meg and her damn dog ears caught it anyway.

"*He* wasn't paying attention? *He?*" The shrill tone of her voice and the way her foot began tapping wildly told Grace there would be no quick dropping of this topic. Meg wanted every last detail.

Grace tried to remain unaffected and stoic, but a goofy smile came across her face before she could stop it. Her head bobbed up and down in answer to Meg's question.

"Eek!" Meg screamed as she clapped her hands together. "Oh my God, you've got to tell me everything."

Taking a deep breath, Grace prepared to come clean. "The reason the front of me is wet is... Oh, Meg, do I really have to tell you?" She was willing to beg, bribe, and threaten her way out of it, but the stubborn set of Meg's jaw told Grace nothing would work. "OK, fine. So he *may* have gotten out of the tub while I was in the bathroom, and he kind of started kissing my neck."

"Oh my God, Grace! Was he naked?"

Grace clamped her hand over Meg's mouth to quiet her high-pitched shouting. "Shh! They're right across the hall. Stop screaming," Grace hissed. "Does the whole hotel have to know that Michael had me pressed up against the bathroom door while he was naked and asked me to go to bed with him?" The words flew out of Grace's mouth before she could stop them.

Meg's eyes were enormous. With a warning look, Grace lowered her hand cautiously from Meg's face and allowed her to speak. "Did you guys … did you … are you out?" she asked quietly.

With obvious disappointment, Grace shook her head. "No, Ryan showed up just in time." She sighed, half in relief, half in disappointment, and then muttered something about 'perfect timing.'

Two arms wrapped around her. "Oh, Grace, I'm sorry. If you want, Ryan and I can make ourselves scarce and you guys can pick up right where you left off."

"Am I out of the bet?" Grace asked, wondering if she had pushed the rules to the max with that little display in the bathroom.

Meg looked at her suspiciously. "I'm not sure, since I wasn't there. Do you think you should be out of the bet?"

"No, I don't think so. There wasn't a specific 'no nudity' clause in our boycott." Meg rolled her eyes at Grace. "Fine, but I didn't see anything, I swear! I didn't peek, not once, even though, God, I wanted to." She suddenly burst into laughter.

"Fine, if you say you're still in, then you're in. I believe you."

"So what did you two do while I was being seduced? And why does it reek of nail polish in here?" Grace sniffed the pungent air around her.

Meg proudly threw out her pink fingers and toes. "Ryan painted my nails. He did a really good job, don't you think?"

Each nail was perfectly painted, smooth and even. Grace paused to admire his handiwork. "Did you scream for him?" she asked casually as she stood up from the bed, looking for the remote control.

"What?" Meg asked as her head snapped in Grace's direction. "What are you talking about?"

"When Ryan walked into the bathroom and scared you, did you scream?"

"Oh that, yep, I screamed," she admitted sheepishly as she fidgeted with her fingers.

"I tried to warn him."

Their conversation was interrupted by a ringing phone. Meg flipped around and grabbed hers off the nightstand. "Hello? Hi. Really?" She glanced over at

Grace and smirked. "Yeah, I think she could use one too. OK, give us a few seconds and we'll be ready." She closed the phone and was on her feet, heading for the closet. "Apparently, Ryan thinks Michael needs a drink after your 'alone time,' so we're all going to go down to the hotel bar. We need to hurry up."

"Meg, I have nothing to wear! Look at me." Grace showed off the damp shirt and jeans she was currently wearing. Her other shirt was in no better shape.

Pausing to assess the situation, Meg looked at her with a critical eye then smiled. "You are so lucky the shirt dress is back in style. Come on, let's get you ready. Michael will love this!" Laughing, she dragged Grace into the bathroom and aimed the hairdryer directly at her chest to dry the oversized shirt. Next, she rummaged through her bag and found a pair of black leggings that were mostly Lycra, so Grace was able to wear them without difficulty, and a pair of black patent leather heels. She finished the outfit off with a thick red belt that she cinched high on Grace's waist to help accentuate her chest.

Grace did a little twirl so show off her handiwork. "Meg, you are simply amazing." She gave her friend a reverent bow.

"All in a day's work. It was also the least I could do since it's my fault your clothes are buried under three and a half feet of snow in the car." Meg smirked as she pulled the red baby doll dress over her head and grabbed the white sweater that was on top of her suitcase. There was a loud knock on the door.

Meg skipped to the door and opened it. "Come on in!"

Ryan and Michael walked into the room, looking downright delicious.

Both opted for more casual clothes; Ryan in a form fitting brown crew neck sweater that had cream-colored stripes down the center of his chest and dark brown pants. Michael was wearing a black button down shirt with white pinstripes and a pair of black jeans. If his clothes didn't make him look sexy enough, the smirk on his face sealed the deal.

"Would you like to explain why you opened the door without asking who it was first?" Ryan interrogated Meg as she took one last look in the mirror.

"Because we knew you big, strong men were on your way over." She gave his chest a flirty tap and kissed his cheek. Ryan gave her a stern look but wisely decided to drop the subject.

As Michael made his way over to Grace, she felt the blush rush into her cheeks as his eyes raked over her body, admiring her outfit. "You have no idea how lovely you look," he whispered as Grace wrapped her arms around him. "You really are irresistible in my clothes."

"You look pretty yummy yourself, even with clothes on." The way his cheeks turned pink made Grace laugh.

"About that, I'm sorry. That wasn't very gentlemanly of me to do that to you back in my bathroom. I don't know what got into me. I promise, it won't happen again," he said as he stared intently at the carpet.

Grinning, Grace lifted his face so she could look him in the eye. "It most definitely better happen again in, say, one hundred twenty-three hours?"

In the matter of a few seconds, the embarrassment in his face vanished and was replaced by a very sexy grin. "If you insist." His lips came to hers as his arms wrapped around her. Then he lowered his hands so they settled on her rear, to which he gave a firm squeeze.

Across the room, Meg cleared her throat. "My offer still stands, Grace. We can vanish," she said with a giggle.

She gave Michael a tap on the chest and broke the kiss before things got out of hand again. "Let's go get a drink," Grace said decidedly as she fanned her face, trying to make her flushed cheeks cool down. Hand in hand, they headed out the door behind Meg and Ryan.

The hotel bar was packed. All the people who had been trapped by the snow filled the room, looking for a way to pass the time until the snow passed and they could return to the roads. Ryan found a small semi-circle shaped booth they could sit at. Grace and Meg slid into the middle, with Michael and Ryan on the ends. They started flipping through the drink menu when the waitress came over to the table looking slightly frazzled.

"Hi, my name is Tiffany. Can I get you something from the bar? We're running low on scotch, so if that's your drink of choice, speak now or forever hold your peace." She glanced over her shoulder at the bartender, who was filling drink orders at a fevered pace.

Michael leaned his head toward the waitress and whispered something in her ear that made her smile.

What the hell?

Meg smacked Grace's leg and questioned her with her eyes. Not having a clue what they might be chatting about, Grace shrugged her shoulders, trying not to be jealous of the fact that Michael was inches away from this Tiffany chick, having a private conversation.

When she giggled, Grace kicked him—hard—on the shin under the table. He winced, but made sure he finished chatting with Tiffany before he turned away. "Ouch!" he said, rubbing his leg while his new friend scurried away from the table. "Sweetheart, are you jealous?"

Childishly, Grace glared at him and moved as far away from him as possible in their cramped space. Before she could tell him off, that floozy Tiffany was back, whispering something to Michael that made him leave the table. As he turned his back to walk away, the sound of Grace's hand slamming into the table top made him pause, turn back, and grin. "Relax. I'll be right back." Without another word, he wandered off with the hussy whose name Grace had forgotten. She decided she would refer to her as "the slut."

"What the hell is he doing?" Meg hissed in Grace's ear.

"I have no idea, but I may need your help burying a body later."

"Hers or his?" Meg asked as she shook her head from side to side, watching the pair saunter over to the bar.

Overhearing everything, Ryan snorted with laughter.

"What the hell is he doing?" Grace threw up her hands in disgust.

Grace watched Michael as he shook the bartender's hand and had a quick conversation with him. The bartender slapped him on the shoulder, and the next thing Grace knew, Michael had gotten behind the bar and set four glasses in front of him. Ryan decided he wanted to get in to the action and left the table to join Michael, the bartender, and the slut.

"Where do you think we could find a shovel?" Meg growled as her eyes shot laser beams into the back of Ryan's head.

The slut put her hand on Ryan's back, her trampy red fingernails rubbing across his back. Grace had to hold Meg in place since she was ready to climb over the table and rip the girl's head off.

Ryan stepped behind the bar and took two of the glasses from Michael, filling them with ice and two different clear liquids, and finishing them off with a lime wedge in each.

While he did that, Michael was measuring and mixing multiple ingredients as the bartender and the slut watched his every move.

"If I wasn't so mad at them right now, I'd mention how hot they look when they're behind the bar like that, but since I'm pissed … Oh hell, they're hot. There's no denying it." Grace rested her face in her hand in frustration.

Meg let out a small sigh, seconding the opinion. Grace watched Michael pour an orange concoction into the two glasses; then he reached for a third from under the bar, where he poured the remainder of the contents from his shaker.

He offered the third glass to the slut, who tasted it and smiled. Then he offered the cup to the bartender, who laughed and downed the rest of the drink. He gave Michael a slap on the back, and the two men started back toward the table with four drinks in hand.

Annoyed beyond words, neither woman made any attempt to hide their irritation. Grace sat back into the booth, her arms tightly folded across her chest, an undeniable scowl on her face. Meg dug into her purse and pulled out a compact which she used to fix her hair and makeup while completely ignoring Ryan as he sat down beside her.

"I made something," Michael said as he sat down.

Grace narrowed her eyes at him. "A new friend?" she snapped as she glared over at the slut, thinking up a hundred different ways to make her bleed.

Michael laughed when he realized she was staring at Tiffany. "No, sweetheart, I made you and Meg a drink. The bartender didn't know how to make it, so I showed him." He slid a glass in front of both of the girls. Then his hand slid off the table discretely and found its way to Grace's upper thigh, causing her to blush as his fingers played with the hem of his shirt. "Taste it," he whispered, anxiously awaiting their opinions.

The girls exchanged a suspicious glance and then Meg stared at the glass on the table. Very dramatically, she rolled her eyes, put the compact away, and raised the drink to her lips.

Grace followed suit, realizing she needed a drink pretty badly when she felt Michael's hand snake up under the bottom hem of the shirtdress she was wearing and continue higher up her thigh. She took a big swig of the drink and was surprised by how good it tasted.

The glass appeared to have orange juice, cranberry juice, and something red, maybe strawberry, in it. It was cold and sweet, and it tasted so good, Grace drank some more. Meg had sucked down half of hers before turning to Ryan and asking if there was alcohol in it. He just laughed and nodded his head yes.

Licking her lips, Grace said, "This is really good. I definitely want more of it."

Michael and Ryan laughed out loud.

"What is this?" Grace took another sip, trying to figure out the remaining ingredients. She could definitely taste the alcohol. Whatever it was, Michael had made them really strong, she knew that much. Grace couldn't imagine how Meg had missed the alcohol in it.

Michael couldn't help but grin. "I'm really glad you like it. The drink is called 'Screaming Sex with the Bartender.'" That sexy twinkle was back in his eyes as his finger grazed the edge of Grace's underwear, making her jump at his touch.

To stop Michael's undercover explorations, Grace clamped her hand down on top of his and pushed it toward her knee. "Well, it is very good, but it's a lot to live up to," Grace said as she raised her glass to her lips for another desperate sip.

Meg's glass was empty and she was already in Ryan's lap, whispering in his ear before the second drink hit the table. The alcohol was starting to do its job. The grin of masculine satisfaction on Ryan's face was priceless.

With everyone's inhibitions fading, Michael saw his opportunity and took it. He bent his head and started whispering to Grace. "Don't forget I have amazing skills in certain areas. I don't think I'll have any problems making you scream if I put my mind to it, Grace."

As if her heart wasn't already flying in her chest, that comment kicked it into overdrive. She felt Michael's hand moving along her leg again, making her mind race back to that bathroom and the feel of his wet body against hers when he'd had her pressed against the door. What she wouldn't give to go back upstairs and pick things up where they left off.

"Ladies, the gentleman in red sends you these drinks with his regards." The slut, Tiffany, pointed toward the door, where they caught a glimpse of Mark before he dashed into the crowd.

Michael and Ryan began swearing as they tasted the drinks that Mark had sent over, slamming the glasses onto the table.

"Orgasms?" Ryan hissed. "He sent you orgasms? When I find that little—" Ryan was on his feet until Meg put her hand on his arm, pulling him back into the booth.

"The guy has a slight crush. Let it go. I like the screaming sex with the bartender much better than a boring old orgasm anyway." Her loud, flirty giggle got his attention, and he relaxed back into his seat.

Michael, however, still looked ready to kill. "Michael, come on, he's a kid. Leave it at that. Nothing to be worried about." Grace tried to settle him by running her hands down his arm.

"I'm not at all worried; I'm just going to strangle the little twerp the next time I see him."

An hour later, they left the bar. Meg was completely drunk, and Grace was definitely tipsy. Michael had made another round of "screaming sex," and they were so tasty they didn't last long at the table.

When they arrived back at the rooms, the girls needed to take a nap and sleep off the alcohol. Michael said he'd come get them around eight-thirty so they could go to dinner. He scooped a wobbling Grace up into his arms and carried her to the bed so she wouldn't fall and hurt herself. Ryan did the same to Meg. Then they tucked the girls in, gave them a quick kiss on the head, and quietly headed back out the door.

"They really are dreamy, aren't they?" Meg sighed from her side of the bed.

"Yeah, we got pretty lucky, didn't we?" Grace tried to close her eyes to sleep, but every time she did, she saw Michael, wet and glistening in the bathroom. Her eyes flew open and instead of sleeping, she found herself staring at the cracks in the ceiling. Meg was tapping her foot anxiously beside her. "We aren't going to get any sleep, are we?"

Grace laughed and sat up in bed, leaning back against the headboard. "What should we do instead?"

Meg scooted out from under the covers and grabbed the remote off the nightstand. "Let's find a movie. That should kill some time until they come back." She started flipping the channels in search of the pay per view movies. They were trying to decide between a horror movie and a comedy when there was a loud knock on the door.

Meg squealed and flopped off the bed, still a bit drunk. "It's Ryan! I knew he couldn't stay away for too long." She took off toward the door, and as she threw it open, she said, "Hey, sailor, come here often?" in her best, husky voice.

Chapter 22

Grace laughed at Meg's flirting until she heard a man's voice—one that most definitely wasn't Ryan's or Michael's.

"Hey, there, little lady. You going to invite me in?" Mark's gruff voice was unmistakable. Grace could hear Meg stammering, her head too foggy from the alcohol to come up with a quick comeback.

Grace scooted to the end of the bed and looked toward the door to find Mark already standing inside the doorway while Meg was leaning against the wall, trying to block his path with her body. He took another step into the room, and Grace's survival instincts took over. She leaned across the bed, grabbed Meg's phone, and called Ryan.

"Hey, baby…" he answered.

"Ryan, get over here now! That Mark guy is—" She didn't get to finish before the phone clunked to the ground on his end and she heard Ryan yell at Michael to get his ass out of bed, followed by a nasty string of profanity.

Grace closed the phone and tucked it under her leg just in case she needed it again. She peeked over to see what Mark was doing. He had moved closer to Meg, who was nervously looking back over her shoulder at Grace for help, using her blond hair as a shield between her and Mark. Grace held up the cell phone, and she saw Meg sigh in relief.

Not even a second later, the door across the hall flew open, and in the blink of an eye Ryan had pushed his way past Mark, swept Meg up into his arms and carried her over his shoulder back to his room.

Instead of a hasty retreat, Michael barreled inside and held Mark by the shoulder against the wall. He looked Grace in the eyes, pointed his finger at her, and said in a lethal voice, "Don't move an inch."

Numbly, she nodded her head and sat back on the bed.

Michael barked "In the hall!" to Mark and dragged him out the door. Grace waited until she heard the door slam shut to leap out of bed and press her ear to the door, not wanting to miss a second of the conversation between the two men.

Out in the hall, she could hear Ryan asking Mark what he thought he was doing while Michael paced back and forth on the phone. Grace guessed from his tone that he was talking with the front desk, insisting they send a manager up to their floor immediately to deal with Mark before they did. Ryan was cursing at Mark and threatening to wipe the smirk off his face.

As the shouting continued, Grace decided to call across the hall.

"Hello?" Meg said.

"Are you listening to this?" Grace whispered as she peered out the peephole, trying to see their faces.

"Of course, but I can't see them out the peephole, can you?"

"No, not anymore…Oh, there's another voice! That must be the manager." Straining her ears, Grace heard Michael insist that Mark stay away from their girlfriends and their rooms.

The manager quickly agreed and said he'd escort Mark off the floor himself.

Michael and Ryan came back into her view and were deep in conversation when Grace moved away from the peephole and sat down on the floor by the door.

"Well, I guess they took care of everything. Are you all right?" Grace realized she had no idea what Mark had said to Meg earlier.

"Yeah, he was just telling me that he liked my dress and he wanted to come in and hang out with us. What a creeper. Oh, hi, Ryan. Grace, I gotta go."

There was a noise outside the door. *Shit, Michael's coming!* She tried to scramble to her feet and run to the bed so he wouldn't know what she had been up to, but the door opened just as she started to get up. Michael stood in the doorway with his hands on his hips, towering over her.

"Hi, honey." She waved from the floor, smiling.

"What part of 'don't move an inch' did you have trouble with?" he asked with a scowl on his face.

"Oh, get a grip." Grace rolled her eyes. "I was perfectly safe on the other side of this door. I just wanted to hear you and Ryan lay into the jackass. So, is he gone?" Lamely she tried to change the subject.

He held his hand out and helped her to her feet. "Yes, he's gone. Hopefully fired. Even so, Ryan and I don't want you girls in a room alone. He's worked here for a few months and he could have a master key. So you have a choice, either I stay in here with you or Ryan does. Who would you prefer?"

This wasn't a lame ploy to get Grace alone; his concern was genuine, and he made it clear that he would do whatever made her more comfortable.

Without hesitation, Grace blurted out, "You, of course. That is, as long as you don't snore." She giggled, remembering the horrific noises Jack made when he slept.

"I can assure you I don't snore." He turned and headed for the door. "I'm going to go get my suitcase and I'll be right back. Stay put!"

Grace saluted him like a good little soldier and lay back on the bed, butterflies erupting in her stomach at the thought of spending the whole night alone, with Michael … and a bed.

There was a knock on the door, and Meg was standing there, waiting to claim her clothes. She skipped in, grinning from ear to ear, and quickly packed a pair of pajamas and a change of clothes. She went in the bathroom and gathered her toiletries before springing onto the bed next to Grace. "You two kids have fun tonight. Don't do anything I wouldn't do," she said with a giggle.

"Yeah, don't worry. I have every intention of still being in the bet come the morning, Meg. I'll sleep in the bathroom with the door locked if I have to, but I'll behave myself," Grace boasted, hoping she would have the strength to actually do it if necessary. Silently she prayed that Meg would be the one to cave and by morning, the whole bet would finally be over.

Meg grinned and kissed Grace on the cheek. "Love you! Sleep well!" she said with a wink as she ran out the door.

Grace began busying herself in the room, trying to kill time until Michael returned. She was about to pick out a movie when the hotel room phone rang. "Hello?" she said, assuming it was Michael calling from across the hall.

"Oh, um, hello, Mrs. Andris? This is David from the front desk. Is your husband there?" the man asked nervously.

Not feeling like launching into an awkward explanation of the fact that she and Michael weren't married and really not even technically dating, she just went with it. "Um, Michael isn't here right now. Can I take a message?" She scrambled to find the pen and notepad by the phone.

"Yes, please let him know that the gentleman who was harassing you and your friend has been escorted off the property, and I wanted to apologize for any distress he may have caused you. If Mr. Andris has any questions, he can contact me anytime. I'll be here all night." Just as David finished his apology, Michael walked in the door wearing a tight gray T-shirt and black sweatpants, holding a small suitcase in his hand and looking absolutely edible.

"Hang on, David; he just walked in the door." Grace held the phone out to him and said, "The front desk."

With a curious expression, he took the phone and put it to his ear as he stood next to the bed. "Hello?" He listened as David introduced himself. A second later his eyebrows shot up and he looked at Grace, grinning. "I'm sorry, you were telling *my wife*, what?"

Oh, hell. Her cheeks turned bright red and she tried to distract herself by flipping through the movies on the television until he was done talking.

He mumbled a few words of thanks to the manager, and then said loudly, "I don't know, let me ask my *wife*." He turned toward Grace with a raised eyebrow. "Oh, *wife*, David would like to know if you're hungry. He'd be happy to send up some room service for us so we can have a private dinner in our room. What should I tell him?"

Her grumbling stomach answered for her. "Tell him your beautiful bride is starving and that would be lovely, *dear*."

He shook his head, laughing, and thanked David for his generosity before hanging up the phone.

Feeling the inquisition coming about the 'wife' thing, Grace kept her eyes on the carpet. As a last ditch effort to avoid the topic, she started rambling about the first thing that popped into her head. "What movie do you want to watch? Meg and I were going to watch one before we were interrupted. You in the mood for a comedy, drama, or horror?" She stared at the television and stretched out on her stomach, moving her head to the foot of the bed.

The mattress dipped under Michael's weight as he crawled onto the bed next to her. "I'll watch whatever my dear wife wants to watch. Isn't that what good husbands do?" He reached out and brushed her long black waves over her shoulders and then ran his hand down her back.

"OK, so he called me Mrs. Andris, and rather than explain every-thing…I…I just went with it. I'm sorry I forgot to warn you." Grace didn't know how he would react to the whole marriage thing, and she didn't want him thinking she was some psychotic woman, already shopping for a wedding dress. His silence only made her more flustered by the second.

He sat there and smirked while Grace continued to flounder, trying to make a coherent sentence. "Relax, Grace. I was only teasing you. Of course, if you're ready to tie the knot, I'm sure we could get Ryan online and have him become a minister and make it legal by dawn, *Mrs. Andris*. I don't think that would break any of the rules of the bet, do you?" The look on his face was absolutely sinful.

"Yeah, but I think Liz and Susan would kill us if they didn't get to plan the wedding and drive us crazy." She laughed at the thought of the two of them running around making wedding plans. *What the hell am I thinking about mar-riage for? Shouldn't we go on a date first? Snap out of it, Grace.*

Michael leaned over, his face only inches from hers. He raised an eyebrow and smiled. "You're right. *When* we get married, we should let them have their fun."

When we get married? Did he just say when? I must still be buzzed from all those drinks; that's the only explanation that makes sense. Breathe, Grace, breathe…

"How about we go on a date before we get married, there, lover boy?" she murmured, trying to calm her heart which was currently trying to leap out of her chest.

He sighed. "If you insist."

Grace scanned the movies until she found the perfect show. "Can we watch this one? I love this movie," she said as she began hopping up and down on her knees on top of the bed.

"*Planes, Trains, and Automobiles*? Sure. Seems appropriate, considering the day we've had. Now can you please stop bouncing before I throw up?" With a playful gleam in his eye, he tackled her back onto the bed.

With Grace happily trapped beneath him, Michael started kissing her neck as she squealed in delight. Soon, she wasn't laughing anymore, though; she was enjoying the sensation of his heated lips on her skin way too much. A game that started playfully had turned into something hot and dangerous. Her hands ran down his sides, settling on his hips. She gave him a shove and took off for the bathroom, gasping for breath.

"Shower!" She gasped as she leaned against the wall, trying to breathe.

"Are you asking me to join you in the shower?" Michael stalked closer with a mischievous grin on his face.

"No! You stay. I'll shower. Set up the movie." Grace retreated into the bathroom and slammed the door shut, hiding from the sexy man in the other room. She turned on the shower and drowned out the sound of his laughter as the steam filled the bathroom. The leggings were stripped from her legs first, followed by Michael's shirt. She laid them on the counter with her underwear, which she decided to simply wash in the sink.

Steam filled the bathroom, and when she could hardly see where she was going, Grace slipped into the shower, leisurely lathering her hair with the coconut shampoo the hotel provided. It smelled good as she rinsed the bubbles from her hair, making her think of the beach or the tropics. Quickly, she washed her body and conditioned her hair. When her stomach growled, Grace decided shower time was over and it was time to brave some more one-on-one time with Michael. She was hopeful that the room service had come while she was showering and she could eat soon.

With the water off, Grace grabbed two fluffy towels. One, she wrapped around her hair and spun into a pile on top of her head. The other she used to dry her arms and legs before wrapping it around her body.

Crap, no clothes, Grace thought as she took a deep breath and opened the door a crack. "Michael, can I borrow some more clothes?" There was a rustling sound then she heard him hop off the bed and head in her direction.

He stopped and admired her revealing outfit through the crack of the opening, then pushed open the door and wrapped his arms around her. "You're toasty warm, aren't you?" he asked as he kissed her bare shoulder.

"I am. But right now, I need clothes. Can I borrow a shirt, please?" Without hesitation, Michael smiled and headed back to his suitcase, but before he could open it, Grace stepped out of the bathroom and stopped him. "Wait, I already know which one I want, if you don't mind." Grace went right up to him and tugged on the hem of the gray T-shirt he was wearing.

"Sweetheart, I have a ton of clean shirts in here." He motioned to the suitcase at his feet.

"But this one will smell like you; those won't."

Unable to resist her sexy little pout, he lifted the bottom of the shirt over his head, exposing his bare chest to an already aroused Grace.

God, he's stunning, she thought as he came closer.

"Here you go. Is there anything else you'd like me to take off? Just let me know, I'd be happy to oblige," he said as he draped the shirt around her neck then tugged on the side of her towel.

Grace broke out in goose bumps at his gentle touch. "No, nothing else off your body, but I do need some shorts or underwear." He quickly went to his suitcase and rummaged through it for something she could borrow.

With a pile of clothes in hand, Grace slipped back into the bathroom to get dressed. There was a knock at the door, and she prayed it was room service and not another lunatic stalking them. When she heard the cart rolling in, she quickly finished getting dressed and brushed her hair. After a quick once over in the mirror and checking to make sure the T-shirt covered her ass as it barely hung above her mid thigh, she walked back into the bedroom.

The gentleman from room service said, "I hope you and your wife have a lovely dinner." Grace couldn't help but snicker.

When she finally came out of the bathroom, she was blown away by the elaborate dinner, complete with a bottle of wine, salad, two steaks with potatoes, and an entire dessert sampler tray. There was even a vase full of flowers in the center of all the food. "Holy cow!" she mumbled as she peered under each of the lids, her mouth watering. "He sent up all this food? I would have been happy with a burger and fries. Apology accepted, David."

Making herself at home, Grace sat down at the table and started cutting her steak while Michael poured the wine. It was the most delicious steak she had ever eaten, cooked to perfection. She didn't realize how hungry she was until she finished off her potatoes and started eating a few off of Michael's plate.

After dinner, Grace was stuffed to the gills and stretched out across the bed, moaning.

Michael threw a pillow at her head and said something about her eyes being bigger than her stomach.

"Start the movie while I digest. I need to make room for that desert tray." She eyed the mountain of chocolate mousse with a raspberries on top that Michael was about to dig into. "Drop the spoon, Mikey, and no one gets hurt. No dessert for you until I make more room in my stomach."

Grace propped her head up on the pillow and rubbed her stomach. He put the spoon down and came over to lie down next to her on the bed.

The movie started and Michael laughed when Grace would moan every few minutes from eating too much. After a half hour, though, she started to feel much better. When the part came on where John Candy and Steve Martin were in bed together, Grace laughed. "Look, that could have been you and Ryan!"

"I don't think so. We would have done rocks paper scissors to see who got the bed. Loser takes the floor. It is a 'guy's unwritten rule.'"

"Well, you guys are stupid. Meg and I would have shared the bed, no problem." She rolled up onto her elbow smiling. "However, I'm much more excited about sleeping with my new roomie, I have to admit." Grace smirked as she ran her fingers across his incredibly sexy and still bare chest.

"Grace." She could tell from the tone in his voice it was a warning of sorts, one that told her she was starting to test his limits like she had in the bathroom.

"Michael." She used his same warning tone as she leaned over and kissed the center of his chest.

"I'm trying hard to behave, Grace, but you're not making it very easy." Grace watched his body twitch as she dragged her fingernails across his stomach.

One of his hands gripped the sheet so tightly, his knuckles started turning white.

"Oh, come on, Michael, I'm just having a little fun with you. Surely you're man enough to take it." Grace bit her lip to keep from laughing as she wrapped her thigh around his and laid her arm across his chest. She could hear his heart pounding and felt the quickened rise and fall of his chest.

When his phone rang, Michael jumped up to answer it. "Hello? Hey, man. No, I got everything. She is? Ha, OK, no, we're good. Watching a movie. I'll talk to you in the morning. Bye." He put the phone back on the nightstand and chuckled. "Meg's out cold. David sent the same spread to their room, and she drank one glass of wine too many. Ryan says she's sound asleep. He just wanted to make sure I didn't need anything from over there."

Shit! Meg's asleep which means she won't be losing the bet tonight. Now I really do have to be good.

"I think it was those drinks you made in the bar. She normally can drink like a fish. The 'screaming sex with the bartender' must have been too much for her." Grace sat up, glancing at the desert tray that suddenly was calling her name.

Walking over to the cart, Grace stopped and stabbed her spoon into the thick mousse before Michael had a chance to stop her. As soon as the spoon hit her lips, she heard him utter her name. He then came barreling over to the cart and spun her away from the desserts, grabbing the remaining mousse and holding it high over his head.

"Come on, Michael, give it back. It's delicious." She tried jumping for it, but he was too damn tall for her to reach.

"You little sneak. You knew I wanted to try this and then you tiptoe over here and try to eat it all? That's not a very nice thing for my wife to do," he scolded as he lowered the mousse and took a huge spoonful of it, holding it up to his mouth like he was going to eat the last bite.

"Don't make me come after the mousse, Michael. I don't want to hurt you, but I will. I'm a woman, and we really like our chocolate." Grace slowly climbed up onto the bed and crouched like a tiger preparing to launch an attack.

He stood his ground, not believing she would dare to jump at him.

"Last chance. Hand over the dessert and no one gets hurt." Bouncing gently on the bed, Grace tried to calculate how hard she would have to jump to make it all the way over to him.

As she thrust herself forward, launching herself off the bed, Michael suddenly realized she was serious about coming after him. He dropped the glass the dessert had been in onto the cart and took the smallest step backwards. Instead of landing in his arms, Grace crashed into the hand that was holding the spoon of mousse and flung it all over his cheek and neck. As she slid down his chest and onto the floor, she clamped her hand over her mouth to keep from laughing.

Michael stood there like a statue, with mousse dripping ever so slowly off his chin and onto his chest.

Uh-oh, now I did it. He's mad. Suddenly her little game didn't seem so funny anymore. "Michael, I'm so sorry." Grace scrambled to her feet, searching for a napkin.

He remained silent and dropped the spoon onto the cart with a loud crash as it hit the tray.

"Are you mad?" She nervously bit her fingernail and looked up into his unreadable face.

After what felt like an eternity, he took an unexpected step toward her, causing Grace to stumble backward. The next thing she knew, his hands were on her shoulders and he gave her a stiff shove backward.

Grace's knees hit the edge of the mattress and she flopped back onto the bed as he towered over her, a wicked smile on his face. *OK, so maybe he isn't mad,* she thought to herself as he leaned over her, his chocolaty face hovering over hers.

She reached up and scooped a bit of the mousse off his cheek with her finger and licked it clean. "Yum, tasty." His eyes watched her tongue swirl around her finger, sucking and licking as it wantonly moved in and out of her mouth. While he was distracted, Grace flipped over, scrambling back to the headboard of the bed. In an effort to catch her, he crawled up the bed toward her like a sleek jungle cat.

"You know, Grace, I still haven't gotten to taste the mousse." He stopped when he reached her legs and smiled. Lowering his head, he kissed her knee, making sure his cheek brushed against her leg, smearing the mousse all over it.

"What are you doing?" Grace gasped as she watched his tongue dart out of his mouth and slowly move toward her leg.

"I'm simply tasting the mousse. Relax, Grace." His sinful wink sent her body into overdrive, and relaxing was definitely out of the question. His fingers crept up her leg as he held her calf firmly against his chest. His hot breath washed over her skin as he dipped his head and started licking the side of her thigh.

It took every ounce of strength and focus Grace had to stay still. Occasionally her whole body would tremble in anticipation of his touch. When she felt his lips sucking on a patch of skin just above her knee, she moaned loudly, causing Michael's eyes to look up, a devilish grin firmly planted on his face.

"You OK, sweetheart?" He laughed as Grace fanned her face, looking anywhere but into his darkened eyes. If she saw a hint of the desire she was feeling for him on his face, she would get caught up in the moment and do something she might later regret.

"I'm fine. Finish your mousse, please. I'll just be watching the movie." She turned away, staring at the television instead, but out of the corner of her eye, she saw his smile grow then he lowered his face back to her leg, working his way higher up her thigh.

Z, Y... X, W, V, U... T... She started saying the alphabet backwards in her head to keep her focus anywhere other than on his naughty tongue working its way up her inner thigh. *That feels so amazing. Stop it, Grace, now before it's too late.*

"OK, dessert's over, Michael. Stop playing with your food and clean up the mess." Running to the bathroom, Grace dared not look at him. She threw a washcloth under the running water, wrung out the excess water, and put her foot on the edge of the tub to wipe the sticky mousse off her leg.

Michael strolled into the bathroom, laughing to himself as he leaned over the sink and splashed water all over his neck and face, removing the last remnants of chocolate off his body.

When Grace looked over at him, he still had a smear of mousse across his chest so she gently ran the washcloth over his pecs, removing the last traces of the tantalizing dessert. She felt him intently watching her every move as she reached over and grabbed a towel off the shelf and dried the excess moisture off his chest and neck.

He took the towel from her hand and used it to dry his face. Then he surprised her by dropping down on one knee and drying her thigh which was still wet from her earlier clean up.

"There you go, all clean and dry." He got up off the ground, smiling. "I don't think I've ever enjoyed eating mousse so much before."

Grace rolled her eyes at him. "I love you." As she wrapped her arms around him, she could still smell the rich-tasting chocolate on his skin. "And you smell delicious, too."

Since they were in the bathroom already, she grabbed her toothbrush and quickly brushed her teeth before bed. While she was combing her hair out, Michael took a minute to brush his teeth at the adjacent sink. Suddenly, Grace became very sleepy and a yawn escaped her lips.

Michael laughed. "Let's go to bed." Hearing him say those words sent her mind plummeting into the gutter. There were so many things Grace wanted to do with him in bed, and sleep was toward the bottom of the list, but she grudgingly followed his platonic lead. She took his hand and then turned out the bathroom light. Michael stopped at the front door to make sure the latch was securely in place and that they were safely locked in together. The only illumination remaining in the room was the flickering light from the television.

"What side of the bed do you like?" Grace asked, suddenly concerned about the sleeping arrangements.

"The right side. Why?" he asked as he pulled the covers back.

She quickly crawled across to the left side. "Just checking. Because if you'd said left, I'd have had to call off the wedding before you even proposed." Trying to get comfortable, Grace slid her legs under the fluffy blankets, laying on her side so she could watch him get into bed. Michael found the remote and clicked off the television, putting the room into complete darkness before climbing into bed beside her.

Under the covers, Grace slid her body right next to his, snuggling as close as possible. He wrapped his arms around her and sighed. "I love you, Grace. More than you could possibly know." His lips brushed against her forehead and she smiled.

"I love you, too. Being with you, like this, just feels so right." Turning her face up to his, Grace kissed him. His hand went to the back of her neck, pressing her tightly against his lips.

"Sleep, Grace." He sighed in the darkness. She felt her body relaxing, comfortable in his arms. He tenderly stroked her hair, and occasionally she'd feel his lips kiss the top of her head. As she drifted off to sleep, she heard him whisper, "I will marry you someday…I promise."

Chapter 23

The early morning sun peeked into the room from between the heavy curtains. Grace was asleep next to Michael, her raven-colored hair falling across her face. She was still curled up, deep asleep. Feeling the warmth of her body was the most glorious way to start his day.

His memory flashed back to just before they had fallen asleep, and Michael couldn't help but chuckle quietly. Grace had started talking about produce, possibly making a shopping list in her dreams.

He gently brushed her black locks out of her face, revealing a small smile on her lips as she slept. How he wished he could know exactly what she was dreaming about at that moment, to know what had put such a contented smile on her face. She truly looked like a sleeping angel; a more perfect creature couldn't possibly exist.

Michael's thoughts drifted back to the previous night—the Jacuzzi, dinner, dessert, and finally, crawling into bed with her—and he found himself smiling. There was also the promise he had whispered to her as she fell asleep. Deep down in his heart, he knew that he would marry her one day. A huge realization had hit him in the wee hours of the morning, and he couldn't explain how, but he understood that without her, he was nothing. She was his other half, his better half, and when he was with her, he was finally the man he wanted to be.

Lifting his head, Michael read the clock and saw it was 7:00 a.m. He knew that Ryan wanted to get an early start, so he reluctantly tried to wake his sleeping angel. "Grace? Sweetheart, it's time to wake up." He tenderly kissed her forehead as she stirred under his lips.

"Five more minutes, Mom … just five minutes," she mumbled as she buried her head further into the pillow, pulling the covers over her head.

"It's time to get up, Grace." He said the words a little louder, and at the sound of his voice, she stretched her hand out from under the comforter, toward his mouth and pushed on it, trying to silence him like an alarm clock.

"Shh, Mikey. I'm sleeping. Be a good boy and be quiet," she whispered without opening her eyes.

"You need to get up so we have time to shower and get dressed. Ryan wants us to get on the road soon." Michael peeked under the comforter and gently pulled it down from her face. In another attempt to awaken his sleeping beauty, his hand ran up and down her arm, giving her a gentle shake.

"Michael," she whined, scooting her body closer to his and wrapping her arms and legs around his body. "Shh, let's go back to sleep. Hold me please. Let's just stay here forever. Send Meg and Ryan back to Portland." Her warm cheek pressed onto his chest as her warm breath tickled across his skin.

Knowing he couldn't possibly resist her, he sighed in defeat and hugged her tightly. "Five minutes, Grace. I'll give you five minutes." Needing to touch her, he ran his hands along the length of her arms and down her side. Michael's T-shirt was twisted around her, exposing the soft skin of her stomach and lower back. He couldn't resist the opportunity to touch her. Slowly his fingers traced across her lower back, making her shiver.

"Michael," she sighed, her voice still sounding half asleep, "I love you."

"I love you too." They kissed and lay in each other's arms for five more minutes, before Michael tried to wake her again. "We really have to get up. Ryan will be banging on the door any minute now." As much as he hated to do it, Michael started to pry her tiny arms and legs away from him.

"You shower first; I'll just lie in this big bed, all by myself. Hmm …" she sighed as she batted her eyelashes, the corners of her mouth turning up into a seductive grin.

Michael's mind immediately flashed back to the previous day in the bathroom when he'd had her pressed up against the door, his shirt barely draped over her shoulders, hanging open, inviting him to touch her soft skin.

The phone rang loudly, snapping him out of his daydream.

"Come on." Grace groaned as she threw the pillow over her head. "Can't a person get a little sleep?"

"Hello?"

"Mike, it's me. Meg's refusing to get out of bed. We're going to be a bit later than I thought." In the background, Michael could hear Meg begging Ryan to close the curtains before she was permanently blinded.

"Well, seems like we're in the same situation because Grace has her head buried under her pillow as we speak. Give me ten minutes to shower and I'll meet you downstairs for breakfast," he suggested. Ryan was very receptive to the idea and agreed. Michael hung up the phone and lifted the pillow off Grace's head.

"Sleeping, Michael. Still sleeping," Grace grumbled as he kissed her cheek.

"I'm going to shower and then grab some breakfast with Ryan, so you can sleep a little longer."

"See, I knew there was a reason I love you so much." She giggled as Michael tapped her on the head with the pillow. She puckered her lips out, asking for a kiss, and he was more than happy to grant her request.

She looked so gorgeous sprawled out across their bed, her hair tousled and sexy. Instead of a quick peck, Michael flipped her onto her back and allowed his chest to press her down deep into the mattress as he kissed her with more enthusiasm than she was expecting. The soft moan she made as she wrapped her arms around his neck let him know he had gotten her attention.

"I'm going to shower," Michael said as he quickly hopped off the bed before he listened to what his body was begging him to do rather than what his head was telling him was right. It was getting harder and harder to behave around Grace.

After a nice hot shower, Michael met Ryan downstairs at the hotel restaurant for breakfast. Quickly they ate and then checked road conditions to Portland; they were pleased to find that road crews had been out all night, making the highway drivable once again. They hurried back up to the girls, eager to get on the road. Michael wished Ryan luck at waking Meg and went into his room.

Grace was still lying in the middle of the bed. The sun was streaming through the curtains, illuminating her skin in a soft glow. Her right leg had slipped out from under the covers and Michael could see the length of her creamy skin against the white sheet. The gentle curve of her hip was hypnotizing as he walked closer. Her arm was extended out and resting on his pillow as if she were reaching out to touch him in her sleep.

Michael sat on the edge of the bed and took in every inch of her body, allowing the vision before him to be burned into his memory. Glancing at his watch and doing some quick math in his head, Michael realized that the next one hundred and fourteen hours were going to be the longest of his life. He started to chuckle to himself, and the light shaking of the mattress woke her from her slumber.

"Michael?" she whispered, one eye was still closed as she spoke. She patted the pillow, wanting him to lie down next to her. Even though he was supposed to be getting her out of bed, Michael lay down for one last minute of bliss before they were trapped in a car with Ryan and Meg for three hours.

"Good morning…again. The roads are clear. So, unfortunately, it's time for you to crawl out of bed," Michael said as he stroked her cheek.

He was expecting her to protest again, but what came out of her mouth threw his body into a frenzy. "Oh, Michael. Make love to me."

His body began responding before his brain could stop it; his heart raced, his breathing increased, blood coursed through his veins and pooled in his groin. His fingers began unbuttoning his shirt at lightning speed, and then Michael's brain kicked in and put the brakes on everything.

"What did you just say?" Suddenly he realized he must have misunderstood her because there was no way she would just blurt that out.

"You said it was time to get up," she put her hand over her mouth as she yawned, "and I said 'Make me!'" She opened her eyes and immediately her brow furrowed when she saw Michael's unbuttoned shirt. "Why are you stripping? Not that I'm complaining; it's just…unexpected."

Well, crap. Now what do I say? Sorry, Grace, I thought you just invited me to have sex with you? Or, I was going to take advantage of you while you slept? Think, Michael…

"Um, I thought you might need a shirt for today and I was going to offer you this one," he said, hoping the panic in his voice wasn't too obvious.

She smiled and ran her warm palm down his cheek. "That's sweet, Michael, thank you. But if we're going to be stuck in the car for a few hours, I think I'd be more comfortable in a T-shirt. So while I'm in the shower, can you find me one?" She rolled onto her stomach, resting up on her elbows and kissed his nose.

Dumbly, Michael nodded his head.

"Fine, I'll get up. But for the record, I'm not a morning person, Michael. I'm a grump until I have my morning coffee." She squealed as she glanced over

Michael's shoulder and found the coffee and pancakes he had bought at the restaurant for her.

He couldn't help but laugh as he rolled off the bed and fetched her coffee and breakfast from the table, placing them in her lap. She sat straight up and took a large swig of coffee before cutting into the pancakes.

The next ten minutes were spent watching Grace devour her breakfast. When she popped the last bite of pancake into her mouth, he cleared away the trash as she climbed out of bed.

"When you find a shirt, can you bring it into the bathroom for me?" She gave a flirty wink over her shoulder then headed across the room.

Michael's mouth hung open in shock as he watched the seductive sway of her hips as she walked away, her glossy waves of hair bouncing down her back. When he heard the click of the bathroom door, he closed his eyes and buried his face in his hands, trying to slow his now thundering heart. *You can do this, Michael. Just find her a shirt.* Rummaging through his suitcase, a green sleeve peeked out and Michael knew that it was the perfect shirt for her.

He pulled out one of his old Oregon State track T-shirts from college. On the back was printed 'Andris' and he couldn't help but smirk. She had enjoyed pretending to be his wife last night, so he figured the least he could do was make her an Andris for the day.

Be a gentleman. She wants to win the bet; it's important to her, so behave, he reminded himself as he took a deep breath and tapped on the bathroom door. The shower was running, but she didn't answer.

When he opened the door a crack, he could see the steam from the shower had covered the mirror, and he wondered if she was in there and naked, wet, or both. *She wants the shoes, Michael. Why? I have freaking no idea, but she wants them, so hands off.* "Grace, I found you a shirt." He kept his eyes locked on the floor in front of him.

It had sounded like a good idea at the time, staring at the floor. But he quickly realized it was a huge mistake when he saw his shirt along with the shorts she had borrowed in a pile at his feet. He groaned with that confirmation that she was approximately seven feet away and completely naked. Michael took a deep breath and was placing the shirt on the counter, ready to make a hasty exit, when he heard her voice.

"Michael? Are you still in here?" she asked so sweetly, he was instantly suspicious.

Run, Michael! Get out while you can. "Yes. I, um, just put your shirt on the counter. I'm leaving," he said quickly as he made his way back to the door, giving her back her privacy.

"No wait!" Reflexively, he turned at the sound of her voice and saw Grace's bare arm waving from the glass shower door.

He inhaled sharply and stumbled back against the wall, trying to avert his glance from her deliciously naked form behind the foggy glass.

"I need you—"

"What?" He gasped loudly, unable to believe what she was saying.

She chuckled at his response. "I need you to hand me the bottle of conditioner that's on the counter." Her dripping finger pointed over toward the vanity, where a tiny white bottle with a blue lid sat. "Do you see it?"

"Yes, I-I see it," he said as he closed his hand tightly around the small bottle, keeping his eyes fixed on the counter. "What do you want me to do with it?"

Grace's laughter rang through the bathroom. "I need you to bring it over to me. I'd get it myself, but I'm all wet and I'd probably slip and break my neck on the marble floor. Oh, and grab a washcloth on your way over here too, please."

"What?" *Surely she didn't expect me to…*

"I forgot a washcloth. Calm down. Can you just hand me one, please?" Her bare finger beckoned him toward the steam-covered shower door.

With the bottle in his hand, Michael turned to the towel rack and snatched a washcloth and called out, "Catch!" He didn't know what possessed him to do it, other than the fact that he didn't know what he would do if he actually saw her body through the glass or came close enough to touch her. So, like a coward, he hurled the tiny bottle of conditioner at the shower, trying to aim it into the gap of the door.

"Ouch!" Grace cried, and then she started cursing. "Damn it! What the hell has gotten into you? Why are you throwing things? That's going to leave a bruise."

He glanced apologetically toward the shower—which was a big mistake.

Out from the gap in the door, Grace thrust her long, naked leg, showing him the damage. The water was slowly trickling down her thigh and calf. He watched the moisture drip off her heel, pooling underneath her foot. Her skin glistened in the light.

"Look at this!" Her hand shot out, pointing to her knee, where she indicated the point of impact for the conditioner bottle.

"Sorry, I just didn't think you would want me to come all the way over there and see you, you know… naked. And we really need to work on your catching skills. That was a pretty decent throw; you should have caught it." As he rambled, his eyes refused to leave her toned, bare leg that was taunting him from the shower stall.

"I had no idea you were throwing it. You could have warned me."

"I'm sorry… I just… Are you OK?" There was a small welt forming on her knee. As he fumbled with his words, he instinctively took a step towards her.

"I'm fine. Could you please hand me the washcloth? I'm still a bit sticky from the mousse."

She had to mention the mousse…

Images of her, lying back on the bed as he crawled up her curvaceous body, licking and tasting her leg, danced through his head, making being a gentleman even more difficult. His body tightened as she tuned to the side and he saw the exquisite profile of her body. He stopped dead in his tracks and closed his eyes for a second, begging God for the strength to respect her wishes and keep her in the bet.

"Michael? I really need to wash up. Don't make me come out there and take the washcloth from you." She was only teasing, but a big part of Michael hoped she would throw open the shower door and invite him in. But then she'd lose the bet, and he was desperately trying to respect her wishes rather than dragging her back to bed and having his way with her.

"Grace, don't you dare come out of that shower."

"I'm just kidding. Relax. Bring me the damn washcloth or throw it, whatever you're more comfortable with, but I'm turning into a prune in here!" Her hand stretched out further from the shower so he could see her bare shoulder now, and as he squinted, he could barely see the outline of her breast through the glass door. Michael's eyes shot to the ground, his heart racing.

Slowly, he made his way toward her, careful to look anywhere but at the floor. When he could see the lower edge of the door, he blindly extended his arm with the washcloth and felt her slippery fingers groping for his hand. Her skin was warm from the hot water of the shower.

"Gotcha!" she laughed as she grabbed his wrist and playfully tugged on it, the water streaming off her body and onto his.

"Grace," he warned as he tried to shake free, but Michael found she had a pretty strong grip for a girl.

Grabbing the washcloth from his fingertips, she closed the door. "Thanks." Her singsong voice echoed from the shower stall. "You're a lifesaver."

"Any time I can be of service." As Michael turned to leave, he did the one thing that he swore he wouldn't do: he peeked at the door, and through the steam; he saw her. There was no mistaking what he saw—the silhouette of her gorgeous, naked body. He watched her profile bend over as she began lathering one leg, then the other. She was washing her stomach before he realized that he was still standing there, ogling her.

"Wow," he quietly sighed.

Maybe she'd heard him or she'd felt Michael's eyes on her body. Either way, she stood straight up and turned in his direction. "Are you still out there?"

"Um, nope. I left a minute ago." He turned his back in embarrassment and headed for the door. Once safely outside the bathroom, he began pacing around the hotel room. *Do not go back in there,* he told himself.

She was the most irresistible woman he had ever met, and yet he had to keep away from her for another … one hundred and ten hours. *This is going to be impossible. Stupid bet.* With a groan, he threw himself onto the bed and punched the pillow.

He draped his arm across his eyes as he listened to the sound of the shower turning off. *She's standing in there naked, drying herself.* He allowed his wild imagination to take over, and visions of her toweling off and sliding her panties up her legs and over her hips raced through his head. His groin screamed for release, his body very aware of how close she was and how very little clothing she was currently wearing.

Unable to think of anything but Grace naked, Michael distracted himself by listing the states in alphabetical order until he heard the door to the bathroom open. Grace had dried her hair, which now cascaded over her shoulders in black, shiny waves. She wore her jeans from the day before, which he had to say, fit her like a glove. The most staggering thing about her outfit was seeing her in his shirt. She had cinched the side of it to make it more form fitting on her body.

When she saw that Michael was looking, Grace swept her hair over her shoulder then turned around and proudly pointed to her back. "Look! I'm an Andris today!" She spun back around and had the loveliest smile on her face.

Michael climbed up off the bed and went to her, needing to feel her in his arms if nothing else. "You have no idea how sexy you look right now," he whispered as he buried his face into her hair. Her skin was still warm from the shower as her body pressed against his. Michael's lips trailed down her neck, kissing and tasting every inch of it.

"Sorry about in the bathroom. It wasn't very nice of me to tease you that way." She bit her lip to keep from smiling. "But it was a lot of fun, I have to admit."

"Just be happy I was raised to be a respectful young man or you would be underneath me in that bed and out of the bet by now," he growled as he kissed and nipped at her neck with as much passion as he dared. Of course, kissing Grace was always a very dangerous thing because every time he did, he wanted her more.

"I think that's the problem. Part of me was hoping that maybe you wouldn't be so respectful in there," she sheepishly admitted, her eyes not daring to meet his.

For one of the few times in his life, Michael was at a complete loss for words. A million thoughts were running through his head all at once, most of them involving Grace and the bed that was only a few feet away.

She misunderstood his silence as a bad thing and started stammering. "I'm sorry, never mind, Michael. Let's just pack." She quickly brushed past and started jamming things into her suitcase, her cheeks bright red with embarrassment.

He swiftly went over to her and swept her up into his arms. "I love you and would thoroughly enjoy making you lose the bet. As a matter of fact, I've been thinking about nothing else for the last few days. You have a gorgeous body that I want to take my time and memorize every inch of. I have a long list of things I want to do to you, Grace. Never doubt how much I want you." He stepped closer to the bed and, as Michael lowered her onto the sheets, it happened again.

"Grace! Michael! Let's get a move on!" They heard Meg yell from outside the door.

Michael looked down at an extremely exasperated Grace. "Does she have built in radar or something?"

"If I didn't love her like a sister, I swear I would kill her right now," Grace growled through her clenched teeth.

Michael had to laugh at how cute she was when she was frustrated. To work off some of his frustration, he began pulling the suitcases out of the closet and putting them on the bed as they added the last of their toiletries. Grace threw open the door, glaring at Meg.

"Well, that sexually frustrated look speaks volumes: you're still in the bet. Love the shirt!" Meg giggled from the doorway. "Come on. Ryan's pacing a hole in the floor, ready to go."

"We'll meet you in the lobby," Grace said with a moan. She closed the door and flopped down on the bed. "Back to reality."

"Come on, let's go, Mrs. Andris." Michael extended a hand out to her, which made her crack a smile. She rolled over and stroked Michael's cheek, kissing him sweetly.

"Thanks for being the best roomie I've ever had."

"Hey, you know, I do live alone. Anytime you want to be my roomie again, all you have to do is come over. You can stay as long as you like." *A night, a week, a month … forever.*

She threw her head back and laughed. "Oh, I'm sure you'd get sick of me pretty quick."

"I could never get sick of you, Grace."

The two of them gathered up their bags and headed down to meet Meg and Ryan, who were huddled together on the couch in the lobby. The line to check out was really long from all the stranded guests.

As Michael and Grace waited in line, David saw them from behind the counter. "Mr. and Mrs. Andris, please come here." He held his hands up and waved them over.

Grace buried her face in Michael's arm when she heard Meg squeal from the couch.

"I hope everything was to your liking last night," David said as he printed up their receipt.

"Everything was lovely last night. Thank you so much," Grace said softly.

Michael wrapped his arm around her shoulders. "Dessert was especially tasty wasn't it, sweetheart?" He snickered while Grace looked every bit the blushing bride.

"The chocolate mousse is my favorite," David commented.

"Mine too," they both answered together, laughing.

They settled the bill and packed all the bags back into the car, heading off to Portland. The storm had ended and the roads were still somewhat empty, so they were able to make good time on the trip home. Grace let Michael drive home without any complaint. She knew he drove faster than she did, and when he let her know they had a meeting this afternoon with the developer of the site they really wanted for the bar, she was happy to ride shotgun.

Portland looked like a winter wonderland, covered in a thick blanket of snow. The trees looked like something out of a story book, beautiful and pristine.

Michael needed his car and assumed it would still be with Jack at the girls' apartment. He didn't even bother checking anywhere else. Sure enough, it was sitting right out front, covered in snow. They parked nearby, unloaded the girls' bags, and helped carry them up to the door.

"Maybe we should knock or call before we go in there," Meg said apprehensively, sounding afraid of what they might find on the other side of the door. Ryan nodded in agreement.

"Oh, how bad could it be?" Grace laughed. "It's eleven o'clock in the morning." She pushed open the door and yelled, "Hi, honey, we're ho— Oh my God! Jack, what the hell are you wearing? And where are your clothes?"

Chapter 24

The two couples crowded in the doorway, too stunned to move. Inside the kitchen, with his back to them, Jack stood, completely naked, except for the apron he was wearing around his waist. Like a hospital gown, it hung wide open in the back, giving them quite a view of his muscular, round backside and the tattoo across his back. He was happily making pancakes on the stove top, a large pile of them stacked on a plate.

"Hey, guys! Want some pancakes?" he asked offering a batch in their direction, not even phased by the fact that he was half naked in front of them.

"Jack," Grace growled through clenched teeth, "please tell me what the front of that apron says?"

Jack stepped back from the cook top, looked down, and laughed. "It says 'Grace is Baking in the Kitchen.' How cute." Her glare wiped the smile off his face in record time. "What's the big deal?"

"What's the big deal? You're standing in our kitchen, naked, wearing *my* apron! There's so much wrong with this picture I don't even know where to begin." Michael's hands came to rest on Grace's shoulders as he tried to massage the building stress from her body.

From the other side of the apartment, there was the rapid clicking of high heels on the hardwood floor that made everyone's head whip to the right in at the same time.

"Hey, baby, I found the whipped cream. It was in my room. We must have left it next to the bed from last ni—um, oops. Hey, guys." Bianca quickly hid the whipped cream behind her back, while holding her tiny, black silk robe shut with her other hand. On her feet was a pair of shiny, red Manolo Blahnik shoes.

"Bianca Quinn! Why is he naked, in the kitchen, wearing *my* apron? It's eleven o'clock in the morning, and we *did* call you from the road to let you know we were on our way." Grace turned her attention to Jack. "And would it have *killed* you to put on a pair of boxers?"

Behind her, Meg started laughing. "Nice butt, Jack. A little hairy for my taste, but a good waxing would do wonders."

Michael burst out laughing at Meg's candid assessment, while Ryan clasped his hand protectively over Meg's eyes, shielding her from the glare off Jack's ass.

A normal person would have been embarrassed by the whole situation; Jack, however, grinned unrepentantly and shook his naked rear in their direction, sending them all into hysterics. Michael's head dropped to Grace's shoulder as his body quaked with laughter.

Bianca stormed into the kitchen. "Jack, the girls are only human, and you're a lot of man for them to admire. Now quit mooning them and go throw some clothes on." She pointed her finger toward her bedroom. Jack sadly dropped his spatula and sulked off.

With a smirk on her face, Grace looked Bianca up and down. Her robe barely reached her upper thigh, and at the bottom of her long, sexy legs rested a fabulous pair of stilettos. "Nice shoes, Bianca."

Meg ripped Ryan's hand from her eyes and stared in awe. "Where did you get those?" she cried as she dropped to her knees to inspect them more closely.

Bianca laughed and pointed her toe out toward Meg. "A Christmas present from Jack."

Right on cue, Jack emerged from Bianca's room wearing only a pair of faded blue jeans that hung dangerously low on his hips and carrying a T-shirt in his hand. He strode over to Bianca and wrapped his arms around her. "Anything for you, baby." He kissed her cheek then put his shirt on in the middle of the kitchen like they weren't even there.

"I'm going to put my bags in my room," Grace groused as she started dragging the heavy suitcase past the kitchen. Michael quickly rushed to her side and took it from her. As they walked into her room, they heard Jack offering pancakes to a starving Ryan.

Grace reached out into her dark bedroom and turned on the lamp next to the bed. When the light filled the room, she let out a bloodcurdling scream. Michael dropped the suitcases on the floor with a loud thud and hurried to her side. "What's the matter?"

Her horrified finger pointed at the tousled bed. Before she'd left for Spokane, the bed had been neatly made, with all the throw pillows lined up across the headboard. But now, pillows were cast off onto the floor, the comforter was pulled down and tangled with the sheets. It had obviously been slept in—or worse.

She wouldn't dare.

"Bianca, you and the naked guy better get your asses in here now!" Grace stomped her foot furiously. Not only did Bianca and Jack rush into the room, but Meg and Ryan came flying up behind them, curious about all the commotion. With her hands on her hips, Grace glared at them. "What did you two do in *my* bed? Wait! Don't answer that! Just tell me—do I need to buy a new mattress?"

Meg and Ryan's mouths were slightly open, shocked that Bianca and Jack might have been so bold as to defile Grace's bed in that way. Amused beyond words, Michael was biting his lip to keep from laughing. Grace's eyes darted from Jack to Bianca then back again.

"Grace, relax. We did not have sex in your room. I swear." She held her hand up and crossed her heart. "He was snoring one night so I slept in here for a few hours. That's it, I promise. Don't worry, the virginal mattress can stay." Grinning, she reached for Jack's hand.

"Yep, Grace, that's the truth. My penis has been nowhere near your bed." Bianca smacked him in the back of the head. "Um, and it never will be. That's Michael's territory—ouch!" Bianca punched him in the shoulder for running his mouth. While Michael brought his hands to his face and shook his head, Ryan let out a loud snort.

Blushing, Grace suddenly found herself screaming. "Get out! All of you!" She threw her arm toward the door, motioning them to all leave. Meg and Ryan dashed out, laughing. Bianca and her formerly naked cohort shrugged; they apparently felt she was overreacting. When Grace saw Michael turn to leave, she grabbed his arm and smiled. "You, stay."

He leaned against the dresser with a laugh. Grace walked around her bed and began stripping off all the sheets, including the pillowcases. She wadded them up into a big ball and threw it at Michael.

"We're going to burn those," she said in a serious voice, "along with the apron. Now come here and help me flip this mattress over." Grace had her hands buried under one corner of it and managed to lift it a few inches off the box spring.

Michael rolled his eyes at her, but was by Grace's side in a second, hiking the mattress up and over onto the floor. Together, they scooped it up and laid the freshly flipped mattress back into place.

From the closet, Grace pulled out clean set of sheets, and in a matter of minutes, all traces of the possible debauchery that may have occurred had vanished. She lay down across the newly made bed and sighed.

Michael climbed up next to her, chuckling at her little tirade. "Feel better?" He brushed the strands of long black hair back off her face, kissing her gently on the forehead.

"Not really. I swear I will be having nightmares about them having some depraved tryst in my room for the next few months." Grace shuddered at the thought when the idea hit her. She jerked herself up on the bed and started clapping. "Tryst! That's it!"

His brows furrowed together as she jumped off the bed and began jumping around the room. "You actually want them to have a tryst in your bed?" he asked, utterly confused. "Should I be jealous?"

Grace rushed over to him and pulled him off the bed. "No, God no. Listen, you said if I ever thought of a good name for your bar to tell you, so how about... Tryst?" He stood there silently, mulling it over in his head.

All of a sudden, her feet left the ground and he was spinning her around, his laughter filling the room. Without releasing his grasp, Michael carried Grace out the door and into the family room. "Jack, Ryan! Come here quick," he yelled as he kissed her face repeatedly. "Do you have any idea how much I love you?"

"Yeah, I think I might have a clue." She laughed as her feet came back to the ground.

Ryan emerged from Meg's room with his cell phone pressed to his ear, holding a finger to his mouth, signaling everyone to be quiet. Jack stayed stretched out on the couch, reading the newspaper, his head comfortably resting in Bianca's lap.

Michael and Grace went over to the recliner and made themselves comfortable. He sat down, pulling Grace onto his lap while they waited for Ryan to finish his call. "We have to go meet with the developer this afternoon to see if we can work a deal so we can lease the location we want for the bar. It is down on North High near all those galleries and restaurants. Perfect location, but that means it will cost a fortune. We're hoping that we can get him to negotiate his price and get lucky. I'm guessing that's what this call is about." Michael's brow furrowed in concern as he ran his fingers lazily across Grace's back, watching Ryan continue to pace back and forth in the kitchen.

Ryan said a quick goodbye and snapped the phone shut, walking to Meg's side. "Sorry, that was the Realtor."

"What does she want?" Jack asked, lifting his head so he could see Ryan better.

"Well, apparently the building was just sold yesterday." The look on Ryan's face was grim. Jack cursed under his breath, and Grace felt Michael tense up beneath her. "The good news is the new owner is going to be in town briefly signing the papers and said he'd meet with us. But we need to be there in an hour with the paperwork from the bank approving us for the loan."

Michael glanced at his watch. "We'll have to hurry, but we can make it. Does he know the bank hasn't approved us for enough to cover the cost of the space?" He shifted nervously in the chair, his fingers repeatedly tapping on the arm of the chair.

"I'm not sure," Ryan said quietly. Then tension in the room was palpable as the men exchanged glances.

Breaking the silence, Jack boomed, "Well, then, we just have to charm the hell out of him. First things first: let's get home and get changed." Jack stood up, kissed Bianca on the cheek, and said, "Ladies, we love you, but we gotta jet."

Grace gave Michael a big hug and a kiss. "Good luck."

"Wait, Ryan, Jack, real quick. Grace had a great idea of what to name the bar. Tell them what you came up with." Michael blocked their exit, forcing Jack and Ryan to turn their attention to Grace.

"Um, well, it's just a suggestion, you know, but how about … Tryst?" She nervously looked around the room at Ryan's and Jack's faces, trying to read them, but couldn't.

After what felt like an hour of silence, Grace looked at Michael who simply winked at her, then nodded his head in Jack's direction. She glanced over and saw a big smile on his face and when she looked back to Ryan, he was absolutely beaming.

"It makes me think of naughty, sexy, and illicit things—like us! Tryst it is!" Jack arrogantly grinned as Ryan shrugged in agreement. Meg and Bianca clapped their approval, too.

"Don't you guys have a meeting to get to? Go charm this guy so you can open yourselves a bar." Grace made her way over to Michael and teased, "It might not hurt to show a little skin." Nimbly she undid the top two buttons on his shirt, revealing more of his chest. "Yep, I'd give you a really good deal on some property if you showed up like this."

As she stood back, appraising his heavenly form, he began snickering. "Would you do anything I asked, Grace, if I looked like this? Anything?" he whispered in her ear as his hand wrapped around her waist before coming to rest very low on her hip.

"Wow, yeah, um … totally." Grace muttered incoherently as she ran her finger down the newly exposed skin on his chest.

"I'll have to remember that," he whispered seductively in her ear.

"Sorry to break up the groping session, you two, but, Mike, we have forty-five minutes to haul ass home, get pretty, and then get downtown. Even with your driving, we're cutting it close. Kiss the girl, and let's motor," Ryan said as he wrapped his arms around Meg and kissed her head.

"I have to go." Michael sighed. "I'll call you and let you know how it goes. I love you."

"I love you, too. Go impress him. Take my car. Yours is buried under five inches of snow. That way you have an excuse to come back over here when you're done." He gave her one last kiss before all three of them raced out the front door.

As the door clicked shut, Grace said, "They're easily—"

"The three sexiest men on the planet?" Bianca sighed as she fell back onto the couch.

"Without a doubt." Meg said, pulling Grace back onto the couch with her. "Of course, now that we're alone, it's time for some girl talk." Meg began bouncing up and down on the couch. Her eyes darted down to Bianca's feet again. "So, Jack got you the shoes? Before or after you slept with him?"

Bianca's cheeks turned pink. "Before …"

"And what did you give him for Christmas?" Meg asked suspiciously.

Grace rolled her eyes and said, "Do you really need to ask?" She turned to Bianca, who was biting her lip, trying not to smile. "I'm guessing you, no clothes, and a big red bow were involved."

"Well, for your information, Miss Smarty-pants, you're wrong." Bianca tried to act offended, but her dancing eyes gave her away. "I also wore the shoes…" Girly screams and squeals echoed through the apartment.

Bianca asked what she and Michael had exchanged for Christmas. Grace told her the story of the running shoes and what Michael said about his endurance. More giggles and squeals ensued.

Grace ran into her room and brought out the dress that Michael had bought her for their date, holding it up for her inspection. Bianca complimented it repeatedly, impressed with Michael's taste and was already planning what shoes and accessories she should wear with it.

"Meg got the most beautiful bound journals from Ryan for Christmas. He must have written something super sweet inside too, because she burst into tears after reading it."

Bianca's eyebrows perked up in curiosity. "Care to share with the class what he wrote? I bet it was a sappy poem; he looks like the poem type."

"It wasn't a poem," Meg said quietly. "He just made an entry in the journal." Tears welled up in her eyes. "Oh, here, let me get it and read it to you. It's too beautiful for me to mess up." She scurried into her room and came out clutching the leather bound journal in her arms. She opened it to the first page and cleared her throat.

December 24

Today, I am giving Meg, the love of my life, this journal. I've known from the moment that I laid eyes on her that she was the one I was meant to be with. My heart sang and my knees went weak at the sight of her. I still get butterflies in my stomach when she is near. I love her smile, her exuberance, her mind, her heart, her kindness, her loyalty, her friendship and her spirit. Without her, a piece of me is missing. Together, we are a perfect fit.

I give her this journal in the hopes that from this day forward, all her entries will be filled with the stories of our lives together. I hope that our names appear together a thousand times over on these pages, filled with memories to pass on to our children. The story of our love affair will be spelled out as an example to them of what true love looks like, feels like, and acts like.

Finally, I hope she smiles when she opens her gift because nothing can compare to the beauty of her smile. My Meg, my love, my life. I will love you forever.

Ryan

When she closed the journal, she couldn't help but smile. Grace and Bianca also had tears streaming down their faces, touched by his words to their friend. They sprung up off the couch and hugged her.

"We're very lucky," Grace said softly as the three friends broke their embrace and wiped the tears from their eyes.

Trying to lighten things up, Meg asked the question she'd been dying to ask for hours now. "So, Grace, would you like to explain why the guy at the front desk called you Mrs. Andris this morning when we were checking out?" Meg snickered. "Is there something you'd like to announce to us?" Bianca shot up; Meg's little comment catching her attention.

"Do tell, Mrs. Andris, do tell. I'd like to hear about *everything* that happened at the hotel last night." Bianca grinned evilly at Grace as she leaned back into the couch, making herself comfortable and ready to watch her friend blush.

"Oh, wait! Instead, why don't you start at the part where Michael was naked? Bianca didn't hear about that," Meg squealed. Bianca's eyes bugged out of her head and Grace nearly died of embarrassment on the spot.

"It's not as bad as it sounds, really." Grace tried to downplay the whole naked thing, unsuccessfully. "He was in the Jacuzzi and with the bubbling water; I couldn't see *much*." They both let out a scream as Grace buried her face in her hands.

"She didn't see much until he jumped out of the tub. And didn't you say something like he had you pinned against the door?" Meg asked innocently, while Grace felt her cheeks heat up. Bianca's mouth hung open in surprise.

"Wait, wait, wait! He was naked and kissing you, and you … resisted that?" Bianca asked in wonder.

"Well, no. I kind of, um, moaned his name and was ready to do whatever he wanted, but then Ryan showed up and screwed the whole thing up by busting into the room."

"Fine, he interrupted *that* moment, but you can't tell me nothing else happened between you two all night," Meg said, leaning in to not miss Grace's soon-to-be embarrassing answer.

"Well, there might have been a little something before and after dinner," Grace mumbled softly.

"What?" they screeched in unison.

"Get to the Mrs. Andris thing!" Bianca begged.

"Well, the manager called to apologize after the whole Mark incident." They quickly told Bianca about the creeper who bought them drinks and how he came up to the room. "I answered the phone because Michael was talking to Ryan, and the guy from the desk called me Mrs. Andris. So rather than explain that I was Michael's girlfriend, I went along with it. And then Michael got on the phone and the manager said he'd spoke with his 'wife.' So then Michael started referring to me as his wife, and it was the biggest turn-on, I can't even begin to tell you." Grace shook her head back and forth to try and calm herself down. *God, he was sexy though.* She remembered the butterflies that exploded in her stomach each time he called her his wife.

When Grace continued on and told them about the mousse incident, they both were stunned. Bianca kept saying, "I can't believe you didn't crack. All for a pair of shoes…" She shook her head from side to side, impressed by Grace's resolve.

"Don't forget eternal bragging rights," she said smugly. "And then, he said something before I fell asleep. He said … well, he promised he would marry me someday." If Grace thought their prior screams had been loud, the silence that hung in the air between them was deafening.

Bianca's eyes were huge while Meg was on her feet, her hands clasped over her mouth as she said "Oh my gosh, oh my gosh" over and over.

"And if all that wasn't enough, I decided to have a little fun with him in the shower this morning." Grace grinned from ear to ear as she told them of how she'd teased Michael with her wet and naked limbs.

"Grace, I can't believe you were brave enough to do that. I'm thoroughly impressed. I love how he panicked and threw the conditioner at you. Poor guy … Of course, it was pretty risky of you. What if he'd climbed into that shower with you? Then what would you have done?" Bianca gave Grace's shoulder a playful shove.

She thought about it for a second and then confessed, "Honestly, I would've said 'screw the shoes' and had the best sex of my life without a single regret. I think part of me was kind of hoping he would. Of course, Meg, if you hadn't banged on the door and told us it was time to go … We were about to … you know…"

Meg gasped. "Why didn't you tell me? Ryan and I would have gone shopping for an hour. Well, maybe a few hours—you guys have been waiting a long time.

However long you needed, we could have occupied ourselves." Meg felt terrible about interrupting their romantic interlude.

"It's all for the best. Besides, I'm in it to win. We only have one hundred and five hours to go. Piece of cake." Grace tried to sound confident, but she knew this was going to be a dog fight till the end with her stubborn friend, Meg.

Changing the subject, Meg turned to Bianca. "So, do we need to make an official house rule about 'no naked men in the kitchen' or do you think can you keep your man under control?" Meg snickered.

"Oh, I can definitely keep him under control," Bianca said with a wicked grin. "By the way, we need more whipped cream."

Over the next few hours, they unpacked their suitcases, cleaned the apartment, showered, answered emails, and paid the bills.

Meg sat on the couch, glancing out the window any time she heard a car door close. Bianca paced past the phone, picking it up to make sure there was still a dial tone. Grace busied herself by reorganizing their DVD collection in the family room, but she checked her cell phone to make sure she hadn't missed a call more times than she wanted to admit.

At 3:00 p.m., Bianca finally burst. "What could possibly be taking so long? The waiting is driving me crazy!"

Just then, the door flew open and a booming voice said, "Did someone say crazy?" Jack's firm body filled the doorway, his sunglasses still covering his eyes.

"Move, you big oaf!" Ryan growled as he pushed Jack aside, trying to make his way to Meg. She was off the couch and flying into Ryan's arms before he made it a step further. He picked her up and carried her over to the kitchen counter.

"So, tell us, tell us!" Meg squealed.

Grace peered around Ryan, trying to find her man. "Where's Michael? You didn't have to sell him into slavery, did you? He isn't sleeping with some rich lady to make a quick million dollars, is he? Wait, did he wreck my car? I'll kill him." She was craning her neck past Jack when a flash of brown came through the doorway and two arms nearly crushed her as they wrapped around her and squeezed.

"We did it!" he whispered in her ear as he began kissing Grace enthusiastically. "That's wonderful!"

From behind her, Grace heard Meg and Bianca start screaming too as they found out the good news. When the joyful screams subsided, everyone gathered in the family room to hear the story.

"So, did you have to charm him? Was he a jerk or a nice guy?" Grace asked, unable to contain her excitement any longer. They started chuckling at the question and had the most peculiar looks on their faces.

"What?" Bianca snapped. "Oh my gosh, was it a woman? Did she hit on you?" Bianca wheeled around and glared at a now hysterical Jack. "Did you flirt with her?" She was fuming as she grabbed him by the ear and led him off to the corner where he defensively threw up his hands in front of his chest.

"No, no, no, Bianca. It was a guy, not a girl. Calm down, baby. Is it wrong that I get turned on when you act all jealous like that?" He picked up a lock of her hair and began twirling it around his fingers.

"So, explain. He met your price? Out of the kindness of his heart, this guy agreed to give you a discount?" Meg said skeptically.

"Actually, yes. That's exactly what happened." Ryan smiled at Michael. "We pitched our idea and explained the financial situation we were in, and he agreed to it. By the way, Grace, he loved the name."

"And he wanted nothing in return?" Grace asked Michael, who still had a goofy grin on his face.

Michael shook his head side to side. "He didn't want anything. So we insisted he be our partner."

"You did what?" Bianca shrieked, swatting away Jack's hand. "You don't even know this guy. He could be a total sleaze. Please tell me you didn't sign anything. You need a lawyer to go over everything with a fine-tooth comb and make sure you guys are protected."

"We signed everything already. He was only in town for a few hours, so we went with our gut on this one." Jack put his arm around her shoulder, but Bianca just shrugged it off.

"Um, I know it's not really our business, but how can you be so trusting of someone you just met? Have you lost your minds?" Grace asked Michael.

"Don't you trust *my* judgment?" When he saw her wariness, Michael reached in his pocket with a sigh and pulled out his phone. "I told him you wouldn't just let this go. Do you want to talk to him? He said to call him if you didn't believe us."

"Me? Why would he talk to me?" Grace watched Michael quickly punch a series of numbers into his phone. "It's me. Yeah, I think you'd better, because they think we've lost our minds. No, they think you're a crook and that we signed away our firstborn sons in the deal. Yeah, here she is." Michael smiled as he held the phone out to her. "Here you go. Ask him anything you want."

"Hello?" Grace said apprehensively. Michael could hardly contain his laughter, so she shot him a dirty look. *What the hell has gotten into him?* Her mental tirade was interrupted by a male voice on the phone.

"Grace Marie Park, do you really think I would steal that bar from Michael? You hurt me. Haven't I been a good uncle to you all these years? And wasn't it Evelyn who got you those gold hoop earrings Susan said you couldn't have when you turned twelve? I think you can trust me, of all people," the voice on the phone teased.

"Uncle Frank? *You* bought the building? Are you crazy?" Grace nearly dropped the phone in shock.

"Actually, I'm quite sane. Why are you questioning everyone's mental faculties today?"

"But, then, why did you do it? Who just buys a building?"

"Because, Grace, Michael and Ryan are wonderful young men. And five minutes after meeting Jack, he impressed me not only with his wit, but with his intelligence. The three of them are very sharp and have great ideas. Michael and Ryan told me all about their plans for the bar at your mother's house, the direction they wanted to take it. They mentioned their financial predicament. That night, I spoke with Evelyn, and she convinced me they would be a good investment. To tell you the truth, I think she's a bit smitten with the two of them." He chuckled. "So we decided to invest in a piece of property that just happened to be the one they had their eye on. Of course, I wasn't expecting them to insist I be their partner, but that just goes to show what kind of men they are."

"Uncle Frank, are you sure about this?" Grace still couldn't believe all of this was happening.

"The only thing I'm more certain about is how much he loves you."

She glanced up at Michael as he stood a few feet away with an endearing look on his face. "Thank you, Uncle Frank, you're the best. I love you."

"Love you too, Grace. Have fun celebrating tonight. Oh, and have a Happy New Year."

"I'm quite certain that I will." She closed the phone and ran into Michael's awaiting arms. "I'm so happy for you!"

Michael looked over at Ryan and Jack "Let's go celebrate. Would you ladies join us?"

"That depends. Where would we be going?" Bianca giggled as Jack tipped her back and kissed her neck.

"Are you ladies any good at pool?"

Chapter 25

The guys left to give the girls a chance to get dressed. They rushed through the apartment, clothes flying between the bedrooms. Meg and Bianca, of course, spent twenty minutes on their outfits. Grace, however, threw on her favorite jeans, a pair of knee high black boots, and her most comfortable black T-shirt, and waited on the couch for the fashion plates to finish dressing.

She breathed a sigh of relief when she saw they were dressed in similar clothing. Of course, Bianca's "Nice Rack" shirt from the local barbeque restaurant, tied in a knot at the waist, made Grace laugh out loud.

When Grace heard Michael's horn sound from in front of the apartment, her heart skipped a beat and she called to Meg and Bianca as she grabbed her keys.

The girls all piled into Grace's car and followed them to the pool hall.

❧

Bumpers wasn't very crowed on a Thursday night. Only one of the seven pool tables was being used by two gigantic, biker guys. Over at the bar, there was a group of guys watching a hockey game on one of the plasma televisions. Off to the side, the banks of pool tables were surrounded by tall bar tables that each sat four people. They pushed two of them together and sat down while Jack went to get a few beers.

Soon Jack was back, balancing two pitchers of beer. Carefully, he poured each of them a glass. Ryan strolled across the room to look at the pool cues, Meg at his side.

"So, you never answered the question. Are you ladies any good at pool?" Jack asked with an air of challenge in his voice.

Bianca gave him a coy smile. "We aren't too bad are we, Grace?"

"Nope, we aren't too bad at all. We take the sticks and hit the balls into the holes on the table. It's all algebra. Want us to show you our skills?" Grace laughed, waving her hand at the table.

What she failed to mention was that they were actually quite good—real "pool sharks." Before they met the guys, one of their favorite pastimes was finding a pool hall, playing dumb, and letting guys challenge them to a game. They won more free rounds of beer that way than Grace cared to admit.

"Please, show us what you can do. I'd love to see you bent over the table—with the cue stick in your hand, that is," Michael whispered as Grace's body came alive.

"You're so bad," Grace said as she poked his rock hard chest with her finger. "Behave yourself or we'll never make it until New Year's."

"Would that really be so bad?" he asked as he placed a lingering kiss on her neck, his warm breath skipping across her skin.

"No, it wouldn't, which is why *you* need to behave, because I don't think I can do this much longer." Grace kissed his cheek and ran over to the wall where the pool cues were hanging, trying to put some physical distance between them while she pulled herself together.

"Grace! Come here," Meg called across the room. "Girls versus boys; losers buy the beer. Will you grab me one of those pole thingies?"

Grace bit her lip to try to keep from laughing; Meg was playing her part perfectly. By the time she made her way back to the tables, Ryan was very sweetly explaining the rules of the game to her like she had never played before.

If only he knew how deadly she was with a pool cue!

"OK, let me see if I understand this. I hit the balls in the holes, but not the boring black or white one. Ryan, I don't want to be stripes. I want to be the cute solid ones." Meg clapped her hands excitedly and when the guys turned their backs to laugh, she shot Bianca and Grace a sly wink.

"Honey, when you break, whatever ball you hit in the pocket first decides if you're stripes or solids," Ryan patiently explained, while Jack puffed out his chest a little more, sensing an easy victory. Michael gave Grace a smug look out of the corner of his eye.

Hook, line, and sinker, she laughed in her head. *This is going to be fun.*

Jack set up the balls and Michael broke. As Michael leaned over the table to take his shot, Grace shamelessly stared at his firm, sculpted ass. Meg got her wish; the guys were stripes and girls were solids.

"Jack, you have high balls," Bianca called over her shoulder.

Jack immediately looked between his legs, grabbing his crotch. "Really? How can you tell from there?"

Bianca rolled her eyes in irritation. "You have stripes, Jack. Your balls are striped."

"Should I see the doctor about that?" he said with a grin.

Bianca shook her head. "Smart ass." Then she turned her attention back to the game.

Grace's turn was after Michael's. Calmly, she went to the table and banked the cue ball off the bumper, sinking the two-ball with ease. She made a big deal to get excited and clap, claiming "beginner's luck" on the amazing shot. Then she purposely missed her next attempt—badly. The cue ball didn't even make it all the way across the table.

"It's all geometry, ladies. Watch." Jack strutted around the table, trying to decide which shot would be best to take. Arrogantly, he decided to get fancy as he tried a very difficult shot to impress Bianca, missing it by a hair.

Bianca stepped up to the table, and the three women began to run their elaborate game. She missed her first shot to make their claimed inexperience look believable. Meg, of course, made a spectacle of herself, playing the ditzy blond and trying to use the wrong end of the cue to hit the ball. She, too, missed her shot, nearly sinking the eight-ball. The guys cleared a few more balls and were starting to get cocky.

"You're terrible!" Jack teased. "I thought you'd at least make this interesting." He slipped his sunglasses back over his eyes and juggled two of the balls from the corner pocket.

Michael grabbed his cue and carefully examined the table. The ladies had six solid balls still on the table to their two striped ones, plus the eight-ball. He and Ryan took a second to discuss strategy, gesturing with their arms what was the best way to make the shot he was considering.

Being experienced, Grace knew what shot he was going to take and casually stood nearby—within distracting distance. Bianca smiled from across the table, knowing what was coming. Grace needed to make Michael miss his shot or their victory was going to be tricky to pull off.

After the conference with Ryan was over, Michael walked to the table and stood right in front of Grace. He leaned forward to line up his shot. Just as his cue stick came back, she stepped up behind him and when his elbow began to move forward, Grace put her hands on his ass, one per cheek, and gave him a firm squeeze.

Michael let out a yelp and jumped. His cue stick flew and nearly went through the felt on the table. "What was that?"

Grace bit her finger innocently. "Sorry, Michael, you just looked too cute standing there, all bent over and sexy." She glanced over his shoulder and saw Meg and Bianca were laughing. Even Ryan was gasping for breath after Grace's antics. "I couldn't help myself."

Sensing her game, Michael pulled her close, his velvet voice tickling her ear. "So, is that how you want to play this game, Grace? Because I've been behaving myself like you asked, but I can always stop and make everything much *harder* for you as well." His hands slid from her waist and landed snugly into the back pockets of her jeans. He pressed Grace tightly against his groin and she stopped breathing, suddenly understanding what his statement meant. He leaned closer, his nose running along her jaw as her heart sputtered. "Your turn to shoot, love."

Grace cleared her throat and stepped away from him, flustered beyond all reason. She grabbed the first cue she saw and fumbled her way over to the table. Grace glanced quickly at the table, but then felt Michael come stand behind her and continue his flirtation so she couldn't focus on the game at all.

Trembling and wondering what he might do next, Grace leaned down to line up a shot when she felt the weight of Michael's body covering her. One of his arms snaked around her waist, his thumb grazing the bottom of her breast, and the other slowly came over her shoulder running down her arm, finally resting on her wrist.

"You do realize that you're aiming at the wrong ball, right? Your team is solids." Grace turned her face to look at him then felt his warm lips on her jaw. She nearly jumped out of her skin when his tongue ran down her neck. "And by the way, you really do look *amazing* bent over the table like this." He chuckled when he felt her body drop as her knees gave out when he ground his hips into hers. "I know what you ladies are doing, and all I can say is … game on."

He released his grasp on Grace, but her body continued to tingle after he walked away. She rested her forehead down on the pool table for a second, trying to remember how to breathe. When she peeked up, Michael was across the table, drinking his beer and looking quite smug.

Damn you, Michael Andris. Suck it up, Grace! Time to hustle the hustlers.

Without breaking eye contact with him, she stood up, blew him a slow and sexy kiss that received colorful hoots and hollers from the gang, and then returned her attention to the table, quickly finding her shot and taking it.

The four-ball sank into the pocket like a stone.

Bianca and Meg cheered as Grace stalked around the table with newfound determination and started to methodically clear the table, one ball at a time. With each ball that sank, Jack's cursing increased. Ryan was dumbfounded, especially when Grace pulled out all the stops and jumped the cue ball over one of theirs to sink the one-ball. Even Michael looked impressed, but that damn smirk still remained on his face.

Getting a bit too arrogant, Grace tried to make a really difficult shot, hitting the cue ball off the rail, but she missed her target and scratched. When she left the table, the guys had two balls on the table, and so did the ladies.

Jack downed the rest of his beer and went to the table with his cue stick in hand and a sly smile on his face. He confidently cracked his knuckles before bending over the table, examining the situation. Without even removing his sunglasses, he leaned over the table, pulled back on the cue stick, and fired. The white cue ball rolled across the table, looking like it had missed its mark, until it bounced off the rail and, with all the backspin Jack put on it, rotated, clipping the edge of the ten-ball. In slow motion, it rolled into the corner pocket.

"Woo hoo! Eat that!" Jack screamed as he high-fived Ryan. Michael congratulated Jack, slapping his hand on his friend's back, and then he winked at Grace. Being the mature woman she was, Grace stuck her tongue out at Michael, which only made him laugh harder.

When Jack finally settled himself, he looked down at the table and surveyed his options. He really didn't have a shot at the thirteen-ball, which was their only ball left on the table. It was nestled up right next to the eight-ball, and he didn't want to risk sending that into the pocket. Instead, he took evasive measures and lightly tapped the cue ball into the corner, leaving Bianca in a bind.

"Great, now I have no shot, you asshole. How am I supposed to show off my pool skills? Damn it, Jack," Bianca fumed, her heels clicking loudly as she walked around to look for a good angle.

Jack walked up to the other side of the table and started running his mouth, which was a bad idea when Bianca had a cue stick in her hand. "Oh, come on, baby. Who are you trying to kid? Your aim is really off, and you don't seem to know what you're doing with that stick."

As he waved his arm across the table, Bianca snapped. She picked up the stick, drew it back, and shot the cue ball. It bounced once on the table and then went airborne, hitting Jack squarely in the crotch.

Jack made a small yelp before crumbling into a heap on the floor.

"My aim is excellent, and I didn't get the nickname Ball Crusher for nothing. You better not forget that, *baby*." She towered over his limp body on the floor. "Come on; let's get you some ice for your nuts."

"Note to self: don't piss off Bianca," Michael mumbled in awe as Ryan stood up to find the cue ball which had rolled under Meg's chair.

"I believe that counts as a scratch," Ryan proclaimed as he put the cue ball back onto the table, giving himself the easiest shot to sink their one remaining ball.

"Shit," Grace muttered as Ryan lined up the shot. She gave Meg a what-the-hell-are-you-going-to-do look.

Meg smiled and immediately hopped off her stool, stood across the table from Ryan, and began popping open the buttons on her blouse. Ryan's head started to shake from side to side as he tried to not look at her, but when she bent down so her semi-exposed chest and red lace bra were hanging directly in his line of sight, little beads of sweat formed on his brow.

"Hit it right to momma, Ry," Meg said as she shook her chest in his direction.

"You ladies really are shameless, aren't you?" Michael asked, shaking his head in disgust at Ryan as he watched the cue ball careen off course and miss its intended target by a mile.

"Don't get your panties in a bunch, Mikey. It's just a game." Grace laughed and ran a single finger down the front of his shirt, stopping at the waistband of his jeans.

Jack hobbled back to the table, followed by Bianca, who was carrying an ice pack and rolling her eyes as Jack rambled on. "All I'm saying, Bianca, is if we ever do have kids some day and they aren't too smart, just remember it's because you gave my little swimmers brain damage with that trick of yours." He gingerly cupped himself as he sat down on the stool.

Giving him no sympathy whatsoever, Bianca slammed the icepack onto his crotch. "Yeah, I gave them the brain damage, not the guy dumb enough to piss off a woman with a pool cue in her hand. Sure, it's my fault."

"You know the least you could do is," and Jack started laughing, "kiss them and make them better." Bianca's hand flew up to the back of his head. "Ouch! I think I need more ice…"

"My shot!" Meg squealed as Ryan sulked away from the table, having let down his team.

"Nice focus, Ryan," Michael snarled. "They're just boobs."

"Yeah, well, you did really well under pressure yourself there, Mikey," Ryan spat back as he watched Meg skip around the table and sink the first ball. Groans came from all the guys, but they were overshadowed by the vibrant cheers from Grace and Bianca.

Meg pretended to yawn in boredom before she lowered her body across the table and took her next shot, sinking the remaining solid ball into the far pocket. The only balls left on the table were the cue ball, the eight-ball, and a single striped ball. Meg grinned as she lined up her final shot.

Jack started screaming to try and distract her, Michael coughed, and Ryan tried tickling her, but nothing could break Meg's concentration. She closed her eyes, pulled back the cue and sank the eight-ball with authority into the center pocket. Screams of victory erupted from the ladies.

"Rematch!" Jack whined loudly as he jumped up, dropping his ice pack onto the floor. "Come on," he pleaded with Bianca, who simply shook her head no.

"You guys are buying the beer. Suddenly, I feel very thirsty. How about you, ladies?" Bianca filled her friends' glasses, and they toasted their victory.

"Let's do a little couples tournament," Meg suggested.

"What does the winning team get?" Ryan asked with raised eyebrows.

"Another free kiss," Michael blurted out too quickly, and then blushed.

Um, that works for me. Wait, how about free sex? Yeah, that'd be better. Damn it! Next time, think bigger, Michael.

"Aw, Michael wants to kiss our fair Grace again," Meg teased. She glanced in Grace's direction and found her the same shade of red as Michael. "OK, fine. Winning team gets one no-holds-barred kiss. Only catch is that you have to do it right here, in front of us, so we can judge your skills." Meg glanced over at Jack and Bianca. Just to rub in the fact they could do whatever they wanted win or lose, Jack grabbed Bianca in his arms and kissed her deeply.

"Agreed!" Michael and Grace said in unison.

First up were Meg and Ryan versus Jack and Bianca. While they started their game, trading taunts back and forth, Grace pulled Michael aside to work on their strategy.

"OK, so listen. First of all, drop the beer!" She snatched the glass from his hand. "I really want to win this, so you need to be focused on the prize, namely *me,* and we don't need any beer messing with your aim."

"Oh, don't worry. I'm very focused on you, Grace." He stepped closer and ran his hand down her cheek, brushing it softly and then running his fingers through her long black hair.

"Stop being all sexy, Michael. Now is not the time. I need to be focused on the game. Distractions like butterflies and shaky hands won't win me that kiss. I want that kiss!" She grabbed his shirt and pulled him so close their chests brushed against one another. "I *need* that kiss," Grace whispered breathlessly.

With a devious grin on his face, he asked, "What can I do to help?"

She quickly told him Meg's strengths and weaknesses in pool and what shots she struggled with so he could make sure to take advantage of that when he played. He told Grace that Ryan was probably the weakest player of the guys, which made her feel a bit better; but Meg was the strongest player of the three ladies, so they evened each other out. Michael needed to outsmart Meg with his shooting, and they'd be fine.

Motivated by the prize, Meg and Ryan made short work of Jack and Bianca, beating them handily. After their victory, they went and sat down, watching while Michael and Grace took their turn against Jack and Bianca. Right off the bat, Jack became cocky and miscalculated his angles, sinking the eight-ball. Grace launched herself into Michael's arms in celebration. Bianca stuck her tongue out at them, having been eliminated, and then proceeded to stick her tongue down Jack's throat just because she could.

When Jack collected himself, he strode over to the table and racked the balls for the final round. A coin toss determined that Grace and Michael would break. "I want a clean game, ladies and gentlemen. No distracting, flashing, or goosing the opposing team. You will remain silent while they shoot and the prize for the winner is a big fat smooch, with tongue, and I guess you could cop a feel if you were so inclined, in front of all of us. Do you understand the rules?" Jack asked in his most official voice. The players all nodded their heads in agreement. "Who from team 'Naughty Librarian' is going to break?" Jack teased.

Grace decided to let Michael break, that way his turn would fall right before Meg's. Taking a deep breath, he leaned over the table and gave the cue ball a solid hit, sending the other balls scattering in every direction. Luckily, he sank the four-ball, making them solids which annoyed Meg right from the start.

The game progressed like a chess match. Ryan flubbed more shots than he made, while Michael and Meg were locked in a battle of the minds. Each kept thinking two shots ahead of where they were, trying to leave the other without a move. As Michael gained the upper hand, Meg became so frustrated that it began to affect her play.

Sensing her weakness, Grace too stepped up her game and made a good run, sinking two balls, which left Michael with one solid and the eight-ball when his turn came around. Ryan conferred with Meg before he sank one of theirs and then missed, leaving them two striped balls on the table.

"No pressure, Michael, but it comes down to you. Meg just might be able to run the table if you don't clear the balls, so please, I'm begging you, sink the balls." Grace stood back and held her breath as he considered his options. Meg watched his analysis and crossed her fingers, pressing them nervously to her lips.

"Eight-ball in the corner pocket," Michael called as he took his position at the side of the table. He looked away from the ball for a split second to give Grace a confident wink, and then took his shot. As the black ball rolled to the pocket, Grace nearly passed out, watching it bounce off one corner of the pocket, then the other corner, and finally falling back into the pocket with a dull thud.

"You did it!" Grace flung herself at Michael, a huge smile on her face.

He lifted Grace up into the air and immediately sat her down on the pool table. He waited for her knees to part then stepped between them, his fingers leisurely trailing up her thighs. His hand went to her face, caressing her cheek as his thumb ran across her plump lower lip.

"I'd like to claim my prize right now, if you don't mind," he whispered as she looked into his smoldering eyes. "I don't think I can wait another second." As his face moved closer, Grace felt her heart explode to life in anticipation of feeling his powerful lips on hers. Grace's body burned as his chest made contact with it, his hands grasping her face and tilting her head to the side.

"Michael," she muttered as his lips brushed against hers.

Her mind vaguely registered the screams and clapping coming from their friends. Michael's heated breath on her skin caused her whole body to explode into a million pieces. With each second that passed, she forgot about everything but him.

Once Grace felt his lips part and his tongue stroked passionately into her mouth, she was lost in her desire. The searing heat of his mouth on hers erupted throughout her trembling body. As Grace pulled herself closer to him, her legs locked around his back, their hips making forceful contact. She couldn't contain her moan as his tongue continued to caress hers, the taste of him filling her as no one ever would again. Grace's hands locked around the nape of his neck as she held on tight and refused to let him go.

Michael lowered his hands from her face and ran them along her sides, his thumbs purposely running across the edge of her breasts, sending visible waves of pleasure throughout her body. Grace felt one of his hands on her lower back as he tipped her backwards onto the table.

Grace's hands fell back to support her as Michael pressed the full weight of his body against her, urging her to lie back and let him be in control. She couldn't remember how long it had been since she had drawn a breath and she didn't care. Grace was more than willing to pass out on the pool table before she would dare break the kiss with Michael. She would have kept kissing him all night if she hadn't heard a strange male clearing his throat next to them.

"Um, excuse me there, folks. Sorry to interrupt. My name is Jason and I'm one of the bartenders here. Listen, I hate to break it to you, but she can't be up on the pool table like that. Her weight will throw off the balance, and we'll have to take the whole thing apart to get it level again."

Can't you see we're busy here?

Grace was prepared to ignore the unfamiliar voice and kept right on kissing Michael until this Jason guy forcefully removed her lips from Michael's, but Michael had other ideas. She felt the corners of his mouth turn up into a smile, and a second later, she felt herself being lifted up off the table with her legs still clamped around his waist in a death grip.

Michael reluctantly pulled his lips from hers to address this lunatic. "Sorry, Jason, my bad."

There was nothing bad about that kiss, Michael. It was really, really good ... Bad, Grace, bad!

She wasn't at all amused by the situation and was still a bit tipsy from the kiss and her lack of oxygen. Grace began her usual nervous rambling. "Jason, let me ask you a question. Have you ever made a bet? A stupid bet you regret about two weeks into the flippin' thing, and yet for some strange reason, you stay in the bet simply to win a stupid pair of shoes and eternal bragging rights, whatever the hell that even means? Of course, the catch is, in order to win the shoes and bragging rights, you can't go on a date or kiss the person you are madly in love with. You ever do something that stupid? Because I did, and that kiss you just interrupted for the sake of a pool table was the last kiss I'm going to get until New Year's, damn it! And that was a *really* good kiss you interrupted, right judges?" She looked over her shoulder at their friends, who were all hysterical.

Meg held up a napkin with a large number ten boldly written on it. Bianca held up ten fingers and waved them in the air. Jack and Ryan were on their feet, applauding the spectacle they had made. Grace glared at Jason with a raised eyebrow, waiting for his official score.

"Um, it looked pretty good. I'd give it a nine." Jason's evaluation irritated Michael.

"Why'd we only get a nine?"

"Because you didn't lay her down on the pool table, man. Now that would have been hotter. Her sprawled out up there, with that long black hair spread out around her head. That's what I would have done if it was my girlfriend," he said nonchalantly, like he had spent a lot of time thinking about it. "Anyway, stay off the table or I gotta throw you guys out. Next round is on me for cutting things short. We good?" Jason held his hand out to Michael and tipped his head apologetically in Grace's direction.

As Jason left, she leaned her head against Michael's chest. "If you kiss that well, I can only imagine how good you are at other things," she thought out loud, fanning herself.

Glowing with pride, he lifted her chin up to his face. "I'll be happy to show you, just say when … and it doesn't matter where," he whispered, his eyes looking as mischievous as the grin on his face. "Just not on the pool table or Jason will throw us out."

"Grace, are you going to hang onto Mike like that all night?" Jack boomed from the table as the free pitcher of beer arrived, just as promised. "And if you are, I'd suggest ditching the clothes; it'd be much more fun that way."

An image of her and Michael, naked on the pool table, flashed briefly in her head, sending an erotic shiver down her spine.

"Are you all right?" Michael asked as he watched her cheeks turn red with embarrassment.

"Yeah, I'm fine. Just counting down the hours. Hey, do you realize we only have ninety-seven hours to go?" They were going to be the longest ninety-seven hours of her life, but the end was in sight. Grace just had to behave a little longer. She grabbed the nearest glass of beer and chugged it, suddenly feeling very hot.

The group played a few more games, but then it was time for everyone to head home. Michael followed the girls to make sure they made it back to their apartment safely and then dropped Ryan and Jack off at their place. He teasingly invited Grace over for a "sleepover" if she wanted, but she politely declined, thinking it would be a very bad idea after that not-so-little kiss. Her heart was still fluttering wildly in her chest when she thought about it, and her self-control was at an all-time low.

Grace washed her face and was sitting on her bed in her pajamas when there was a small knock on the door.

Bianca stepped in, dressed for bed. "Hey."

"Missing your giant bed warmer?" Grace teased until she saw how sad her friend looked. "What's wrong?"

She crawled into bed with Grace, laying her head on the pillow. "I just got used to having him around these last few days. I miss him. I even miss his obnoxious snoring and the way he spent twenty minutes spiking his hair in the morning. God, I know I sound lame and I hate feeling this way, but I need him. I feel like there is this terrible ache in my chest right now, do you know what I mean?" A single tear fell from the corner of Bianca's eye.

Grace sighed, understanding completely. Last night, she had been curled up in Michael's warm arms, and tonight, she would be in her big bed, alone. "I know exactly what you mean, Bianca. You love him and never want to let him go. Why don't you just call Jack and ask him to come over? I'm sure he'd be here in less than five minutes."

"No, I don't want to sound like some helpless, lovesick girl. I'm a grown woman, damn it, and I can spend one night alone." She gave a small sigh and then asked, "Actually, would you mind if I stayed in here with you?"

"Not at all." Grace laughed. "As long as you don't mind me mumbling about Michael in my sleep." As she reached out to turn off the light, her hand brushed along the picture frame Liz had given her.

"Can I see it?" Bianca leaned over and held out her arm, wanting to get a better look at the photograph she had heard so much about. "Oh, Grace, look how sweet you two are! And his hair has always been messy, hasn't it?" She giggled, and then became very quiet. "You two were meant to be together, Grace. I'm so happy for you." Bianca leaned over, placing the picture back on the nightstand. She gave Grace a kiss on the cheek and laughed. "And by the way, that kiss on the pool table tonight was so hot. I can only imagine the night you two are going to have on New Year's. And I expect details—lots and lots of details."

Chapter 26

"Meg, I *know* there are dresses in this store with more fabric on them," Grace growled from behind the dressing room door. "Go find me one of those, please. I want something that screams sexy, not slutty."

They were at the mall once again, searching for the perfect dresses to wear to the New Year's Eve party at The Vault. The theme this year was black and white, so the girls were scouring the mall for the perfect outfit for the evening. So far, most of the dresses Meg picked barely covered Grace's body, and she didn't think it was wise to wear something that short around Michael during the final hours of the boycott.

Everyone had been busy since the night at Bumpers. The guys were diligently working at The Vault every night until close so they could have New Year's Eve off. Not to mention how busy they were making all the preliminary arrangements to help get Tryst up and running.

Meg and Bianca had spent the better part of the weekend returning phone calls from clients and arranging appointments for after the holiday, while Grace had to get ready for the new semester that would be starting only a few days after New Year's. Before they knew it, New Year's Eve had arrived, and there were only hours left in the agonizing bet.

There was a loud knock on the door with Meg grousing from outside the dressing room. "Quit your complaining. Here, try this one on. I think it'll be perfect." A black and white dress flew over the door, landing on Grace's head.

There was a loud ruckus from the dressing room next to her as Meg began barking orders at Bianca too. "Bianca, this is the dress for you, trust me. I want to see them when you have them on," Meg ordered from her position near the triple mirror.

Grace quickly stripped herself of the spandex nightmare Meg had given her previously and took a moment to look at the second dress in her hand. It was a bit bolder than what she might have normally chosen for herself, but if ever there was a night to be bold, this was it. Whatever dress she chose, she would only be in it until just before midnight; then she was planning to change into the dress Michael had given for their date. She didn't want to risk it getting ruined; she wanted everything about the night to be perfect.

"Let's shake a leg, ladies. We have manicure appointments in two hours. Move it, move it!" Meg rapped her knuckles on the dressing room doors, hurrying her friends as much as possible.

Grace swiftly stepped into the dress, secured the zipper, and when she looked up into the mirror, there stood a beautiful, sexy woman with a confident smile on her face. She barely recognized herself in the reflection. "Meg, this is the one!" Grace squealed as she thrust open the door to make a dramatic exit.

"Let me see… Oh, it's perfect on you! Come here." She grabbed Grace's hand and pulled her over to the mirror. "Your ass looks fantastic with the way this dress is cut." Meg admired her friend from behind as she spun in front of the mirror. "And look at your curves, girl." She ran her hands over Grace's hips and gave them a little shake. "Michael will love you in this."

The dress was spectacular; it was a short, mid thigh, sleeveless, sequined dress. The sequins made a cool geometric black and white print of squares and triangles which covered the dress. It was cute, flirty, and sexy—exactly what she had been searching for. Grace was amazed at how a simple piece of fabric could make her feel so confident and almost powerful.

"Are you ready for tonight? Or do you still think he'll disappear at the stroke of midnight?" Meg joked as she leaned against one of the mirrors, waiting for Grace's answer.

"Honestly, before Christmas, I would have put money on him vanishing. But now, after spending this last week together, I can't explain it. I just know that nothing is going to be able to keep me from him and he would never leave me. Does that make sense or do I sound like a crazed stalker?" The two women started laughing together at the lame explanation.

"Well, I want you to know that I am so happy for you, Grace, and very proud of you for putting yourself out there and trusting Michael with your heart. I think you finally see how amazing you are. Michael helped you see that; he's a great guy." She gave Grace a big hug when they heard grumbling from behind them.

Bianca came out of her dressing room in the most form fitting black dress they had seen her in all day. The dress had thin, adjustable spaghetti straps and hugged every one of her glorious curves. She was fidgeting with a bow that hung from the sweetheart neckline, cursing its existence.

"We can cut this thing off, right?" She bent over and let Meg examine the stitching that held it in place.

"Yeah, three snips and it'll be gone. God, you two look amazing. So, do you like the dresses?" The two women nodded their heads vigorously.

Meg had, immediately upon arrival, found a beautiful white sleeveless dress with the most spectacular bead work along the bottom hem of the dress and around the neckline. It was the first and only dress she tried on, and she looked like an angel in it.

"Good, now take them off and meet me at the cashier. Then it's on to the shoe department." As Meg went to grab her purse, her phone started singing a new tune…about keeping "dirty little secrets." She quickly opened it. "Hey, there," she purred into the phone.

"Who was that?" Grace asked Bianca as they walked back to the dressing room.

"Ryan." She giggled.

"When did he make that his ring tone? She never told me he changed it. "

Bianca glanced over her shoulder at Meg, smirking. "Well, I just found out the other day. Apparently, they did it quite a while ago." She gave Grace a gentle push toward the door. "Come on, let's get changed. We have a lot to get done before tonight."

Grace gave her a small salute before slipping obediently into her dressing room to change back into her clothes.

Bianca's voice carried over the wall dividing their dressing rooms. "And we're making one more stop to get you something sexy, black, and lacy to wear under that little number, Grace, so be prepared—and no complaining. If I have to wrestle you into it myself, you *will* wear it."

❧

With freshly painted nails and a brand new outfit for the party hanging in her room, Grace was trying to keep herself occupied the rest of the afternoon by watching a movie. Michael, however, had started texting her every hour on the hour with his countdown.

Meg had left to drop off Ryan's shirt for the party, so Bianca and Grace were alone when Michael's next message arrived.

Seven hours until I get to have to all to myself. I can hardly wait.
You have no idea.
I love you,
M

"So, how are you holding up, Grace?" Bianca asked as she watched her friend blush at the latest message.

"I'm really excited, but I guess a little nervous too. I've wanted this date for so long. I just hope I don't do anything to embarrass myself—like hyperventilate or pass out."

Bianca laughed out loud. "Just remember to breathe, Grace. I think we might have some smelling salts in the first aid kit in the kitchen if you want to slip those into your overnight bag."

"Wait, overnight bag?" Grace panicked. That was something she hadn't even considered.

"Um, well … I was just assuming you would stay out all night with him and sleep there. I'm sorry, my mistake." Bianca looked very apologetic. "You do whatever you're comfortable with, Grace. I shouldn't have opened my big mouth."

"What? No, it's not that. I mean, I *hope* he wants me to spend the night. I want to spend the night. I just … don't have anything *good* to wear. And what should I pack? Is it terribly presumptuous if I show up with a bag in my hand?" Grace jumped up in a panic and started racing off to her room to rummage through her drawers. Flannel pants and boxers tumbled onto the floor at her feet as she searched for something suitable for the occasion.

Bianca calmly walked up behind Grace with a small, pink bag in her hand. "Did you really think we'd let you go off on a date this important unprepared and inappropriately dressed?" She extended her hand with the bag dangling from her index finger.

Relieved, Grace took the bag and emptied the contents onto the bed. There was a brand new white lace bra and panty set for the following day, a short green nightgown and a toothbrush. She spun around and hugged Bianca with all her might. "Thank you. I love you!"

"And what am I, chopped liver?" a whiny voice said from the doorway behind them. Meg had just returned and wanted a little love for her part in the purchases. She stuck out a pouty lip until Grace burst out laughing.

"I love you too, Meg. Now, I need a bag so I can pack this stuff and a change of clothes. Any suggestions?" Grace gave her a knowing look, quite certain that Meg had the perfect bag sitting over in her room with all the tags still attached.

"As a matter of fact…" Meg grinned and skipped off to her room only to return a second later with a small black suitcase just bigger than a briefcase, but very subtle so Grace wouldn't look like she was moving in or anything. Meg ran to Grace's closet, picked out a few clothes for the following day, folded them, and pressed them into the bottom of the suitcase. She carefully laid the lacy garments on top, tucking Grace's toiletries and toothbrush off to the side. With the straps clasped tightly, holding everything in place, she zipped the case closed and set it on the bed.

"There, you're all ready for your hot date. I threw in an extra shirt in case you make it an *extended* stay. Do you even know where he's taking you?" Meg asked as she bounced up and down with excitement.

"I have no idea. He won't tell me anything. All I know is that I'm supposed to wear my dress… and that's it. I feel like a bunch of butterflies have taken up permanent residence in my stomach, and he keeps sending me these messages, each more sexy than the last. I just hope I can control myself at the club." Grace had to sit down as her pulse skyrocketed, just thinking about Michael and how tempting he was going to look tonight, especially knowing that at the stroke of midnight, the bet ended.

"How are you holding up?" Grace was a trembling, sputtering mess, while Meg sat there, perfectly composed and looking like she didn't have a care in the world.

"Me? Oh, I'm getting rather excited. I can't wait for tonight. It's going to be amazing." She looked over to Bianca. "Full of fun surprises, I think."

"You've been so quiet about things. What do you and Ryan have planned? For, you know, after midnight?" Grace asked suggestively.

Meg blushed. "Well, I assume pretty much the same thing as you and Michael. Bianca, is Jack spending the night over here with you?" Bianca nodded her head, grinning. "Then I guess we'll go over to Ryan's for some, um, privacy." She giggled, refusing to make eye contact with Grace.

In the middle of their laughter, Grace heard her phone beep with Michael's latest message.

Six more hours until midnight.
Are you ready to come with me?
On our date
I love you,
M

"Argh! He's killing me, totally and completely killing me. Hide my keys please so I don't go over to his place right now." Grace went to the wicker basket in the kitchen and grabbed the set of keys that were inside and tossed them over to Bianca, who promptly stuffed them down the front of her blouse. Leaning against the granite counter top, Grace took a shaky breath. "OK, I'm better. Come on, I need to eat a little something and feed this flock of butterflies."

About an hour later, she was in the shower, letting the hot water work its magic and soothe her overly tense muscles. It did absolutely nothing to kill the butterflies, quench her insatiable desire for Michael, or slow her thundering heart, but when she stepped out, Grace did find herself significantly more relaxed. During her shower, the smell of the coconut shampoo made her smile, mainly because she lost herself in a few naughty thoughts about Michael that involved drinking daiquiris, in bed, naked. Of course the image faded instantly when, in her daze, Grace let some of the shampoo trickle into her eye, causing a horrible, burning pain. She turned into the water jet and rinsed her eyes clean of all traces of soap before she was permanently blinded.

Grace climbed out of the shower and started to dry off. She'd barely managed to wrap the towel around her body when the phone rang. She dashed out of the bathroom and grabbed the phone off the bed. "Michael, if you're calling to leave me some sexy or suggestive message about all the things that we're going to be doing in," she glanced at her watch, "four hours and twenty nine minutes, I will scream. I can only resist you for so long. Keep it up much longer, and I'm going to come over to your place and—"

"Grace?"

No, no, no. This isn't happening.

"Um, hi, Mom. Wow, this is awkward. What I just said … yeah, it was … um, a joke. Ha ha ha, right? … Shit. What do you want?" Grace buried her face into her hands and wished she could suck that little rant back onto her mouth.

"Well, no need to curse at me, dear. We were just calling to say Happy New Year. I figured you and Michael had *plans,* so we wanted to catch you before you went out for the evening." Grace's stomach sank when she heard giggling on the other end of the phone and Susan's muffled laughter.

"Tell me I'm not on speaker phone, Mother. For the love of all that is holy! You know I hate being on speaker phone," Grace growled.

"Happy New Year, Grace!" yelled the other laughing female voices in the background.

"Mother, who else is there? No. Please don't tell me you're spending New Years Eve with—"

"Liz and Evelyn, dear."

"Kill. Me. Now." Grace covered the phone and a string of profanities flew from her lips.

"Oh, dear, now stop. We were all young and in love once. Weren't we, ladies?" There was a loud chorus of yeses in the background. "We remember what it was like. Just make sure that you two are … you know, careful and well … use protection, dear. You do have condoms, right? Or wait, Liz, do you know if Michael has some condoms at his place?"

"Stop!" Grace screamed into the phone, causing the women on the other end to laugh hysterically. "I'm going to hang up now, Mother, and we will *never* speak of this conversation again. Liz, Evelyn, I love you both. Happy New Year. "

Grace heard Susan sing "You kids have fun!" into the phone as she hung up. Again, Grace buried her face into her pillow and screamed as loud as she could.

Get them out of your head, Grace. Tonight is about you and Michael. Not Susan, not Evelyn or Liz. Think about Michael. Hunky, sexy Michael. Her mind, of course, went straight into the gutter which didn't help her already flustered state.

"Grace? Why are you screaming in here? Did Michael send you another message?" Meg asked as she cautiously opened the bedroom door. "Oh my gosh, why aren't you ready? They'll be here soon," Meg yelled as she ran to the bed, grabbed Grace's arm, and dragged her into the bathroom to begin frantically working on her hair.

"Sorry, I got sidetracked humiliating myself on the phone with my mother, Liz, and Evelyn." Meg froze with the brush hanging in mid air, a confused look on her face. Grace held up her hand to stop her question. "Don't even ask. If I tell you, I might burst into tears. All I can say is the word condom came up in the conversation." Meg's mouth fell open in stunned silence; then she focused and went back to work, drying Grace's hair.

Twenty minutes later, Grace looked beautiful, her hair cascading over her shoulders in big, black curls which had a stunning shine to them. Bianca had helped get her makeup perfect before she rushed back to her room to put on her dress and touch up her own makeup. Meg had cranked up the music in the apartment and was apparently dancing around the family room to pass the time. While Grace was applying one last coat of mascara, she heard her phone beep with Michael's latest message. With a trembling hand, she picked it up and took a deep breath before reading it.

Four more hours until you are all MINE.
Are you bringing the condoms or do you just want to use the ones I have here?
Yes, they called me, too.
I love you!
M

Laughing, Grace rolled her eyes and started searching her room for the shoes they had bought earlier at the store. Her eyes lingered on the dress Michael bought, which was hanging on her closet door, waiting for midnight. Grace could hardly wait to come back and slip into that dress for their date. *Just a few more hours,* she told herself as she crouched on her hands and knees to look under her bed for the shoe box. Out of nowhere, she heard a husky voice behind her.

"Nice view," he said, followed by a whistle.

"Michael!" Grace squeaked. *Oh God, was my butt hanging out?* "You're early," she sputtered as she scrambled to her feet, nearly tripping.

His stunning, muscular form filled the doorway as she turned around. Michael pushed himself off the door jamb he had been leaning against and walked over to Grace, his eyes taking in every inch of her body. The more he looked, the wider his smile grew. By the time she was in his arms, his eyes were on fire with desire.

"You look spectacular, Grace. You are downright irresistible in this dress. How am I going to control myself around you tonight?" He ran a single finger slowly along her jaw line as her mouth hung open.

"Michael … four hours … please." She was barely able to whisper the words as he brushed her long black curls over her shoulder and began kissing the newly exposed section of her neck. "Two hundred forty minutes. Just a little bit longer."

Goosebumps covered her body, and when Grace felt him start gently sucking on her neck, her legs buckled. He quickly wrapped his arms around her waist, holding her in place. She felt his warm laughter against her skin. "Grace, you're trembling."

"Hey, you two—oops. Never mind, I was never here." The sound of Bianca's voice snapped Grace out of her Michael-induced haze.

She gave him a small shove and looked around his chest to see her friend. "What do you need, Bianca?" Grace leaned forward so Michael couldn't see her face as she mouthed the word "Help!" behind his back.

Being the good friend she was, all Bianca did was flick her long red locks over her shoulder and laugh. "I thought you might be looking for these." In her hand was the box with Grace's shoes in it.

She escaped from Michael and scooted to the door to retrieve the footwear. "Thanks, Bianca," she said loudly, grabbing her wrist so she couldn't leave. "Help, he's being super sexy," she whispered, "don't leave me alone with him. Help me resist him!" All her pleading got her nowhere; Bianca rolled her eyes, and Grace knew she was on her own. "Traitor," Grace hissed as Bianca wrenched her wrist free and left the room, giggling.

"Let me see the shoes you picked out." Michael had sat down on the edge of her bed and was holding out his hand.

It was impossible to not notice the defined muscles of his arms or the way his shirt clung across his chest, reminding her of his most delicious body underneath. Grace became distracted imagining him without a shirt, hovering over her body.

Instead of walking over to him, she tossed the box, trying to keep herself a safe distance away. Grace bit her lip when he let out a low whistle as he opened the box. "Nice." He patted the bed beside him. "Sit down and put them on."

Cautiously she approached the bed, keeping a suspicious eye on him at all times. He handed her the right shoe, which she quickly slipped onto her foot. She bent over to fasten the strap around her ankle and after a few seconds of wrestling with it, she was finally successful. As she reached for the other shoe, Michael tightened his grip on it.

"Here, let me help you with this one, sweetheart." He slid off the edge of the bed and knelt down on the floor at her feet. He gently lifted Grace's foot off the ground and placed it into the shoe. She expected him to just fasten the strap around her ankle and be done with it, but instead, he surprised her by hoisting her foot higher onto his upper chest.

She let out a yelp as her foot went up into the air. Grace felt his fingertips linger on her calf before sliding down to her ankle and begin working on the strap. He took his time, slyly glancing from the buckle up to her face and back again.

Grace started losing her balance, so she leaned back onto the bed and braced herself back on her arms, waiting for him to finish and trying not to think about how good his fingers felt as they ghosted over her skin. She thought about telling him to hurry up, but was afraid the only thing that would come out of her mouth was a desperate moan, so she pressed her lips together tightly and tried to focus her attention on the bedroom door over his shoulder rather than how delicious he looked kneeling between her legs.

"There you go. Perfect." She tried to move her foot, but Michael was holding it in place, the tip of her shoe wedged under his chin. His blue eyes ran up the length of her long, bare leg before finally locking one her brown ones. He paused as if collecting himself, and then let out a huge sigh. "Black lace?"

Grace slid her foot off his shoulder and tugged her skirt lower over her thighs. "What are you talking about?"

"Your panties, they're black lace, right?" He ran his fingers slowly through his hair as he wedged his body further between Grace's legs. His hands settled on her knees before they started to make the tortuously slow climb up her thighs. His fingertips had just dipped under the hem of her dress when they were summoned.

"Michael, Grace, let's get a move on!" Jack hollered from the other room.

Springing to her feet, Grace was desperate to put some small distance between them before things got out of hand, but she couldn't move from the bedside because Michael was still on his knees, at her feet, completely blocking the exit.

"And where do you think you are running off to?" Michael asked as he stood up, his hands running up the sides of her legs before coming to settle on her hips. "I'm not quite finished with you yet..." He clasped his hands behind her back and started kissing a fiery trail up her neck, carefully working his way toward her plump, red lips. His pace was agonizingly slow, each touch of his lips making her that much closer to losing the bet.

She needed to put a stop to all of the temptation that Michael was literally putting in front of her. He'd started with the text messages earlier in the day and now this erotic assault on her body … Grace knew she was only human and wasn't going to make it much longer if she didn't put the brakes on.

She decided to try and bluff by pretending that his advances weren't affecting her in the least. "Listen here, Mikey-boy, I only have two hundred thirty-four minutes left in this stupid bet, and I'm *not* about to lose now. So you can try and seduce me as many ways as you want, but I'm winning those damn shoes tonight." Grace made every effort to look self-assured and slightly annoyed, but he saw right through her and gave her a dimpled smirk.

"I can try to seduce you?" he asked, exuding sensuality with every word. "I accept your challenge." He took her hand and slowly lifted it to his lips, kissing the top of her hand, his blue eyes sparkling.

Well, that backfired. How stupid am I? I just dared the man I can't keep my hands off of to entice me into his bed before midnight. What the hell was I thinking?

Chapter 27

The gang pulled up to The Vault where they found a long line of people waiting outside. Michael parked the car around back so they could use the employee entrance, avoiding the wait and the crowd. Ryan and Jack were pulling into the lot as Grace climbed out of the car. Michael held out his hand to her, her teeth already chattering in the cold December air.

"I knew I should have worn more clothes," Grace grumbled as Michael led her toward the building, her free hand buried deep inside her coat pocket, the other tingling from the contact with Michael's hand.

"I think you still have a few too many clothes on for my liking," Michael said as he pulled her closer and walked through the doorway.

"Yeah, I had a feeling you were going to say that." Grace laughed and threw her coat at him. "I'm watching you, mister." They piled their coats on the couch in the break room before heading out to the bar, hand in hand.

The club had truly been transformed for the evening. Black and white fabric was draped everywhere: along the bar, across the ceiling, and down the walls. Even the napkins were all black and white. Every table had been removed from the upstairs section and instead, black and white leather couches and chairs created cozy seating areas away from the crowds on the dance floor. The music was so loud you could feel it pulsing throughout the place.

"Wow." Bianca stopped in her tracks to admire all the decorations. "This must have taken you guys forever." She and Grace were both staring up at the ceiling, trying to figure out exactly how they got the yards of fabric draped so elegantly in a perfect checkerboard pattern.

"You don't even want to know." Jack shuddered at the memory. "It took us until six-fifteen this morning. Ryan nearly broke his neck somewhere around four a.m., didn't you?" Jack smirked.

"It might have had something to do with the fact that you were snoring instead of holding the ladder steady, Jack." Ryan glared at his friend as he took a generous sip of the gin and tonic the bartender had just set on the bar next to him.

"Ladies!" they heard someone shout from behind them. Out of nowhere, Vicki came marching over, dragging a huge, burly, and extensively tattooed man behind her, who Grace instantly knew had to be Steve.

"Vicki!" They squealed and ran over, wrapping her up in their arms. The girls were so excited to see her that without thinking, they stood on their tip toes and kissed Steve on the cheek. The public display of affection by three gorgeous strangers took him completely by surprise. Vicki laughed at seeing her big, strong man flustered by a flock of girls.

"Oh, by the way, I'm Meg. The redhead that just kissed you, her name is Bianca, and the raven here is Grace. We probably should have introduced ourselves before we slobbered on you. Sorry!" Her eyes fixated on his arms. "So how many tattoos do you have, Steve?" Meg asked as she grabbed one of his arms and began counting. "I bet this one hurt like a mother." She cringed pointing to the snake tattoo that ran along his elbow.

"I see what you mean about them, Vic. I like them. And they are perfect for those guys. They'll definitely keep them on their toes." Steve winked at Vicki before heading over to the bar to join Michael and the guys. He shook hands with them and whatever he said had all of them cracking up.

Vicki looked great tonight. She was wearing a black tube top and white jeans that were neatly tucked into the sexy black leather boots they'd given her for Christmas.

Steve was in a white button-down shirt with the sleeves cut off and a pair of black jeans with a giant silver Jack Daniels belt buckle. Both of his arms were covered with colorful tattoos, but the most prominent one was Vicki's name in bold black letters on his right forearm.

"So, your boycott ends tonight, ladies? Any *exciting* plans?" Vicki asked, a knowing smirk on her face. "I hope you're able to find some *decent* guys in town now." She looked from the girls over to the bar, where the guys and Steve were deep in conversation, an occasional laugh coming from one of them.

"Hey, don't look at me. I already found my man, and that girl over there better stop looking at his ass or I will be knocking her down onto hers." Bianca glared at a tall bleached blonde who was chewing on her straw while batting her fake eyelashes in Jack's direction.

Feeling the need to mark her territory, Bianca marched straight over to the unaware Jack, spun him around, and planted one hell of a kiss on him before smugly looking over her shoulder to make sure the other girl caught the show.

She rolled her eyes at Bianca and headed onto the dance floor. Jack, not caring what the reason for the kiss was, gave Bianca a playful swat on the rear in thanks and possessively wrapped his arm around her shoulder.

"I knew they'd be perfect together," Vicki laughed as she watched Jack and Bianca tease one another. She nudged Grace and tilted her head in Meg's direction. "And those two fell in love the first night she was here." They watched as Meg stood next to them, completely lost in Ryan as he leaned back against the bar, simply smiling at her. "The idiot forgot how to speak when he saw her." After a few seconds, he held out his hand, and Meg instinctively rushed to his side.

"They do make cute couples, don't they?" Grace laughed.

"And look at you. This dress is very sexy, my dear. You wouldn't be trying to get the attention of anyone in particular this evening like, say, a hunky guy with unbelievable ice blue eyes?" Vicki grinned as Grace looked away, trying to hide her embarrassment. "Yeah, from the looks of it, I'd say you *definitely* got his attention."

Grace peeked over her shoulder to the bar and found Michael standing a few feet away with his arms folded across his chest, his hair slightly in his eyes, dimples blazing, and a gorgeous smile on his face. When their eyes met, he winked and Grace immediately looked away and spun back to face Vicki, who was simply shaking her head from side to side.

"Yeah, I hope you slept in this morning, because from the look on his face, he's got *big* plans for the two of you tonight." Vicki teased her, making Grace's heart beat faster in anticipation of her night with Michael. "And I doubt you'll be doing much sleeping."

Dumbfounded, Grace felt a hand settle on the small of her back as Vicki grinned and quipped, "Speak of the devil. Hello there, Michael. I was just telling Grace how cute she looks tonight."

"She looks beyond cute, Vicki. I think she looks absolutely delicious. And did you know that she gave me permission to try and seduce her this evening? Speaking of which, I think I need to get busy." Before Grace knew what was happening, Michael was gathering her black waves into a ponytail that he held in place with one if his hands as he started gently kissing the sensitive skin along the back of her exposed neck. His free hand slid down Grace's back and settled on her curvaceous rear.

Vicki's eyes grew huge as she and Grace stared at each other in disbelief. Instead of helping Grace, though, all Vicki did was stand there and mouth "Oh my God..." and then fan herself as she walked back to Steve and the rest of their friends at the bar.

"Michael?" Grace said breathlessly, feeling his hand make its way up her side.

"Mm-hmm?" he mumbled as he continued kissing the sensitive skin along her collarbone.

"I think I'm going to have a heart attack if you don't stop that..." His lips were now skimming up the side of her neck and moved near her ear. "I said you could try to seduce me, not stop my heart."

"Aren't you enjoying yourself?" he asked softly as he took a small break from nuzzling his nose against her cheek.

"Oh, I'm enjoying this more than you can imagine." Grace grabbed his hand and placed it over her heart so he could feel the thundering in her chest. "But *this* is what it's doing to me. I really need to breathe for a second there, lover boy." Having his hand half on her breast made her heart race even faster.

"You are rather excited right now, aren't you?" He laughed.

"You have no idea."

"Well, I think you better sit down. Come with me, sweetheart. I know just the place for us." He slowly slid his hand down from the center of her chest and reached for her hand, leading her through the crowd.

With their fingers laced together, they climbed the staircase that led to the table Vicki had reserved for them. The regular furniture had been replaced by a black leather loveseat and two oversized white chairs. The reserved sign was sitting on the small table in the middle.

"I guess it pays to have connections here tonight, doesn't it?" Grace glanced around the rest of the area to see wall to wall people packing all the other sofas and chairs. And in the middle of all of that chaos was a tiny section all for them, an oasis set away from the crowds. Grace noticed there were even long black panels of fabric hanging from the ceiling on either side of their seats to give them more privacy.

"You guys really thought of everything."

"I assure you, we've been planning this evening for a very long time now." Michael said teasingly, pulling Grace onto the loveseat with him.

While they sat there alone in relative quiet, she felt her body being drawn to him as if by some sort of magnetic attraction. In no time at all, Grace was pressed against his chest while she played with the little black buttons that ran down the front of his shirt. His hand was skimming up her side, his thumb barely grazing along her breast, making her jump.

"Have I told you just how handsome you look tonight?" His snug black button-down shirt hugged him in all the right places. Grace could feel the outlines of his muscles through the thin fabric as she eagerly ran her hands over his chest.

"No, you haven't, but come a little closer and you can show me just how attractive you find me." He reached his hands around her waist and pulled her on top of him. Instinctively her legs spread and Grace found herself straddling his lap.

She let out a loud gasp when she realized the precarious position she placed herself in with him. "This is such a bad idea," Grace said, trying to pull the sides of her dress down lower on her thighs before her underwear was on display for the entire upper level of the club, not to mention Michael.

He leaned forward, pressing his chest to hers and whispering into her ear. "I'm sorry; the music's very loud. You're going to have to get really close to me tonight so I can hear you." His hot breath swept across her cheek as his hands came to rest very, very low on her back.

"I said, I think sitting like this is a very bad idea." Grace was nearly gasping for breath as the words came out. *That's the understatement of the century!*

"Actually, I think having you straddle me like this is a very good idea and I wouldn't mind doing this again, a little later tonight, without so many clo—"

Not wanting to hear him actually utter the words that were about to come across his lips, for fear of undressing him right there on the couch, Grace tried to move off his lap, but he wouldn't let her. His strong hands locked her in place with absolutely no chance of escape.

"If you keep wiggling around like that, sweetheart, we might have a little situation on our hands soon," he whispered as his hands moved a few inches lower down her back. He slid her farther up his lap, their chests now touching. There was no missing the way his pants were beginning to tent out toward her body.

If that's the 'situation' he's referring to, there is nothing little about it, Grace thought to herself, blushing. She tried to settle down, but then he moved his hands to her upper back and began running his fingertips through her long mane of hair, wrapping his fists in it. Grace's head tipped to the side in delight, allowing him better access to her neck. "Michael," she sighed, gripping onto his shoulders for dear life.

I don't know how much more of this I can take.

"Hey, guys, do you mind if we join you, or do you want to some 'alone time'?" Jack's voice boomed from the side. Grace didn't have to turn to know there was a smug grin on his bearded face. She felt Michael's hands slide to her rear, to block any view her hiked-up dress might be flashing to their friends at the moment.

"Sit down," Grace said loudly, happy for any distraction. *Save me...from myself.*

"Go away," Michael said at the same time, grinning.

"Don't listen to him. He's just mad he hasn't been able to seduce me yet." Grace gave Michael a playful swat and gracefully attempted to detach herself from his lap, trying not to completely expose herself to everyone.

"Yet..." he added as he ran his hand up the curve of her thigh, inching higher, as she sat beside him. "The night is still young, Grace, don't forget that." A round of cat calls came from the gang as Michael's fingers continued to feather along her thigh.

Thankfully, over the next few minutes, the conversation moved away from Grace and onto Meg and Bianca. More specifically, they talked about the crazy clients they'd dealt with in the past and the amazing fits people would throw over the interior finishes of their homes. Some of the stories sounded so far-fetched that if Grace hadn't been there when they came home from work, she might not have believed them.

Twenty minutes later, Meg got antsy. "I love this song!" she squealed. "Come on, girls, let's go dance." She grabbed their hands and scurried down the stairs while the guys stayed behind.

❧

Hundreds of people were packed onto the floor; the heat from all the bodies made the temperature at least fifteen degrees higher there than in the rest of the club. Meg led them through the tight crowd, looking for a less congested area to dance. They found a small haven close to the bar and began dancing, laughing, and having a great time. Vicki even came and joined them for a while. Steve, however, just watched from his position at the bar.

From the second floor railing, Michael, Ryan, and Jack watched the trio dance. When Bianca tried to wave them down, they shook their heads no and laughed, preferring instead to simply enjoy the view. The ladies even got a good laugh when a couple of pathetic barflies planted themselves next to the guys at the rail, flipping their hair and giggling, desperately trying to get their attention, only to be ignored. When their more subtle attempts failed, they became more brazen in their advances, but with a wave of a hand, Jack dismissed them and sent them stomping away.

Vicki watched the whole thing go down, grinning like a proud mother. "Wow. I guess they don't need my fly-swatting services any more. They did just fine on their own. Maybe my boys are finally growing up." She wiped a pretend tear away from the corner of her eye. Glancing over to the bar, she saw Steve waving his thumb towards the door. "You ladies have fun; Steve and I are going to split. Happy New Year!" Vicki threw her arms around them to say goodbye; then the girls all turned to wave furiously at Steve. He returned their silliness with a smile and salute.

As Vicki walked away, Grace noticed that Meg was craning her neck around the crowd. "Now where did those boys run off to?" She was looking toward the section of the bar that Vicki and Steve had just abandoned when she was suddenly lifted high into the air. "Ryan!" she screamed as her legs sailed upwards.

"You looked like you were having fun, so I decided to join you." Ryan wrapped his arms around Meg and the two of them began dancing away. Without missing a beat, Meg melded her body to his and the two of them were lost in each other amidst the loud music and screaming crowd.

With Meg occupied, Grace and Bianca partnered up to dance. A couple of cheesy club guys tried to cut in and join them, but the pair managed to run them off by completely ignoring them and paying a lot of attention to one another. As the rejected males sulked away, Ryan pointed to the bar where Jack and Michael were proudly applauding the girls' efforts.

The DJ was playing a great mix of dance songs and the crowd loved every second of it. People swarmed to the floor as the music and lights picked up. The room was wall to wall bodies, all moving together in unison to the rapid beat of the music. Even more and more people rushed onto the dance floor when one of their favorites blasted over the sound system, the red lights flashing over the crowd.

"Meg, it's your song!" Grace called over. Meg simply squealed and began dancing even more enthusiastically, with Ryan laughing at her exuberance.

As Grace started dancing, she felt two strong arms wrap around her from behind, crushing her against a warm chest. "Mind if I join you?" Michael said in her ear as he planted his hands firmly onto Grace's hips and began to slowly move them in unison with his without missing a beat.

She immediately flashed back to that first night when she had unknowingly danced with him and remembered how well he moved their bodies. "Um, nope. Not at all." Grace knew she'd have to keep her heart in check, but having him that close made it incredibly difficult. She leaned her head back onto his chest and let him take the lead, surrendering control and moving her body with his, following his lead.

The tempo of the song changed and Grace wanted to try something. She crooked her finger at Michael, encouraging him to follow her lead. Together, they swiveled their hips down to the ground then slowly back up again, keeping in constant contact with one another. Grace was acutely aware of everything about his body, each muscle she felt moving underneath her fingertips, every curve to his body, every ripple of muscle and just how well they fit together. He couldn't have held her any closer if he tried, making their two bodies move as one under the flashing lights of the dance floor.

"How did I do?" he asked in Grace's ear as his hands drifted upwards, hiking up her dress while sending chills down her spine. As the tempo of the song increased, so did the speed of their movements together.

Grace spun around to face him and pulled his head down so his ear was right next to her lips. "Oh, you definitely know how to use your hips." She gently bit down on his earlobe which made him grind his hips harder into her. "Let me show you a little something the girls taught me."

When she pulled her cheek away from his, Grace saw his blue eyes were on fire. "Go for it." He licked his lips and continued gracefully rocking their bodies together to the beat.

As the music continued to pulse through the club, whenever the notes began to drop low and the beat slowed, Grace would slither her body down to the floor, keeping contact with Michael the whole time. Her hips swiveled and swayed all the way down. He stood in silence and watched as she seductively crawled back up his body, knowing the sole goal of her actions was to drive him crazy. She finished her little display by pressing her lips against his chest.

"Wow…" was all Michael could manage to say before he scooped her up into his arms and kissed her.

The way they moved together became more erotic with each passing minute. Every time they had their bodies pressed together, Grace could feel him moving with her in perfect unison. If she closed her eyes, Grace could imagine how it would feel to move this way with him later that night, minus the clothes. Her cheeks flushed at the naughty images while her head fell back in pleasure. Grace gasped and couldn't breathe when she felt the incredible sensation of his tongue running along her neck.

With each touch, each caress, Grace wanted him more. His hands felt like velvet as they glided over her skin, his full lips begging to be kissed. She remembered how sweet he'd tasted at the pool hall when they kissed, and she wanted nothing more than to feel the warmth of his mouth on hers again. Grace wanted his hands all over her. She wanted him naked. She wanted him *now*!

Screw the shoes.

Grace raised her head and quickly checked over her shoulder to see Bianca and Jack with their hands all over each other while Meg and Ryan were off dancing in their own little world. *No one would miss us if we left before midnight. Hell, they might even thank us.*

I'm OUT, her head screamed.

As the song was coming to an end, and with her confidence soaring, Grace decided to play dirty and get Michael's undivided attention. She brazenly put her hands on the front of his chest; then she slid not only her body down his, but also her hands. Her fingers trailed down his chest, his abdomen, and then Grace carefully slid them all the way down the front of his thighs, doing her best to tease him as her thumbs slid over the zipper of his pants.

He froze when she crouched at his feet. Her big brown eyes looked up at him through her thick eyelashes. It seemed as if he held his breath as he waited for her to begin her graceful climb back up his body, and part of him wondered what she might do next.

Instead of moving slowly, she grabbed onto his belt buckle, her fingers reaching partway into his pants and pulled herself up in one swift motion. With her hand still on the buckle, Grace stood on her tip toes and as the music lulled, she said, "Don't move an inch." Grace ran her free hand down his cheek, her finger slowly grazing over his lower lip.

All he could do was nod his head as his eyes smoldered with desire.

Without releasing him, Grace turned to Meg and whistled to get her attention. Meg turned and leaned her head into Grace's and heard her say the magic words. "I am out."

Meg pulled back, a look of shock on her face. Then she leaned in again and asked, "Are you sure, Grace?"

"Oh yeah, I'm sure. I'm done waiting. I want him. Screw the shoes. I'm out." Grace kissed her friend's cheek and caught the brilliant smile that came across it as she realized her victory. Spinning around, Grace turned her attention back to Michael, who was still standing there, stunned. "You, come with me." She placed both her hands on his chest and pushed him backwards until he bumped into a nearby wall.

"What's wrong, Grace?" He was still trying to fully understand her odd behavior, but a knowing smile started to creep onto his face.

"I'm out."

"Out of what?" He smirked, dimples blazing as he waited to hear her say the words.

Grace didn't even bother to answer him. She put her hands on his face and quickly pulled him to her. Her lips crashed into his, and he responded with equal enthusiasm. Grace's mouth opened, allowing his tongue to plunge inside, the sensation igniting a fire deep inside of her. With a surge of emotion, she ground her hips against his, their bodies melting together. Her hands slid from his face down to his chest, gripping his shirt, as one of his hands knotted into her long hair and the other tightly clutched her around the waist.

He pushed himself forward from the wall and spun Grace around so her back was now flush with the coarse brick wall. She felt the weight and power of his body as he sank into her. Reflexively, she arched her back, pulling him closer, trying to eliminate any distance between their bodies. His hand left her waist and gently cupped her breast, making her gasp in pleasure.

"Michael, let's get out of here, please. Take me somewhere—anywhere," Grace said breathlessly as he devoured her neck, making every hair on her arms stand on end as his tongue teased its way down her neck.

Grinning, Michael stepped back from her and started rummaging in his pocket. His phone flew up to his ear and it sounded like he said "She's ready," and then he hung up.

"Who were you calling?" Grace asked as she straightened out her dress and tousled hair. Now was not exactly the time for phone calls. Now was the time for taking the extremely aroused girl in front of him back to his place for a long night of wild sex.

He saw the look of frustration on her face and pulled Grace into his arms, kissing her once more. "Do you trust me?" he purred in her ear.

How can I say no when he says it like that? she thought.

She nodded and stared at his glistening lips, wanting nothing more than to feel them all over her body.

"You won."

"Won what? Most sexually frustrated girl in the room contest? Most likely to beg for sex? What exactly did I win, Michael?" Grace scoffed, completely confused at this point.

"You won the bet, sweetheart. We both did." He brushed her hair back over her shoulder and pressed his lips to her cheek. "Go with them now, and I'll come get you in a bit. Then we can be alone, finally. God, you have no idea how badly I want to be with you." He grabbed Grace and passionately kissed her, letting her get just a taste of the desire burning in him at that moment.

Meg and Bianca appeared out of nowhere and scooped her up, directing Grace to the door. Reluctantly she went with them, but Grace glanced back in time to see Jack and Ryan patting Michael on the back and shaking his hand. As the girls ushered her into the break room, Bianca grabbed their coats and hurried Grace into the car in record time.

Flying down the road in Jack's truck, Grace turned to Meg and threw up her hands. "Would one of you like to tell me what the hell is going on?"

Chapter 28

The girls pulled the truck up in front of their place. They hadn't spoken a single word to one another since Grace had asked for an explanation a few minutes earlier in the club, and they walked up to the building in silence. Meg and Bianca occasionally exchanged nervous glances but gave Grace no further clues.

As soon as they walked through the door of the apartment, Grace felt Meg grab her wrist and drag her to the very couch where they had spent countless hours not only sharing the horrific stories of their dates, but also their most secret hopes and dreams. Grace landed on the couch with a thud and looked at Meg, her face begging for an explanation.

"Before I say a word, I want you to know that I love you and what I did was because I love you."

Well, this must be bad for her to start like that.

"Fine, Meg, you love me. I get that. Now, explain one thing to me. How did I win the bet? Michael said I won. Was he telling the truth or was he just trying to make me feel better for attacking him back there in the club?" Her eyes danced between her friends' faces, hoping for a straight answer from one of them.

"You won." Meg said the words, looking extremely guilty, while behind her, Bianca's face was absolutely beaming.

"How? Oh my God, did you and Ryan have sex at the club? Tonight? In the break room?" Grace gasped, trying to make sense of the baffling situation, her hand instinctively covering her now gaping mouth.

Ewww! Our poor coats!

"No!" Meg said, insulted.

Grace racked her brain trying to figure where they might have been able to sneak off to tonight. Her nose crinkled as she continued her guessing. "In his car?"

It would be a little chilly, but this is Meg we're talking about so you never know…

"Grace, it's twenty degrees outside. Do you think I'm crazy or that the prospect of hypothermia is somehow appealing to me?" Meg winced at the insinuation. Bianca, however, was doubled over in laughter.

Grace pressed her fingers to her temples, thinking. *Where could they have had sex at the club? Where?* All of a sudden, it hit her. Right away, her eyes flew to Meg's in horror.

"Oh my God, please, please don't tell me you and Ryan had sex in the bathroom of the club. Meg, I'm sorry, but that's just revolting," Grace shrieked, trying not to gag.

"Grace Marie Park," Meg snapped, "I most certainly did not have sex with Ryan in the bathroom of the club. What do you take me for, a twenty-dollar hooker?" Offended at the speculation, Meg's eyes became narrow slits as she glared at Grace. "You know I don't even sit on public toilet seats to pee; I hover because they're so disgusting."

"Then where did you and Ryan have sex?" Grace felt utterly lost as she threw up her hands in frustration. *It wasn't on the dance floor… was it? How could I have missed it? That might actually be worse than the bathroom…*

"Thefirsttimewehadsexwasatahotel," Meg blurted out in frustration.

Slowing down the sentence, Grace repeated it in her head a few times, trying to separate the jumble of words… *the first time…* "What do you mean 'the first time'?" Grace growled, her jaw tightly clenched. Meg's eyes grew wide with alarm. Bianca instantly stopped laughing, confirming to Grace that she had caught the most important phrase in Meg's rambling sentence.

"Spill!" Grace commanded.

"Well," Meg started, "I went out of the bet, um, a while ago."

"Define a while ago."

Her words were barely above a whisper. "Before Bianca."

"What? You went out of the bet before Bianca did? Are you kidding? You are, aren't you… you're just trying to make me feel better, right?" Grace's head began to throb as she attempted to process all the information being thrown at her. Meg fidgeted nervously in her seat as Grace sat stoically, keeping her anger under control. For now. Sensing Grace was about to explode, Bianca moved closer and rubbed her friend's back to try and help settle her nerves.

Oh my God, it's true…

Meg took a deep breath and began explaining. "OK, here's the truth. I slept with Ryan the night of the bar show. Remember when I was late coming home?" She was nervously wringing her hands together in her lap as she waited for Grace's reaction.

She thought back to that night, remembering how she and Bianca got ready together, and how Meg came flying in the door at the last minute, complaining about work.

"So you didn't spend the day with a client?" Grace asked, waiting for her to look up. Meg's eyes remained firmly focused on her hands as she shamefully shook her head no.

"So you and Ryan…"

"We met at a hotel." She bit her lip in a desperate attempt to hold in the goofy grin that was threatening to spread across her face before she finally chanced a look at Grace. "Are you going to yell at me?" She cringed as she asked the question.

"No. I mean, I don't think so… but why on Earth didn't you tell me? Bianca, how long have you known?" Grace tried very hard to keep her voice calm, wanting to hear every detail, but there was an accusing undertone as she spoke.

Bianca immediately threw her hands up in front of herself. "Hey, I swear, I just found out two days ago. I had no idea, but after we talked about it, I agreed that we should wait until tonight to tell you."

Grace opened her mouth to say something, but then she shut it without uttering a word. After pausing for another second, she tried again. "But why wait? You both know how hard the last few days have been on me. I don't understand. Was it a joke? Did you enjoy seeing me blush and hurling myself into cold shower after cold shower?" Grace didn't bother to hide the anger in her voice this time.

"Grace, I would never do that to you! I swear! No, ugh, this isn't coming out right again. I did the same thing when I talked to Michael," Meg mumbled—and then slapped her hand over her mouth when she realized what she just let slip.

"You told Michael?" Grace seethed. "So basically everyone knew except for me? Did you all have a good laugh at my expense?" She was starting to put the pieces together in her head, the picture becoming clearer. "So that's why he was so seductive tonight, with touching me and the things he was saying. He was trying to get me to cave, wasn't he? I saw him shaking hands with the guys as we left. They must have had a bet about how long it would take Michael to break me." Tears were streaming down her cheeks as she shook her head from side to side in disbelief. "I wonder who won *that* bet," she hissed as she turned and stormed to her bedroom, slamming the door as hard as she could.

"Grace!" Meg's strangled cry came from the family room. Grace could hear her running over to the door as she fell onto her bed, sobbing.

Meg and Bianca didn't even bother to knock; they walked right into the room and sat down on the bed beside Grace, waiting silently, unsure of exactly how to proceed.

"Grace? There was no bet, I promise," Meg said quietly as she coaxed Grace into lifting her head up to look at her. She reached her hand out and softly wiped away the tears that were streaming down Grace's cheeks. "May I please explain?"

With a little sniffle, Grace nodded her head, ready to listen to her reasons but not sure how she was going to react to the whole ugly truth. She saw Bianca give Meg an encouraging smile before she started speaking.

"It all goes back to the beginning of the boycott. You need to understand that the Grace who agreed to the bet is not the same woman who is sitting here right now. Back then, you would go on all of those disastrous dates with men who were the dullest, most uninteresting people on the planet because that's the kind of guy you thought you deserved—the only kind of guy you thought would be interested in you. How many times did we have to call and save you on one of those dates? Bianca and I knew you were so much more than what you saw when you looked in the mirror. We saw the amazing woman inside who is funny, smart, beautiful, and witty, but you didn't even realize she existed. You were so unsure of yourself." She reached over and brushed Grace's hair back over her shoulder so she could see her face.

"Then, a few weeks ago, we made this silly bet. And when you had absolutely nothing to lose, you started putting yourself out there with men. You began talking to guys you otherwise wouldn't have dared to approach. You flirted, you … how did we put it?" She glanced at Bianca and smiled. "You tasted the different flavors of the buffet. And slowly your confidence grew."

"Then, one day, an amazing man walked into your life." Bianca took Grace's hand in hers as she took over explaining things. "You haven't been the same since. You are a different person when you're with him. Confident, self assured, funny, playful, sexy—*really* sexy, Grace." She gave her friend's hand a tight squeeze as she winked reassuringly at Meg.

"But at Christmas, you were still so unsure of everything. I found you crying in the kitchen, again, wondering what Michael could possibly see in you. And even after he walked into the room and told you exactly why he loved you, part of you *still* thought he would disappear, that you weren't worth his time." Meg left her side and walked over to the nightstand and brought over the picture Liz had given to Grace. "Then, little by little, day by day, you realized that this," she tapped her finger on the glass of the frame, "was meant to be."

Compelled by Meg's words, Grace looked down at the sweet sleeping faces of the two toddlers in the picture and started to process all the information that she had just heard.

She *was* insecure and did lack confidence; that was a fact. Grace's self-esteem was embarrassingly low, but all of that was before she met Michael. She had spent nights crying, thinking how she wasn't good enough for him or that he deserved someone better. Then she recalled how certain she had been that this was all a dream that would vanish at the stroke of midnight.

It was only over the last week, after Christmas, that she knew … that she felt it was real. She and Michael were truly meant to be together, and if something happened, she wouldn't give up on them; she would stay and fight. That was something Grace never would have done before. She looked up into Meg's and Bianca's loving eyes and offered them a shaky smile, letting them know that she was slowly beginning to understand their motivations.

Meg spoke first. "You said it today, Grace. You finally said that you wouldn't just let him walk away. The things you said, those were the words of a confident woman who knew exactly what she wanted and was willing to fight for it. You let him in; you finally trusted him with your heart. I simply wanted you to have time to get to that place on your own." Meg's face was hopeful, waiting for Grace to say something.

As she glanced back down at the picture in her hands, Grace could hear her cell phone beeping in her purse. Bianca picked the small, black leather clutch up off the floor and took out the phone, peeking to see who it was. "You might want to look at this."

Grace,

Don't be mad at Meg. Whatever her reasons, everything that happened over the last few weeks led me to you. I thank God every day that I have you in my life. Her choices gave us the time to get where we are today, and I for one am extremely grateful to her. She loves you almost *as much as I do.*

I'll be there soon, sweetheart.

M

Taking a moment, Grace reflected on Michael's words. Her friends hadn't kept things from her maliciously or tried to hurt her; they'd had good intentions. Misguided, yes, but they came from a place of love and support. Would she be as certain of her relationship with Michael if she hadn't taken these last few weeks to get to know him and to begin believing that he actually did love her? Would she have put herself out there and taken such a huge step? Probably not. Without the time, Grace wasn't quite sure where she and Michael would be today.

Grace hid the smile that was threatening to break out across her face, instead replacing it with a serious façade as she addressed her two deeply distressed friends. "The last few weeks have been really hard, almost hell on Earth for me. You both know that," she said, watching their faces fall slightly, "but I also can't say that I didn't enjoy every second of it. I love Michael, and he loves me. And getting to know him has been an amazing experience. I don't doubt his love in any way. I feel it in my heart, and you're right, Meg, if I had known earlier, I just might have tried to push him away to let him find someone better, someone I *thought* he deserved. But now," Grace let out a dark laugh, "anyone who tries to get between us will be in for the fight of their life."

She was different; they all were. The woman smirking confidently at her dearest friends in the world was not the same person who, six weeks ago, thought all she deserved in life was average and dull. Now she knew that anything less than her heart's desire was settling, and that was something the new Grace Park refused to do.

She winked at Bianca and then turned her attention back to Meg. "So, tell me about Ryan and this hotel…"

Meg's face stained itself pink as the blood rushed to her cheeks. "Well, it was actually your fault, you know." The surprised look on Grace's face made her laugh. "That night Bianca and I were out of town, and you let the guys rummage through our rooms. Ryan found my journals, but he didn't read through them or anything like that. He simply opened the most current one, and on the first blank page, he wrote me a letter."

"And we know that boy can write!" Bianca interrupted, remembering the romantic message he had included in Meg's Christmas present that had them all bawling.

"Yes, he certainly can. In the note, he told me that he loved me from the moment we met and he didn't care about the bet anymore. He said that I was worth far more to him than two hundred dollars, and then he asked me to meet him at the hotel on that Wednesday. There were also a bunch of very sweet and personal things that I'm not going to share with you. I made up a 'meeting' so you wouldn't wonder why I was dressed to the nines, and I was ready to play off my nerves on meeting a new client, but neither of you asked. I think you were a little distracted yourselves."

"When I got to the hotel, he was waiting in the lobby with a huge bouquet of roses. He came over to me, kissed my hand, and then he took my arm in his and led me to the elevators. I don't think we said a word to each other; we just looked into each other's eyes. When the doors opened, he led me down the hall to the most amazing suite I'd ever seen. There were flowers everywhere and a steaming bubble bath waiting in the bathroom with rose petals floating on the top." Meg got lost in a dreamy haze as she recalled the day. Grace and Bianca exchanged knowing smiles while she blushed.

In a hushed voice she continued her story. "And I don't even know what happened. I mean obviously I do, but he just led me into the bathroom and started undressing me, telling me how much he loved me the whole time. He untucked my blouse and before I knew it, his fingers were slowly unbuttoning the front of my shirt. I just remember staring up into his eyes as he bent over me—and nearly passing out when I felt his warm hands on my skin. And then the way he kissed me… Before I knew it, my skirt dropped down to the floor. Eventually, I was standing there in my panties, breathing like I had just run a one hundred yard dash or something, just waiting for him to reach out and touch me. I remember I was trembling when he finally. . . Oh my gosh, too much information, I'm stopping right there." Meg was fanning herself furiously while Grace and Bianca blushed right along with her. "That's far more than I ever planned on telling you!" she squealed as she buried her face in her hands.

"Well, it sounds like you two had, um, fun!" Grace replied, and they all burst into laughter. As the giggles subsided, she asked, "So is there anything else you feel the need to confess?"

Meg bit her lip. "Well, I also might have 'arranged' a few of the times we just bumped into the guys. Like that time at the movies? And I might have suggested to Ryan that Michael and Jack should send you the text messages about the gym that one day so I could go to the mall with him." Their mouths hung open in shock as the list of Meg's crimes against the boycott grew and grew.

"Margaret Elizabeth Tomlin, you little sneak!" Bianca shrieked in mock horror, but the smile on her face gave her true feelings away. She leaned over and hugged her friend. "Thank you."

"Before we hug this all out, I might have one more thing to confess." Meg began to nibble on the tip of her thumb as she dropped her chin to her chest. She cringed and waited for the yelling to begin, but when her comment was met by silence, she peeked up found her friends staring at her, speechless.

"There's more?" Grace looked warily over at Bianca.

"This afternoon," Meg started slowly, intently watching Grace's every reaction, "I went to see Michael."

Grace sat up straight on the couch, alarmed. "What did you *do*?" The words fell from her mouth in a rush of breath.

"We...talked?" Meg's voice cracked, making her response come out more like a question than a statement.

A loud bark of laughter echoed through the apartment. "You told him, didn't you?" Bianca was on her feet, laughing. "He knew all night that he'd already won the bet. No wonder his libido was in overdrive, Grace. Michael was trying to drive you out of your mind to make you quit the bet. The sooner you caved—"

"—the sooner they'd get to the good stuff." With a wink, Meg joined in Bianca's raucous laughter. But when Grace remained silent, the two apprehensively turned and faced their friend.

"He knew...all night?"

Meg slowly nodded her head.

Grace's heart pounded faster in her chest as she remembered all the wicked things Michael had said and done over the last few hours. Fanning her face, Grace smirked. "Well, that explains a hell of a lot." She jumped up and wrapped her arms around her friends, pulling them into a hug. "For someone so sweet, you sure do cause a lot of trouble, you know," Grace teased. "But thanks to you and all your scheming, we have three wonderful men in our lives. Speaking of which, I'd better get dressed!" The clock on the wall said it was ten till eleven. Michael would be there any minute.

Meg and Bianca squealed when Grace leapt off the bed and started running around her room in a panic. "He'll be here soon. Oh my God! I have so much to do." She ran into the bathroom and saw how her tears had made her eye makeup come streaking down her cheeks. "Bianca!" she screamed, and a second later the beautiful redhead appeared in the doorway with her makeup bag in hand.

"Breathe, Grace. We'll get you cleaned up and ready to go." She sat the panicked woman down on the toilet lid in her bathroom and got to work, getting Grace ready for her big date with Michael.

Fifteen minutes later, Grace was standing in front of the full length mirror in the hallway, admiring the way her dress flared out as she spun in circles. Her long black waves were twisted up and off her shoulders into a clip with small wisps of hair softly framing her face. All signs of the tears she had shed earlier were erased by Bianca's skilled hands.

Meg placed Grace's overnight bag on the kitchen table alongside the much larger one she was planning on taking over to Ryan's. Grace was digging around in the hall closet for her black wool trench coat when she heard the clicking of heels behind her.

Meg and Bianca stood there grinning. In their hands was a box, neatly wrapped in shiny silver paper with a red bow on top. "Congratulations," Bianca said as she handed Grace the beautifully wrapped package.

Like a child at Christmas, Grace quickly tore into the wrapping paper and gasped when she saw the pristine white box that had been hidden underneath the layers of paper and the crisp black print that said "Manolo Blahnik" across the top. Her eyes darted up, only to see her smile reflected on her friends' faces. Grace let the paper fall onto the floor and gently lifted the lid off to reveal the shoes inside.

"Oh my God. They're magnificent." Gingerly, Grace lifted out a beautiful black ankle-tie pump. The suede shoe had cutouts along the sides and heels with a silver tie in the front of the ankle. "Are these the Carmines?" Grace barely croaked the words out; she was in a state of shock. The limited edition shoe in her hand was the one she had been fantasizing about for weeks.

"The very ones," Bianca said proudly. "You don't even want to know how many favors I had to call in to find this in your size, in two days' time." Laughing, she took the box from Grace's hand and stooped down to slide the shoe onto her foot.

Grace held onto Meg's shoulder to steady herself as Bianca tied the ankle straps tightly. "They're a perfect fit," she said softly as she stared down at her feet, tears welling up into her eyes. "Thank you both for finding them." Grace was overwhelmed that they would both go to the trouble to find the exact shoe she had dreamed of.

"The deal was a fabulous pair of shoes to be worn on your first date of the New Year, Grace," Meg said as she wrapped her arms around her friend. "Would we let you down?"

Once more, Grace glanced at herself in the mirror and let it all sink in. The last few weeks, the fun, finding Michael, and falling in love—it was all culminating in this evening and she found herself suddenly quite flustered.

"How do I look?" Grace spun around to face her friends. "Is my hair OK or is it too much? Do I need a necklace? What about a bracelet?"

"You look beautiful, Grace. Absolutely beautiful." The awe in their voices made her blush. "Are you ready? He'll be here soon."

"I'm not sure. I think I might throw up. That would be bad … Oh God, look at my hands." Tremors were raging though Grace's body as she tried to pull herself together. Her nerves taking over completely, Grace started pacing back and forth through the family room like one of the tigers at the zoo.

"You're going to wear a hole in the floor. Sit down," Bianca said sharply as she patted the empty seat next to her on the couch.

In a daze, Grace wandered over, sat down for thirty seconds, and then was back on her feet again, pacing.

"Grace! You're making *me* nervous, now sit down!" Meg yelled from her chair as she yanked her blond locks in frustration. She watched Grace sit, then pace, sit, then pace, two more times before she finally exploded out of her chair and grabbed the phone. "Where the hell are you? She's about to have a stroke! You know you shouldn't keep a lady waiting. Hurry up!" she snapped into the phone before slamming it down onto the table. "Jackasses."

"You didn't," Grace hissed.

"I did. And for your information, they just pulled onto the street. Give him five minutes." Meg quickly ran her fingers through her hair, smoothing it down as she looked at her reflection in the window. Bianca made herself comfortable on the couch and flipped through a stack of DVDs since she and Jack were staying in for the rest of the evening.

"I'm going to throw up," Grace mumbled as her stomach flipped over violently. "Do we have a bucket?"

"Don't you dare vomit!" Bianca said sternly from her perch, waving her finger at Grace. "Then I'd have to fix your makeup all over again. Suck it up, girl. Please don't make me slap you." She picked up an issue of *Cosmo* off the coffee table and flung it directly at Grace's head.

Catching the magazine before it could hit her, Grace fell into the nearest chair and began flipping though the three hundred-plus page issue at lightning speed until she found the monthly quiz which was titled "Are you good in bed?" She grabbed a pencil off the table and was about to gain some very important insight about herself, when a loud knock on the door made Grace jump and clutch the edge the chair. Her heart nearly jumped from her chest as Meg ran to answer the door. The magazine fell to the floor with a loud thud as Grace nervously glanced over at Bianca and stood up, visibly trembling.

"Well, it certainly took you long enough. Oh … OK, I guess you're forgiven." Meg giggled from the front door. "Come in."

Ryan was the first one to step inside. He handed Meg a huge bouquet of roses which she immediately buried her nose into before kissing him. She led him into the kitchen and promptly rummaged for a vase.

A laughing Jack burst through the door next, with a pizza in one hand and a bottle of wine in the other. He walked right past Grace, setting the pizza down on the coffee table before sweeping Bianca up into his arms. They shared a tender kiss, getting lost in each other's eyes, the rest of the room falling away.

Grace was still captivated as she watched Bianca and Jack start arguing over what movie they were going to watch when she felt someone standing right next to her. She closed her eyes and waited for the silky sound of his voice.

"Hello, sweetheart," Michael said softly, making her entire body tingle. He moved to stand in front to her and held her arms out, taking a moment to soak in the sight of her in her dress. "I knew that would look spectacular. You truly take my breath away, Grace. I've never seen you look more beautiful." He leaned even closer and whispered, "I can't wait to get you out of here."

"Hi," she said shyly as she blushed at his compliment. Suddenly Grace felt like a teenager being picked up for a first date. "You look pretty amazing yourself."

Michael looked stunning. He was wearing a black leather jacket with a white button down shirt underneath. The first three or four buttons of the shirt remained open, showing a tantalizing sliver of his chest. The scent of his spicy cologne reached Grace's nose, making her want to throw herself at him right then and there.

Grace's eyes moved from his chest back to his face, settling on the perfect curve of his lips. She felt him move closer. "Happy New Year," Grace purred as he wrapped his arms around her waist and kissed her ... *really* kissed her. At first the contact was gentle, but the longer their lips stayed connected, the more urgent the kiss became until Grace felt her legs wobble. The only thing that made her pull away was knowing that they were being watched.

"Are you ready to go?" Michael asked as his fingers softly swept a stray hair out of her face. When she nodded, he walked over to the table, picked up her coat, and held it out so Grace could slip her arms into the sleeves. He lifted the coat up and over her shoulders, then spun her around to make it easier for him to button the coat. His fingers slowly brushed against her neck as he wrapped the green cashmere scarf around Grace's neck as he kissed her cheek.

"Are you bringing anything with you?" he asked hopefully, eyeing the bags on the table.

Suddenly feeling quite timid, Grace picked an imaginary piece of lint from the front of her dress, knowing that by grabbing one of these bags, Michael would understand that she was planning on spending the night with him. She looked up at him as he stood there, his hands innocently tucked into his pockets and a hopeful expression on his face, and then she didn't care about being embarrassed. Spending the night with him was exactly where she wanted to be, and instead of being shy, she was going to go after what she wanted. And she wanted this night with Michael.

As her fingers wrapped around the handle of the bag, she felt Michael's eyes on her, his face now glowing as she gently set it down at his feet.

He crouched to pick up the bag, and Grace was taken by surprise when she suddenly felt his fingers skimming over her ankle, examining her new shoes. With a smirk on his face, he stood up and held his arm out. "Your shoes are beautiful."

"Thank you." Grace returned his smile with a kiss on the cheek. With a twinkle in her eye she added, "Now, let's get out of here."

Grace didn't have to repeat herself. The moment the words crossed her lips, Michael squeezed her hand and started briskly walking them over to the front door, oblivious to Meg and Bianca screaming "Wait!" from the family room, until they nearly tackled him.

"Where are you two rushing off to without saying goodbye?" Bianca asked smugly. "Got a hot date or something?"

"Don't do anything I wouldn't do!" Jack called from the couch, earning himself a dirty look not only from Michael, but Bianca as well.

"Have fun," Meg whispered in Grace's ear as she kissed her cheek.

"Details…" Bianca reminded, as she wrapped her friend up into a big hug.

Waving over her shoulder, Grace yelled, "I'll call you." Then Michael coaxed her out the door.

They walked in comfortable silence past the wall of mailboxes to the front door of the apartment building. "So are you going to tell me where we're going?"

Michael smiled smugly, holding the door open as a blast of cold air hit her face. "Nope."

Chapter 29

Grace took two steps outside and stopped dead in her tracks. In front of the building, parked at the curb, was a shiny black stretch limo. The driver was bundled up in a winter coat and scarf, holding the door open. Michael placed his hand on the small of her back and led her to the limo. "What did you do?" Grace hissed in shock as she reached for the driver's outstretched hand. He simply shrugged his shoulders and winked. As she slid onto the leather seat, Grace heard the door close behind her and then the sound of two muffled voices speaking softly as the trunk closed.

Excited by her surroundings, Grace was fiddling with all the different buttons on the ceiling when she felt a sudden chill as Michael climbed into the limo.

"A limo?" she asked, waving at the astounding accommodations. "Michael, you didn't have to—"

His finger came up and pressed to her lips, stopping any further discussion of the topic. "I plan on spoiling you every chance I get; you need to understand that. And I just recently came into some money." He lowered his finger, but when she opened her mouth and tried to protest, his lips took the place of his finger, again silencing her.

Their kiss was interrupted by the buzzing of the opaque divider being lowered. "Mr. Andris, Miss Grace?" the driver called over his shoulder. "Are we ready to head out?" He glanced at the two of them in the rear view mirror, smiling warmly.

"Yes, George, thank you," Michael replied.

"If you need anything, just lower the divider." George pointed into the backseat. "It's the blue button on the console."

"Thanks, I think we'll be fine." As the divider went back up, Michael slid closer to Grace across the leather seat. His fingers rapidly unbuttoned her jacket, revealing the gorgeous dress underneath. He mumbled something under his breath that she missed, but by the way his eyes devoured her, she was certain he was pleased with what he saw.

As he adjusted the temperature controls, Grace slipped her arms out of her jacket, laying it neatly on the seat. Michael made himself more comfortable and took off his jacket as well, tossing it with hers, before reaching for the bottle of champagne. Grace watched as he peeled the foil back and began loosening the tiny lacing of wires that held the cork in place. He pressed a button and the sunroof opened as he aimed the top of the bottle upwards, wiggling the cork back and forth until it exploded, flying out into the night sky. He closed the sunroof quickly, and then laughter tumbled from Grace's lips as a tiny trickle of bubbles spilled onto Michael's hand while he tried to fill their glasses.

"Here, let me help." Grace grabbed the glasses and held them steady as he filled them. She handed him one of the glasses, keeping the other for herself. As she looked into his baby blue eyes, she raised her glass. "To our first date."

"To the beginning of forever," he replied as he clinked his glass against hers, never taking his eyes off of hers. Grace's heart melted at his words.

She took a small sip of the champagne and then set the glass into a nearby cup holder. Michael leaned back into the seat, looking very relaxed and content, so Grace scooted over and curled up next to him, resting her head on his chest. "I love you," she murmured as her fingers began to explore the section of his chest that was exposed by the unbuttoned portion of his shirt. He jumped as her nails teased their way across his chest. "I'm sorry, are my fingers cold?" she asked, quickly trying to pull them away but his hand covered hers, holding it in place against his chest.

"No. God no, Grace. That just feels so good. You have no idea…" He released her hand and relaxed when she went back to her somewhat timid exploration of his body. His hand ran up and down her back in a steady rhythm, slowly soothing away her nerves. "Come here, you." He put his hands on her hips and repositioned her so that she was once again in the very pleasant position of straddling his lap.

As he looked lovingly into her eyes, his hand moved up to her hair and touched the clip that was holding it up off her shoulders. "May I?" His normally silky voice had turned low and husky as he spoke, sending a delicious tingle down Grace's spine.

"Whatever you want," she said softly, biting her lower lip.

There was a gentle tug on the clip, and then her hair fell down, cascading across her shoulders.

"Exquisite…" he whispered as he ran his fingers through her thick waves letting his fingers explore the softness of the strands. "I'm sorry; I just had to touch your hair. You have no idea how sexy you look right now."

He took her face in his hands and pulled her to him. Their lips gently brushed once, twice, and then no longer able to stand it, Michael's lips collided with hers.

A moan escaped Grace as she felt the warmth of his tongue brush against hers. She could still taste the sweetness of the champagne in his mouth. A fire spread throughout her body when his kisses became more passionate, more urgent. The need between them was growing exponentially with every second that passed. Grace could feel just how much he wanted her with every stroke of his tongue, every touch of his lips.

"I love you, Grace…so much." He dropped his hands to her bare shoulders and arms, sliding them further down until he ended at her fingertips. Teasing her almost to the point of madness, Grace felt both of Michael's hands shift and begin creeping up her thighs, finally slipping underneath the hem of her dress.

Grace gasped when she felt his fingertips meet the edge of her lace panties, her legs tightening on either side of him. As his fingers moved over the round curve of her bottom, tracing the delicate pattern of the lace, Grace whispered his name as she clutched the front of his shirt. "Michael…What are you doing?"

"I've been imagining how this lace would feel all night. I couldn't wait any longer to find out. Do you want me to stop?" he asked as he looked into her eyes, which most certainly revealed the raging desire she was feeling at that moment. The sexy curve of his lips let Grace know he liked what he saw.

"No, don't stop. Don't ever stop." She threw her body against his, wrapping her hands into his hair and kissing him without any inhibitions as a wild current of excitement poured out of her. Grace's breathing grew erratic as she became more and more caught up in Michael and how good he felt in her hands, on her lips, and against her skin. She forgot they were in a car, or that there was another person a few feet away. Only Michael existed. He filled her every thought, and the rest of the world simply disappeared.

His fingers touched her shoulder, and Grace felt one side of her dress glide effortlessly off her shoulder, coming to rest near her elbow. His eager kisses covered the newly exposed skin of her collarbone and trailed his fingertips down to the lacy curve of her bra. The heat of his breath on her skin set everything in its path aflame. The tingling in her chest immediately spread out to her arms and down to the rest of Grace's body, filling her with desire.

Michael moved to the edge of the seat and without separating their lips, he rolled her onto her back. The slight chill of the leather sent goose bumps up her arms, making Michael laugh. "Cold, sweetheart?"

"No." She kissed his neck. "Actually, I feel incredibly hot right now." Grace smiled as she felt him hike her skirt higher, his hand now running along the smooth skin of her abdomen.

"We'd better do something about that then." He lowered his body onto her, pushing Grace deeper into the seat, and she gasped in pleasure at the sensation of his body against hers. She only wished he wasn't wearing so many clothes. "Do you have any idea how badly I want you right now?" he asked, as he slid his tongue slowly down the center of Grace's chest.

Her hands frantically tugged on his shirt, untucking it from his pants and allowing her better access to his chest as she moved her hands under the fabric. The smooth muscles of his abdomen were so soft, yet solid underneath. As her hands moved over his skin, Grace heard him moan her name in a deep, husky voice that made her body quiver.

Once she heard that, Grace couldn't get the buttons on the front of his shirt freed fast enough. Her fingers fluttered over the tiny plastic circles, and as the last one popped open, she paused to drink in the sight of his bare chest only inches away from her. Just as her lips made contact with his now heaving chest, she felt the limo come to a stop.

Michael must have felt it too, because he gave her a quick kiss then sat up in case the divider lowered a crack.

"We're here, Mr. Andris, and they're just about to start," George said over the intercom, wisely giving them their privacy.

Grace let out a small groan of frustration, but Michael easily kissed her irritation away before he paused to button his shirt. As Grace ran her fingers over her swollen and freshly kissed lips, Michael reached over to retrieve their coats which had been knocked onto the floor in their romantic haste. He helped Grace back into her jacket and pulled a blanket from a hidden shelf before opening the sunroof again.

"What are we doing now?" Grace watched as Michael popped his head up through the top of the limo, holding a hand out for her to join him. She squeezed out through the hole in the ceiling to find them parked along the river downtown, with a perfect view of the cityscape. They were the only car in the parking lot as Grace looked up at the beautiful starry sky.

Michael wrapped the blanket around her shoulders and pulled Grace to his chest in an effort to keep her warm. "It's almost midnight," he whispered against her cheek as he glanced down at his watch. "Five, four, three, two, one. Happy New Year, Grace." He ran his fingers through her hair, bringing them around to her chin and then drawing Grace's body closer to him. "I love you."

"Happy New Year. I love you, too. More than you could possibly know," Grace replied seconds before his lips found hers in the frigid, now January, air. As they kissed, Grace heard a loud booming noise near them. Her head snapped around to see Portland's annual New Year's fireworks exploding directly overhead. As the sky lit up all around them, Grace was simply overcome with love for the man holding her in his arms. "You're amazing."

They spent the next fifteen minutes watching the fireworks explode overhead, the colors swirling to the ground around them. Even in the freezing temperatures, Grace felt warm and protected in Michael's strong arms, and she knew that she always would. As the finale began exploding above them, Grace and Michael dipped back into the car, sealing the sunroof shut once more. He gave a quick tap on the divider and told George to take them to their next destination, giving Grace no clue as to where they were going. When he didn't help her out of her coat this time, though, she assumed the destination was somewhere nearby.

Michael pulled Grace into his lap, needing to hold her. His hands rubbed up and down her back vigorously, trying to warm her from the chill in the air. Grace pressed her cheek to his chest and let out a contented sigh as her fingers twirled around the buttons on his jacket. His warm lips pressed against her forehead and whispered, "Just a few more minutes, sweetheart."

A comfortable silence fell over them as they rode through town in the limo. Michael held her snugly to his chest, the blanket still wrapped around her shoulders, assuring that she was warm enough. They held hands, their fingers tightly interlocked, and occasionally, Michael would pull Grace's hand to his lips, placing a soft kiss across her knuckles or on the center of her palm.

When the car came to a stop, George lowered the divider for the last time. Michael climbed out of the car, asking Grace to wait inside until he settled things with George, insisting he didn't want her to get cold standing outside in the frigid air.

Grace took the brief separation to check her makeup in the small compact Meg shoved into her purse at the last second. She was happy to see most of her makeup was safely in place, except for her lipstick, which Michael's incredible kisses had easily removed. Grace pulled out a tube of lip gloss and had just finished lightly brushing it against her lips when the door opened and Michael's hand reached into the car.

"Ready?" he asked as his head dipped down into the car, his smile making Grace's pulse quicken.

"Absolutely," she said as she grabbed his hand and slid her way across the leather and into his awaiting arms.

George was standing at the door, smiling. He handed Michael Grace's overnight bag as he passed. "Thank you, George," she said and gave him a quick hug, her giddiness getting the better of her. "Happy New Year!" Grace waved to the driver as Michael led her up the snowy steps to his apartment.

"Happy New Year to you too, Miss Grace. Enjoy your evening." George slammed the door shut, headed to the front of the car, and climbed back into the driver's seat. She heard the engine of the limo start up as Michael opened the door and ushered her inside.

His apartment was dark when they came through the door, but Grace could immediately smell something delicious, the scent of tomatoes and garlic wafting through the air. There was music softly playing in the background as they moved down the hallway. Michael turned on the light and took Grace's coat, hanging it in the closet before taking her hand and leading her into the dimly lit kitchen. He carried her bag in and set it on a nearby chair.

"Now what did you do?" Grace asked in astonishment while she watched him peek into the oven and check on whatever was cooking inside. In the other room, she noticed that the table was beautifully set, with two plates, wine glasses, linen napkins, and a huge bouquet of flowers in the center with two candlesticks, one on either side of the flowers. A bottle of wine was chilling in an ice-filled bucket on the corner of the table.

"I thought you might be hungry, so I made you dinner." He laughed as he saw her stunned face still staring at the beautiful table in the other room. "It's almost ready, but in the meantime, come here. I have something I want to give you." He came up behind her and wrapped his arms around her waist, leading her toward the couch.

As they passed the table, Grace paused to get a closer look at the flowers, and then froze. "Those flowers…" She gasped. "Those are the same flowers you sent me that day, after the gym." Grace went over to the table and ran her fingers over the soft, satiny petals.

"The day when I first started falling in love with you," he whispered as he pulled her into a warm embrace, kissing the top of her head before leading her to the couch. When Grace sat down, he took a small rectangular box off of the end table and set it on her knee. "This is for you."

She stared at the tiny white bow on the box for a minute before slowly unwrapping the paper, wondering what could possibly be inside. She paused before she removed the lid. "Michael, you didn't have to get me anything."

"Actually, someone gave this to me a long time ago, and I only bought one tiny thing for it. So please, just open the box." No woman could resist his pleading eyes and dimples, least of all Grace. "Open it," he urged one final time before she obeyed.

Her trembling hand clutched the lid, working it back and forth as she lifted it up. A flash of silver immediately caught Grace's eye as the dim light hit the chain. Inside was an exquisite charm bracelet, with five charms already hanging from the sturdy chain that Michael was wrapping around her wrist.

"My mom started this the day I was born. The sun charm is for my birthday being in summer, the M is obviously for my name. Those two charms were on there since the day I was born." He rotated her wrist to show the tiny black music note charm hanging from the side of her wrist. "This one she added when I was sixteen. And this one, she added very recently." Right next to the music note was a tiny silver book charm, for Grace's degree in literature. "And this one…I added." Beside the aged "M" was a shiny new silver "G."

Grace was speechless. With tears threatening to spill out of her eyes at any second, she looked up to his face to find nothing but pure love looking back at her. Her eyes drawn to the bracelet, Grace began playing with the tiny charms, still unable to believe that Michael had given her something so precious.

"My grandmother started a bracelet just like this one for my dad when he was born. She gave it to him on his eighteenth birthday and asked him to someday give it to the woman he wanted to spend the rest of his life with. My mother has worn his bracelet every day for the last thirty years. When I was getting ready to leave her house, I asked her for my bracelet because I wanted to give it to you." He gingerly took her hand and watched the charms reflect the light as he put it to his chest and smiled. "Of course, imagine my surprise to find out not only had she already slipped it into my suitcase, but she had also attached a new charm to it. I hope that you'll accept it and wear it, always."

Trying to keep her overwhelming emotions under control, Grace began stammering and failing miserably. "I don't know what to say. You're such an amazing man and this means so much to me, I can't even begin to put it into words. All I can say is… I truly love you, with every fiber of my being. I love you, Michael. Forever." Grace leaned over and pressed her forehead to his. "Thank you." As she tenderly raised her hand to the side of his face, the charms of the bracelet tinkled together, making his smile grow even wider.

"That sound reminds me of home. You are my home now, Grace." As they kissed, Grace couldn't contain her tears anymore. They glided down her cheeks and Michael sweetly kissed each of them away. "I love you," he whispered as he wiped the final tear from her face.

From the kitchen, a timer started beeping. "Sounds like dinner's ready!" Grace laughed at the distraction, using the time to try and pull herself together. Taking one last glance down at her wrist, she followed Michael into the kitchen and suspiciously asked, "So, did you *really* make this or is it something Liz made and put it in the freezer the last time she was in town?"

Her skepticism only made Michael laugh. "I made it, thank you very much, with my own two hands this afternoon. Just wait until you taste it, you'll see. Breakfast isn't the only thing I can cook." He laughed as he slid the hot tray from the oven and placed it on the counter top to cool for a few minutes. "Can you open the wine?" he asked, holding out a corkscrew. "And maybe light the candles?"

"No problem." Soon the candles began to glow brilliantly, accentuating the delicate colors in the flower arrangement. In no time at all, Grace had opened the wine and poured each of them a glass of Merlot. She took a generous sip, hoping to calm the final few butterflies she had. The dry red wine slid smoothly down her throat, warming a trail deep into her chest. "This is really good," she said as she joined Michael in the kitchen and handed him his glass. He dried his hands on a towel next to the sink and smiled in thanks. "You have good taste in wine."

"And other things…" He smirked as he too took a sip of the wine, his eyes fixed on Grace's lips. "Would you like to taste the lasagna?" He rummaged through a nearby drawer for a fork, and then carefully dug into the bubbling tray of pasta, pulling a small bite onto the fork. He gently blew on it before offering it to her. "Please?"

Grace leaned over and slowly wrapped her mouth around the fork, watching Michael's eyes twitch when she peeked up seductively at him through her thick eyelashes. She pulled her lips off of the fork and smiled at the effect she had on him. Like a statue, Michael's hands remained frozen in mid air as his eyes lingered on hers for a second before he cleared his head.

"So, how is it?" he asked smugly, already knowing it was perfection.

Delicious would have been an understatement. It was the best lasagna she had ever tasted. He really was an excellent cook; Grace couldn't even pretend he wasn't. It was yet another reason to love the wonderful man standing in front of her. She let a small moan escape her lips as she enjoyed the flavors on her taste buds. The next thing she knew, there was a loud clink as the fork Michael had been holding fell sharply onto the counter top.

"Do you like that?" he purred, his voice thick with lust. His darkened eyes darted from her full lips to her eyes repeatedly. She swallowed the lasagna in one gulp and took another huge sip of wine as a bit of a distraction. The intense desire in his eyes sent shivers down her spine.

"It's delicious," Grace mumbled into her wine glass, taking another sip before Michael stole the stemware from her now-trembling hand and set it down on the counter.

"Would you like to sit down and eat?" As he posed the innocent question, Michael took a step closer and wrapped his hand around the back of her neck, tangling his fingers deep in the hair at the nape of Grace's neck and bringing her face within inches of his.

No, dinner can wait. I don't even need to eat again. Food? What's that?

At that moment, Grace knew exactly what she wanted. "There is something I would really like to do, but it doesn't really involve food, at least not right now." Grace stifled a laugh when she saw his eyes light up, the excitement plainly written all over his sexy face. "Would you mind terribly if we put dinner on hold for now?" Not able to keep her hands to herself, Grace started kissing his chest and neck allowing her body to seek out his.

Michael's breathing became more ragged as her trail of kisses crept higher up his neck. He pulled back just long enough to look over his shoulder and make sure both the oven and stove were off so the apartment wouldn't burn to the ground. "Screw dinner," he said as a devilish smile broke across his face.

He turned off the kitchen lights leaving the soft glow of candlelight as the only source of illumination in the apartment. Michael kissed Grace with increased vigor in the darkness as her body responded and started to tingle with excitement. As they stumbled out of the kitchen, their lips still locked together in a passionate kiss, Grace heard it: Meg's ring tone.

"Meg…" Grace muttered against Michael's lips as the music continued to play.

"Meg who?" Michael replied as he tugged at the zipper on the back of her dress, but the damn song kept playing. "We don't know anyone named Meg. Not right now."

"I have to get it or she'll come barreling through the door next, and that would be far worse." Growling, Grace snatched her purse off the counter and flipped open the phone inside. Michael came up behind her and wrapped his arms around her stomach, his lips continuing their exploration of her shoulders.

"Do you have a death wish?" Grace snarled into the phone rather than saying hello, but her anger was immediately diffused when Michael leaned in and began sucking on the side of her neck. "Wha- what do you want?" She was paying very little attention to the phone anymore; all of Grace's focus was on Michael's lips feathering up her neck.

"Well, you've been on your date for an hour so Bianca and I were making the customary call to see if you needed to be rescued? How's it going?" Meg giggled over the phone.

Bianca was laughing in the background, and had Grace's brain been functioning properly, she would have started screaming at them. Instead, she continued stammering as Michael's tongue swirled over her skin "Amazing… good… No rescue needed… but thanks for… oh my God… asking." Grace gasped and nearly dropped the phone when Michael's hands slid from her stomach down the front of her thighs and began hiking up the hem of her dress.

"What's going on?" Bianca asked when she heard the breathy response.

"Um, nothing. Well, that's not true. He's … wow … his hands are … and he's kissing my neck. Now, he's doing that thing with his tongue … the thing Jack did, Bianca …" Grace was trying to concentrate on the conversation, but Michael was doing everything in his power to take her mind to other places.

He laughed when she became more flustered, barely even able to hold the phone.

"Ew! We don't need the play-by-play, Grace," Bianca whined.

In the background, Jack was laughing. "Yes, we do."

"Hey, you called me. Oh, man …" Grace moaned again as she felt Michael's hips grind against hers, his arousal obvious.

"Are you sure you don't need any rescuing, Grace?" Meg teased. "Because we'd be happy to come over there and get you."

"No … Just stop. No, no, not you, Michael. Meg … Oh, forget it. You talk to her. I can't think straight when you do that." Grace shoved the phone at Michael's head as her body collapsed into his.

"Ladies, I promise to make sure she, uh, enjoys herself … all night, to the best of my abilities." Giggles poured out of the receiver. "She will be well taken care of. And just so you know, I'm keeping her for a few days, so I don't want you to worry and don't expect her home anytime soon." He nuzzled his cheek to hers so Grace could hear their reaction.

"But, Michael," Meg started so seriously, "she didn't pack enough clothes. I can run a few things over in the morning."

"I have a feeling she'll be rather busy in the morning. And actually, Meg, what I'm planning to do with her for the next few days really doesn't require any clothing, so she'll be fine. Say bye, Grace." He held the phone out and Grace heard Meg and Bianca squealing on the other end.

"Bye, Grace." She laughed, running her hands down Michael's chest.

"Good night, ladies," Michael said sweetly as he turned off the phone and shoved it deep into a nearby drawer. "Now, where were we?"

Holding his intense gaze, Grace held his hand and led him to the table where he blew out the candles, complete darkness suddenly surrounding them. A hint of light from outside streamed into the room through the front windows, allowing the two of them to safely navigate their way down the hall toward his bedroom.

After a few steps, Michael gave her arm a quick tug, stopping Grace in her tracks and bringing her body to his. When she looked up at him, she felt his lips crush into hers, instantly taking her breath away. Grace felt the smooth coolness of the wall against her back as he pressed himself further into her. Content to be trapped in his arms, Grace smiled against his lips.

Michael wrapped one arm around her waist and lifted Grace off the floor. With his other hand locked around the back of her neck, he carried her down the hall, his heated kisses making Grace's head spin. His hand slid from her hair just long enough to push open his bedroom door, then returned to gently stroke her silky curls as they swayed across her back. He kicked the door shut and gently lowered her feet to the floor.

Once inside his room, their bodies brushed together in the dark as Grace nimbly unbuttoned the rest of his shirt and ran her hands over his chest. As the fabric hung open, the moonlight poured in through the window and created subtle shadows that danced across his skin.

Grace's body ached for him, to feel the warmth of his body surround hers. She pressed her lips to the center of his chest and tasted the sweetness of his skin on her tongue as she savored the strength and power of his body. Her hands found their way to his back and lightly stroked the well defined muscles, feeling each ridge and dip of his body. Grace giggled against his skin when she felt him twitch from the contact, a low moan escaping him at her soft caress.

In a powerful rush of emotion, Grace gave his shirt a tug and slid it off his shoulders allowing it to fall onto the floor. Her eyes lingered on his bare chest, taking in the perfect shape of his broad shoulders, and the sexy way his pants hung low on his waist, accentuating the V-shaped muscles of his lower abdomen that dipped down below his belt. When her eyes finally flickered back up to his face, she saw the same desire and hunger she was feeling reflected back in his eyes.

"You are so beautiful." He sighed as he stood in front of her, his hand slowly sliding up her back. Eventually his fingers reached for the zipper of her dress. At a snail's pace Michael lowered the zipper down her back, which only served to prolong the ecstasy of him undressing her, until Grace didn't think she could stand it another second.

With the back of the dress hanging wide open, Grace realized that all that kept it from falling were the two thin straps of fabric over her shoulders, both of which were dangerously close to falling down. Michael's fingers lightly ran up and down the bare skin of her partially exposed back. His touch was so gentle and smooth, barely a whisper across her skin as he took his time, investigating every supple curve of her body.

By the time his hands crept up over her shoulders, Grace was trembling with anticipation. He slipped a single finger under the straps on either side of her dress and gave them a gentle tug, allowing the dress to spill downward and pool at her feet. She felt a rush of cool air on her legs as the fabric rushed to the floor.

"Exquisite," he whispered as he looked down and admired Grace's body. He gently ran his fingers down the lace of her bra straps, his fingers lightly brushing over the swells of her chest as she moved closer, suddenly overwhelmed by the need to feel his skin on her. "Grace, you're so beautiful. I love you."

Her feet left the floor again as Michael scooped her up into his arms in one fluid movement. The wicked grin on his face sent Grace's heart into overdrive. She lay comfortably in his arms, wearing nothing more than her black lace panties and bra, plus her new shoes still dangling from her feet. As he closed the distance to the bed, their eyes locked, the deep love and passion they felt for one another flowing freely between them.

Being with Michael felt so right, so comfortable to Grace. Even in a moment as intimate as the one being shared between them now, she felt like they had been together for years. The familiarity Grace felt around him was staggering. She knew him in ways she didn't know another soul on Earth, and she could tell it was the same for him.

He was able to make her feel things she never thought possible, and for the first time, Grace felt truly alive. From the top of her head to the tip of her toes, every part of her wanted him, needed him, and she knew she was exactly where she belonged. Michael was her home.

A fluffy pillow slipped under her head as Michael eased her down onto his bed. He leaned over her quivering body and whispered words of love and adoration in her ear as his hands moved skillfully across her torso igniting a fire in their wake. Grace's stomach twitched as his lips tickled against the sensitive skin below her belly button, her fingers snaked deeply into the hair at the back of his head. She found herself writhing at his every touch, unable to hold still, constantly wanting and needing to feel closer to him.

Michael showered her body with kisses, trailing down her arms, her legs, over her stomach and across her breasts as he memorized every inch of Grace's body. The smooth, warm feel of his lips made her wild with desire. He sat up and took her foot in his hand. With his teeth, Michael tugged on the delicate tie holding her shoe in place. The silver bow quickly came undone, the shoe dangling off the tips of her toes. He cupped the shoe in his hands, and with a thud, Grace heard it fall onto the floor next to the bed. The other one left her body in much the same fashion; however, this time, when she heard the thud, she sat up, crawled toward Michael, and sat at the foot of the bed, facing him.

She wrapped her legs loosely around his calves as she started unbuckling his belt, wanting to see more of his perfect body. Grace slid the long leather belt from the loops on his pants and let it fall to the floor into the ever growing pile of clothes beside the bed.

When her fingers went for the button of his pants, a low growl escaped his chest, which only turned Grace on more, making her work faster. Adrenaline coursed through her veins as her breathing went off the charts, the passion completely overtaking her body, every cell craving Michael's touch. A hiss escaped his lips as she lowered his zipper, grazing over his obvious arousal.

He pushed her back onto the bed, and as he inched his way up her body, Michael worked himself free from his pants, revealing his long muscular legs. His rock hard body pressed deeply into her, letting his presence be felt by every inch of Grace's skin. His hands found their way to her chest, slipping between her full breasts. With a gentle tug, she felt her bra clasp open and she gasped as Michael's masterful hands began to work the scrap of fabric off her body, his mouth eagerly kissing the newly exposed flesh.

Their bodies drew together as they shed the remainder of their clothes and they found themselves naked and entwined in one another's arms. His skin was warm and smooth as it slid across her, causing her body to respond to the slightest touch. Grace's back arched as her lips covered his, tasting him again, unable to get enough of his kisses, each one sending her further over the edge than the kiss before.

"Michael," she murmured as he hovered over her, his lips turned up into a smile at the husky sound of her voice. "Make love to me." Grace all but begged, not even trying to hide the need in her voice. "Please…"

Without hesitating, Michael's eyes darkened, and he answered her request. She felt a wonderful pressure as he entered her, filling her completely. Their hips rocked together, the resulting sensation more than anything Grace ever imagined it to be. All of her fantasies about him paled in comparison to actually being with him now. She couldn't believe all the emotions she was feeling as they made love. Michael made her feel sexy, beautiful, and loved with every touch, every erotic movement of their bodies.

Grace didn't feel inhibited or embarrassed in any way with him. Instead, she found herself feeling bold and positively daring in their lovemaking. Everything felt right. She could say or do anything, completely confident in her own skin for the first time in her life, when she was with Michael.

Each time she heard her name cross his lips, her skin would ignite and her heart would soar. Michael needed her; he wanted her, just as much as Grace wanted him. That knowledge empowered her, washing away any lingering fear or insecurities.

The intense and erotic movements they had shared together on the dance floor were nothing compared to the ways they moved while making love. The brush of his skin, his undulating hips, and the feel of him between her legs was so electric; the current between them was palpable.

Together, their emotions continued to grow as their kisses became more passionate, the sensations taking them closer to their limits, until finally they were unable to hold back any longer and climaxed together, both of them crying out at the peak of their ecstasy. Together they called out one another's names and then collapsed in exhaustion.

Grace knew in that moment that Michael was the only man who could ever make her feel this way, the only one to make her feel this high, this fulfilled, this complete. When they made love, Grace had given him every part of herself—mind, body, and soul. She held nothing back. She was now Michael's, forever. Grace had been waiting her whole life for him to find her, and now, here he was, his intense blue eyes looking lovingly down at her. She vowed to herself that she would never let him go.

Michael's body surrounded her, the weight of it calming the tremors that were still surging through her. Both of their chests were heaving as they tried to catch their breath. A sexy sheen of sweat covered Michael's body, evidence of their enthusiastic love making.

Grace wrapped her arms and legs tightly around him, never wanting the moment to end.

He leaned closer and began whispering how much he loved her as he tenderly caressed her cheek, his eyes remaining locked on her, full of love and adoration. "You are amazing," Michael said softly as his exhausted body finally rolled off of her, a thoroughly satisfied grin on his face. He held his arms out and Grace happily crawled next to him, resting her head on his chest, her naked body pressed against the side of his warm, glistening torso.

"Well, that was definitely worth the wait." Grace giggled as Michael's fingers tickled her side.

They spent the rest of the night making love, unable to get enough of each other. Every time with Michael was pure bliss, her joy and love growing with every experience they shared. When their lovemaking finally ended in the wee hours of the morning, Grace glanced out the window and saw the first hint of sunrise breaking over the horizon. A pink tinge crept up in the distance, making the snow along the window sill sparkle.

Michael took her hand and raised it to his lips, the charm bracelet tinkling in front of his face. He tugged on Grace's arm, coaxing her over onto his chest. He sighed contently as she lay on top of him, her face nuzzled in his neck, his arms tightly wrapped around her fatigued body. "Let's stay here all day." Michael sighed as he stroked her tousled hair.

"I'm not going anywhere. I'm right where I want to be—forever."

Utterly exhausted, Grace drifted off to sleep in Michael's protective arms. Sweet dreams filled her mind, making it the most peaceful night's sleep she'd had in a while. Grace wasn't quite sure how long she had been asleep, but she woke up to the sound of Michael hissing into the phone.

"I am not talking to you about that! No, I will not do that either." Michael glanced her way and noticed her raised head peeking out from underneath the blanket. He threw Grace an apologetic smile, and then a devilish grin when she sat up, revealing her still naked body to him.

Grace stuck out her tongue and quickly pulled up the sheet, motioning to the phone with a confused look on her face as she tried to figure out who it could be. "Meg?" she mouthed to him, but he shook his head.

Michael rolled his eyes and let out a loud sigh in response to whatever was being said on the other end of the line.

"Jack?" Grace asked softly, and Michael pressed his index finger to his nose and nodded his head yes. "What does he want?"

He was becoming more visibly irritated until suddenly an evil grin danced across his face. Michael covered the receiver and winked at Grace. "Feel like having some fun with him?"

Grace beamed at the thought of having a little fun at Jack's expense for a change. "Absolutely." She snatched the phone from his hand and cracked her knuckles as she prepared for battle. "Jack, what can I do for you?"

Michael watched the gorgeous woman in his bed brush her hair over her shoulder and roll her eyes at whatever question Jack had the balls to ask her, and he assumed it was pretty bad based on the red color creeping into Grace's cheeks. To her credit, she kept her composure, her voice never giving away embarrassment.

"You really want to know?" Her voice dropped an octave and took on a sultry tone. "It was fantastic. Your boy is an animal in bed. The man can go for hours." She sent a playful wink in Michael's direction, and his heart clenched with absolute joy. Nothing rattled her. She took things in stride, she knew how to have fun, and was the most genuine person he had ever met. Plus, she loved giving Jack shit, and he couldn't have loved her more.

Playing along with her game, Michael leaned in and whispered into the receiver, "Sweetheart, come back to bed. I have something to show you." The suggestive tone of his voice made Grace's eyes grow wide. He winked and ran his fingers over the swell of her breast and grinned.

"Jack, I gotta go. Michael's calling me—again. No wonder he has all those sports drinks in his refrigerator." She giggled and sighed into the phone. "He's definitely got stamina."

As Jack stammered an awkward goodbye, Michael's body shook violently with laughter beside her.

"You're incorrigible, Michael Andris."

He rolled himself on top of her and paused to enjoy the way her black hair contrasted with the light sheets beneath her. "That's not what you said last night. You said I was actually quite…what was the word you used? Oh yeah, magnificent." He continued kissing her as his hands dipped under the covers and ran along her bare thighs. "I think you may have actually made Jack blush with that little performance. And you," he ran his tongue along her neck, "are perfection."

"All right, Mr. Magnificent, don't let it go to your head. It just means I have very high expectations now." Grace tried to laugh, but all the air flew out of her lungs as she felt him slip out of his pajama bottoms, his body settling over hers. "What do you think you're doing?"

"I'm keeping you in bed all day, just like I planned," he murmured, his lips brushing against the swell of her breasts.

"You sound so sure of yourself." Grace laughed, wrapping her legs around his waist.

"I am quite *confident* in my abilities." He grinned mischievously.

"Really? Care to make a bet?" Grace asked with a twinkle in her eye.

"No. Never ever again."

The End

Victoria Michaels once again delivers a can't-put-it-down novel loaded with engaging characters, cheeky dialogue, and powerful emotions. *Trust in Advertising* is a cleverly woven tale about two people getting to know each other and ultimately themselves. Turn the page for a sneak peek from …

· TRUST IN ADVERTISING ·

Lexi's alarm started blaring at six a.m. sharp. With her mouth feeling like it was full of sawdust, she cracked open one eye just wide enough to see the irritating contraption and hit it with her fist, sending it crashing to the floor. The body beside her moaned.

"Shh, sleeping," a raspy voice growled into the pillow.

"Shh, head hurts," Lexi whispered in response.

"Maybe you should lay off the vodka next time." A hand patted Lexi roughly on the head. "It makes you do crazy things, darlin'."

Lexi groaned and rolled over, coming face to face with her bedmate. "You snore."

"I do not!"

"Hope, trust me—you snore like a hairy wildebeest. I think that's half the reason why my head hurts so much this morning." Lexi pressed on her temple in an effort to relieve the throbbing.

A feather pillow smacked Lexi square in the face. "Your head hurts because you drank half a bottle of vodka in less than an hour, just because your new boss happens to be a hunky guy who you had a huge crush on in high school."

"Bite me, Hope." Lexi rolled herself out of bed and fell onto the floor. "It's not too late for me to quit."

"Don't you dare!" Hope sat straight up in bed and glared at her friend crumpled up beside the bed. "I stayed up past three this morning convincing you to stay at Hunter Advertising, and you *promised* you'd give it a try."

"Hope," Lexi whined as she stood up on her still wobbly legs and brushed her hair out of her face.

A yawn escaped Hope's lips, then she laughed. "You promised me. And you, my friend, are a good person. You wouldn't break your word to me or leave Hunter high and dry. So, get your little butt in the shower and quit your whining."

Lexi's feet thumped angrily against the hardwood floor as she stormed off into the bathroom to shower and get ready for work. When the door slammed shut, Hope slowly rolled over with a satisfied grin on her face and went back to sleep.

✦

Still annoyed at Hope for making her act like a grown up and return to work, Lexi began texting her every five minutes after leaving the apartment. When Hope shot off a message with every curse word known to man, Lexi felt victorious.

"Look who's here bright and early." Leigh beamed as Lexi stepped of the elevator.

"Good morning, Leigh." Lexi laughed, pausing to tuck the BlackBerry into her purse.

"Go get yourself settled. I have a feeling today will be a busy one." Leigh seemed to be trying a little too hard to sound nonchalant.

With a suspicious look on her face, Lexi sighed. "Okay, I'll get a few dozen cups of coffee in me, twenty or so ibuprofen, and then I should be good to go. I'm going to mess around on the computer today and try and look through some current projects and proposals so I have an idea what everyone is talking about in meetings."

A huge grin broke across Leigh's face. "That sounds like a great idea, Lexi. Don't let me keep you." She waved her hands dismissively, and then busied herself behind her desk.

Lexi said good morning to a few of the other assistants on her way to her desk. Each of them wished her luck, which Lexi found odd, but she had so much she wanted to get accomplished that she shrugged it off and headed for her desk.

She no sooner sat down than the sound of her chirping bird ringtone filled the room, making her head throb. Suddenly, her heart nearly leapt out of her chest, when she wondered if it could be Vincent calling to check in for the day.

"Lexi White," she said nervously into her phone.

Hope's laughter rang out. "Lexi White? That's how you answer the phone now, not 'Hey, Hope'?"

Lexi let out the breath she had been holding. "Hope, I'm hung over, exhausted, and about ten minutes away from a nervous breakdown, and you called to give me grief?"

"Absolutely." Hope chuckled. "You need to lighten up and breathe, Lexi."

Drumming her fingernails on her desktop, Lexi waited. "Are you done?"

"Has the hunk called you yet?"

"Hope!" Lexi looked over her shoulder to make sure no one heard the little outburst. "His name is Vincent, and no, he hasn't called yet."

"So, what are you doing?"

Lexi shuffled the papers on her desk. "I'm looking over one of the files from his desk to find out what projects we're working on."

"Sounds exciting," Hope said sarcastically. "So, are you still nervous to talk to him?"

"No, I figure I'll keep my head down and my mouth shut."

Lexi heard Hope snort over the phone. "Whatever you say, Lexi. I'll let you get back to work. Text me later if anything exciting happens. I'll be at work with the meatheads."

"Give them my love. Bye." Lexi ended the call and flipped the phone around in her hand as she continued reading through the papers on her desk.

For a solid hour or two, Lexi poured over file after file, learning every detail of the projects Vincent was currently working on and the accounts he was in the process of acquiring. She was taking a pile of files back into his office when her phone chirped. Lexi rolled her eyes, wondering what Hope could possibly want now. When she saw "Vincent Drake" in bold letters on the display, she nearly dropped everything she was carrying onto the floor.

Lexi's hand started trembling, her mouth going completely dry at the thought of having a conversation with Vincent. She breathed a much needed sigh of relief when she saw it was only a message.

Alexandra,
Welcome to Hunter Advertising. I hope that you are more competent than
your predecessor. You have three minutes to reply to this message.
Vincent Drake

Lexi rolled her eyes at the obnoxious message. His clipped introduction, laced with a haughty arrogance, helped her push aside any leftover fantasies she had of him from high school, and her already throbbing head lowered the chances of a tactful response. "Leigh wasn't kidding. You are a prick now." Lexi typed out a quick reply and hit send.

Vincent,
Thank you for the warm welcome. I'm sure you'll find me more than competent.
Lexi

ACKNOWLEDGEMENTS

A special thank you to the amazing ladies at Omnific Publishing for making my dream a reality. To my wonderful editors Lynette McCann, Kimberly Myers and Cindy Campbell, thank you for all your hard work, guidance, and polishing of my endless ramblings. To my cover designer Barbara Hallworth, your talents truly know no limit, nor does your overwhelming generosity. To CJ Creel and Micha Stone, thank you more than I could ever say for your expertise and for all you have done to make this day possible. And finally, to the woman behind it all, Elizabeth Harper, thank you for your vision and for your friendship and faith in me, even when I didn't always have it in myself. Without these incredible ladies, none of this would have been possible.

ABOUT THE AUTHOR

*V*ictoria Michaels is a wife, and mother of many who lives her life in what seems like a constant state of motion. Kids' sports, meetings, homework and general family fun take up twenty-seven hours of her day. In her thirty seconds of free time, Victoria likes to read, write and travel the country with her husband.

She most enjoys writing about love and laughter, two things that are central to her everyday life. If you would like to know more about what's coming next from Victoria, please check back at www.victoriamichaels.net for updates, news and sneak peeks of future releases.